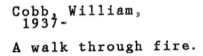

Cobb, William,
193?-

A walk through fire.

$21.50

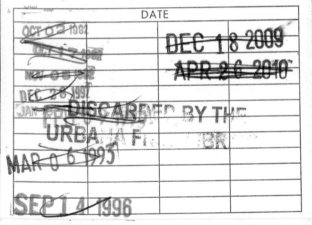
BAKER & TAYLOR BOOKS

A WALK THROUGH FIRE

Also by William Cobb

THE HERMIT KING

COMING OF AGE AT THE Y

A WALK Through FIRE

A NOVEL

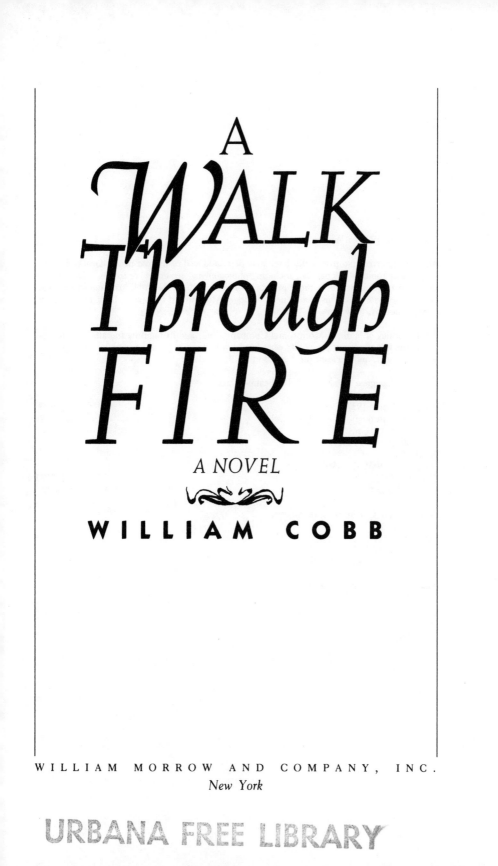

WILLIAM COBB

WILLIAM MORROW AND COMPANY, INC.
New York

F

9-92 BT 2200

It is the policy of William Morrow and Company, Inc., and its imprints and affiliates, recognizing the importance of preserving what has been written, to print the books we publish on acid-free paper, and we exert our best efforts to that end.

Library of Congress Cataloging-in-Publication Data

Cobb, William, 1937–
    A walk through fire / William Cobb.
        p.   cm.
    ISBN 0-688-11366-4
    I. Title.
  PS3553.0198W35   1992
813'.54—dc20   92-7199
                                                                            CIP

Printed in the United States of America

First Edition

1 2 3 4 5 6 7 8 9 10

BOOK DESIGN BY RUTH KOLBERT

I am grateful to the following people: to my wife, Loretta, and my daughter, Meredith, whose faith sustained me; to my fellow writers Fred Feldman, Sandra Ray, and Eileen Goudge, all of whom read the manuscript in its earlier stages and made valuable suggestions; to my dear friend and colleague Barbara Belisle, whose close reading gave me a perspective I needed; to Norman McMillan, whose encouragement and confidence were steady; to Susan Leon of William Morrow and Robert Mecoy of Avon Books, who were the perfect editors for me; and—finally—to my tenacious and talented agent, Al Zuckerman, without whom this book, quite literally, would never have been written.

*When you pass through the waters I will
be with you; and through the rivers,
they shall not overwhelm you; when you
walk through fire you shall not be
burned, and the flame shall not
consume you.*

—ISAIAH 43:2

Hammond,
ALABAMA

1 9 6 1

PART 1

WINTER

Chapter One

~~~~~~

O. B. Brewster, in his winter daydreams, escaped into baseball. He had decided, after many painful years away from it, after the longings and the yearnings, to give in. The local American Legion Post had been after him for years to coach its team, and this spring they had some good ball players, a couple even who were pro prospects. O.B., sitting quietly in the cramped little office of his farm-implement dealership, could almost smell the new-mown grass, hear the sound of cowhide on leather. It was what he wanted now. Baseball might bring back the way he used to feel. He had begun to think of himself as middle-aged, and Martha, his wife, was drinking again. By spring he didn't know what would be happening. He needed to allow himself some freedom to do what he wanted, what he liked. He closed his eyes and imagined what it was going to be like, the warm sunlight, the feel of good sweat on his brow. His reverie was interrupted by loud and angry voices.

O.B. tensed. It was his mechanic, Rusty Jackson, and Buddy Ed. Buddy Ed's small tractor had been in for repairs just last week, and O.B. remembered that Rusty Jackson had worked on it. O.B. had considered himself lucky to be able to hire Jackson, who was one of the best mechanics around, even though he was not very likable. Small

13

and wiry, an angry little man from down around Dixons Mills, Rusty had worked for O.B. for only a few months. His clothes were always grease-stained and rank, and he never laughed and joked with the other men in the shop.

"The goddam thing'd already been nigger-rigged," O.B. heard Rusty say, his voice ringing in the high-ceilinged shop, "what'd you expect?"

"I wants to speak to Mr. Brewster," Buddy Ed said, his voice respectful but hard-edged.

O.B. had known the old Negro for years, since he, O.B., had been a boy. Now O.B. could imagine Buddy Ed standing stooped over and shuffling his feet, edging toward the front of the shop toward O.B.'s little dusty office.

"Well, he's busy," Rusty said.

"I wants to talk to him," Buddy Ed repeated.

"Can't you understand what I'm sayin to you, nigger? Now, bout this tractor, you musta run over a stump with it. That what you did?"

"I ain't run over nothin with it. I ain't done nothin to it."

"Well, it was runnin fine when it left here. What you tryin to say?"

There was a brief silence. *Maybe they'll stop on their own.* O.B. studied his hands on the desk, feeling the tenseness in his arms, his shoulders. He dreaded becoming involved in this. He could all but see Rusty's smug face. *Why did people like Rusty always have to do this?* He knew that Rusty would assume that O.B. would automatically be on his side because he was white. Old Buddy Ed would look to him as an old friend, a man who had always been fair to him. O.B. swallowed. *Maybe they'll resolve it on their own.*

Then he heard Buddy Ed's voice. "I ain't tryin to say nothin. I just be talkin to Mr. Brewster, then—"

"You ain't talkin to nobody! You tryin to say I didn't do a good enough job on it, ain't you?" Rusty's voice twanged with hate.

"I ain't tryin to say nothing, Mr. Rusty," Buddy Ed said.

"You tryin to git me in trouble with O.B. Anybody talk to O.B., it'll be me. I bet you ain't even paid for the damn thing, have you? What you owe this place, huh?"

"That be's between me and Mr. Brewster."

"Don't you sass me, nigger! Who you think you talkin to?"

O.B. was standing now. He shook his head. He was imagining Jackson, his pale gray eyes and his mouse-colored hair cut short, his bony wrists hanging out of his splotched and spotted, ill-fitting and greasy, blue work shirt. Jackson would be strutting, aware now that the other two mechanics were watching. O.B. felt like kicking his cluttered desk. *It makes no sense.* He *needed* a mechanic as good as Rusty.

"I ain't sassin you, Mr. Rusty," Buddy Ed said. "All I know is my tractor broke down again."

"After *I* worked on it?"

"I ain't sayin who worked on it. Whoever worked on it ain't none of my business. It broke down, thass all I know."

"Goddammit! And I'm sayin you broke it down. A nigger don't know how to treat a tractor. You need a goddam mule!"

The air in the office was overheated, heavy. The afternoon light was pale and gloomy. O.B.'s desk was lighted with yellow light from a gooseneck lamp. He stood there, feeling both disgust and anger now. Old Buddy Ed was a good man who never meant any harm to anybody, O.B. knew that, and yet the sound of his voice irritated O.B. with its hint of whimpering.

"What you been doin with it?" he heard Rusty say. There was a cold sneer in his voice.

"We be clearin," Buddy Ed said.

"You ran over a goddam stump, didn't you?"

"I ain't run over nothin. I needs to speak with Mr. Brewster."

"He can't do nothin to help you, nigger. You been draggin logs with that thang. You shoulda been usin a mule. Ain't that right?" The voice was slightly raised on the question, and O.B. knew that Rusty was asking the two other white men in the shop.

There was no response that O.B. could hear. He stood rooted by his cluttered desk, brooding on how things had been going so well, especially now that he had at least one good, experienced mechanic. Rusty could teach Clyde and Ernest a lot. Why did he have to turn out to be this worst kind of white trash? O.B. had known Rusty Jackson types all his life, and they always made him nervous. They were so angry at the world, angry at whatever had made them what they were. There was never any telling what awful thing they might do.

I need Jackson, but I can't let him walk all over Buddy Ed Webb, O.B. thought as he made himself go through the swinging door into the shop. The smells of motor oil and harsh cleanser hit his nostrils; the air around his head seemed even more stuffy and hot back here, but the concrete floor and the air just above it were cold.

"O.B., we got a problem," Rusty said when he saw O.B. walking up.

"I see we do," O.B. muttered. "How you doin, Buddy Ed?"

"All right," Buddy Ed said.

"What's the problem?" O.B. asked.

"My tractor broke down—" Buddy Ed started to say.

"He come in here claimin I ain't fixed his goddam tractor right,"

Rusty said. "Shit! The goddam rust is holdin the thang together. I ain't no goddam miracle worker."

"I ain't said nothin like that," Buddy Ed said.

"You callin me a liar, nigger?!" Rusty sneered.

"I ain't callin you nothin."

"Goddam!" Rusty said. He looked at O.B.

O.B. saw that the mechanic had picked up one of his large monkey wrenches. His pale eyes, the color of lead, glinted.

"Just calm down, Rusty," O.B. said, hearing the tightness in his own voice. He took a step toward Rusty.

Buddy Ed was backing away toward the door to the front of the shop. Then he just stood there, impassive, resigned. O.B. felt weighted down with the knowledge that Buddy Ed had given it over to him, transferred the burden to the white man, the same as always.

"You hear me?" O.B. said to Rusty. "No sense in all this. Just—"

"Shit! Don't tell me nothin," Rusty said. "A goddam nigger come in here and accuses me of bad work, I don't—"

"Nobody's accusin you of anything," O.B. said. He tried to keep his voice normal. "Buddy Ed, the tractor stopped runnin on you, huh?"

"Yessir." Buddy Ed looked at his heavy brogan shoes on the dirty floor. He wore overalls and a huge, heavily lined denim coat with a worn brown corduroy collar. His close-cropped hair was oily and tinged with gray.

"Yessir," he repeated. "It ain't run right since—"

"Goddammit!" Rusty moved toward Buddy Ed, but O.B. stepped between them. Rusty hefted the wrench, letting it tap against his grimy palm. His face was contorted with hatred as he glared up at O.B. "Git outta my way."

"You got it outside?" O.B. asked Buddy Ed, watching Rusty out of the corners of his eyes.

"On the trailer, yessir."

"All right. Clyde, you help Rusty roll it off the trailer and get it inside. Check it out, Rusty."

"It's a piece of junk, O.B.," Rusty complained. He had called his boss by his first name from the start. The other two mechanics were younger men, and they called him "Mr. Brewster."

"Just fix it," O.B. said. This was the deciding moment.

"I'll be fucked if I will," Rusty said.

"Fix the goddam thing, Rusty," O.B. repeated. He could feel the mechanic's brooding resentment, as palpable as the stale air. If only there were a way to let Rusty back down, to let the man save his distorted sense of dignity. But no, it wouldn't work. Rusty wouldn't let it go.

Rusty took a step closer, hefting the wrench. The other men watched in tense silence. He was close enough for O.B. to smell his sour odor. O.B. knew he had to do something, so he reached out and pushed Rusty's shoulder, hard, and Jackson, losing his balance for a moment, backed up. He looked up at O.B. with hatred, his eyes squinted, but then his lips parted in a tight grin, revealing his crooked teeth, tinged with green. "I'm tired of fixin goddam nigger stuff," Jackson said.

He made to go around O.B., but O.B. slid his feet to block him. He poked Jackson in the chest with a stiff finger, not as hard as the push. It stopped him in his tracks.

"Drop the wrench," O.B. said. The man scared him, but now he was almost sure, having seen Jackson's mock-cocky grin, that he was all talk, that he would not use the wrench on him.

Jackson hefted it again. There was a tense silence. The wiry little man looked barely in control now, and O.B. stiffened, watching him carefully, imagining the crunch of the cold cast iron against his head.

Jackson took a step back. He dropped the wrench to arm's length.

"He's a customer," O.B. said, letting his breath out in a long sigh. "He's been my customer a hell of a lot longer than you been workin here. Now you gonna fix it or not?"

"I tell you," Rusty Jackson sneered, "I never saw a white man had more nigger customers than you. I been hearin bout the great O.B. Brewster all my life, so I come up here and go to work for the man, but he's got two nigger customers to every white one. Shit. It's a disappointment, I tell you, a big-time baseball star like you."

"Shut up about that, Jackson," O.B. said. "Fix it, or pack up your tools and get outta here." *What am I doing?*

"Any nigger that calls me a liar, I ain't workin on his tractor," Jackson said.

"Then get the hell out."

"I reckon I can find me a shop that ain't run by a nigger-lover," Jackson said. "Shit!" He looked sideways at O.B. out of the corners of his dull gray eyes.

O.B. felt disgust and a sense of relief that the monkey wrench had been all bluff. Only the two half-assed mechanics would be here now, but he'd worry about that later. He felt his stomach relaxing.

"Ernest, help Clyde with the tractor. Come on in my office, Buddy Ed," O.B. said.

"Shit. Look at that. Bowin and scrapin to a nigger."

"Git your tools and git, Rusty," O.B. said.

"You owe me money. This is Thursday."

"All right, goddammit," O.B. said. He took out a roll of wrinkled bills. He counted them out in Rusty Jackson's dirty palm. "Here's three and a half days. Don't be hangin around here, you hear?"

"Don't worry about that. You," he said toward where Buddy Ed stood just inside the door. "You better watch yourself, nigger," Jackson warned.

"Come on, Rusty," O.B. said. "He ain't done a damn thing to you."

"He better watch hisself, that's all," Jackson said, as he went over to the corner where the men hung their coats. The others had street clothes hanging there, too, but Rusty wore his shop clothes to work and wore them home in the afternoons. He grabbed an oily-looking black overcoat from a hook. "Goddam niggers," he muttered.

O.B. watched him go out, his narrow, bony shoulders hunched under the black wool against the weight of his battered toolbox. O.B. knew that more than likely some shop tools were walking out with Rusty. He would have to drive to Tuscaloosa and put out money to replace them. He started to call to Jackson, thinking to search the toolbox, but his heart wasn't in it.

Where will I find another mechanic as good as Jackson? O.B. wondered.

He looked at Buddy Ed, standing with his hands clasped in front of him, his eyes as wide and clear and trusting as a child's.

"Come on in, Buddy Ed," he said, "and let's talk." Buddy Ed stepped aside to let him pass, bowing slightly, shuffling his feet on the dirty floor.

·~·~·~·

Buddy Ed sat across O.B.'s desk from him, looking down at his gnarled fingers twisted in his lap. "I can't pay you nothin on it right now," he said. "I just need to get that field cleared before plantin."

"All right," O.B. said. "But you got to pay me when you can. I got to stay in business, too." His irritation over what he had been forced into doing had not gone completely away. O.B. looked at Buddy Ed, remembering that when he had been a boy, he had worked in the fields alongside the Negro. They'd chopped cotton together and had fished in the bar pits and along the river.

Buddy Ed stood up to go.

"Just sit there and wait. It'll take those two a coupla hours. Just make yourself comfortable."

"I thank you." He sat back down. "How your peoples?"

"Mama and Daddy are doin fine," O.B. said. "My girl is about to graduate from high school."

"Lawd! No!"

"Yep. Time flies."

"Seem like it was yesterday when you lived with yore mama and daddy out there on the Hubbard place. I remember when you wasn't no bigger than a hoppergrass."

O.B. laughed. "Yep. Those were good days." He felt better now, more at ease. He would not worry about Rusty. His boys could probably carry it okay. Or maybe he could find somebody. *But where?*

"Sho was. Sho was," Buddy Ed said, shaking his head.

The old man sat there, his coat bunched in his lap. O.B. knew that any payments coming from him before next fall would be few and skimpy. Buddy Ed shook his head, chuckling and sighing, relaxing in the chair. O.B. looked around the tiny room. His office was in the old part of the shop, low-ceilinged and cramped. Back where the mechanics were, clanging away on something—maybe it was Buddy Ed's tractor—was the new part, the part financed by the Planters and Merchants Bank, the note for which was coming due and would need to be refinanced. A tight knot of worry formed in O.B.'s gut. Mac McClellon, the president of the bank, was an old friend, but they had not exactly remained close over the years. He could be hard-nosed. O.B. would have to find an experienced mechanic to replace Jackson.

"Mister Rusty had it right about your baseball," Buddy Ed said. "I sho remember that."

"Yeah," O.B. said.

"You was somethin else," the old man said.

Was, O.B. thought. Could I ever have been a really great player? "I'm gonna coach, Buddy Ed," O.B. said.

"You is? Sho nuff? Dat's good."

O.B. nodded. Just thinking about it was like a tonic on this gray winter day: the crisp dream of deep green grass between the white lines; the sounds: *smack, crack*. It seemed an eternity since he had signed a pro contract out of Hammond High School, where he had played third base, caught, and pitched, and his senior year had batted .645. Mac McClellon had once told him that he was the closest thing to a hero Hammond had ever produced, but that had been long after O.B. had come home with a busted-up knee, his career ended before it even really began after four years of Class A and then Double A ball, and a dream-short half-season with the Yankees. He'd been astonished by Mac's comment, and only gradually came to accept that people in the town did consider him just that, a hero; they were proud that he had at least played in the majors. *What could I have been if it hadn't of been for my knee?* . . .

Buddy Ed was smiling at him. "Who you gonna coach now?" the old man said.

"American Legion." O.B. grinned back.

"Yore girl," Buddy Ed said, after a minute, "graduatin from high school. What her name now?"

"Ellen," O.B. said.

"Ellen. I bet she love her daddy, don't she?" The old man grinned. He had only one upper tooth, right in the middle of his mouth.

"Well," O.B. said, "yeah. She does." He leaned back in his swivel chair. Ellen did love him. He was confident of it despite his bitter confusion about Martha's drinking. He felt warmth when he thought of Ellen. And sadness. She wanted to go North to college; he had a brother-in-law who lived in Vermont, and Ellen had gotten it into her head that she wanted to go up there to Middlebury College to continue her schooling. She had never been there, even to visit, but she knew all about it from her cousins. The problem was, he didn't see any way possible for her, financially, to do it. The State Teachers College over at Livingston would have to do. She could live at home; O.B. could afford that. Live at home. That made him think once again of his wife's alcoholism, and he blinked, looking at Buddy Ed.

"I bet if you'd kept playin baseball, you'd be up there with Willie Mays," Buddy Ed said.

"He's in the other league." O.B. smiled at the old man.

"Still, you played up there where Willie play. Thass plenty."

"Well," O.B. said.

Buddy Ed shook his head. "You played," he insisted. "Baseball ain't *but* baseball."

O.B. didn't answer. The old man had made him wistful and sad. It was true; he *had* played up there in the big leagues, but for a tantalizingly, cruelly short time. Willie Mays. There had been no Negroes at all in professional baseball when O.B. came along. *But now* . . . He thought of the team he was planning on coaching. There were no Negro boys on that team, even now, but how *could* there be? It was the American Legion Post, after all. He supposed the idea had floated through his head because the old man had mentioned Willie Mays.

O.B. was tired, his muscles sore from the tension. He leaned back and stretched, wishing that he could go back and capture his afternoon reverie, but he could not. It was gone.

·~·~·~·

Eldon Long pulled his old black Chevrolet into a space in front of O.B.'s shop. The building sat out on Highway 80, a couple of miles from the three-block-long main business district on Washington Street that was downtown Hammond. O.B.'s place was built of dark red brick, except for a lighter, newer part, which was concrete block painted to match the dull crimson of the old brick, the attempt at matching not very successful.

Eldon sat there for a moment, the motor idling, the heater running. The weather had turned clear and sunny, but it was cold, probably the last real cold spell of the winter. Eldon read O.B.'s worn and faded sign: BREWSTER TRACTOR COMPANY, in large red letters, and under that: *New and Used Farm Implements, Parts.* He listened to the purring of the motor. He straightened his tie, brushed at the knees of his dark suit. He was one of only two black men in the town who wore suits and ties, the other being Gus Levy, who owned a large Negro funeral home on the outskirts of town. Eldon was pastor of the Mount Sinai AME Zion Church, the largest black church in town. And he had come out here to do something that he dreaded, but that he felt he had to do: He was determined to get his old friend—his old enemy—O.B. Brewster to run for mayor of Hammond against Mac McClellon. After much prayerful contemplation, he was convinced that O.B.'s running for mayor was destiny, was God's will, and he was prepared to move heaven and earth to make it happen. It was the only way, and God would help him, just as God would help his people overcome.

He cut the engine and got out, slamming the door. He stood for a moment, breathing the cold air. *Lord, don't let me mess this up. It is comin, Lord, it is comin!* Excitement hammered his chest. He could feel it in his blood. He was just back from a weeklong session in Montgomery, with Martin King and Abernathy, and E. D. Nixon. Now Eldon knew the fire was coming. And one thing was a fact: If, in these towns where it was all starting, you had even a moderately sympathetic local government, then you were a long way toward heading off the potential bloodshed that might come when things really started moving. It had been while he was pondering that fact that the idea had come to him in the night: O.B. He had lain awake, tense, with Cora breathing steadily beside him in the bed, contemplating on how O.B. running for mayor was a crazy idea and also a stroke of genius. O.B. was the only white man Eldon knew who could or would understand what it was all about for the black man, because they had been like brothers. He would be able to see the truth. How they even had a special election for mayor in Hammond, in the summer, had for years, because it was a white folks election, like electing the president of the country club. O.B. did not belong to the country club. He was not like that. They had truly been like brothers.

Had been . . . Eldon's eyes tickled and burned in the winter sunlight. He had been just thirteen when he had begun to suspect that there was something precarious in his friendship with O.B. The suspicion began that day Eldon came upon his father, sitting in the sandy backyard of their cabin, under the chinaberry tree, crying like a child. Eldon had stood there, stunned, his legs trembling beneath him, as he watched his tall and bulky and powerful father bent forward, the tears coursing down his cheeks. His eyes had been full of a terrible and profound agony that Eldon, in his youth, had never dreamed existed. He had never seen his father cry and never would again.

"There ain't nothin she can do. Ain't nothin I can do," his father had said. Eldon had known that the "she" was his mother, and cold, quivering fear had gripped him. His mouth was as dry as dust, his young soul confused with mounting dread. "I ain't nothin but a nigger, God knows," his father had said, and then he'd told Eldon what was tormenting him. It had been Mr. Hubbard, the white man who owned the large farm they lived on. Eldon's mother worked in the man's kitchen during the day. He had touched her, finally. Had forced himself upon his mother. It was rape, Eldon now knew. His father had wiped at his eyes with the sleeves of his flannel shirt as he'd told him, his voice growing stronger, "Course, Mr. Hubbard would just deny it. And a nigger's word against a white man . . . Well." His father had sat there, not having to explain. "The waitin was worse," his father went on. "The waitin and knowin what he was gonna do, and knowin that there wasn't a goddam thing she could do about it, nor me neither, short of killin him, cuttin his goddam white heart out with my razor. She said it was almost a relief when it finally happened. It was the livin with it, day to day, the way he looked at her, knowin that she was his to do whatever he wanted to with her. I'm talkin bout your mama, son. She ain't just another hound dog he can kick when he pleases. She my wife. But that don't matter."

Eldon's own eyes blurred with tears, and he had felt his young heart bleeding. The pain and anger was so welled up inside him that he could hardly breathe.

"I could kill him" his father had said, "an go to the prison farm and get my back broke and never see neither one of you again. I ain't gonna do that. You understand that, don't you? *Don't you—?*"

"Yessir," Eldon had said, feeling dizzy, knowing that he could never look at his mother again without thinking of her sorrow and her shame. His young manhood, *his very being*, narrowed at that moment, became focused on his mother's and his father's and his own pain. He knew that the image of his father weeping under the tree, the shiny tears on his ruddy black cheeks, would be with him forever, that when he closed his eyes to sleep, this was the image he would see; that here was his legacy, his flag, his still and steady rallying point in his leadership of his people. And then it happened again, like fate had been determined to deal him a double blow. O.B. and Cora. But that had been different, that had been another kind of rape. That had been something that he, himself, had almost willed, and he had been willing to share the guilt. And to forgive.

He took a deep breath and walked through the front door of O.B.'s place. He went back toward the little offices, stopping in the doorway, and the girl behind her typewriter looked up. She stared at him, her face flat and blank. Her lower jaw rolled on the piece of chewing gum in her mouth.

"I want to see Mr. Brewster," Eldon said, hearing the tenseness in his own voice. The girl just looked at him for a moment. She was heavy and young, probably just out of high school, Eldon guessed.

"Uh-huh," she said. She popped the gum. "He's in there," she said, pointing.

"Thank you," Eldon said, and the girl looked at him with open hostility as he passed through. He stopped in the doorway. O.B. was sitting behind his desk, writing something. Eldon watched him for a moment; he looked tall, even sitting down, and his fine blond hair was only slightly highlighted with gray. He was lean and muscular, stooped a bit as he concentrated on whatever it was he was writing. Eldon cleared his throat, and O.B. looked up, blinking.

"Hey, Eldon," he said. "Long time no see! Come in. You takin up farmin?"

"No," Eldon said. He sat in the chair across the desk. There was barely room for it in the office, and Eldon's knees were flush against the desk. "I need to talk to you."

There was the slightest, barely noticeable pause. "Okay," O.B. said.

He dropped the pencil on the desk. His blue eyes flicked over Eldon's face. "What can I do for you?"

"Do you have a few minutes?"

"Sure," O.B. said. "Like I say . . ."

"Do you mind?" said Eldon, getting up and closing the door.

"No, 'course not," O.B. said. He had a curious, interested look in his eyes. Eldon said nothing for a minute. He could never look at O.B. without thinking of him and Cora together. It was almost as though he forced himself to think it, knowing that somehow, if he thought it enough, the pain would ease, go away, but it didn't. He knew it never would.

"Hey, I heard your mama'd been sick with the flu," O.B. said suddenly.

"Yeah. She's okay now." Eldon shifted in the chair and crossed his legs. His mouth felt dry, and he cleared his throat. "Listen. I feel like I can talk to you, O.B. We go back a long way, in a whole lot of ways." He paused. O.B.'s face was a blank. "I'm takin a chance talkin to you," Eldon said.

"How so?" O.B. said.

"Well," Eldon said. He shook his head. "Wait till you hear what I've got to say. I don't know how you stand on all this, but I've got a pretty good idea."

"All what?"

"Wait."

"Git to the point, Eldon."

"All right." The point. *His father's tears and his mother's shame. What do you know of that, white man?* He sat thinking, knowing that it was O.B. he was talking with, and he remembered suddenly the way O.B. had looked in his faded overalls, remembered their boyhoods together, the November hunts and the fishing over the long summers of their youth, his lean arms tanned and rawboned and lightly downed with hair, his blue eyes fading in the sun. Eldon swallowed, feeling again a flash of the love he had felt for him then. "Here it is. You remember the bus boycott over in Montgomery, all that?"

"Yeah. It's long over," O.B. said.

"It ain't *over*. Nothin's ever over. You know what's goin on, up in Rock Hill, South Carolina, and all. Right?"

"You mean all that demonstratin, all that stuff?"

"Yes. And it is coming here. That was in honor of the first anniversary of Greensboro. The Rock Hill jail-in. There will be a Hammond jail-in."

"Here? Come on!" O.B. said.

"That's right. Demonstrations and marches and all like that. Colored people goin to white restaurants and bus-station waitin rooms and movie theaters and such. It's all about to really get goin, O.B. It's gonna be somethin." He looked at the white man across the desk. The bitter sense of betrayal began to grow within him, to drag his enthusiasm down. *We were like brothers, and now I feel the anger of betrayal between brothers, but I have forgiven, I have forgiven.* O.B. just sat slumped in the chair, looking back at him. Eldon thought he had a slightly embarrassed look on his face.

"So?" O.B. said.

"So it's comin to Hammond," Eldon said. O.B. didn't say anything. He picked up the pencil from the desk and chewed the eraser. "I've been to some workshops in Birmingham and Atlanta. SNCC is sendin in a couple of civil rights workers, two white college boys that they've trained in Washington, and we're gonna have a voter registration drive."

"Here?" O.B. said.

"Here. We're gonna set up what they call citizenship classes, at the church, and we're gonna organize a demonstration at every white-only establishment in Hammond."

"Shit," O.B. said softly. Eldon peered at him, trying to read him.

"Whattaya mean?" Eldon said.

"Nothin. Go on."

"Okay." He paused. O.B. seemed relaxed now, easy. Eldon felt more tense, his mouth dry. He had the beginnings of a headache. "One of the problems we're faced with—by 'we' I mean Negroes—is local officials. You see . . ." Eldon paused again. O.B. would not understand, but it seemed to Eldon that he could be made to. That if O.B. could somehow be the leader of the white community, everything would fall into place, and he could put in operation all that he had learned. "One of the problems with enforcin the law, people's rights, is a matter of what's called 'jurisdiction.' " There was a long silence, and Eldon felt himself shifting in the chair. All that he was saying sounded stiff and cold and diffident. O.B. *had* to understand, because they had slept in the same bed, eaten the same food. "Meanin that the federal people, the FBI, can't just come in here and take over what the local police and authorities ought to be doin but are not."

"I don't follow you," O.B. said.

"Well. The way the voter registration process is run, for one thing. The local officials, if a white person comes in to register, they just sign him up. Let a colored go in, they make him read the Constitution and then interpret it to em, whatever that means. Then turn em away. And the county officials support that. It's an abuse, but it's supported, and there ain't any way the federal government can get in here and—"

"Wait a minute. I don't know about this federal government business—"

"—get in here and find out the truth and make things right." O.B. He had prayed intensely that O.B. would still be someone he could tell anything to. But he had never told him about the time of his father's crying over his mother in the white man's kitchen, the fear and the despair. And yet he knew that O.B. would understand it, because he was a white man. It was the way things were. He felt his heart begin to pound again. "Surely you don't think that that kind of abuse is right?"

"For one thing," O.B. said, after a minute, "I don't know if it happens. I know you come in here and tell me it does, but I don't know that that's true."

Eldon felt his frustration growing, the beginnings of an old familiar and helpless rage. "Oh, for heaven's sake, O.B. I thought maybe you—"

"Hold on. Just hold on. I'm hearin you out." O.B. smiled at him, his head cocked to the side.

Eldon stared at him across the desk. *What are you so proud of yourself about? Don't you patronize me, you son of a bitch.* He felt a sudden remorse. *You are my brother.* He tried to speak firmly but calmly. "I think you owe me that much," Eldon said. O.B. met his eyes, then looked away. He picked up the pencil and doodled on the pad in front of him. Eldon swallowed. *White skin and brown skin.*

"Go on," O.B. said, and Eldon blinked, trying to refocus.

"There are Freedom Riders comin into the South—"

"Who? What?"

"Freedom Riders. People, colored and white, get on buses in Washington and ride down through the South. Get off and go in waitin rooms together. They're gonna need protection—"

"Hah! Damn fools! You can say that again!"

"And if local officials won't protect em, there's gonna be bloodshed. Bad bloodshed." He paused again. He licked his dry lips. He felt his tight muscles quivering. "There's gonna be a lot of blood spilled in the streets before all this is over, O.B. Colored blood. And white blood. You and me, we got a whole lot in common, ain't we? We—"

"Say what you came to say, Eldon. Don't start goin on about that."

"All right," Eldon said. He felt a hot ball of nausea, like a tight burning in his belly. *White skin on brown skin, moving. Honeyed whispers. Secret endearments that locked the world out. Locked him out.* He swallowed. "Hear me out, then. I want you to run for mayor."

There was a silence. Eldon could feel his pulse beating steadily in his ears.

"What?" O.B. said. He laughed. "What?"

"Just hear me out! You owe me that."

O.B. grinned at him. He shook his head. "All right. Go on," he said.

O.B. seemed not to hear the last part, about owing. Or he pretended he didn't. "Mac McClellon's comin up for reelection, right? This summer. Now he's been mayor for how many years? Too many to count. Nobody runs against him—"

"Who the hell wants to be mayor of this little town?" O.B. was chuckling, and Eldon kept speaking rapidly. He did not want O.B. to spoil his excitement at coming up with this plan.

"—so he's got the police chief and the city council and everybody else in his hip pocket; all the county people kowtow to him because he controls the northern end of the county. He's also Klan, O.B., and you know this as well as I do—"

"Whoa! I don't know that!"

"—and he's the power behind the Citizens Council, the *White* Citizens Council, if they called it by the right name."

"Okay. So you think I could beat him? I never ran for anything, Eldon. And I sure don't want to start now. Besides, I already decided I'm gonna coach some baseball—"

"Baseball?!?" Eldon said. He could not believe his ears. "Baseball?"

"Yeah, baseball. You know what that is, don't you? No. Not me. *You* run."

Eldon laughed dryly. "Hammond ain't ready for *that*. But you. You're white. You're popular. And this is important. Not like baseball. Everybody likes you, O.B. You were important to this town once. People looked up to you. You could be a hero again, a new kind of hero. You don't have any idea how much my people's lives could be improved with just a tiny jot of fair treatment—"

"I could be a *dead* hero, too. You got the wrong man, Eldon."

"No. You're wrong. I got the right man. Are you scared of Mac and his trash? Of Rooster? Don't give me that shit."

"Yeah. I'm scared of em. Me and Mac, we ain't exactly bosom buddies, Eldon."

Eldon looked down at his shoes; they were shined, bright and glinting almost like patent leather except for a smear of red mud across the toe of the right one. He concentrated on the smear of mud, trying not to let his excitement, his energy, slip away. He knew how important this was to him, to his people; he sat there reliving the agony of all it had taken to come here: the vacillating, the rehearsing what he would say, the gathering of his courage. He did not fully understand it, but it seemed to him that O.B. held his destiny in his hand. Eldon was unaccountably drawn to him. And repulsed by him at the same time.

"Yeah, you got the wrong man, Eldon," O.B. mumbled.

The words, and the finality with which they were said, cut into Eldon like a knife. O.B.'s white shirt was open at the collar, and it was wrinkled. It had not been ironed, Eldon realized.

I will not give up. Not so easy as that. "How's . . . Mrs. Brewster?" Eldon said, a slight tremor in his voice. He watched O.B.'s face. He was thinking of Martha, all her troubles that he had heard about. He was being mean-spirited, but he wanted to be mean.

"She's . . . not doin all that good," O.B. said. "How's Cora?"

"Fine," Eldon said. *You dare to ask about her. You dare to even mention her name!* He looked away, not meeting O.B.'s eyes, hating himself for doing it. "Great, matter of fact."

"Well, good," O.B. said. Eldon raised his eyes. O.B. was looking levelly at Eldon. His blue eyes seemed a shade darker. "Forget all that, Eldon," he said. "Ain't any use carryin around somethin like that. We were children."

"Not the second time," Eldon said.

"It's history. There ain't a goddam thing we can do about it. I'm sorry. I was foolish. What more can I say?"

"Say you'll run for mayor."

"Jesus! Come on, Eldon. You're talkin about two different things here. I ain't any politician. I don't know anything about that. Get serious."

"I *am* serious," Eldon said.

"That's right," O.B. said. "You're always serious. You always *been* serious. Maybe you ought to loosen up."

The pain of rejection was so intense now that Eldon could barely speak, but from somewhere deep down inside came a new determination. "You know," Eldon said thinly, "when I came out here, I thought you might consider this. I don't know why, but I thought you might." In place of his tingly excitement was a cold hollowness.

"Well, I won't, so forget it."

Eldon felt the anger begin to burn inside the hollow. "Maybe you're not as decent as I thought you were. I thought you were, O.B., in spite of the fact that you fucked my wife."

"Now wait. That was a long time—"

"Fucked you a nigger gal. 'You want to fuck, fuck a white girl. You want to *get* fucked, fuck a nigger!' Ain't that what they say?"

"I never said anything like that, Eldon. Not me."

"Maybe not you. But you've heard your white brothers say it. And you haven't said a thing to em." Eldon was aware suddenly that his hands were shaking in his lap. Old Mr. Hubbard. And then O.B. *No. It was not the same thing! I could never forgive old Hubbard!* He clasped his hands tightly. They were hidden from O.B. by the desk. His headache pierced his brain.

"Eldon," O.B. said, "you're talkin about ancient history. We were all children. It was—"

"My wife was a maid in your house, O.B.," Eldon said, his voice taut and trembling. "I don't think I can ever forget that. I can forgive you for it, but I can't forget it."

There was a long silence. O.B.'s face had darkened, and his eyes were steady, glinting.

"You've got a long way to go," Eldon went on, "before you can put things back right." He gripped his fingers tightly together in his lap. "Before you can forget 'ancient history,' as you call it. A long way."

"I'm not responsible for all that, Eldon," O.B. said. His hands were flat on the desk. His body looked tight, ready almost to spring. He still had the look of an athlete.

"Yes, you are," Eldon said. "You and all your white sisters and brothers. And mothers and fathers. From the beginning of time."

The two men stared at one another across the desk, the air heavy and silent between them. Eldon's fury, his helpless rage, was like ashes, heavy ashes smothering his earlier exhilaration. But he knew that he would do anything for his people, that he would work day and night to get O.B. to help him, because it was destiny, a destiny that had been sealed a long time ago. *You owe me. You owe me. I am not finished with you yet!*

~~~

O.B. parked his red International pickup on the street in front of the house. Martha's old black Ford, with the bent right rear fender, was parked at least three feet from the curb. O.B. sat there in the evening quiet, looking up the walkway at the neat brick house, the porchlight glowing in the early darkness. The house was small and compact, yellow brick, with a screened front porch across one side of the front; the screen was dull gray, not shiny anymore, and it seemed to absorb what was left of the day's light rather than reflect it. In the early dusk, he could not see the peeling paint on the window frames, the dry-rotted sill on one of the front bedroom windows that he had not gotten around to repairing. He was afraid to go in. He knew that Martha was drinking again. She had been on the wagon for less than two weeks this time. He had a familiar hollow ache at the base of his chest, a premonition, a feeling of helplessness. He knew he would not leave her, because of Ellen. He had resolved to kick her out if she started drinking again, force her into going home to her parents—maybe *they* could do something with her—but he knew he wouldn't; he had made that vow before, and even though he hated her when she drank, hated her with an intensity that surprised and troubled him, he knew he would only take care of her. Even in his anger. He rubbed his temples, taking a deep breath. He felt that he was beyond forgiving her, beyond loving her in any real sense, and yet he felt attached to her. She was the mother of his daughter. Somewhere inside her now was the high school sweetheart that he had gone with and married; therefore, as he reminded himself over and over, the only woman he had ever loved. It did not work to tell himself that, because he always thought of Cora then, and he was overwhelmed with sadness. He knew now that she was the woman he had truly loved, still loved, but he could not allow himself even to think about that.

His wife had called the shop that afternoon, out of the blue.

"She didn't to out for cheerleader," she had said to him, her voice loose and mushy, making his stomach sink. "I know that was just to spite me. To make me look silly. She hates me, O.B."

"Good God, Martha," he had said. "That was way last spring. Forget it. What are you doin?"

"I was a wonderful cheerleader," she had said, "the best goddam cheerleader Hammond High School ever had! She hates my goddam guts," she had said. He could tell that she was crying.

"Look," he had said, "why don't you take a nap? I'll be home around seven."

"Seven?"

"I've got to run out into the country. Keep everything warm. What are we havin?"

"Havin?"

There had been a silence on the line.

"Why don't you take a nap?"

"Chicken, maybe," she had said. "All right. A nap."

Now he sat looking up the walk. He liked this little three-bedroom house that they'd lived in since right after the war. Martha wanted a new house out in the new subdivision that was opening up south of town. O.B. saw nothing wrong with where they were, a quiet side street near the river, close to the swimming pool in the summer and only ten blocks from the schools, so that Ellen had always walked. He had no idea how he could afford a new house, though many of his friends were building them. Martha had come home from her bridge club talking about all her friends' new houses, and O.B. had been shocked when she told him what their new house payments were. In his lean months, the payments were more than the total that he brought home. Martha had talked about going to work herself, at a dress shop downtown or something, but he knew that was just talk. He opened the door of the pickup, breathing deeply in the chilly evening air. *I will put my foot down. I will make her stop.* It seemed to him that their future together was doomed if she didn't stop drinking. *We cannot continue to be husband and wife if she doesn't stop.* This time he would do it.

She was sitting in the dim living room, watching *The Gale Storm Show*. The only light was the flickering gray from the television screen and the light spilling from the kitchen. He looked to see if she had a drink; an empty coffee cup sat on the end table beside her. She looked at him; her face seemed pale, her eyes slightly unfocused. The tinny laughter erupted from the television.

"I took a nice nap," she said.

"Good," he said. He stood there, not saying anything. He had to stifle his anger, to suppress his abiding hatred.

"What's the matter?" she said.

"You know what's the matter."

"What? What are you talkin about?"

"Oh, come off it, Martha. Where is it?"

"Where's what?"

"The liquor. Where is it?"

She stared at him, a hurt expression on her face. She shook her head and pushed a strand of her black hair behind her ear. It was only slightly flecked with gray, still thick and heavy. He had once loved to put his hands in it, to feel it between his fingers.

"What are you talkin about, O.B.? I haven't been drinkin."

"Shit," he said.

"I don't know what you mean," she said. She turned back to the TV.

"You promised, Martha," he said, "after that last time at the PTA meetin, you promised. Ellen was never so embarrassed in her life, not to mention me."

"You have no right to throw that up to me," she said. He saw that her hands were gripped tightly in her lap, so tightly that her fingers were white. She stared at the TV. He flipped on a light. Her hair was brushed back, loosely. She wore heavy black wool slacks and a wrinkled red sweater. His heart softened as he looked at her. She was still somehow the girl he had loved, still the woman who had completed his life.

"Do you have to turn that on?" she said, squinting. She put her hands, too casually, on the arms of the chair. He could see them shaking. She held her body stiffly.

"You can get your booze out," he said. "You can have another drink. Why do you have to pretend like this?" He looked at her. She stared at the television. "In fact, I'll have one with you. Where is it?" She didn't answer. "What'd you buy this time? Early Times? Vodka? What?" He spat the words at her. He rarely drank, and she looked at him in surprise.

"You want to have one with me?" Her face had brightened.

"Yeah," he said. Maybe it would make it easier for him to do what he had to do.

"A nice drink," she said. "It would relax us both. I picked up some bourbon. It's on the floor in the front bedroom closet. Want me to get it?" She smiled, her face very bright now, gleaming. "No reason in the world why we shouldn't have a drink. Everybody in town's havin a drink. Right?"

"I'll get it," he said. The dull hatred lay like a lump in his belly.

.~.~.~.

She was giggling, almost girlish. She sipped the drink, looking at him over the rim. The television set was turned down, droning on, *The Real McCoys* now, canned laughter coming in spurts and jerks, as she said:

"Ellen won't be home until late. She's studying somewhere."

"Where?" he said.

"Somewhere. Somebody's house. I don't know. Lacy McClellon's, maybe."

"I thought they weren't gettin along these days," he said.

"Who knows?" She smiled at him.

He sipped his second drink. She had bought a half-gallon jug of Old Crow. It now sat openly on the kitchen table.

O.B. felt the bourbon relaxing him, the tenseness going out of his shoulders. Maybe he had failed her. He had carried her off to the North, a young bride, expecting as much as he did. The disappointment was as great for her as for him when he got hurt. Those years of tiny, dingy apartments in the minor-league cities, of smelling like motor oil all winter from his mechanic's job—they told each other that that was just paying dues. And then they got the big break: New York! She had been excited, delirious. Young and beautiful. And then . . . He thought, then, of his decision to start coaching, And he started to tell her about it, but he was afraid she wouldn't think it was important. He was afraid she would spoil it for him, and it was something he wanted badly, wanted even more now that he was here with her, so aware of her drinking. *I have failed her. A long time ago.* He looked at her. She had started drinking when they had come back to Hammond, and he remembered the first binges, after he and Cora—

He wanted to be close to her, to share something with her. To recapture something. He had been thinking about Eldon all the rest of the day. *Cora!* The fact that Eldon thought he would be a good mayor secretly pleased him immensely. But thinking of Eldon brought with it the image of Cora, the image that he fought so hard to cleanse from his mind. It seemed to him that he almost visibly shuddered when he thought of her almond eyes, her soft and yet firm skin, and he was afraid that Martha would see it, would know. Memories of Cora, when they were together, in his youth, were so painful! The older he got, the more painful they became. He was drawn to her body, the heat and intensity that he knew was there, but it was her quiet strength that haunted him. He knew that Eldon loved her for the same reasons. It was wrong for him to feel the way he did. They moved in different worlds. He rarely saw her. And yet he knew the truth of it, too. He knew, in his secret soul, that he had never felt the way he felt with Cora with any other woman. Not even Martha.

He looked over at his wife again. Something in him ached to reach out to her, touch her; he wanted her, *needed* her, to save him from himself. "Eldon Long came by to see me today," he said.

"Oh?" She seemed instantly alert, though she did not look at him. "What about?"

"You won't believe this. . . ."

"What? Yes, I will. Come on."

"He wants me to run for mayor."

"Mayor? Of Hammond?"

"Yes, of course, of Hammond." He leaned back in the chair. He pushed the lingering thoughts of Cora from his mind. He smiled, then looked at Martha. The idea, ridiculous as it was, made him feel good to contemplate. Not *running* for mayor as much as holding office. Maybe it wasn't such a bad idea after all. He was as qualified as Mac. He thought he had the time. He could just *take* the time if he had to. Of course, it might take time away from coaching. . . .

He remembered what Eldon had said about the "Freedom Riders," the other stuff, and he wished that the colored people would just leave well enough alone, but he would probably be a good mayor if all that happened. He thought of the orderly way he would go about the job, the same kind of orderliness that he loved on the baseball diamond; it was a game in which everything made its own kind of sense.

He stopped thinking. He suddenly realized that Martha was laughing. Almost silently, but her head shook with it.

"What?" he said.

"You? God! That's funny," she said. "That's hilarious!"

"Really? Maybe not," he said. The offer to run plus the booze, had put him in a good mood, but he felt his enthusiasm give way to dullness. He sat his drink on the table beside him, staring at her as she laughed.

She stopped her almost silent laughter and looked sideways at him. She shook her head. "Are you serious?" Her eyes seemed amused. He didn't say anything for a moment.

"No," he said, after a moment, looking away from her broad, bloated face.

"Because you couldn't be a mayor like Mac. He's . . . well, he's at least *sophisticated* and all. You? Well, it's kind of funny. Don't you think?"

"Yeah," he said. "I guess." He tried to force away the feelings of resentment, tasting his bitter anger on the back of his tongue. He felt wounded by her attitude, even though he knew from the thickness of her voice that she was drunk. He wondered about how often she was drinking now. Sometimes she would buy several bottles of whiskey and hide them all over the house.

"Martha," he said evenly, "you're gonna have to go to A.A."

"Don't start that again. Come on. We're havin fun."

"I don't know how much more of this I can put up with."

"You're not havin fun? Come on, O.B."

"Okay. But you won't stop here, Martha. You won't quit. You—"

"Yeah, I will. You watch me. This time I will. I can tell. I can feel it. I know about things like that. Really."

He looked at the flickering gray images on the television screen. He could not understand the words of the program; the laughter was like distant tinkling glass. It was absurd, how many times she had made the same promise. He looked at her and realized she actually believed the words.

"I'm not an alcoholic, O.B.," she said. "I'm not."

He didn't answer.

"I couldn't bear to go to that meetin," she went on. "With all those old people. Can't you just imagine who'd be there? Nasty old drunks. I can't believe you'd want me goin to somethin like that. No. People would find out."

"What about the people at the PTA meeting?" he said. He had been pained, embarrassed; she had worn a blouse and skirt that even he could tell did not go together—something that she had blindly thrown on at the last minute; her hair had been mussed and dirty, and she had insisted on standing and commenting on everything that came up, as though that would somehow prove to everyone that she had not been drinking. Or maybe it had been to prove it to herself. During the refreshments after the meeting, she had gone into the ladies' room and puked in the toilet, and one of the teachers had come out and told O.B. that she was ill and he needed to take her home.

And after they were home, she had hurriedly tossed down a couple of jiggers of whiskey, O.B. gagging just to watch her, and then she had slipped and fallen to the kitchen floor, her eyes vague and rolling, and he had stood over her, refusing to help her up, knowing that if he helped her, it was only helping her to stay as she was. "Please," she had said, softly, and he had looked down at her, both rage and heartbreak churning within him. "No," he had said, and he had left her there and gone to bed. In the morning, she was there beside him, her breathing ragged, the sour odor of whiskey hovering over them.

Now, sipping her drink, she said, "The PTA, it just . . . slipped up on me. An empty stomach. They . . . they would understand."

She relaxed back into the chair, stretching her legs out in front of her. She sighed, smiling at him. The color had returned to her face. He could see the tiny wrinkles around her eyes, the puffiness underneath. Her face was round; she had gained fifteen pounds in the last six years. He could see her stomach pushing at the waistband of her slacks. She stood up and stretched, her arms over her head, and a strand of dark hair fell across her face. The old steady anger of their lives gnawed at him. He looked away from her, not wanting to see her.

"We've got plenty of time," she said. She pulled the sweater over her head; then she shook her hair out and stood, hands on hips, looking at him. He looked at her heavy breasts, her large dark nipples. She pushed the wool slacks down her legs and stepped out of them. She wore no underwear. Her large black triangle of pubic hair was right in front of his face. He felt a stirring, a movement, in his groin.

He thought that Ellen might come in anytime. They should at least be in the bedroom.

"Martha," he said. "I don't . . ."

"What?"

He wanted to resist, but he knew his sex was betraying him. She took his hand and pulled him to his feet. She put her arms around his neck, grinding her body against his; she kissed him, hard, and he could taste the whisky, smell it. Her tongue was cold and wet. His hands, almost of their own accord, dropped and cupped her buttocks. He felt curiously outside himself, detached, an observer. He was aware of his tight erection, but it seemed not a part of him.

He stepped back, then, looking into her swollen face, at her lop-sided grin. He could smell the harsh fumes of the whiskey and hear again in his mind her laughter. How he resented her easy dismissal of the idea of him running for mayor, even if he had scoffed at it himself. He backed away. The grin faded from her face, and her eyes became hard and dull. "You bastard," she hissed.

"That's right," he said. "You're goddam right!"

She looked at him, her face contorted, her eyes puzzled.

"I've had it, Martha," he said. "I'm movin into the guest room."

"What?" she said.

"You heard me! We'll share a roof, but not a bed. Until you quit drinkin, go to A.A., get straightened out, then—"

"Wait—"

"No, that's the way it is." He was edging toward the door, away from her. He could see tears in her eyes.

"But . . . Please!" she said.

His body moved to the door and out, almost of its own accord, and he felt the cold night air on his face, almost startling him after the close warmth of the house. Thoughts of Cora exploded in his mind like a vivid dream suddenly remembered, and he felt his heart shriveling within him. Cora, as she had looked when they were young, almost children and yet as tragically adult as they could ever be, the faded

flour-sack dress clinging to her ripe body, the sunlight dancing darkly
in her laughing, taunting eyes, her skin like the richest, sweetest syrup,
not sweet but salty and pungent on his eager, boyish lips. She had
stood before him like a statue, a madonna, with tufts of tightly curled
black hairs beneath her outstretched arms. Her palms had been almost
white, creamy and smooth in the summer sun.

When we were young. Martha had been young once, too.

He meant it. He could not, would not, live with Martha as husband
again until she came back to him from the depths of that hell that had
taken her away, taken their youth and their innocence, he vowed,
hugging his arms tightly against his chest, walking toward the river,
feeling the tears begin to sting his eyes in the darkness.

Chapter Two

❧

ELDON DROVE HIS BLACK '53 CHEVROLET DOWN THE MAIN STREET of the town that had been a part of him all his life, so much so that he could not imagine living anywhere else—past the stores, most of them closing now, past the segregated movie theater, the Dauphin, at the end of Washington Street. It was showing *Please Don't Eat The Daisies*. He turned north, and after a couple of blocks the pavement ran out and the street was gravel and mud, rutted, with potholes. Limerock ditches lined the street and reflected the late afternoon winter sunlight. He passed his church, whitewashed brick, fairly new, and he felt the familiar warm gush of pride. It had been built in 1949, and it sat back on a large lot, between the shanties crowded around it. He loved the church because it was a symbol to his people, with its simple steeple pointing upward. Not only to heaven, but upward on this earth, too, he often told them. He turned onto Ashe Street, a muddy, narrow street lined with cramped maroon cabins with steep roofs. He could smell open privies and hog pens, coal fires and cooking smells, greens. In the middle of the block was their little house, their place— more than a shanty, more like the lower-class white houses in Short- leaf—dark brick veneer, with a screen porch across the front. It had been built by a man who, for twenty years, had been principal of

U. S. Smith High School, the colored high school; they had bought it after he had died. Eldon guided the car down the narrow limerock driveway and around to the back.

Eldon called his wife's name when he came into the house. "Cora?" There was no answer. Her name echoed in the empty house. This was the next step. He was going to have it out with her about the boys, the young white men from the North. He wanted them to stay down here in Frogbottom with them, and she was against that. Stubborn. He had his own ideas about what the boys were going to do when they got here, and he thought it was vitally important that they saw life, *lived* life, as close to the way his people did as possible. He wanted them to smell the hog slop, the acrid, nauseating stench of burning garbage, the seeping dampness of the limerock ditches. He wanted them using the privies, tasting food cooked on coal stoves.

He took off his suit coat and went through the little hallway, back to their bedroom. There were no closets in the bedrooms, and they kept their clothes on racks in the corners; why would anybody ever build a house like this without closets in the bedrooms? Eldon took off his tie and slung it over a ten-penny nail that he kept in a wall beam for that purpose. He had exactly ten neckties, dark blue or black striped, and they were draped over the nail. Eldon looked at his lean face in the small mirror over their chest of drawers; his eyes looked strained, and his thin mustache looked ragged and uneven as he brushed it with his finger. The house was overheated; he noticed that the gas heater in the corner was turned up full blast, and he could see the heat waves in the air, radiating out from it. He went into the bathroom, feeling the floor give slightly; it had been added to the house, and the floor had never been completely steady. Their daughter, Sally, had the small bathroom next to her bedroom on the other side of the hall; for years it had been the only one in the house. Eldon splashed cold water in his face and dried it carefully. The towel was coarse, and it smelled of detergent. He patted his cheeks and his forehead, then looked at his teeth in the mirror over the sink. They were startlingly white against his dark skin, and he always took pleasure in that. He noticed that the collar of his stiff white shirt was frayed.

Eldon went back to the living room, sat down, and picked up *The Birmingham News*, scanning the headlines. He wondered if Kennedy, just inaugurated last month, would make any real difference way down here. He doubted it. He turned to the sports pages and looked at the basketball scores. He wondered where Cora was. He had no idea how he was going to get her to agree about the boys from up North. He would use logic. He smiled to himself, but then he frowned. He did not want to bully her, and thinking of her he felt a wave of sympathy. But he would not give in. It was his responsibility, and he would simply tell her that that was the way it was going to be.

His mind wandered back to his conversation with O. B. Brewster. The man was bull-headed, all right. But he could make a lot of difference. Eldon just could not allow himself to think about O.B. and Cora. Instead, he focused on that moment—it seemed hundreds of years ago—when he had known that God was calling him, when he had suddenly and without forewarning realized that he was in this world for a purpose. At first he had realized it in the heated, sweaty, heavily perfumed air of a little frame church in the Flatwoods, caught up in the shouting and singing, the rhythms, the very heartbeat of his people. God was there, in the air, in the walls and behind the pulpit of the sagging wooden building. Then he began to feel special, some-how singled out, and while he did not understand why, he did not question it. When he had decided he was a minister of God, he had expected miracles to accompany the decision, the lightning and thun-der promised him on Jordan's stormy banks. He had heard an old minister named Ned Clay, who reeked of cheap whiskey and spoke so rapidly that he was hard to understand, weaving and stumbling in the pulpit, his eyes unfocused, whether by whiskey or his passion Eldon couldn't tell.

"De Lord tole Nicodemus, you muss be bone again. Nicodemus say to the Lord, he say, how I done be born again affer I done been born outta my motha? The Lord say, you believe, you done been born again. You believe, you in the church! Lord Jesus!"

These words were a sudden revelation to Eldon, and God's presence suddenly was like fire in his breast. He had been seventeen years old. *"Don't worry about all them Ten Commandments,"* the old man had said. *"Jesus, he say don't worry bout em. They axed him, say, what about them Ten Commandments? He say they ain't but two, ain't but two commandments! Love the Lord! The Lord thy God! And den go outchere and love yo neighbor. Love yo neighbor as yoself! Amen! On them two, he say, hang all them others, all them laws of prophets and such! Love yo neighbor, friends, and you loves God! You love yo neigh-bor, you ain't gone do harm to him, you ain't gone covet and such, nor murder and steal! Lord Jesus! Love him! Love everybody! Love the white man that don't pay you doodlem, treat you like yard-dirt! Love him! If you love him, den you can love the Lord!"*

Eldon had sat there, stunned, looking about at the faces around him, some amused, some rapturous, some bored, and he had known that only he had heard the message, only he knew. He had heard it expressed better in later years, just recently by Martin King himself, but he had never felt it so clearly and so eloquently as he had at seventeen, and he had known then his mission in life. He would serve God, but he would serve Him by serving his people, by putting Jesus' message into action. Social action. Now he knew he had a lifetime of work ahead of him, and he did not believe in miracles anymore. He knew that he could not rely on God to help him. He knew that miracles, if they were possible, could occur only in the hearts of men.

He thought of Sally. He was conscious of the fact that he focused his dream on Sally. His vision was that within his lifetime, she would be able to go to the University of Alabama, be the Phi Beta Kappa she was capable of being, and then be able to do anything she wanted to do, be any person she wanted to be. She could eat in restaurants, drive down the highway and stop at filling stations to use the bathroom, sit anywhere she damn well pleased in a moving-picture show. More than that, she would never again be "niggered," never again be treated like something less than human, and the pain and the bitterness he was already seeing building in her, young as she was, would disappear into the air. He dreamed that he would be able to see that, to know the happiness that would bring.

The two civil rights workers were due in from Atlanta at the end of the week, and Eldon would not allow any of the bad things he had heard about, over in Mississippi, for instance, to happen to them. He lowered the paper to his lap. He licked his dry lips. He knew that he could expect only indifference and hostility from Mac McClellon and his police chief, Lester Sparks. And Rooster Wembley and his cohorts were capable of all sorts of intimidation, even bloodshed. He knew it was going to be a long spring and summer, and he knew it would be crucial, might even make the difference between success or failure, if he could throw some of the attention onto O. B. Brewster and the race for mayor. The more he had thought about it, since it had first occurred to him, the more he had become convinced that O.B. had a chance to win. He was respected, even adored, by everybody in town because of the baseball when he was young, and all the Negroes who were registered to vote, not very many, Eldon knew, but some—and there would be more by that time—would vote for him, along with a lot of whites.

He heard someone at the front door. Cora came in, shedding her heavy coat. She saw him and said, "Oh."

"I surprise you?"

"I just didn't know anybody was home." She draped the coat over a chair next to the door. "Sally home?"

"No."

She sat down on the sofa across from him and sighed. "Rough day?" he asked, and she nodded, rolling her eyes. Her beauty still almost took his breath away. His heart still sometimes pounded like a schoolboy's when he was first with her. She was tall, a couple of inches taller than he was, and her skin was slightly lighter and smooth. Her color reminded him of rich molasses. She was a lean woman, with youthful, plump breasts and wide hips, but no fat at all. She still had on the dress that she had worn to teach in. Pale blue, with a satiny finish. She seemed ageless; he imagined that if he had not known her so intimately, it would have been difficult for him to tell her age. Sometimes he felt . . . that she was not really his. That their almost twenty years together had been a strange dream, a cruel trick that God had played on him. It was because of O.B., he knew, and as he sat admiring her, he felt the bitterness and sadness that had always tinged his dizzying, steadfast love for her.

"I'm tired," she said. "I get very tired."

"I love you, Cora," Eldon said, and she glanced over at him, her eyebrows arched, a curious smile on her face. He dropped the newspaper to the floor. "Well, listen," he said, "we might as well talk about it. Before Sally gets home."

Her face was puzzled. "About what?"

"About the workers. The boys."

"Ohhh," she groaned. "I thought we'd settled that."

"No, we didn't. We've got that back bedroom back there—"

"That old bed ain't fit for—"

"They need to live in the quarter. With us. They need to live nigger, Cora. They want to, and the organization wants em to." He tried to make his voice forceful, final.

"The Youngbloods said they'd put em up. I think that's mighty brave of em, myself," Cora said.

"The Youngbloods are white."

"Yes," she said, "they are. So?"

"Those boys need to stay down here with us. Close to the church. For the citizenship classes. They need to know what it's like livin in Frogbottom."

"They're *white* boys, Eldon. Comin down here from God knows where."

"Yale. They both go to Yale."

"Wherever," she said. "Don't make any difference. They don't know a thing about us. What you think the white people in this town'd say about two white college boys from the North livin down here with us colored folks?" She looked at him.

"They can say what they want to," Eldon said, turning away from her.

There was a silence in the room. Eldon could hear the hissing of the gas space heater. He felt anew some of the humiliation and rage that had plunged him into the depths twelve years ago, when Cora had come to him and confessed that she and O.B. had given in to the temptation again, had renewed their old lust. The pain was still too real for him. *I have forgiven! I have forgiven!* He could not let it go. *I must surrender, give it up to Him.*

"All right," she said, "I hear what you're sayin. But I'm dead set against it, Eldon. We don't know those boys. Sally's livin in this house. A seventeen-year-old girl, and you want to move these boys in here?"

"They wouldn't be comin down here if they wasn't serious about it."

"But college boys? No." She crossed her arms across her breasts. "They stay with the Youngbloods. They'll be safer there."

"You know Sally can take care of herself with— Wait!" He squinted at her. "What did you say? Safer? With those crazy people?"

She was staring at him, her black eyes flashing. "You think I want em *here*? Some of these trash white people might take it in their heads to blow somethin up. And it just might be this house. No, sir. Ain't no way."

"They're stayin with us."

She stood up. "No, they're not, Eldon. If they stay in this house, it'll be with just *you*." She looked down at him, her dark eyes intense. "It won't be with *us*."

"What you mean?" he said. For the second time that day, he knew that his confidence had sunk so low that he felt the old familiar sense of hope deferred descending on him. *Even Cora . . . Even Cora!*

"I don't want em here, Eldon," she was saying, her voice pleading now. "I don't like all this."

"All what?"

"The movement. The way it is now. It scares me. You . . . you can't think of anything else. Since you got back—"

"We're talkin bout freedom here," he said, his voice tight and strained. "We're talkin bout justice and dignity."

"We've always talked about that. All of a sudden you—"

"Justice and dignity." He held himself erect, liking the way the words sounded, grasping at them. They could bring him back, bring him up.

She stared at him for a moment. "Those words don't mean a whole lot to me, Eldon," she said. "They sound like just words. I'm talkin bout survival. I'm doing what I can. I go to that school every day, try to cram math into those heads. Their folks don't even want em there, can't wait till they get out. They don't see any need for addin five and three. Five and three what? You think they care about dignity? They care about findin some fatback and collards. Enough to feed a child and get her through the day. That's what I care about, too."

He ached with the disappointment of what she was saying. "Don't you care about your daughter's future?" he demanded, but his voice sounded weak in his own ears.

"Yeah, I do," she said, "but I got to get her to it first."

"With that kinda thinkin, we'll never get there," he said bitterly.

She sighed, looking at him. "You take too much on yourself, honey," she said. "You take it all on your shoulders. You lettin it take you over."

"I'm gonna pretend I don't hafta do that? That's like a catfish sayin he ain't in water. He is. All the time. That's what makes him a fish." He detected a whine in his voice, and he hated it. He sat very erect.

There was a long silence. She looked away.

"I ain't the only one that thinks like that, you know," she said.

"I know," he said. "And I'm gonna hafta change you, every one of you. I can't rest, Cora, until I bring justice to all my people, whether they know they want it or not."

He rolled his sleeves up, then picked up the paper and fanned himself. "It's hot in here," he said, and she got up and went over and started to adjust the space heater. He watched her as she bent over, her long flank clearly visible under the fabric. Her strong, sturdy hands twisted the lever. She chewed on her lower lip, concentrating on the level of adjustment. Noticing little details like that could still fill his chest with an almost choking love for her. He still considered her the most beautiful woman he had ever known, and he knew that was rare after almost twenty years of marriage. Sometimes, he thought he loved her too much.

"I talked to O. B. Brewster today," he said, and he saw her stiffen.

"What about?" she asked softly, looking at him quizzically. So that's it, her eyes seemed to say. So that's the pebble in your boot!

"I'm trying to talk him into runnin for mayor," he said. "Against

Mac McClellon. He doesn't want to, but I'll convince him." He tried to be casual, businesslike, but his voice almost trembled.

"No, you won't," she said.

He cocked his head. His eyes searched her face. "What do you mean?" he said.

"You know O.B. as well as I do. He ain't gonna run for *mayor*, for heaven's sake." She sat back down, not looking at him.

Eldon ran his fingers lightly across his forehead. His mouth was dry. "No," he said, "I won't rest until I accomplish that, either. He'll run." He was thinking of O.B. and Cora together, and he could tell by the look on her face, facing the wall, that she knew he was. *White skin. Brown skin.* "I don't think I'll ever be able to get all that out of my mind," he said.

"You got to, Eldon. It doesn't do any good. It was a long time ago."

"I can understand when we were children. Children do things like that. But then the second time . . ."

"You forgave me that a long time ago. That has to be enough. For us," Cora said softly.

"I forgave you. God forgave you. But He won't let me forget it." He looked away, tears burning his eyes.

"Are we gonna go through our whole lives tensin up like this every time one or the other of us mentions or sees or thinks about O. B. Brewster?"

He swallowed. He tried to blink back the tears. "It looks that way, Cora. I can't help it. I try."

"I love *you*, Eldon. That's the end of it. Maybe you ought to just . . . avoid O.B. Don't think about him. Don't go around him."

He sat looking back at her now. "Maybe I'll do that," he said. He could tell from the look on her face that she knew he wouldn't. Her look was puzzled, curious and hurt at the same time. She sighed.

"Well . . ." she said.

He wanted to say, *But I can't not think about you, not go around you,* but he didn't. After a minute, he smiled weakly at her, feeling stiff and awkward. She did love him. *Of course she loved him. Only him.*

·~·~·~·

Cora was in the kitchen when she heard someone on the porch, and she came up the little hallway and into the living room just as Sally came through the front door, slamming it behind her. She had on what looked like men's khaki pants and an old, worn flannel-lined denim jacket that she had found somewhere. Her hair was clipped short. She nodded and started through the room toward the hallway. Cora did not move aside.

"My God, Sally, you're dressed like a field hand," Cora said.

"That's the idea, muh-dear," Sally said. She stopped.

"Don't you even say hello?" Eldon gently chided.

"All right," she said. "Hello." She stood awkwardly, first on one foot, then the other. She was small and thin, as he was, and she had his hair, thin and fine, forming tight curls around her face.

"Where you been?" Cora said.

"Why?" Sally's lips were narrow and dark. Today her face looked sullen, clouded.

"I was just makin conversation. How was your day, that sorta stuff," Cora said. "Excuse *me*." The girl had changed so much, just in recent months. As though she had suddenly become someone Cora did not know. And someone she knew all too well.

"Around." Sally paused. Then she looked directly at her father. "I been hangin around with Nathaniel," she said.

Cora saw quick anger on Eldon's face. He gripped the arms of his chair, then looked away. Sally knew they didn't approve of her going around with Nathaniel Pierson. He had not finished the eighth grade, and he worked out at the veneer mill. He wore a woman's stocking tied around his head, and he had been involved in a couple of fights, even a cutting at the Silver Moon Cafe.

"Trouble," Cora said. "Trouble walkin round." She didn't think she sounded very convincing. She well knew what Sally saw in the boy. She had noticed him, the way he walked, almost stalking. She had seen their youthful bodies, side by side.

"Maybe," Sally said. "he's a black man, ain't he?"

"Sally," Eldon said, softly, "don't start—"

"He's mad," Sally said. "He's got a right to be. He's pissed off. So am I."

Cora snorted. "You can't be just *generally* pissed off."

"Yes, you can," Sally said, looking at her, eyes flashing.

"What good does it do? He's fulla hate, Sally," Cora said.

"So am I," the girl said.

Sally looked very small in the oversized jacket. She looked young and vulnerable, little more than a baby. Cora felt a fervent protectiveness toward her, knowing what she was feeling. *God knows I know. It hasn't been so long since . . . since . . .*

"There's a new day comin, honey," Eldon said gently.

"Shit," Sally said. "It's comin too slow."

"Sally," Cora said, "don't you talk to your daddy like that." Her voice, she knew, lacked conviction. She, too, was tired of talk of the "new day," but for different reasons from her daughter's. It frightened her, made her feel timid and cautious.

"It's all right," Eldon said.

"Who are *you* to tell me anything?" Sally said to her mother. She spit the words. "You so busy tryin to be white. Oreo."

"That's enough!" Cora said. The intensity of her daughter's anger these days always surprised her when it surfaced.

"I got to live in the house with Uncle Tom and Aunt Jemima—"

"I said that's enough, Sally. Now stop it!" Cora was looking down at the girl. "Go on to your room."

"No," Sally said. She eased toward the door. "I'm goin back out."

"Honey," Cora began, her voice softer, pleading. "Honey, don't act like—"

"Sometimes I feel like I want to bust," Sally said bitterly. She went out the door, slamming it behind her. They heard the screen door's rattle, then silence. Cora sat down. They sat there in the quiet for a few minutes. She could hear a clock ticking, back in the kitchen.

"What are we gonna do with her?" Cora said.

"She'll grow out of it," Eldon said.

"Will she?" Cora said. They looked at each other.

"She's just a child," he said.

"No," Cora said. "She ain't a child." She stared at the flowered rug. Images of her own girlhood suddenly flooded her. *I know what you feel, Sally, I know.* She had known that burning, that intensity. That fierce recklessness. After a minute, she stood up. "I'm gonna fry us some eggs. You want bacon?"

"Yeah," he said.

She paused by the door. He had picked up the newspaper. "Eldon, those boys? They not stayin here. I don't care what you do, I don't care where you go. Go stay with em if you want to. But don't bring em into my house." She was not looking at him, and there was only silence from where he sat. She stood there a second, then moved back down the hall and into the kitchen.

She took a deep breath, smelling the faint, acrid scent of the butane gas from the heaters, the warm-quilt smells of the house. The kitchen was still, afternoon empty. There was, in these days, a fire in Sally's eyes that had once been so much a part of her, Cora, that it was almost like looking in a mirror, seeing a long-buried other self staring back at her out of some lost time. It excited her. It stirred her, frightened her. The fire was untamed, wild, and she knew that it was her own.

◆·◆◆·

Mac McClellon sat looking at the man from Gulf International Paper Company, who sat in the chair across the desk from him. He was admiring the man's suit and trying to recall his name at the same time. They had just shaken hands, the man mumbling his name, and the man had placed his black leather attaché case on Mac's desk. He sat there, his legs crossed, looking around Mac's spacious office, out the windows that looked out across Washington Street to the park, with the fountain, and beyond that, clearly visible through the leafless trees, the tall Confederate monument. Mac's office was on the third floor of the bank, in an old, remodeled mercantile building. There were tasteful prints that his wife, Belinda, had chosen, scenes from the town and its history, on the walls; his desk was massive, dark-stained, and heavy, the carpet thick and plush. The man across the desk from Mac wore the kind of suit that Mac had always envied: dark gray with light pinstripes and a matching vest. Mac had bought at least twenty suits just like this one over the years, but they never looked right on him; the vests were always too tight and uncomfortable, with a corset feeling that annoyed Mac all day long. He always looked chunky and square in his suits, no matter how much he paid for them.

What the hell am I thinking about? Mac forced his concentration back to the meeting. And its purpose. The man's name was . . . Byrd. Carleton Byrd. Mac remembered his flowery signature. He spoke with a clipped, midwestern accent. Like a newscaster.

Mac sighed, grinning, nodding his head. He was nervous, and he hoped it didn't show. He was hoping, *praying*, that he could get a commitment out of the man. Gulf International Paper was very close to announcing that they were building a new $84 million paper mill south of Hammond, along the river, and Mac wanted desperately for the deal to go through. He took his position as mayor seriously. He had been a leader in Hammond ever since he had been in high school, where he had been president of the senior class and voted most likely to succeed. And not only for the town did he want it. He himself had some land parcels and building projects that would make him a rich man if everything worked out. And if things *didn't* work out . . . He shivered. He did not like to think about that. It was mostly his secret, just how much he was gambling on this deal. He was borrowed and mortgaged to the hilt, not only what

little money he himself had but his wife's family money, and the
resources of this bank, which had been founded back in the last century by his wife's grandfather.

Yeah, Mac brooded. My ass is on the line.

"That's a nice suit," Mac said. Carleton Byrd looked quickly at him,
his lips poised in a half-smile. He seemed to find that remark funny for
some reason.

"Thank you," he said, "Mr. McClellon."

"Mac."

"Mr. Mayor," he said, still smiling, "Mac."

"Nobody's ever called me 'Mr. Mayor,' to tell you the truth," Mac
said.

"I guess not." Carleton Byrd nodded. He looked very clean-shaven.
Mac could detect the faint scent of a shaving lotion or cologne. It
smelled expensive. Mac coughed discreetly. He detested men who
wore expensive-smelling shaving lotion. Who talked down to him as if
they were aristocracy and he were nothing.

Mac knew that even more than the wealth he stood to gain, he
wanted to be a part of the aristocracy. He wanted to be from an old
family, to have a "pedigree," and live in a grand old house with
painted ceilings and a parlor with those family portraits with eyes that
followed you all over the room. Such a house, and the genteel life it
represented, had always been painfully foreign, and closed to Mac, but
it seemed to represent a time, an Old South, that was the very model
of decency and graciousness.

What Mac wanted, more than anything else in the world, was to be
invited to the annual Shady Grove Deer Drive, out at Shady Grove
Plantation. It was held every fall, dating back to the Civil War, and it
was presided over by old man Thomas Jonathan Merriweather, who sat
on the board of directors of Planters and Merchants Bank and who
looked coldly at Mac down his thin nose, speaking to him as though
to a clerk. Senators went to the hunt, and wealthy landowners. Even
the governor came occasionally. You had to be somebody to be invited, and it was not so much just having money. Hell, it wasn't like
the country club, where you could just buy your way in. No, the
Shady Grove hunt was something else entirely. A memory that still
rankled Mac was the fact that even O. B. Brewster had once been
invited, the fall after he came home from playing in the major leagues
(not that he ever did a goddam thing but just be up there!). Ever since
then, Mac had secretly resented him for that, since O.B. came from
even lower beginnings than Mac did.

Mac's parents were both dead, his daddy boozed and worked to death as a laborer in a veneer mill before he was fifty, his mother an old woman worn-out and tired in her early thirties. His father had put him down constantly when he was a boy, and Mac had wanted desperately to prove that he was not as sorry and resigned and hopeless as his father was. He had studied hard in high school, mostly in secret because he didn't want the other boys to know; he furtively collected books of jokes so that he could make people laugh, and he went out for football when he was not a very good athlete and had to work doubly hard even to make the team, finally excelling enough in his senior year to play guard and make all-conference. He had worked his way through the commerce school at the university. When he graduated, he married the girl he'd dated in high school and then at the university, the girl who represented the world for which he longed. Belinda had not wanted to live in her family's old house where she had grown up, so they'd sold it and built a new one out near the country club. Mac had known almost immediately what a mistake that was. He sensed it more than he knew it. It was like a sin to sell that old antebellum home, and that had something to do with his being snubbed by the Shady Grove Hunt Club. He had married into a good old family, with money. He was well liked still. As mayor, he had shepherded Hammond as it had grown from a sleepy little river village of about six thousand people to a town of ten thousand, now on the verge of a huge economic boom, but he was still not invited to the Shady Grove Deer Drive. He had gotten the idea that maybe he would be accepted by the aristocracy if he made money on his own, by his own wit and cleverness, instead of relying on his wife's money. The idea had grown, becoming the driving force of his life. Now here he was. This was the big gamble. He had put everything, *everything*, on it.

He smiled at Carleton Byrd, his mouth as dry as sand. "Was the hotel all right last night?" Mac asked. "There's a motel outside of town—"

"Oh, yes. Fine. Quite charming, actually. The Hammond Inn. That's unusual in the South, isn't it?"

"What's that?" Mac said.

"Inn. New England has a lot of inns, but in the South, they're usually hotels."

"We got both, I reckon." Mac had never thought about it before. He wondered what the man was getting at.

"I've spent quite a bit of time in southern hotels," Byrd said. "Of course, as you know, we've looked at quite a few places."

"Yeah. And you won't find one any better than Hammond. We got it all, Mr. Byrd." *You son of a bitch.* Mac's grin felt stiff, like crinkly paper. *You prissy asshole.*

Byrd settled back in the chair. He took out a package of Marlboros and extracted one. Mac fumbled around on the desk and found a book of matches. PLANTERS AND MERCHANTS BANK. *Home Owned and Operated!* Byrd accepted the matches, lit his cigarette, and blew the smoke at the ceiling. Mac could see that his fingernails were very neatly manicured. *At least he put the goddam matchbook in his shirt pocket.*

"Mac," Byrd began, smiling. "We were about ninety-five percent sure we were going to build this new plant over in Montgomery. It was perfect. Montgomery's larger than Hammond, with better schools—"

"Oh, now," Mac said, "I wouldn't say—" but Byrd held up his hand, stopping him.

"I said we *were.* This plant will employ eight hundred to a thousand workers once it's finished. Its economic impact on wherever it's located will be almost immeasurable. Now, you know, of course, *why* we're not building it in Montgomery, don't you, Mac?" Mac started to answer, but Byrd held his hand up again. "We're not building it because of all the racial troubles over there. You understand that it's very frustrating for our company, all this racial business in the South. Since the Supreme Court decision about the Little Rock schools, all that? All these rumblings. We like the South. We *love* the South. Our company has doubled its production of pulp in the last three years, and in another three, by 1964, we'll double it again." He paused. "The south has been good to us. We like the labor costs, the tax structure, the cost of living, everything about it. Almost. Let me put it bluntly. You must, at all costs, hold down the . . . uh . . . racial troubles, or we will reevaluate the situation."

Mac blinked. *What the hell was all this double-talk?* "You mean," he said, "you've already . . . evaluated it?"

"Not quite," Byrd said. "Not completely. We are looking at a lot of places, as I say."

"You said 'reevaluate.' "

"I misspoke myself. I don't want to get ahead, here. There's still the matter of the land."

"I told you, it's all taken care of," Mac said. "It's next to the old airport. The city owns half of it already. I'm workin on the rest." Actually, he had bought it, sinking several hundred thousand in limerock-strewn pastureland full of clumps of Cherokee roses and scrub cedars, land that wouldn't grow doodly squat but that was strategically located.

"The airstrip will have to be lengthened and resurfaced, of course."

"Of course," Mac said. *Of course! Say it prissy!*

"Our corporation is buying a jet," Byrd said.

"Is that right? A jet plane? One of these big suckers?" Mac was impressed in spite of himself. This *was* a big company.

"Big enough. I think they said it would be eight-passenger. But never mind about that. Everything about the land will have to be signed, sealed, and delivered before any announcement is made."

"Yeah. Well." Mac leaned back in his chair. There were no problems there. It was all lined up. "That'll be no problem, no problem at all." Mac cleared his throat. "Actually, it's more like, well, private assurance that I want. You know?"

"I beg your pardon?" Byrd said.

Asshole. He knew what Mac was talking about.

"Those houses we talked about?" Mac said. Byrd had told him earlier, in a phone conversation, that Tendall Construction Company, a large multinational company out of Birmingham, would build the plant, and they would soon be sending in executives and supervisors who would need houses to live in. ("Nice houses," Byrd had said, "ones that can then be resold to our own people when they come in. And some middle-range homes and apartments as well, Mr. McClellon, for the employees. Real estate is going to boom around here!")

Now Mac said, "To the man ownin the right land, buildin on speculation . . . well, we got the potential for some real money here. Like, the right businessman is gonna become a millionaire, right? You understand that kinda talk, don't you Mr. Byrd?"

"Indeed I do. We, of course, are not in the housing business."

"Just between me and you, Mr. Byrd, I am. Just recently, I have definitely gone into the real estate and housing business. Me and another guy, we're startin in to build some houses."

"Good," Byrd said.

"I don't mind tellin you that I am investin some heavy cash in it, too. And it would help me a lot if—"

"I can't give you anything definite, Mac. I can't commit for a multinational company like ours on the basis purely of . . . well, local economy."

Mac leaned back in his chair, watching his hands shake slightly as he fiddled with the edge of a blotter on his desk. He had thought about this, planned it in detail. ("What are you schemin about now?" Belinda had sarcastically demanded, just last night.)

"I don't suppose that you, or . . . well, any of your friends, would like to get in on this, would you?" Mac asked. Byrd drew on his cigarette, looking off out the window. Mac felt almost hatred for the man. He felt alone, dangling out on a precarious limb. "I could make it real attractive to anybody with just a little tiny bit to invest. Real attractive." Maybe this was a crude gesture, not what people of quality would do, Mac worried. Maybe this was the wrong way to go about it.

"I'm not here to talk about that," Byrd said, dismissing Mac with a wave of his hand. "I'm here to tell you that the one thing we can't have, and it's in all the papers, it's everywhere, is racial turmoil. Publicly, we have to take a particular stand on that."

Mac, stinging over Byrd's casual rejection of his offer to cut the man in, waved *his* hand, but it was a hesitant, halfhearted gesture. "Seems to me like this is America. You can take any stand you want to."

"There is only one stand that is publicly feasible at this time, Mr. McClellon."

"What's that?" said Mac, genuinely puzzled.

Byrd smiled. He crushed out the cigarette in the large glass ashtray with the University of Alabama seal on Mac's desk. Mac felt uneasy, suspicious. "I can't get over the naïveté of you southerners, Mr. McClellon."

"Mac. Whattaya mean?"

"If we were simply a southern company, that would be one thing. But we are multinational. Your . . . way of life is very 'special' shall we say. But it is a thing of the past. Our investment is in the future. The world is changing, Mac."

"Yeah, well," Mac said. He almost blustered on, then he caught himself. He took a deep breath. It would be very important what he said on this subject. He concentrated, hard. "Let me tell you somethin," he said. "This is a nice little town. The nig— The Kneegrows here are happy. They don't want to go to school with the white people. They got one of the best colored schools around right here in town. They don't want all this integration stuff these outside agitators are forcin down their throats. I know that, Mr. Byrd, cause I've talked to em. I'm their mayor. They voted for me. They talk to me straight. It's not them that wants all this. Martin Luther Coon don't speak for the . . . colored people in Hammond. Pardon me for callin him that, maybe you don't know he's a communist."

"That's not my concern," Byrd said. "I'm just telling you. My company wants to build this plant. My company *needs* to build this plant, and build it now. But we will hold off indefinitely if we have to. We don't know what's going to come of all this—"

"Nothin," Mac said. "It won't amount to a hill a beans."

"Well, we don't like what seems to be happening in Montgomery, and up in Greensboro. It would not be good for our . . . corporate image."

"Them places ain't like here. Hammond is a good town. We've got good people, colored and white. I know ever' body in town, call em by their first name. I can guarantee you, *double-ought guarantee* you that there ain't gonna be any crap like that goin on in my town." Mac slammed his flattened hand on the desk, and it made a louder noise then he had anticipated. Mr. Byrd flinched. Mac hoped he was getting across to the man. Most outsiders didn't know how it was hereabouts.

"For your sake, and for the sake of your . . . ahh . . . investments, Mac, I hope you're right." Byrd smiled, and Mac squirmed. He heard his swivel chair creak under him. *Was that some kind of threat?*

Mac's stomach felt hollow, tingly. For the first time, he wondered if he was right about the niggers, as he realized that Byrd was going to keep him on a string. He had hoped to get it settled, to know something definite. Now he had to worry about the niggers.

They shook hands, and Byrd left, leaving the faint scent of his cologne lingering in the air behind him. Mac stared out the window, across the park to the Confederate statue. Maybe, when the invitation to the Shady Grove Deer Drive came, he would tell them to stick it up their aristocratic asses. They were the sons of the men who had been the officers in the Civil War. The men who rode fancy horses and wore tailor-made uniforms, and had the nigger-slave body servants. They'd sent *his* antecedents into battle to fight and die for *their* right to own land and slaves, and after the war they'd worked those foot soldiers, the ones who managed to survive, half to death before their time. *They will say, Come on in, you are one of us at last.* And then he would decide, Mac told himself. The important thing now was that he had to have that invitation, to make his life whole.

·~·~·~·

Mac was coming back from lunch at Maud's Cafe, a toothpick jutting from his lips, enjoying the nippy, clear air, when he spotted Eldon Long walking toward him. He didn't know the preacher well, but knew him to be a leader among the colored. Eldon was talking with two

young white men whom Mac didn't recognize. One of them was tall
and blond, and the other was short and Italian-looking. Mac decided
that he might as well start being friendly.

"Well, Eldon, weather turned off nice, didn't it?" he called. Eldon
seemed startled. He stopped, chewing on his lip as he stared at Mac.
He had on the same dark suit that Mac always saw him in. Or he had
several like it, Mac guessed, as he wondered what the preacher was up
to, talking to these white boys.

"Y'all doin all right?" Mac asked, looking at the two young men.
They looked to be about twenty years old. The Italian-looking one's
hair was long in the back and curled down over his collar. They both
had on blue denim work shirts and baggy, wrinkled pants. *Who in hell
are they?*

"Mr. McClellon," Eldon said. He hesitated, looking around, up
and down the street and over in the square. "This is . . . well, I'd like
you to meet Paul Siegel." The tall blond one stuck out his hand, and
Mac took it and shook. "And this is Joe Mancini."

"Well, you fellows new in town?" Mac said, shaking Mancini's
hand.

"Yeah," Mancini said.

"This is Mac McClellon, our mayor," Eldon said.

"The mayor? Well," Mancini said.

"Yeah. The mayor," Mac said. He didn't like the young fellow's
tone. "What you fellows up to?" He had a vague feeling of unease.
Yankees.

"We're here to start a voter registration drive," the tall blond said.
He grinned sheepishly at Mac. Joe Mancini stared at him, his dark eyes
piercing. Mac felt confused.

"A what?" Mac said. The term meant nothing to him.

"They are going to . . ." Eldon said, "well, educate people to vote."

"To vote? What the hell you talkin about, to vote?" Mac looked
back and forth at the men's faces. He felt anxious, a growing fretful-
ness.

"We're going to register Negroes to vote, Mr. McClellon," Siegel
said. "We work for SNCC. You know what that is, don't you?"

"No, I don't," Mac said testily. "But I think I'm gettin the idea."

"The Student Nonviolent Coordinating Committee," Siegel said.

"I know what it means," Mac said. *Okay. Keep calm.*

"You said you didn't—"

"It took me a minute," Mac said. "Well. We got us some outside
agitators, huh?" Mac grinned at them, hiding his nervousness. He was

looking at the boys closely, examining them. They looked harmless enough, but Mac felt unsettled by them.

Joe Mancini laughed. Eldon looked nervous.

"A voter registration drive, Mr. McClellon," Eldon said. He smiled, his lips looking rigid. His eyes were not smiling; they looked frightened.

Mac got his balance. He leaned back, his hands on his hips. "Y'all gonna register our darkies to vote, huh? Well, a lot of em already vote. They vote for me, I oughtta know!" Mac chuckled. "Them that can read and write. I don't know what they need y'all for."

"Many of them are not registered," Mancini said.

"Whites, too. We got illiterate white people, too. Uh-huh," Mac said. He thought the Italian was laughing at him, and it made him angry. *Who the hell does this dago think he is, looking at me like that?* "Ignorance don't know any color. Why, some of my finest supporters are Kneegrows. I'm proud of it."

"That right?" Mancini said.

"Yeah, that's right," Mac said. The boy was a smart-ass. Long looked a little embarrassed by him. "So I think you fellows got the wrong town. No need for you here. Ain't that right, Eldon?"

"Well . . ." Long said. "There have been some abuses, Mr. McClellon. When some of my people have tried to register, they have been turned away—"

"Anything like that happens, you know all you got to do is come to me, don't you?" Mac said. He squinted at Long, and the preacher looked away.

"Well, no," Long said. "I didn't know that."

"You do now. Hell, I'm the mayor of all the people."

"That . . . that's news to me," Long said. He turned back to face Mac, to meet his gaze. Mac peered at him in the sunlight. Long seemed to have pulled himself to his full height, which put them eye-to-eye. Mac was aware that the two young men were watching them closely. Mac felt a kind of vulnerability; he felt exposed on the afternoon street.

"It looks to me like the two of us need to have us a little talk," Mac said.

"Fine," Long said.

"How about, say, around four this afternoon? My office at the bank?" Mac tried to make it sound threatening, ominous.

"Fine," Long said. He didn't seem to notice Mac's tone.

"In the meantime," Mac said, and he struck a stance like an old

western gunfighter, about to draw both guns, "I'll give you hombres till
sundown to git outta town!" He threw his head back and laughed. The
blond boy, Siegel, laughed with him. "Naw. I tell you, enjoy yourself.
We got a nice little town here. We all git along just fine. Where you
boys from?"

"Harrisburg, Pennsylvania," Siegel said.

"New Jersey," Mancini said.

Figures, Mac thought. "See, you fellows don't know how we do
things down here. Everything in its place. Everybody's more comfortable that way. Y'all come down here, you mean well, I ain't gonna
take that away from you, but you don't know doodly squat. You git
yourself in trouble. And there's no cause for it. No, sir. No reason in
the world."

They stood there awkwardly, a strange group. All three of them were
staring at Mac. He cleared his throat. "Four o'clock," he said to
Eldon, and he nodded at the boys and continued his walk back to the
bank. His legs seemed stiff, creaky, as though his muscles were
clenched like fists. *Naw. I can take care of this. Outside agitators!* He
realized he was sweating under his collar.

⁕⁕⁕

Mac sat behind his desk, leaning back in his chair. He reckoned that
he had known Eldon Long, who was about his own age, just about all
his life. He remembered that he came from a part of the county, out
south of town, down in the Tombigbee River basin, called the Flatwoods, given over to large farms, both dairy and cotton. Now Long was
pastor of the Mount Sinai AME Zion Church. Mac recalled the
preacher was heard sometime on a fifteen-minute program on the
radio on Sunday morning, sponsored by Levy Funeral Home, one of
the two black funeral homes in town. *The Sick and Shut-in Show*, they
called it. He and Belinda and the children had heard it while driving
to Sunday school and church, and they had gotten a laugh over it. It
consisted of a short sermon, some spirituals, and a seemingly endless
list of people who had "passed," with their funeral arrangements.
Dudley, his teenaged son, had remarked that that was just what the
sick and shut-in needed: other people's funeral arrangements. Mac also
knew Eldon was married to that good-looking nigger woman Cora
Long, who taught over at U. S. Smith High School. Beyond that,
though, he didn't know much. Was there family? Surely, they had
children. . . .

He didn't really *know* Long, of course, except to speak to him. He didn't really feel he *knew* any niggers well. Just like most darkies, Long seemed sullen, sneaky. It was just like him to bring in some outside agitators, to try to stir up some trouble. *Outside agitators!* Mac had had no idea that there was that kind of stuff going on in Hammond, and now he could have kicked himself, because he *should* have known. There's always a rotten apple like Long in the barrel, Mac thought as he wondered what the preacher was up to. He was going to find out. And he was going to nip in the bud anything that might threaten Gulf International's coming in. He would threaten Long if he had to, remind the man of the presence of the Ku Klux Klan in the area. Just a reminder ought to do it. Mac loved this little town, and most of the people living here did, too, except for a few misfits like Long. If the preacher broke the law, he was going to jail. *Under* the jail, by God!

Mac was suddenly aware that someone was standing in the open door of his office and looked up. Long stood there, in his dark suit, looking hesitant to come through the door.

"Come in, Eldon," Mac said. "Sit down." Long came on in slowly, and sat in the chair across the desk, looking nervous. Mac smiled. Long looked as though he were about to ask for a loan, which usually made people very nervous. Of course, all the loans arranged across this desk were for white people. It seemed odd to have Long sitting there, just looking levelly at him out of his sunken, slightly bloodshot eyes. Mac wondered if he might be a drinker. He had a scraggly-looking little black mustache.

"Eldon, I'll get right to the point," Mac said. "Who were those boys?"

"I told you," Long said. "They're here to do a voter regis—"

"Yeah, you told me that. But what I wanna know is who brought em in here?"

"Well, they were trained by SNCC in Washington."

"Trained?" Mac said. "Like a seal?" He snorted and chuckled at his own joke, but his amusement faded as he noticed Long staring at him. "You're responsible for bringing em in here, ain't you?" he said to Long after a moment, making his voice firm and authoritative.

"Well," Long said, "in a way, yes."

"Whattaya mean, 'in a way'?"

"I made the arrangements. They're fannin out all over the . . . uh . . . South. There'll be a lot more this summer."

"This summer? Jesus Christ! This summer? Here?" Mac was suddenly alarmed, imagining hundreds of them crawling around while Gulf International was trying to make up its mind.

"Oh, no, not necessarily here. All over. Mississippi, Alabama, Georgia, Louis—"

"I git the picture," Mac irritably interrupted. He picked up a ball-point pen and rolled it around in his fingers as he peered at Long, who seemed uneasy, frightened. "How long are they gonna stay?"

Long shrugged. "As long as it takes," he said.

"What the hell is that supposed to mean?" Mac demanded, momentarily thrown by the shrug, the tone of Long's voice.

"We have no strict timetable. They are going to teach a series of citizenship classes at the church. Responsible citizenship. Then we're gonna register people to vote, in groups."

"Citizenship classes? Jesus!" Mac shook his head, grinning. *Citizenship classes! Wasn't that just like a bunch of niggers.*

"Yes. When we attempt to register them, they'll probably be turned away, and then . . ."

"And then?"

"Well, we try again."

"Have any of em actually been turned away?"

"Oh, for heaven's sake, Mr. McClellon. You know they have."

"Whoa! No, I don't. You got that documented?" Long seemed to squirm on the chair. *Got you there,* Mac thought. There was no way Long could have proof of anything.

"I tell you what," the preacher was saying, sounding strained. "Let's just don't worry about what's happened in the past. Let's just worry about what's gonna happen now."

"Gonna happen now," Mac repeated. He paused, thinking. He didn't want to make Long mad if he could help it. Maybe the man could be reasoned with. He said, "You know, 'course, I don't have a goddam thing to do with county voter registration rolls. That's the probate judge's business, the county registrar, all that."

"Yes. Maybe this all doesn't have anything to do with you, then."

"You're doin it in my town," Mac said. "Anybody that wants to register to vote can register to vote here. Ain't any use makin a federal case out of it." Mac smiled at his own joke. "Everything is just hunky-dory here, Eldon. There just ain't a bit of sense in stirrin things up. You tellin me the Kneegrows here are upset about somethin?"

"Wouldn't you be? If everywhere you looked you saw 'White Only'? If there wasn't a single place downtown where you could take a piss? If people patronized you all the ti—"

"Not if I was a . . . uh . . ." He didn't know what to call them. What did they prefer? *God only knew.*

"Try 'Negro.' "

"Kneegrow. Not if I was Kneegrow. No, sir. It's our way of life. You grew up in it. You seem to be doin all right. Didn't neither one of us create the world like it is, Eldon. We might as well just accept it and go on." He leaned forward and tossed the pen onto the desk. "Ten thousand young fellows from Snicker, or whatever, ain't gonna change it. It's the natural way. You can't change God's laws. You a preacher; surely you know that"

"God's laws?"

"God made the races. If He didn't, who did? You know the Bible, the sons of Ham, all that." Mac had him on that one.

"That's bullshit," Long said.

Mac leaned back, aghast. He couldn't believe the preacher was saying that. "It's the Bible. The word of God. 'Course I ain't as *up* on that as you are, bein a preacher and all that. I just sit out in the Presbyterian Church every Sunday mornin and *listen*."

"I have no quarrel with the fact that we are of two different races, Mr. McClellon."

"Well, what's your 'quarrel,' then?" Mac couldn't help the sarcasm in his voice, thinking he might as well forget about trying to reason with the man.

"My quarrel, as you say, stems from the fact that because I am Negro and you are white, you think you have the right to treat me like a second-class citizen, and pass and uphold laws to that effect—"

"I never mistreated a Kneegrow in my life. We have had Kneegrows as practically a part of my family for generations."

"I've heard that one before. . . ." Long said, and trailed off. "Never mind," he sighed. "What did you want with me?"

"What?"

"You asked me to come and see you. What specifically did you want to talk about?"

" 'Specifically,' " Mac said. "I wanted to talk to you about this whole thing." He paused, telling himself to try to be reasonable. "You seem like a reasonable man. Just tell me, what do *you* want?"

"Scuse me?" Long said.

"What all do you people want? That's all I'm askin you."

"Well, okay." Long paused. "We want all black people registered to vote. We want all schools, restaurants, the movie theater—every-thing—integrated."

"Hold on, man." Mac forced a laugh. "I don't own the picture show. Henry Davis has got a right to sit anybody wherever the hell he pleases in there. He owns the damn thing, right? And the same thing goes for the cafés. I don't see how you think I can change—"

"I'm not sayin you can. I didn't come here to ask *you* to do all that. You asked me what we wanted, and I told you. We won't rest till we have all that."

"Then you won't rest for a long damn time. Forever. You think white people are gonna give you all that?" Mac felt his face burning. *The very idea!*

"No, Mr. McClellon," Long said, "because it ain't *yours* to give. You can't give me anything. Or anything that I'd want."

"Well, now, that's a hell of a thing to say. I'm not understandin you," Mac said, sensing some confidence in Long that Mac hadn't anticipated. It made him very nervous.

"I suppose not," Long evenly replied. "Well! If that's all, then, I'll—" He started to get up from the chair.

"Hold on! No, that's not all. Just sit down." As Long sat back down, Mac looked off out the window. A lone walker, a man, was crossing the square; the afternoon light was waning toward the brief winter dusk. Long was a little more than Mac had counted on. He still did not know exactly where he stood with him.

"There are state laws, Eldon," Mac said carefully, "and states' rights is a sacred issue around here. But I don't want to argue with you about all that. You got your own way of lookin at things, I reckon. I don't mind tellin you that to my way of thinkin, it's outlaw. And I'm on the side of the law. But be that as it may. That's not gonna solve our problem, is it?"

"Problem?" Long said.

"Well," Mac said. "How shall I put this? You see, as mayor, I'm real concerned about the economic well-being of the people of Hammond. I'm interested in the future. Now, all this is hush-hush, this is privileged information, you understand, but, well, we're on the verge of what you might call a major economic boom around here. I don't mind sharin that information with you. Seein as how you're a leader over in the Kneegrow community."

"How is this 'boom' gonna benefit colored people?"

"Jobs. Good-payin jobs."

"Ha!" Long grinned at Mac, his teeth very white, and all of a sudden it popped into Mac's head that Long and his wife, Cora, had something to do with O. B. Brewster. Then he remembered. They had all come from the same part of the county, even the same big plantation, and he remembered that for a while, some twelve, thirteen years ago, Cora had worked as a maid for O.B.'s wife, Martha, who was a good friend of his wife, Belinda; that was before Cora went off to finish her last two years at that little colored university in Selma, or so he had heard. He remembered Belinda talking about it. Martha had had some kind of problems with the Long woman; but then, to hear Belinda tell it, Martha had always had problems with her colored help. Cora had gotten her degree and taught math now, over at the colored high school. She was a good-looking woman, Mac had always thought. Belinda thought she was uppity.

"I tell you, Eldon," Mac said, "there is . . . well . . . money to be made in the boom. But we got a problem. Ain't any area gonna grow economically with a lot of agitation and marchin and carryin on in the streets. People get hurt in shit like that. It ain't the American way. It's . . . well, it's my duty to prevent any violence, any bloodshed, God forbid. I . . . we . . . ought to head it off before it starts."

"I agree," Long said.

"You do? Well, good," Mac said, surprised and relieved. Maybe the man had been listening to him after all. "Maybe you'll consider just sendin those two fellows packin. Send em on over to Mississippi." Mac chuckled. "They can use em over in Mississippi!"

"That wasn't what I meant. I deplore violence as much as you do. My people won't be violent."

"Yeah, well, some of *mine* will, you go breakin laws and actin like a bunch of Bolsheviks. There's some mean folks around here. Tough. I'm talkin bout trashy folks. You got to watch out for em."

"I know," Long said.

"Don't stir em up. You know, we got the Klan around here. Those boys mean business. I wouldn't cross em if I was you."

"If there's any violence, Mr. McClellon, it won't be us."

"It'll be you if you get to carryin on. Don't take em in groups down to the registrar. Forget about the picture show. Maud'll probably blow your goddam head off if you come around her café. That woman is a pistol ball. You get out here demonstratin around, it'll be like lightin a match in a room fulla dynamite. I can't be responsible for that."

There was a long silence in the room. Mac began to think that his logic, his sense, had at last gotten through to the preacher.

Then Long, his hands on the arms of the chair, said, "That all?"

His tone was cocky, but Mac stifled his anger, thinking, I got one more card to play. "No. That ain't all. I tell you what. Can I speak frankly?"

"Go ahead."

"There *might, might* now, be a way I could cut you in on a very good deal that could make you a lot of money. Cut you in on some things without even any investment on your part. I could arrange it so there's no risk at all, providin there's no . . . well, racial trouble . . . around here. Know what I mean?"

"I think I do."

"Well, then. Can we talk business?"

"I'm not interested."

"You're not?" Mac frowned, fiddling with the pen on his desk. The man was stubborn, all right. Like a brick wall. "Me, I am. See, I got a couple of high school kids live at my house. They want to go off to college, and I got to pay for it. I got a mortgage, I got a wife that likes clothes. You do, too, from what I hear. You got kids?"

"A daughter," Long said.

"There you go! I bet she wants to go to college, bein a preacher's daughter. I bet she wants to go to Tuskegee, don't she? Or Fisk?"

"I'm not interested, Mr. McClellon. Sorry."

"This is like a gift, Eldon. Don't be a fool."

"I don't want your gift."

Mac felt his anger swelling. He had tried to treat this man like an equal, but look what he was getting in return. "I'd appreciate it," Mac said, his face reddened, "if you wouldn't get smart with me. Remember who you're talkin to."

"Yassur." Long's face was passive, blank.

"Well," Mac said, after a minute, getting himself under control, "I shoulda known better than to try to reason with a Kneegrow, anyhow. But you better think about this, boy. It'd be in the best interest of all the Kneegrows around here. And your ass, too. If you know what I mean."

"You're not threatenin me, are you, Mr. McClellon?" Eldon sat easily in the chair, but Mac could see that his hands, folded across his knee, were shaking slightly. He was smiling, all right, but his eyes were smoldering dark.

"No," Mac said. "I'm not threatenin you. I don't believe in violence. I'm trying to prevent it. And I will, too. I just hope you don't go doin somethin you'll regret, thass all."

"I do, too, Mr. McClellon," Long said. "That's my prayer."

Mac felt his stomach start to burn. He shifted in the chair, opened his middle drawer, and took out a package of Tums. He popped one into his mouth. It was dry and chalky on his tongue. He was feeling a sense of frustration, of angry resentment over how difficult this was turning out to be.

"I guess that's all I wanted to talk to you about," Mac said tightly, and Long stood.

"Yassur," he said, drawling. Mac knew that he was exaggerating it. "Evenin, then, Mr. McClellon." And then he was gone. Mac sat there, sucking the Tums against the slow heartburn building in his chest.

"Goddammit," he mumbled to himself. "Goddammit."

He thought he could still smell the Negro in the office, his hair dressing, the stale odor of his suit. Mac, full of apprehension, told himself he would just have to get control. Of everything.

.~.~.~.

O.B. was home from work, reading the paper in the littered, dirty kitchen, when he heard the front door slam. Ellen was home. He went up the hall to the living room. She was sitting on the edge of the sofa; she had just picked up a new magazine, a *Saturday Evening Post*, and she was looking at the cover. He stood there a moment, admiring her. Her freshness. She had on brown corduroy slacks and a thick, bulky beige sweater. Her dark hair was cut short, chopped off in an uneven cut that she liked but that Martha had howled about when she'd come home with it. She was thin and wiry in the arms and legs, almost athletic-looking but with a good figure; the family joked that thank God she'd gotten her mother's boobs. Her eyes were his, and he thought the combination of the blue eyes with the dark hair was beautiful, as she looked up at him, smiling.

"Hey, punkin," he said.

"Mama home?" she asked.

"Yeah. She's home," he said, and his tone made her look questioningly at him. She arched her eyebrows. He nodded yes. The smile left her face, and she stared at the magazine for a moment. Then she looked back up.

"Have a good day?" she said.

"Yep. How bout you?"

"Okay. Mr. Leach told me to come see him tomorrow. We're gonna talk about scholarships. He said Middlebury's hard to get into. I may qualify for a scholarship later on. And there are others."

"Really? Good." He didn't have any confidence in that, but then he didn't know anything about scholarships.

"Well," she said. "There's a chance. Don't worry about it, though. Daddy?"

"Yeah?"

"Did you know about the civil rights workers?"

"The who?"

"The two boys who're in town to be civil rights workers? Everybody is talkin about em."

"I heard somethin. Heard they were here, anyway. Why? You see em?"

"Yeah, I saw em. One of em's good-lookin! Mr. Leach told me that he heard they went to *Yale*."

He smiled to himself. It was like her to be impressed with that. "That right?" he said.

"They're stayin out at the Youngbloods' house."

"The *Youngbloods?*" he said. He might have expected that. They were the weirdest family in town.

"Yeah. Daddy?" she said. Her tone made him look carefully at her. "What's goin on? I mean, why do you think they're here?" she said.

"You know about it. You know what the Negroes are doin."

"Yeah," she said, "in Little Rock and all. But here?"

"It . . . well, it's the same thing here, I guess," O.B. replied. "They want . . . to integrate the schools and things." He realized how uninterested he was in all that. Briefly, the thought of Eldon and his request of him flickered through his mind. He knew what his answer ought to be. *I just want to be left alone. To try to keep whatever pieces of my life I can together.* He stared at Ellen. Now she was even more the most important thing in his life.

"I know about that. But what are those boys here for?" she said.

"I think they're gonna help Negroes register to vote."

"They vote."

"Some of em do. Some of em don't. I'm sick of it all myself. It seems like a lot of stirrin around—"

He stopped, suddenly aware that Martha was standing in the door. She wore a housedress, dark blue and wrinkled. She stood there holding a glass of bourbon.

"Sylvia smarted off to me about it," she said. Sylvia was their maid. "That's why I fired her, really. She was disrespectful to me."

"Sylvia? You fired Sylvia?" Ellen said.

"What'd she say?" O.B. said.

Martha laughed. "She said her sister, that moved to Chicago? She said her sister told her up North she could eat wherever she wanted to. Said she ate with white people."

"Well, what's so bad about that?" Ellen snapped. Martha stared at her, her lips turned down at the corners.

"It was the way she said it. It was sass."

"Good God," Ellen said.

"Now, Ellen," Martha said. "Don't you start that."

"Well, that's crazy, Mama! Sounds like she was just talkin—"

"I know when I'm bein sassed! And I will not put up with it. Not from a nigger, and not from a smart-aleck teenager!"

"Martha," O.B. said. He did not want her to start in on Ellen. He did not want to take sides.

She drained her glass. "You want a drink?" she said.

"No," he said.

"Why not?"

"I just don't. I don't want a drink. The house is a mess." He was angry at her, and he wanted her to know it. *Why didn't he just tell her?*

She shrugged and went back to the kitchen. Ellen and O.B. glanced at each other. O.B. could tell that there was a thin film of tears in Ellen's eyes.

"I want to go to Middlebury, Daddy," she said. "I want to get out of here. I got a letter from Paula, and she said Uncle George said it would be okay if I stayed with em. He said okay. Call him if you don't believe me. I could stay with them. It wouldn't cost that much."

"We'll see," he said. He didn't want this argument again either.

"I know what *that* means." She looked away. "I've got to get out of this town, Daddy, I hate it. I hate this house."

"Shhhhhh," he said.

"You don't want Mama to hear? You afraid I'll hurt her feelins? She doesn't care. Believe me, she doesn't care."

"Just don't get her riled up."

"Who? Me?" Martha said, coming back through the door. "Me riled up? Why would I be riled up?"

"Never mind," O.B. said, swallowing the flash of anger that he felt at her entrance.

"You're not goin to Vermont, Ellen," Martha said. "It's out of the question. You can't live with George and Kay, they can't afford it—"

"Uncle George said—"

"I don't care what he said. We'd have to send them a lot of money. You'll go over to Livingston, and live at home. That's that."

"Can't we talk about this some other time?" O.B. said tensely. Both women looked at him. Dull hunger stirred in his stomach, and he felt vaguely angry at both of them. He couldn't understand why Ellen was so set on going to a college she'd only heard of, off up North where she'd never been before in her life. He was beginning to get a headache, a hunger headache. A tension headache. Martha had gone back to sipping her fresh drink, ignoring him.

"Besides," Martha said, "you don't need to go off to any fancy school; you're not popular, Ellen. You don't fit in. It bothers me that you can't get along with Lacy McClellon. I found out, through the grapevine, that Belinda had a bridge party the other day, and I wasn't invited, and I know good and well it's because you and Lacy can't get along."

"That's ridiculous," Ellen said.

"Is it?"

"If you weren't drinkin, you'd see how ridiculous it is," Ellen said.

"Are you sayin I'm drunk?" Martha said.

"Stop it," O.B. said sharply. This was too painful for him. It was so pointless, so familiar.

"It's because of your drinkin that you didn't get invited over there. Not because of me," Ellen said.

She was spitting the words at her mother, but they hurt O.B., like sharp darts between his eyes. He could not stand to see them go at each other this way.

"How dare you," Martha said. "You deliberately spite me. I know that you refused to go out for cheerleader just to spite me!"

"What's it ever done for *you?*"

"You just better watch your tongue, young lady. O.B.?"

"What?" he said, startled. He had been trying desperately to shut them both out of his mind.

"Can't you do something with your daughter?" she said.

"Me? Goddammit, me? Just shut up! Just leave me out of it!"

"Oh, no—oh, no," she said. Martha shook her head. "No way, brother. No way to leave you out of it—"

"Stop it, both of you!" he yelled. "Good God, Martha, bringing up all that cheerleadin business, out of the blue!" His head pained him; his old baseball injury in his knee throbbed dully.

"It bothers me. It's on my mind," she said, the beginning of a self-pitying whine in her voice.

"It's on your mind when you're drunk," Ellen said, standing up, tears welling in her eyes as she faced her mother. There was a tense silence; O.B. could see Martha trembling, with her lips pressed tightly together.

"Goddam you!" Martha said. Suddenly, violently, she slapped Ellen across the face. Ellen fell back on the sofa, her face full of shock and pain.

"Martha!" O.B. said. He was on his feet, grabbing at her arm, some of her drink spilling on the rug. She tried to pull away, and he gripped her arm tighter, so that she cried out. He knew that he was hurting her; he wanted to hurt her. She struggled, then was still.

"Look what you made me do," Martha said, after a minute, looking at the wet whiskey stain on the rug. She seemed smug, almost pleased with herself. She tried to move away from him, staggering slightly. O.B. struggled with her, feeling her weight pulling against him, steadying her and restraining her at the same time. Ellen lay against the back of the sofa, looking up at them, tears rolling slowly down her cheeks. There was no sound in the house but their collective breathing. Looking at Ellen, O.B. felt a frustrated rage that he knew he had to control or he would hurt Martha. He pushed her away, and she lost her balance and dropped her glass onto the rug before she steadied herself by holding on to the back of a chair, her hair hanging in her eyes, her breathing ragged.

"I hate you, Mother," Ellen said softly. "I hate this house."

"Get yourself together, Ellen," Martha said. She pulled herself erect with shoulders pushed back, but her attempt at dignity was almost comical. She turned and walked out of the room, holding her shoulders rigid and straight, her steps slightly unsteady. O.B. sat back down. He realized that he had been holding his breath and let the air out of his lungs with a rush. He was exhausted; his anger had been replaced by a cold fatigue. He wanted to put his face in his hands as he looked at his daughter, lying awkwardly against the back of the sofa. Helplessness flooded O.B.'s chest. He felt the sting of beginning tears behind his eyes, but he forced them back down.

"We've got to rustle up somethin to eat," he said. His daughter didn't answer.

Chapter Three

EVEN THOUGH THE NIGHT WAS COLD AND DAMP, O.B. DECIDED TO walk the three blocks to the Community House for the meeting. He had not intended going, but Mac McClellon had called him that afternoon to make sure he was coming. "I think you better be there, O.B.," he'd said, sounding ominous. When O.B. had asked why, Mac had burst out, "Why? Why? Goddammit, man, I don't have to explain that to you, do I?" O.B. hadn't answered. "Listen," Mac had said on the phone, "there are a lot of goddam hotheads around here, O.B. We need men like you. You know that I mean?"

Now O.B. pulled his tan jacket tighter around his throat. Already, a block from the river, cars were lining the street, pulled into driveways and front yards. Mac had said every white man in West Alabama would be at the meeting. It was a typical Mac McClellon exaggeration. Months ago, O.B. had told him that he was not interested in joining the Citizens Council, simply because so much of his business was done with Negroes and he couldn't afford to jeopardize that. It was that simple, but Mac had looked at him as though he were insane.

"Jesus Christ, O.B.," he'd said, "who the hell else they gonna give their business to?"

The Community House was a large white frame building sitting atop the bluff, overlooking the river. A dull winter-brown lawn sloped down to an Olympic-sized swimming pool, empty now, its blue painted sides flaked and stained. Cars crowded the driveway, and O.B. could see small groups of men talking on the wide front porch as he cut across the lawn. "Evenin," several men said to him as he crossed the porch. Inside, folding chairs had been set up, and they were mostly filled. O.B. found a chair near the back. He looked around. He knew everybody there. Mac was sitting up front, at a table set up on the small stage, where the bands played at the dances. He looked serious and solemn. O.B. saw Rusty Jackson down near the front; he wore his grease-stained clothes. O.B. had heard that he had gone to work out at Winningham's Pontiac place. The room was hushed, the men speaking in whispers, like in a church before the service begins.

Mac stood up. "Can we git started?" he called out, and several more men came in from the porch to sit, their chairs scraping. O.B. looked at the floor beneath his shoes; he was sitting on a shuffleboard court. He looked back up. Mac wore a gray suit, wrinkled under the arms and around the knees. He had loosened his collar, so that his blue tie hung down the front of his wilted white shirt. "We'll start this meetin with a prayer," Mac said, and the men around O.B. awkwardly and stiffly bowed their necks, their eyes darting about. "Lord, be with us as we gather to make these decisions. Help us to do the right thing. We know you will be with us in your infinite wisdom. In Jesus name. Amen." There was a rustle and then a quiet, as everyone sat looking at Mac. There were no women in the room.

"It's good to see such a turnout." Mac grinned. "Oh, I'm sorry, I didn't see you back there, Brother Larson, didn't know you'd got here yet. Or I'd a' asked you to pray stead a' me." Emmitt Larson was the pastor of First Baptist Church.

"You did all right, Mac!" Larson said, and there were a couple of loud guffaws and some general laughter.

"You'da made a preacher," someone shouted from the back.

"You better look out, Larson, or he'll have your job!"

"Naw, now," Mac said. He smiled. And then he assumed a serious expression. "It ain't no secret that we are faced with some awful bad prospects these days. I don't need to go into it all. Our way of life is bein threatened on all sides; seems like the almighty federal government can't keep their hands off of us and just let us live our lives like we want to. All of us. White and nigger alike." He paused. "Most of you know that one of these organizations, they call it Snicker or something, has sent in some outside agitators right here to Hammond.

The two young white Yankee gentlemen are here right now"—there
was scattered laughter—"ready to do good and spread the word.
Lordamercy! It's more important than ever for us white people to
band together and take care of ourselves. Everybody knows bout what
went on up in Greensboro, and over in Montgomery. We are faced
with some awful times. And we need to make this council strong."
He sat down behind the table. "I have served as president of this
organization for the two years of its existence. I'm happy to serve.
Seems like it's part of bein mayor, kinda. I git all kinds of letters and
such from the groups over in Mississippi, recommendin how best to go
about it, and what they're sayin now is to have a board, like a board of
directors. Five of the leadin white men of the town. You want to pull
all the elements together: education and the ministry and the business
community. And you got to try to work with the niggers—"

"Hell no!" someone shouted.

"Now wait," said Mac, holding up his hands. "I'm just talkin bout
workin together to keep out all this outside interference. It's important.
Most of you people know about the . . . ahh . . . the negotiations with
Gulf International Paper Company. We don't want to screw that up.
Probably by this summer, they're gonna announce that plant for Ham-
mond, and that's gonna be important to us."

"Important to who, Mac?" someone said, down front, and O.B.
leaned out to look around the man in front of him. It was Rooster
Wembley who had spoken. He was standing, leaning slightly to the
side because of his wooden leg. O.B. could see the back of his head,
bald on top.

"To all of us," Mac said.

"They sure as hell ain't gonna hire any one-legged barber to work
out there," Rooster said, and several men said, "Yeah," and there was
scattered laughter.

"But think of all the new heads there'll be to cut," Mac said. "The
economy of the area is goin up. More people. More jobs. More money.
That's the way it works. It filters down to everybody. Now I know, I
have been informed, that Gulf International is interested in us because
we are a good little town, peaceful, a good place to live and raise a
family and go to church and git your kids through school. They have
settled on us, at least for the time bein, because we're *not* like Greensboro or Montgomery. And it seems to me to be this council's job to
keep it that way. If we don't, then we'll have Martin Luther Coon and
all his troops in here clutterin up the streets, and Gulf International
Paper Company is gonna be lookin to go somewhere else. But they

ain't gonna find anyplace better than this: two negotiable rivers, halfway between Birmingham and the state docks at Mobile, the kind of land we can offer em. The only thing that might screw it up is if the niggers get outta hand. Gulf International wants us to stay the way we are, peaceful and nice, with everybody comin and goin as they please. But the niggers, now . . ."

"They askin for it," a voice down front said. "Hell, burn em out!"

"Sometimes that's the only way," someone else said. O.B. thought it was Rooster again. Everybody knew that Rooster was the head of the local Klan. That was something O.B.'d have no part of. No matter what. O.B. had a slight headache now. He was having them often these days. He looked around the room. Way over in the corner, in the back, he saw the teacher, Mr. Leach, whom Ellen was so fond of. O.B. remembered his own English class with Mr. Leach. All those years ago. He could still remember the first part of the Prologue to *The Canterbury Tales*, after all that time. Ellen had had to memorize the passage last fall. She and O.B. had recited the passage together, at the table, until Martha threatened to shoot them if they didn't stop. Martha had never learned it; O.B. had long forgotten how she did in the rest of senior English, but he remembered that she had refused to memorize the Prologue to *The Canterbury Tales*.

"Violence! Violence is what we have to fear," Mac was saying.

"Shit! That's all they understand!" someone shouted.

"Maybe. Maybe so. But you can't fight fire with fire."

"How you gonna handle the outside agitators?" another said.

"I don't know," Mac replied. "I admit that. I don't know. That's why we need a good group of men. Now. I have drawn up a list of five men that we need. They're all . . . leaders in the community. Between us, we can come up with some answers." He took a folded piece of paper from his pocket. O.B. felt suddenly nervous, warned. He had listened to everything Mac had said, and it had gone right by him. He didn't care about all of that. Something told O.B. that he was about to be drawn in where he didn't want to be. Mac's phone call . . . "Here they are," Mac said, and he read from the paper: "Me. I'm willin to serve. The mayor and the president of the bank ought to be on it. Any objections?" Nobody said anything. "Emmitt Larson, pastor of First Baptist. Vester Clarke, principal of Hammond High School. Lester Sparks, our chief of police. And O.B. Brewster."

"Wait now," O.B. said. He was standing, and men were looking at him. "I don't know—"

"O.B., we need you," Mac said.

"Well, listen," O.B. looked around. He felt self-conscious, inadequate to express what he felt. All those eyes on him. "Most of my business is with . . . niggers. I didn't plan it that way, but it is. If they was to all take away their business, I'd go broke."

"Nobody would take any business away from you for just bein on the Citizens Council."

"The *White* Citizens Council," O.B. said. That seemed important. He saw several of the men smile.

"We don't call it that," Mac said.

"Still," O.B. said. "I don't know why you need *me*. Joe Lee, there, or Herschel. What about them?"

"Everybody knows you, O.B.," Mac said. "Not even just in the county, but all over this part of the state. You got a lot of friends."

"Well," O.B. said. He stood there for a minute. He could see Rusty Jackson looking at him, his eyes squinting. O.B. felt tense, apprehensive. He had not expected this.

"I just want to run my business," O.B. said. "I just want to be left alone, that's all."

"That's what we all want, O.B.," Mac said. "Now your name is in nomination. Unless you want to withdraw it."

O.B. sat there, not speaking. The room was quiet.

"Well," Mac said, grinning.

"No," O.B. said.

"What's that?" Mac said. The grin seemed to freeze stiffly on his face, and his eyes were harsh.

"I said *No*," O.B. said. "I won't be on the board. I can't. And . . ." He paused. "Well, I just won't. I'm sorry."

"Sorry?" Mac said.

"I just can't do it, Mac" O.B. said, and there was a heavy silence in the room. O.B. saw several men looking at him, others looking away. He felt suddenly very alone. He sat down. Nervous tingles prickled at his back, as though someone were spying on him from behind, staring holes in his back; he felt the heat of everyone's eyes on him.

"—work out some strategy," Mac was saying. "Then we'll call another general meetin. I think you can count on these fellows you've approved tonight. The ones that were willin to do their job, anyway." He looked back at O.B. for a moment, then down at the table. "I sho appreciate all y'all comin tonight. I know all of you've worked a long day, so why don't we just say this meetin's adjourned and git our asses on home?"

"All right!" someone shouted.

Chairs scraped, and there were myriad voices, some laughing, some angry. No one said anything to O.B. It was as though he were suddenly a plague, and the other men left a hollow, empty distance around him. O.B. slipped quietly out the door, across the porch, and he headed across the lawn toward the sidewalk, zipping his jacket up against the cold. Mac should have warned him ahead of time; then his refusal wouldn't have had to be so public. He knew that Clarence Crane would write the meeting up for the *Hammond Times*. And his white customers, some of them large farmers out in the Flatwoods that he really depended on—

"Hey!" he heard someone shout behind him, and he stopped. "Hey, where you goin, nigger-lover?"

He recognized Rusty Jackson's harsh voice. He could see his slender silhouette, outlined by the lights on the porch of the Community House. He went on down the sidewalk, toward his house. He was not frightened of Jackson, but the man made him nervous. It seemed unfair that he still—even though the man no longer worked for him— had to deal somehow with Jackson's anger. He jammed his hands in his pockets and hunched his shoulders. A *nigger-lover*. He walked quickly, against the cold dampness of the night air. *Eldon called me that, too.*

·~·~·~·

Mac felt the warmth of the bourbon easing into his bloodstream, relaxing him. He sipped it eagerly as he looked around the hunting lodge. There was a roaring, crackling fire in the big stone fireplace around which men were talking loudly, jawing back and forth. Mac found a chair and sat down. He had taken off his tie and suit coat. Someone had let him borrow a jacket, but it was tight through the shoulders. He glanced at his wristwatch: 10:16. Belinda would be pissed off if he got home too late. But he didn't think there was any way he could not have come out here with them. He was not only going to have to keep a close rein on Long, but on these old boys, too. He was just going to have to put the word on them, plain and simple, despite the fact that he was as uneasy around these men as he imagined he might be at the Shady Grove Deer Drive.

He saw Rooster Wembley coming toward him, with his awkward, halting gait. Rooster had had a wooden leg since World War II. His leg was shot off at Peleliu, in the South Pacific, where he'd been a marine. His wife, Mary Katharine, had been after him for years to get a new plastic one that you couldn't tell from a real leg, but he wouldn't do it. Now he was a barber and ran a little three-chair shop on Washington Street. He had been cutting Mac's hair, with the exception of the war years, for as long as Mac could remember. He kidded Mac about not being able to transpose his initials, the way he did everybody else's. He called Billy King, for example, Killy Bing. And so on. O.B. Brewster was B.O. Oyster.

"Well, Mac, sounds to me like the niggers are gearin up for a showdown," Rooster said.

"I don't know now, Rooster," Mac said, standing up; the two men shook hands.

"Don't you wanna git in on the game?" Rooster said. He was referring to the poker game getting started in the next room.

"Naw. Can't stay long." Mac looked around nervously.

"Gotta git home, huh?"

"You know how it is, Rooster," Mac said.

"Sound to me like you getting pussy-whipped in your old age," Rooster said.

"Naw," Mac said. Mac realized that he was afraid of Rooster, in the same way he'd been afraid of his father's drunken behavior, the unpredictability of it.

"This would be a good time, considerin, for you to go on and join up with us," Rooster said, in the same tone.

"Now, Rooster. You know I can't be joinin the Klan. Public servants—"

"Shit," Rooster said.

Mac remembered Carleton Byrd, sitting across the desk, prissily drawing on his Marlboro. His warning had been clear, and Mac knew that violence, if it came, would start right here. "I'll just keep it informal. Like now, for instance. I'm here, ain't I?"

"Shit. This ain't nothin but a party. Little hell-raisin. You need to be in on the sho-nuff fun."

Mac gripped the glass of whiskey, remembering abruptly the disappearance of Lacharles Putney, a slow-witted nigger boy who, Mac knew—from talking with Lester Sparks—had gone into old man Rufus Kirven's store out in Shortleaf and said something uppity to Mrs. Kirven, something about wanting to do the bad thing with her. Lester had promised to pick the boy up and question him, but then the boy had just vanished. This had happened several years ago—about ten, as Mac remembered. There had been blood on the front stoop of the Putney cabin, and the boy's mother had said that men with white sacks over their heads had come and gotten Lacharles in the night. The talk around town—Mac had heard it in Rooster's barber shop—was that the boy had been weighted down with chains and concrete blocks and thrown, still alive and begging and crying, into the lake at the bottom of the old limestone quarry over near Coatopa. Now Mac's eyes flicked over Rooster's face, with its jutting chin. He was bald on top, and the hair around his head was gun-metal gray, thin and plastered against his skull so that it looked painted on. He stood, drifting slightly to the side, favoring his wooden leg. On his good foot, he was wearing a scuffed black wing tip. Mac found it hard to look him in the eyes. In those yellow eyes was a clear acknowledgment of Rooster's position as head of the Klan that anybody who had lived in Hammond all his life could easily read.

"Fun?" Mac said. "Listen, Rooster, like I was sayin tonight . . ."

"Yeah?"

"Well, we don't want anything bad to happen around here. The paper mill—"

"Ain't any way anything we do gonna be *bad*, Mac. Shit. You know that."

"I'm talkin about . . . well, why can't we just do things by the book? You know, till the paper mill announces, and they get started on it. When they can't change their mind, well then, maybe we can . . . whup some tail. You know?" Mac felt the weight of what he was saying, the urgency of it.

"I ain't talkin bout whuppin no tail," Rooster said. "I'm talkin bout stringin up some black asses."

Mac took a long drink of the strong whiskey and water. He was shaking inside. The image of the boy, Lacharles, who used to walk the streets pulling a block of wood on a string, making motor noises with his lips, his overalls fitting him like a comical barrel on a clown in a circus, haunted him. He remembered other instances, the beating of a nigger man from out in the Flatwoods, niggers' shanties mysteriously burning down, and he had never done or said a thing, one way or the other. Now, it seemed, he would have to take a stand. Several men passed through the room. One of them was the mechanic, Rusty Jackson, whom O. B. Brewster had fired. He was going around telling everybody that Brewster was a nigger-lover. O.B. hadn't done himself any favors by refusing tonight to be on the board of directors. But it seemed to Mac that O.B. Brewster led a charmed life, having been a great athlete in high school, a pro-ball player one time, even making it to the big leagues just long enough to bust up his knee and cripple

himself. He was tall and good-looking, and Mac suspected that half the
women in Hammond would jump into bed with O.B. in a minute. He
knew that his own wife, Belinda, probably wouldn't have, but only
because she wasn't that keen on jumping into bed anyway. Mac
frowned as he remembered O.B.'s one invitation to the Shady Grove
Deer Drive. Everybody seemed to like O.B., no matter what, and what
had he really ever done but marry the head cheerleader, good-looking
as she was, play a little pro ball for a while, and then come home with
his tail between his legs and watch his cheerleader go to fat? (When
Mac had played good-enough guard on the football team their senior
year, O.B. was the quarterback, the goddam star of the team. Belinda
had been a cheerleader, too, but not the head.) Despite all that history,
Mac felt that he needed O.B. in the Citizens Council, especially if he
was going to be able to keep a lid on these wild men. The council. He
would use that.

"I tell you, Rooster," he said. "We got a good organization goin
there, the Citizens Council and all. We gonna be able to handle it all.
You don't need to worry. I been on the phone to Montgomery, to the
governor's office. We're in good shape."

The men had cut on a radio, loud, twangy country music. There
was harsh laughter. They were at a counter that lined one wall of the
lodge, slicing slabs from a ham, making sandwiches and drinking beer.
Rooster peered at Mac. He took out a Camel cigarette and let it dangle
from his thin lips. "Shit," he said, "them two Yankee boys. One of
em's a Jew, the other's a goddam dago. And I hear it's this nigger Eldon
Long that's the ringleader."

"Well," Mac said. He leaned closer to Rooster. "Can we talk, just
between me and you?" He felt suddenly shy, unsure of himself.

"Go ahead," Rooster said. He lit the cigarette with a kitchen match
that he struck on the concrete-block wall of the cabin. Mac smelled the
sulfur of the match, the thick, almost choking smell of the cigarette
smoke.

"I've talked to em," Mac said. "All of em. Long, and those two
fellows. They ain't more'n college boys, scared shitless. They know
what's happened to some of these people, come down here pokin
around where they don't belong."

"Goddam right," Rooster said. He flipped the match into the fire.
He seemed amused, his yellowish-brown eyes twinkling in the firelight. "Here," he said. He took a pint bottle of Old Crow from his back
pocket. He held it up, checking the level. Then he made a mark on the
edge of the label with his thumbnail, turned the bottle up, and drank.

Mac could see his Adam's apple jerking up and down. Rooster took the bottle down and checked the level again. He had drunk down precisely to the mark he had made. Mac took the bottle and marked it, then poured into his glass. He checked it. Right on the money. Rooster grinned at him. "Shit," he said. "I don't know about this paper company comin in. If they can't live like we do down here, then maybe they ought to just stay out."

"It ain't that, Rooster," Mac said. "They do business all over the world."

"So?"

"It's just . . . the troubles. We have any of that, then we can kiss the mill good-bye."

"Tell it to the niggers," Rooster said. "Hell, this 'world company' you talking bout probably gonna hire all the niggers anyway, ain't it?"

"Well, I don't know. I don't think so, no."

"You don't 'think' so?"

"We're talkin bout skilled labor here, Rooster."

Rooster drew on his cigarette. Mac noticed that the mouth end was damp and shredded. Rooster released the smoke in two thin steams from his nostrils, then flipped the butt into the fire. He looked, to Mac, as mean as a snake.

"I'm curious as to what stake you got in this company, Mac," Rooster said.

Mac almost physically jumped, feeling his secret bulging inside his head. He looked away, around the room. His stomach, warm from the whiskey, tingled with alarm. He worried that Rooster had seen his reaction.

"Ahhhh . . . nothin," Mac said, continuing quickly. He felt a nameless dread. "Listen, Rooster. I'm a banker. And I'm the mayor. The economy of the area goes up, my business goes up. And it's good for the town. More people, like I said. More depositors. Payrolls. All that. Nothin so mysterious about that, is it?"

"Why, no," Rooster said.

"So," Mac said, looking Rooster in the eyes, "I'm gonna hafta tell you, order you, I guess, to lay off—"

"Order me?" Rooster said.

"I'm the mayor of this town," Mac said, "and I don't want any trouble. No violence, no bloodshed. Let the law handle anything that comes along."

"The niggers—"

"I mean it, Rooster," he said, making his voice as firm and full of conviction as he could muster. He thought it would make him feel better to stand up to Rooster, but his stomach was like ice.

Rooster said nothing for a moment. Then he grinned. On the radio was Elvis, singing "A Fool Such As I." "Listen to him," Rooster said. "The boy's a white nigger. You ever heard a white man sing more like a nigger than him?"

"Lord, no," Mac said. He sighed with relief to be off the subject. But he had to be on it. He had to make sure.

"The music these children listen to, that's tellin us somethin, Mac. It's the same thing used to be on in the afternoon, Mr. Boogie Man show, didn't nobody but niggers listen to it. Nobody advertised on it but nigger business and such. Now you hear it on the television, everywhere. You can't tell me it ain't planned that way."

Mac was thinking of his own kids, Dudley and Lacy, who played this kind of music in their rooms all day long. They bought forty-fives, dozens, no, hundreds, of forty-fives. It didn't seem to him that the music was so bad, but he wasn't going to say so to Rooster. He began to wish he hadn't come out here. He looked at his watch.

"Worried about your wife, huh?' Rooster said.

"No," Mac said, "I'm not." He really wasn't, and it made him angry and nervous that Rooster seemed to want to insist on that point. He shuddered. He had a sudden urge to tell Rooster all about his plans for the houses, his loans, but he had already committed himself to secrecy, and he might as well see it through. Rooster was looking at him, a slight grin on his face, as though he were reading his thoughts.

"Hey, Rooster!" one of the men called, as others were laughing. "Let's go git us a nigger!"

"They ain't in season," Rooster said. He chuckled, looking at Mac, and Mac laughed nervously; he couldn't help it. He took a deep breath, trying to relax. He took a gulp of the raw, strong whiskey.

"We done decided that what we ought to do is go string us up one a them Yankee nigger-lovers," another man said. "Cut his balls off and feed em to the other one!"

"In good time, boys," Rooster said, "in good time."

"Maybe we oughtta git us a scalawag nigger-lover," another voice said, and Mac saw that it was Rusty Jackson. "We got nigger-lovers was raised right here in Hammond," he said, "loves dealin with niggers, makin em feel good. Shit."

"Calm down, boys," Rooster said. "And if you talkin about O. B. Brewster, boy, you better watch yourself." The tone of Rooster's voice made the men fall silent. Then Rooster grinned at them. "Y'all just gittin antsy. We gonna have to arrange a coon-on-the-log contest or somethin, let y'all git rid o all this nervous energy. Or maybe y'all just need some pussy."

"Yeah!"

"Li'l in and out, yeah!"

"Shit!"

"Pussy! Meeow!"

"Wooo! Wooo!"

"Nigger pussy!"

They were laughing, and Mac laughed along with them, though his stomach felt queasy, and his own laughter rang hollow in his ears. The fumes of the whiskey seemed to linger in the back of his throat, at the base of his nostrils. He swallowed, grinning, looking at the men milling about, shoving and pushing each other like schoolboys. It reminded him of being in the locker room back in high school, and he ordinarily liked that feeling, but tonight he felt threatened, frightened. He didn't feel a part of what was going on here. He knew it must be the houses. He had the sudden impulse again to confess his scheme to Rooster, give it up and get rid of it, but he didn't. He glanced at Rooster. The man was still watching him, the look of slight amusement on his face.

"Don't you worry," he said. "You and your upright White Citizens Council. We'll be around to back you up."

"Well . . ." Mac said. He felt a sudden sense of genuine panic, as though things in the town were already out of control. Had he utterly failed in his mission out here? He opened his eyes, looking around at the men, the way the firelight played and danced off their moving forms in the dim light. He drank the last of the liquor in his glass.

"More?" Rooster said.

"Naw," Mac said, a slight sense of calm returning as he felt the whiskey in his belly. So what if he felt apart from all this? He knew he did not want to be one of these men. He wanted to control them. He would do anything he had to do to make everything work out as he had it planned. "Naw. Y'all have fun. I'm done in."

"All right," Rooster said. "Don't worry now, ya hear?"

⋅~⋅~⋅~⋅

On the night of the first big meeting, Eldon walked the four blocks to the church alone. It gave him time to think about it, and he needed it, because in his mind this was the most crucial moment of his life up to now. This was his chance to be Moses, to lead his people through

the Red Sea, to put in motion finally all the things that had become central to his life and his ministry. He knew he had to be
eloquent, persuasive, more powerful than ever. He knew that the
success or failure of their entire movement rested with him and how
he led them now.

There had been a meeting of the Ladies' Auxiliary earlier, and Cora
was already there. Sally was coming with her friends. The street in
front of the church was lined with old cars and pickup trucks, even an
occasional mule-drawn wagon, while groups of men and women stood
about in the churchyard. Eldon was proud of the plain building, and
the even newer two-story educational building built across the back.
Raising the money for it had been an impossible feat, an insurmount-
able task, and yet he had done it, with God's help, and that told him
that he could do more and bigger "impossible" things. It was one of the
largest churches in Hammond, the largest black church, he thought
proudly, the people nodding and smiling at him as he went up the walk
toward the double doors. His stomach tingled with anticipation. The
very air seemed to him charged with excitement.

As Eldon took his place behind the pulpit and looked out over the
crowd, every pew filled beyond capacity, with people standing along
the sides and in the back, he saw the curious and the angry, the
passive, the uninvolved. Several people fanned themselves in the stuffy
air, overheated for this many people. The cardboard fans, from Stoner
Funeral Home, printed with biblical scenes on the back, were bright
splotches of color in the crowd. Eldon felt confident that tonight they
would win over those who were holding out, the older, more conservative people, those who were nervous and frightened by the young men
who were here.

"Bless Jesus," an old woman, Hardenia Moon, said down front.
"Yes," "Amen," came voices from around the church.

Eldon's throat felt swollen as his eyes moved over the crowd. These
were his people, his blood, extensions of his own family. He could pick
out many that he had baptized as children, and he was now beginning
to baptize their children; he always was there with these people at the
most crucial moments of their lives, at their most joyful and at times
of their deepest grief. He had sat by their bedsides, in the dim, poorly
heated shanties, the air smelling of the sputtering kerosene lamps, to
pray with them when they were sick; he had stood by their raw, open
graves when their coffins were lowered into the ground. He had no
idea how many marriages he had performed, funerals he had conducted, catechisms he had taught; he only knew that it all had made

him so much a part of their lives, and theirs his, that they all were like extensions of one body, one living and breathing organism that derived its life's energy from the same heartbeat. He swallowed, tears misting his eyes.

Eldon held up his hand. He let his eyes play over the people's faces. He always felt a sense of power doing that, having them look up at him, hushed, expectant. He could see Cora, toward the back. He could see her eyes and could sense, even at this distance, the withholding of her approval. He could read the language of her body, the stiffness with which she sat on the crowded and cramped pew. He felt as though he were reaching out to her in a pleading, almost begging gesture, but he had not moved at all. He looked away from her then and around the church. Sally was sitting with a bunch of younger people over on the right side. Next to her was Nathaniel Pierson, who wore a dirty white T-shirt with the sleeves torn out. It made him anxious to see her with the angry-looking boy. He swallowed again.

"Tonight I formally introduce you to our visitors," Eldon began, smiling. "Most of you have met em, here and there, and you know what they're here for—"

"Praise God!"

"—and they're gonna talk briefly to you tonight about the classes and the voter registration drive we have planned for the spring and summer."

"What all *else?*" someone shouted, and Eldon looked over at the knot of young people. He felt alarm, knowing from Sally that many were impatient with the idea of classes and failed to see any importance in voting. They had read about the demonstrations in Greensboro and Nashville, the bus boycotts in Montgomery, seen it all on the television news, and now they were hot to get that started in Hammond. They were prepared to act on their own, if need be, but they seemed to have no knowledge of the possible consequences, seemed unaware of the potental for violence out there from the Ku Klux Klan, which was still very real in Hammond. These young people did not know about any of that. Eldon feared for them to have to learn from broken ribs, smashed skulls, or worse. He cleared his throat.

"We'll discuss all areas for action," he said. "Everybody gets a chance to speak. This is an open forum, and it'll remain an open forum from now on. We must have unity, in whatever we choose to do. We have to consider the best tactics, the best course of action, and we must consider the dangers involved—"

"Bless Jesus," Hardenia Moon said again.

"—and that's what our young visitors are here for. They have been well trained. They know the rules, and they know what our brothers and sisters all over the country are doin. We can't just fly off in all different directions. If we fragment ourselves, the white power structure will turn us all against one another, make us operate against one another. It's happened, and we need to take advantage of what folks have learned other places. I myself have been to workshops—"

"Workshops!" someone shouted derisively, and there was scattered laughter. Eldon glanced over at Sally to see how she'd reacted, and sudden anger flushed through him as he saw his daughter look past him toward the back of the church. Eldon caught sight of Edna Blanks, an English teacher at U. S. Smith High School. He saw her broad face and sad, bulging eyes, and told himself, *Lord, be with me. I must go on.*

"Yes," Eldon said. "I don't try to pass myself off as an expert. I don't pretend to know everything. But I do know some things. It just makes sense to share information back and forth, which is what the workshops do." He paused. "I can't stress too much the importance of education to us. We need to grow. You young folks can't just go off half-cocked." He felt that his own voice was unconvincing, lacking in energy. He looked back at Cora again, and she smiled at him, a tentative, reassuring smile. She was being kind. Some of the older, more conservative people, who sat back there with her, had refused even to meet the two boys. Cora herself had been cool to them, even cool to him when they were around. He again glanced at Sally surrounded by young people, one a young teacher at U. S. Smith. They were all slouched there, looking restless, impatient. The air in the church was oppressive, smelling of bodies and perfume, heavy floral scents that were almost funereal. Eldon gripped the podium as scenes from the television newscasts flickered into his mind, shadowy pictures of young black men in white shirts and dark ties in the department-store lunchroom in Greensboro, their eyes wide with fear. The images made him worried and anxious over what was brewing here. He looked down at Hardenia Moon. She sat where she always sat, Sunday in and Sunday out. She was looking up at him, and he remembered when she'd been in the little group that went down to city hall on the day when the county registrar was in town, to attempt to register to vote.

⋅∼∙∼∙∼∙

Eldon had taken Hardenia and two men, Ruston Sinclair and Hal Parker, two dirt farmers from out near Gallion. They had all been nervous, especially Hardenia.

"What I wants to do this for?" she had said, over and over again. "Jesus knows, I don't want to make no trouble."

"It's no trouble," Eldon said. "Nobody's gonna do anything to you. It's your right, to vote." His heart went out to her, but he was annoyed with her at the same time.

"I done all right for a long enough time without doin it, I reckon," she said.

It was a sunny April day. They stood in the hallway at city hall, the two men in their overalls, holding their worn straw hats over their chests. They stood outside an office with a sign on the door: COUNTY REGISTRAR, TUESDAYS, 1 TO 5. They seemed quietly stoic, curious. "I reckon this a good enough reason to git burned alive," Ruston said, and they all smiled. Except Hardenia. "Sweet Jesus," she murmured. She had on a light blue dress with red and pink flowers on it.

A woman's voice shouted "All right" from within the office, and they filed in, Hardenia and Ruston and Hal behind Eldon. Eldon carried his suit coat over his arm, and the woman behind the tall counter became alert and tense the minute she saw them.

"Help you?" she said. She was about fifty, heavyset, with her hair carefully permed and shaped around her head like a helmet. A filter-tipped cigarette was propped in a clear glass ashtray on the counter. A thin string of gray smoke rose straight up from it toward the ceiling.

"These three people want to register to vote," Eldon said.

"Birth certificates," the woman said.

"No birth certificates were recorded for them," Eldon said. It was like a ritual, one he had been through many times before. "Howsomever, the two fellows have drivers' licenses. Hardenia has her family Bible, giving her date and place of birth, which was Spocari, down in the Flatwoods, in this county. You can visually certify that they're over twenty-one." He smiled. It seemed so simple. "And they are residents of this county. I can swear to that."

"And who might you be?" the woman said.

"A registered voter. Eldon Long. Minister of Mount Sinai AME Zion Church. In this city." Eldon felt the beginnings of a familiar impatience.

He saw that two other women, with similar hair, were watching them through a door to an inner office. The woman looked at Eldon, then at the three older people. A small nameplate on the counter said: CLARA KIRKLAND, ASSISTANT REGISTRAR.

"All right," Clara Kirkland said, "fill these out." She shoved several blank forms across the counter to them. Eldon took them, and they went over in the corner. One by one, Eldon filled the forms out, asking the questions of the three. They were hesitant, and Eldon found himself almost snapping at them, then wondering, Who am I angry at, anyway? When they were finished, they went back to the counter, but there was no one there. They could hear people talking and laughing in the inner office. After a few minutes, Eldon called,

"Miz Kirkland?"

She stuck her head out the door, a frown on her face.

"What is it?" she said.

"We're finished."

She came out and snatched the forms up; she put on a pair of glasses with bright blue frames and scanned them. "All these is wrote in the same hand," she said.

"I assisted them," Eldon said.

"I can write," Hardenia said.

"Well, why didn't you write your own then?" Clara Kirkland said.

"The law says—" Eldon began.

"I know the law," she said. She stood reading the forms, chewing on the inside of her cheek. This was so by rote, so monotonous. It always ended this way. Eldon was longing for something more, some kind of more direct action. How patient did they have to be? What more could they do but keep trying?

"You wants me to write it myself?" Hardenia said.

"Never mind. Here," she said, pushing a thick manila-covered book across the counter to them. "Open it." On the front was a seal, and in heavy black letters, *The State of Alabama, The Constitution.* "Well, open it," she said. Ruston moved forward, reached, but Clara Kirkland said, "No. Her."

Hardenia opened the large, heavy book. "Open it where?" she said.

"Anywhere. There. Now read that section. Then I want you to interpret it to me."

"Say what?"

"Read that section right there. Startin where it says Roman numeral seven, number three-oh-one."

"Out loud?" Hardenia said.

"Any way you want to."

Hardenia looked at the book. She glanced at Eldon. Eldon smiled encouragement to her, encouragement that he did not feel. A man and one of the other women came out of the inner office and stood watching them. The man, who was young, in his twenties, held some sheets of blank paper.

"Test time," he said, and he and the woman smiled. "Which ones is applyin? You?"

"No," Eldon said. "These three."

"Okay," the man said. He had a wispy red mustache and reddish-sandy hair. "Here, Uncles," he said, handing Ruston and Hal each a piece of paper. "Now, you," he said to Ruston, "you write down the total number of words in the Alabama Constitution."

"The what now?" Ruston said. He held the paper in front of him like a snake.

"Give or take ten. We'll allow you a little grace. And you," he said to Hal, "you write down what side of the earth the moon's on."

"The outside," said Hal, and the three white people looked startled for a moment, then they laughed. Eldon and his friends chuckled, too, for a moment. Eldon felt a deep affection for the old man. Then they were quiet again, the two men holding the blank pages and Hardenia looking at the book.

"That's the wrong answer, Uncle," the white man said. He had on a red tie. Both the women were dressed up, with high heels and the diligently set hair. They stood looking at Eldon and the others. They were smiling.

"I reckon any answer they give gonna be the wrong answer," Eldon said. Blunted, drab anger covered him like a shroud of smoke. The room was very quiet. An oscillating fan droned on a desk against the wall. Eldon could hear the distant, lazy afternoon traffic, out on Washington Street.

After a minute, the man said, "You said it. I didn't."

"This doesn't make any sense to me," Hardenia said, looking up from the book, and the two women and the man laughed.

"I tell you what," the women who hadn't said anything began, "if the law changes, we'll call y'all up, okay?"

"The law—" Eldon said automatically.

"It's the law. In here, it's the law. You want to talk to the sheriff?"

"No, sir," Eldon said. He was angry now, but his face remained passive. His hatred was leaden, almost lifeless. It was as though he were numb.

"We . . . we'll be back," he said softly.

"What's that?"

"I say, we'll be back. Try again."

"Y'all do that," the man said. "That's what we here for. We aim to please."

They could hear the white folks laughing as they went back out into the hallway. Hal and Ruston had crumpled up the sheets of paper and had thrown them into a trash can next to the front door of city hall. The three older people laughed, as though it were a joke, and Eldon's anger smoldered within him like a cancer.

.~~~.

Eldon stood to the side now, watching Joe Mancini, who stood behind the pulpit. Paul Siegel also stood over to the side, arms folded across his chest. There had been little response when Eldon had introduced them: a hushed silence, full of apprehension, anticipation, restraint. Suspicion. Eldon had expected some cheers, applause. Instead, they were listening with rapt attention.

"—have some advantages simply because we're alien," Joe Mancini was saying. Both of the boys wore blue work shirts and baggy khaki pants. "And we're white. See, these people, these goons, are gonna think twice before they push me too hard." He grinned, looking cocky, confident. Eldon took a little strength from that, but the boy also made him nervous the way he called white people "goons." Eldon smiled to himself, thinking that at least he felt excited. He needed that.

"Now I know some of you don't like the idea of the citizenship classes, but, believe me, they'll pay off. I'm gonna teach one, and Miss Edna Blanks is gonna teach one. Stand up, there." Edna, scowling, got slowly to her feet. She grunted, shifting her weight under her bulk; her blue dress draped her like a tent. "All right," Mancini said, and she sat back down. He looked as though he had expected them to applaud her. "We are gonna train you in nonviolence. We'll set up simulated restaurants. We'll push you around and spit on you, show you exactly what to do. How to turn passive nonviolence into action. Paul and I have been workin some with Miss Blanks and some of you others, and we can show you all what we've learned so far. We got Freedom Riders coming in this summer, and we're gonna be ready for em."

Eldon's mind wandered as Mancini went on, explaining what Freedom Riders were. Mac McClellon had said to these boys that they didn't know how things were done down here, and he was right. Eldon sensed that most of the people here were paying little attention to Mancini. Most could not have cared less what "Freedom Riders" were. They looked skeptical, and the things these boys talked about were still mere intellectual exercises to them. What was real to these folks was who they were in this place, this town. It was what Cora had said about how they reacted to the math that she taught them. Eldon glanced at his wife. She was listening intently to Mancini. *What does she think of me if she thinks so little of my movement?* He had to get through to her, help the boys get through to her, to all of them.

Eldon snapped alert. There were questions now. He recognized Carrie Winter's voice. "The lady I works for," she said, "she beggin me every day, she say don't fool with them communists, Carrie." There was scattered laughter. "You white boys communists, or what?" she said.

"No," Mancini said. "We're not communists. We're Democrats." He grinned. He had told Eldon, over a cup of coffee, that he was a Marxist. "All we're after is freedom and justice. You tell the lady that we're Americans, just like you are and she is. We're Democrats, just like your governor is."

"That's what she was tellin me, though," Carrie said, "those boys is communists." She looked around.

"Dat what they say," someone else said. "Uh-huh."

Joe Mancini's face was strained. He looked momentarily confused. He looked down at Eldon. Eldon shrugged and winked at him. *Let him learn. It'll do him good.*

"When we gonna git started with the demonstrations?" a harsh voice cut in. Eldon recognized the voice. Nathaniel Pierson.

"Soon," Mancini said.

"How soon?"

"Very soon," Mancini said, grinning.

"This ain't no joke," Pierson said. "I'm tired a' this shit."

There were groans. "Don't talk like that in the church, boy," someone said.

Pierson went on, "I don't know what you pale males got to offer us," he said. "I don't need no white man to tell me how to deal with these other white men."

"You tell it, brother!"

"Hush now!"

A cold, clammy fear gripped Eldon. A premonition, a sudden realization, of the great danger of it all. He thought of the day-to-day fear and hopelessness that his father and his mother had always lived under. He remembered suddenly the disappearance of Lacharles Putney, how they had known what had happened to him, they had all known, huddling around the coal stoves, the tables at the Silver Moon Cafe. Eldon recalled the intenseness of his anger, his frustration, the fear that he felt, not for himself but for Cora and Sally, for all their women and children, the Lacharles Putneys among them. Where was there to turn? Eldon knew the rage inside Nathaniel because he'd felt it hammer and pulse in his own veins, but he knew the risks, too. He knew they would pay. He knew they would bleed.

Eldon stood up, holding out his hands. "Please," he said. There was a stirring, a shuffling of feet, and then quiet as the rows of faces looked expectantly at him. The whitewashed walls reflected the light, so that the church was as bright as day. Eldon swallowed, choking back his fear, moistening his dry lips. "Let him speak," he said.

"I don't mind questions," Mancini said. "I don't mind what he said. I don't blame you people for not trusting me. I'll make you trust me, by what I do. Just give us a chance." There was a silence. Eldon knew they were listening now. "Anybody gets his head knocked, I'll be the first," Mancini said. "I'll be the first one thrown in jail, the first one spit on." He paused, looking back toward where Pierson was sitting. "And you're right. I'm white. I don't gotta be here at all. But I am. I'm here with you. Me and Paul both."

There was some scattered applause. Just as it died down, Eldon heard Nathaniel Pierson say, "Shit!"

"Mr. Mancini," someone was saying from the back. Eldon realized it was Cora, and he felt his jaw clench. He did not want to hear her. "Let me ask you somethin," she said.

"All right, Mrs. Long." Mancini smiled.

"I don't wanta sound like I'm as hot under the collar as Nathaniel there"—some laughter, chuckles—"but some of us are worried about this. I mean, yeah, you come down here to help us, and that takes somethin for you to do that, but then we liable to do all these things and you go on back up to the East and leave us down here to deal with it. I mean, we got to live here. This is our home. We got to go on livin with these people."

"I understand that. That's a very real fear."

"I mean," Cora said, "some of these white people are longtime friends." Eldon winced. What would these boys think of her? He felt shame for her, shame for himself. These boys would not understand what she meant by "longtime friends," how, when it came to white people, that word was always qualified. *They must think we're crazy to be friends with our oppressors.* He pressed the bridge of his nose with his fingers, his eyes closed for a moment. The church seemed to him deathly quiet.

"And some of these friendships will be severed," Mancini said into the quiet. "Maybe some'll be repaired later on. Some won't. Who knows? There will be sacrifices. No doubt about that."

"You may not believe this, Mr. Mancini," Cora said, going on, "but some of us have worked hard for what we've got, and we're proud of it. I'm speakin for a number of folks back here when I say that we don't know if we're ready to risk all that for whatever we might gain from these . . . demonstrations and such as that." The words were like hot coals in Eldon's ears. *I do not want to hear this! Coming from my own wife!*

Mancini leaned forward. His brow furrowed, and he looked down at Eldon and then back at Cora. He seemed puzzled.

Her voice was calm, deliberate. "I mean, people can get hurt. Killed. You're askin us to put our lives and the lives of our children on the line, Mr. Mancini."

Eldon held his breath. Then he spoke. "Why do you say Mr. Mancini is askin us to put our lives on the line? We are askin him to put his life on the line, to risk his neck, comin down here for us. It is God who is requiring us all to do what we know is right, to prepare the *way* for our children and our grandchildren. There are risks. There are always risks." The church was quiet, with only the rustling of a few fans.

"I'm not *asking* you to do anything," Mancini said. "Nobody is forced to participate in any of this if you don't want to."

"But colored people are colored people," Cora said. "The Klan don't make distinctions."

"I get your point," Mancini said.

"I say we fight the Klan with the only thing those crackers understand," Mark Price shouted. He was the young teacher out at U. S. Smith, just graduated from Alabama State. He was standing, and so was Pierson. Price was thin; his color was almost light red, and he wore a wiry little black goatee. "They don't scare me," he said. "Hit white power with pure black strength!"

"Yeah!"

"Wait!" Eldon said, and the murmuring and agitation quieted for a moment. "Don't you see that we have to have a plan? Don't you see that if we are going to win against this evil we must all work together?" Eldon could see Sally sitting in the middle of them. His heart was pounding in his chest, his pulse racing. She had on the tattered denim jacket, faded almost white at the elbows. She caught his eye, then looked away. Eldon was worried to death about her. He was baffled that Cora didn't seem more worried about her. Cora seemed almost unconcerned that she and Sally were so divided on everything. Sally looked up and smiled at Nathaniel Pierson; her hair hung in ringlets around her face. It was as though Eldon were watching a play, a detached happening. Of course he was worried about her! That was why he was taking charge. Why couldn't Cora see that?

"I don't see what we just sit around talkin all the time for," Price went on.

"Let's git on with it," Pierson said.

"We need to be organized!" Mancini said. Siegel was standing next to him, looking around, his eyes wide.

"The first cross gets burned down here," Pierson said, "there's gonna be one dead cracker."

"Amen!"

"White-sheet mothafuckers!" Nathaniel Pierson stood defiantly in the middle of the group of young people. Eldon could see the muscles in his bare arms rippling; the thin cloth of the stained T-shirt was stretched taut over his chest.

"I don't blame you for being angry," Mancini said.

"Oh?" Pierson said. "You don't blame us? Well. That's mighty white of you."

"You have every right in the world to be angry," Mancini said. He stood, his body tense, his head cocked forward like a little bantam rooster. "I hear you, man," he said. Siegel had edged closer to the pulpit, and he eased Mancini to the side.

"Can I speak a minute?" he said. His voice was soft, calm, after Mancini's sharp, choppy twang. He stood looking at Pierson and Price, who continued to talk to those around them. Eldon stood there near the pulpit, his body drenched in sweat.

"Stop it!" he shouted suddenly. "Just calm down!" The church quieted, and he could hear faint echoes of his voice hanging in the back of the church. "This young white man wants to talk to you. Can't you hear him speakin to you?" His voice was forceful, strong. "By God, you'll listen to him, in my church, you will." Everyone sat very still. Eldon felt a wave of adrenaline, of new determination. He stepped back.

Siegel looked out over the whole crowd. "I'm a Jew," he said. "My parents and one of my grandparents left Germany in 1934 and came

to this country. I was born here. I'm an American. But I'm also a Jew."
He paused. "I'm one of you."

Eldon listened for a response. There was none. He could hear his
own pulse pounding in his ears.

"We are all brothers and sisters," Siegel went on, "all of us. I stand
here in this Christian church, and my skin is white, and my accent is
different from yours, but none of that matters. Because we are both a
part of a people that has been degraded and victimized, despised and
viciously destroyed, just because of being who we are. I don't need to
understand *you*, because I understand myself. And you don't really
need to understand me, because you understand *yourself*. And we all
understand why we're here," he said. He stepped back. There was still
silence, but now Eldon realized that it was the kind of silence that was
active; they had listened, and they had heard him. The air in the
church seemed less hopeless, less threatening. Less confused.

Mancini moved back to the pulpit. He cleared his throat. He waited
a minute in the silence. "I want you to sign up for one of the classes.
There'll be one on Wednesday night at seven, one on Thursday afternoon at three. Both of them downstairs in the big Sunday school
room. We'll make the children's classes in conjunction with the Sunday schools at the various churches. The one here will be at nine-thirty
on Sunday mornings and will be open to any children who want to
come. I am working with some of the other ministers, but this is the
only children's class we have lined up so far. Reverend Long says that
any of you are welcome. Now," he said, and he paused. "You folks
over here," he said, indicating Pierson and the young people, "will be
glad to know that we are going to begin, right away, planning a demonstration at Maud's Cafe down on Washington Street—"

There was laughter and groans. "Maud's?" "Look out, now!"

"And we are going to do it right. We . . . you, too—all of us
together—will select the people to participate. We'll go through, step
by step, what we'll do and what we might expect, all the different
possibilities. If you're not chosen on this one, remember there'll be lots
more. There'll be a massive push for voter registration later in the
spring. So . . . well, we're getting moving."

"Gone git the heartburn down there," someone shouted.

"Git yore *ass* burned, wit birdshot," someone else said.

The voices were distant, like an overheard drama ringing faintly in
Eldon's ears.

"All right," Mancini said, holding his hands high in the air. "Power
to the people," he said, grinning.

People were suddenly talking among themselves, laughing; Eldon could tell that they felt energized by the prospects of something happening. He felt drained, but he smiled. He stood down front, shaking hands with people who came down, who were going on to shake the hands of the two young men. He was searching over the heads of the people for Cora, and he saw her, talking quietly with several other people at the back of the church, some of those who didn't want to have anything to do with Siegel and Mancini. Cora, looking worried, concerned, saw him looking at her, and she smiled, but tentatively, briefly. Eldon could not bring himself to smile back. The excitement of the moment, the energy level in the church, seemed distant, not a part of him at all. It was the beginning of the culmination of his dreams, and yet he felt an aching emptiness inside, misgivings where he had expected only joy. He felt, somehow, that that was Cora's fault. She was withholding a part of herself from him. He watched her move easily on out the door of the church with the others, and he felt only anger at her, felt betrayed again, her turned back stinging him as painfully as a Judas kiss.

.~.~.~.

Mancini followed Paul up to his room, the two boys laboring on the steep, creaking stairs of the Youngbloods' old house.

"You were great, man," Mancini said. "Wait a minute, let me get my weed. We'll talk a little while." He went down the dim, cold hallway, and Paul went into his own sparsely furnished room. There was a green army-issue sleeping bag on a mattress on the floor, a couple of plastic straight chairs with clothes thrown over them. A gas spot-heater sat against one wall, and Paul knelt and lit it, watching it spurt into life, smelling the pungent scent of the gas.

Paul was tempted to be bitterly disappointed that the people seemed to be welcoming him and Joe Mancini with less than open arms. The people in Washington had warned them about that, and he knew that he had to fight the temptation, to realize how many centuries of oppression had made the black people in the South the way they were. He had learned in the workshops that it would be a long, slow process, but nothing had prepared him for the fear that gripped his heart and the loneliness and isolation that were his daily existence. His room on the third floor of the Youngbloods' strange, dilapidated house was his haven, and Joe was constantly telling him that he spent too much time there, alone and brooding.

"Jesus Christ," Mancini had muttered one night in Paul's room, a couple of days after they'd arrived, "you better get your head together, man." Mancini was only two years older than Paul, but he seemed at least a generation beyond. "We're playing hardball, man. This ain't the goddam French Foreign Legion. Nobody made this thing up for you to forget a goddam woman that's shafted you, for Christ's sake!"

It had been a mistake ever telling Mancini about Molly, he thought, as he watched the older boy take out his clear plastic bag of pot and begin to roll a joint. Paul knew he believed in what he was doing, but he suspected it was all too true that after he and Molly had broken up he had looked for something to lose himself in, something to absorb the pain. He had been ashamed that the pain over Molly was so intense, that he had left himself so open to be hurt, because he had thought, with all his heart, that she loved him as much as he loved her. He had never felt that way about another person before, and when she had told him that they were getting too serious, that she was not interested in any kind of real commitment—she had her life planned: graduate school and then a college teaching career; he had never thought much beyond tomorrow—he had been stunned, un-believing, shattered that she could say it so casually when she had always told him how much she loved him, over and over again. Just the memory of it was so painful that he still could hardly bear it. He had felt foolish and wounded, full of a self-pity that he had never known before. They had both been in summer school, mainly, in Paul's mind, so they could be together; shortly after she told him, he had seen the recruiting poster from the Student Nonviolent Coor-dinating Committee, and he had left New Haven without taking his finals. And now he found himself in this strange land, where winter was marked by black leafless tree limbs outlined against a limp and lifeless gray sky, where damp raw air seemed to promise cold weather without actually becoming it.

He dropped to the mattress, leaning back against the wall, feeling the little heater begin to warm the room. He thought back over what he had said in the church, before the crowd. Joe had said he had been good tonight. But Paul had lied to those people. Paul's parents had not come to this country in 1934; they were at least third-generation Amer-ican Jews. His mother died of cancer when he was ten, and his father was a fairly wealthy clothing merchant in Harrisburg, Pennsylvania, married to a much younger woman, who seemed, to her only stepson, not much older than himself. Sid, one of the directors of the workshop in Washington, had told him to use it; it was not a lie, he had said, it was a "rhetorical flourish," a device.

~·~·~·

His father had been furious that he was dropping out of Yale. "Just for a year," Paul had said to his father over the phone, and his father had yelled at him, "A year? Goddammit!" And his father had hung up. Three weeks later Paul had called him from Washington.

"What?! SNCC? *Alabama?*" his father growled. "Have you lost your goddam mind, Paul?"

"No, it's what I want to do," Paul had said, and he had known that it was. After he had been with the intense young SNCC people for a week, he had known that he was in the right place, that he was born to do something about the injustice and bigotry in the world. "I don't see why you can't understand that," Paul had said.

"How many young men get to go to Yale, paid for by their old man, not even having to work for it? Huh?"

"Dad, I—"

"And you just throw it up! Goddammit, I've had to work for every dime I ever got, and you just turn your back on it!"

"I'm not turning my back on anything, Dad."

"Yale! Your future. And me! You're turning your goddam back on me!"

"Dad, I—"

"All right, then! Do what you feel like you have to do. When you come to your senses, call me." There was a pause. Paul suspected that it was a relief to his father to be able to say that. Since he married Sharon, he had had little time for or interest in Paul and his doings. "But not before."

"Huh?"

"You heard me. You make this bed, you lie in it. You get your ass in trouble, you get it out. Is that perfectly clear?"

"Yessir," Paul said, his voice barely above a whisper.

"Why you'd want to go down to that godforsaken place is beyond me. They hate Jews worse than they hate Negroes. But just go ahead. Don't bother me with it, though, you hear? When you're ready to go back to Yale, just call me. Otherwise, you're on your goddam own."

"Yessir."

"I mean it, Paul. This kind of ingratitude makes me angry! You better know I mean that."

"I know."

"When you come to your senses, call me," his father repeated before hanging up. Paul knew that his father would expect a call within the next week or two. At least a few days after he got to Alabama. Paul would show him.

***·

"I think things are set up nicely," Mancini said. He had pushed some clothes to the floor and now sat in one of the chairs rolling a joint. Paul watched him lick the paper and shape the cigarette with his fingers. "What'd you think?"

"I . . ." Paul hesitated. Mancini glanced at him, then lit the cigarette. Paul watched Joe take the first drag, holding the smoke deep in his lungs. He passed the cigarette to Paul.

"No thanks," Paul said, and Mancini arched his eyebrows. "I don't think that's a good idea."

"What?" Mancini let the smoke out.

"The dope. That's all they need. You get caught with that . . ."

"Shit"—Mancini grinned—"these crackers don't know what weed is. Don't worry about it."

"Well . . ." He *was* worried about it. The fear that ate at him all the time now had begun to wear him down. He felt disoriented enough without smoking the dope; he could not have imagined that a culture as foreign as this one existed in his own country. "I'm scared, Joe," he whispered.

" 'Course you are. You think I'm not?" Mancini took another long drag, then cupped the joint in his hand. As he let the smoke out, he said, "Shit, we'd be crazy if we weren't scared." But Joe seemed confident, at ease most of the time. He seemed to feel an invulnerability that Paul did not share. If he felt fear, Joe never let it show.

"God, it's like . . ." Paul paused. The night was still and quiet. He could hear the distant crying of the Youngbloods' baby down on the first floor at the front of the big house. They were a strange family that seemed to exist in some odd cultural cyst in this town. This quaint river town with its stately antebellum homes and wide streets lined with towering elm and oak trees. And its narrow limerock-strewn back streets, little more than alleys, lined with the leaning, rotting shanties that housed the town's black people, its dark side. It was like stepping back into a lost time, a time and place as distant as another planet from anything Paul had ever known.

It was like a dream, difficult for him to believe that he was actually here. The excited talk in Washington had centered around the new decade that was dawning; the sixties promised liberation and hope for everyone, they said, and Paul had embraced that dream with all the youthful fervor that was in him. And now he felt the brooding menace out there in the darkness, something in the very air that he was breathing. Something silent and palpable. It was as though he could feel its heart beating around him, its regular rhythm like a distant drumbeat that was almost, but not quite, within hearing.

His sense of isolation was steady and strong, as familiar to him now as the feel of a shirt against his skin. "It's like . . . well . . . being alone," Paul said.

"Yeah," Mancini said.

"All alone."

There was a long pause as Mancini slumped in the chair and stared at the faded wallpaper.

"Yeah," Mancini whispered softly.

.~.~.~.

Lacy McClellon had always been Ellen's best friend. The two girls had grown up together, from kindergarten on. Lacy drove a white Ford convertible, and she was free with her rides around town. She kept a package of Chesterfield cigarettes in the glove compartment, and she was generous with those, too. Several times recently she and Ellen had ridden around at lunchtime, puffing the Chesterfields. Today, after school, she had offered Ellen a ride downtown, to Ramsey's Drug Store, where many of their friends tended to congregate on winter afternoons, drinking cherry cokes and eating potato chips.

"Could we . . . I mean, could we talk?" Ellen had asked, and Lacy had looked at her sideways. There was some kind of distance there now, something that had not been there when they were younger. Lacy had driven down to the river landing, where they sat for a while, smoking, listening to the radio, looking out over the river to the greenish-gray swamps on the other side. Lacy had left the motor running, and the heater purred; they were listening to the Shirelles singing "Will You Love Me Tomorrow."

Lacy was a tall, thin blonde. Her lips were narrow, and she wore very dark, almost black, lipstick. She let her hand hang loosely over the steering wheel, the cigarette dangling from her fingers, as she looked at Ellen, a question in her eyes.

Ellen wished there were someone she could talk to. She had found that she could successfully shut her mother and her drinking out of her mind most of the day, deny that her mother even existed, but she needed to replace it with something.

"They're probably nice," Ellen said. "Those boys from up North, I mean." She was fascinated with the young civil rights workers who had come to town, although most of her classmates were angry and hostile about it.

"They're livin with the Youngbloods," Lacy said. "Yuck."

Ellen rolled the window down and threw her cigarette butt out onto the gravel. She didn't answer.

"The Youngbloods are so trashy. And Daddy says those boys are probably some kind of perverts," Lacy said. "He said they usually are."

"I don't think so," Ellen said.

"How do you know?"

"I don't," Ellen said. She had seen the tall, good-looking blond boy again, downtown, the past Saturday. She had been in the A & P with her mother, and the boy had been buying some bread and sandwich meat. He was in the next line over, and Ellen had watched him out of the corners of her eye. She had felt stimulated being that close to him, his mystery, his mission; she had felt almost feverish. She had thought he was noticing her, but she didn't look openly at him. "The tall blond one's named Paul," Ellen said.

"What do I care?" Lacy said, "He's a nigger-lover."

"Please don't use that word," Ellen said.

"What?" Ellen didn't answer. "Nigger? Jesus! What's got into you, Ellen?"

"I just don't like that word," Ellen said. Everyone around her used it, in school, on the street, and she had grown to hate it. It stood for something in her life that she detested, though she did not understand what it was.

Lacy sat looking at her, turned slightly sideways in the seat. She drew on her cigarette and blew the smoke toward the canvas top. The cigarette's mouth end was stained dark maroon. The Shirelles droned on. "All right," she said, after a minute, "Kneegrows, then. Jesus. I don't understand you."

"What's there to understand?" She was thinking about her old friend Sally Long. They had been such friends as little girls. But then . . .

"You sound like a Yankee." Ellen laughed. "Well, you do. Or somethin. Everybody says nigger. Jesus."

"I don't," Ellen said. "You know, I used to be good friends with this girl, Sally. A . . . colored girl."

Lacy drew on the cigarette, her eyes vague and uninterested. "Yeah?" she said, after a minute.

"Anyway," Ellen blurted, "I can't see anything wrong with eatin with somebody of another race, can you? I mean, I think it's wrong."

Lacy stared at her. "How'd you find out his name anyway?"

Ellen looked off out the window, at the river. "I heard somebody call him that," she said.

"You were somewhere where they were? Jesus!"

"At the A and P," she said.

"The A *and P*?"

"With Mom. Saturday morning. I saw him inside, then out in the parkin lot I heard somebody call him Paul." She was staring out the window, feeling a warmth in the car, and it seemed to her that a flush was starting up her neck, a blush, and she looked over at Lacy. Lacy was staring at her, a suspicious, almost incredulous look on her face.

"Well, you better stay away from those people, Ellen."

"For heaven's sake," she said. "I just *saw* the boy."

"Shit," Lacy said. She ground her cigarette into the ashtray on the dash. She sat with her knees apart, her navy skirt hiked up over her slim, muscular thighs. She had a reputation for driving the Ford very fast on country roads.

"What did you want to talk to me about?" she said, tossing her blond hair. Ellen, thinking that she was a complete stranger, did not answer her. Lacy backed up, the tires scratching in the gravel. "Let's go to Ramsey's," she said.

⋅∿⋅∿⋅

They were sitting around the littered table, after everyone else was gone. The tabletop was cluttered with glasses and crumpled napkins and chip packages.

"Jesus, I hate to go home," Lacy said.

"Me, too," Ellen said. Ellen dreaded going home because of her mother. It had not been too bad so far this time. But sooner or later, her mother would slide over the edge. She would get very drunk and mean and stay that way for a long time. She willed the thoughts of her mother from her mind.

"God, I'll be glad when basketball season is over," Lacy said. She had reapplied her lipstick, and she sat there blotting it on a napkin, inspecting the lip marks she made. "All the good-lookin guys play basketball. Nobody plays baseball."

Suddenly, Ellen saw Paul Siegel up at the front of the store, and her heart jumped in her chest. He was at the counter, with something to purchase in his hand. It looked like a can of shaving cream. He had on a gray sweatshirt and tight blue jeans tucked into scuffed boots. His blond hair was shaggy over the back of his neck.

"I'm gonna say somethin to him," Ellen said.

"Who?" Lacy said. "Oh!" She squinted her eyes, peering into the gray late afternoon light that came through the plate-glass windows at the front of the drugstore. "Ellen, you don't dare."

"I do. Watch me."

"Jesus," Lacy said. She frowned. Then she smiled for a moment, then frowned again. "I wouldn't. Not that boy. What'll your dad say?"

"I know *you* wouldn't. But I'm me."

Ellen got her books and her purse and went up the aisle, between shelves of toothpaste and mouthwash and soap, smelling perfume and chocolate syrup. Paul stood with his back to her. Mrs. Ramsey, the pharmacist's wife, was behind the cash register, waiting on him, and she had a tight, thin-lipped frown on her face. She looked at Ellen and rolled her eyes.

"Hello," Ellen said, feeling light-headed, excited.

The boy turned and looked at her. His eyebrows arched, and a questioning expression appeared on his face. He looked back at Mrs. Ramsey, who was glaring at Ellen, and then he turned back around. His blue eyes jolted her. His smile was dazzling.

"Hi," he said.

"Here's your change," Mrs. Ramsey said. She counted it out into his palm. "Anything else?"

"No, thank you," he said. She handed him his purchase in a small white paper sack. He stood there holding it, looking at Ellen.

Ellen could see Lacy in the back, watching them, her neck craned to see around the display cases, so Ellen turned her back on her. She could feel her lips trembling slightly as she smiled up at the boy. Mrs. Ramsey continued to stare at her, making her nervous.

"My name's Ellen Brewster," she said. It seemed to her that she spoke very rapidly, the words tumbling out of her mouth one on top of the other.

"Well, hello," the boy said. "Paul Siegel." He stuck out his hand. Ellen was holding her books with both arms, her purse dangling from one arm, and she paused, awkwardly, thinking *I am hopeless, completely hopeless.* The she laughed and held out her left hand, around the books, and Paul, laughing, took it. "Glad to meetcha, Ellen Brewster," he said.

"Humph," grunted Mrs. Ramsey.

Ellen glanced at her. Mrs. Ramsey made a big deal out of the teenagers hanging out in the back of the drugstore. She and Mr. Ramsey had never had children, and they both taught Sunday School at the Episcopal church. She shook her head at Ellen, mouthing the words *What do you think you're doing?* Ellen turned back to Paul, ignoring her.

"I wanted to say welcome to Hammond," Ellen said, trying to sound mature and sophisticated, and she heard Mrs. Ramsey suck in her breath. "I saw you at the grocery store Saturday morning."

"You did? The grocery store?"

"Yes."

"Oh. Yeah. Okay." So he *hadn't* been noticing her in the line. She could tell that he didn't remember it. She was chagrined.

"Where do you go to school?" she blurted, almost stuttering.

"Yale. I—"

"Because I'm goin to Middlebury College next fall. You know Middlebury? In Vermont?" She knew she was talking very fast, but she couldn't help it.

"Yes. Of course I've heard of it."

"Well, I'm going there in September."

"Really? That's great."

"Well. So what are you doin in Hammond?" she said. "I mean, well, you know." The silence was painful to her, embarrassing.

He grinned. "Visiting," he said.

"Visiting?"

"Yeah. Friends. You know."

Mrs. Ramsey snorted, hovering three feet from them. "Ellen?" she said.

"Yes, m'am?"

"Don't you need to be gittin on home?"

"Why, no, m'am." Ellen felt bold. She felt in league with Paul against the old woman.

"Humph," Mrs. Ramsey said. She moved away from them, then behind the soda fountain. She picked up a rag and began to wipe the counter. She had told a group of them one afternoon that she and Mr. Ramsey might have to take the soda fountain out and quit selling Cokes and milk shakes altogether. It had happened other places, she had said. All because of the niggers.

She felt bolder. "Would you like to . . . sit down? Have a Coke?" she said.

"Well . . ." He looked around. "Maybe I better not. I'm . . ." He looked at his watch. "I'm expected somewhere," he said.

"Oh. I don't want to keep you then," she said, her heart sinking with disappointment.

"No. That's okay. I mean . . . well, I'm not in *that* big a hurry, but I don't have time for a Coke or anything. You know?"

"Okay. Well." Her spirits soared again. They stood there for a moment. Ellen looked toward the back. She saw Lacy's face, high up, and she realized she was standing on a chair in order to see them. Mrs. Ramsey had turned on water in a sink behind the counter. She was washing glasses, glancing up at them from time to time.

Ellen felt more relaxed. She felt bolder still now. Her words tumbled out. "See, I used to have this friend. We played together a lot as little girls. She was . . . my only friend for the longest time. I mean, I guess we're still friends, in a way. But she's a Negro. You probably know her. Sally Long?"

"Sure. I know her."

"Okay, well." She motioned with her head and they moved away from the cash register, over to a wall covered with a magazine rack. She could see Mrs. Ramsey following them with her eyes, gaping curiously at them. "I don't know what I mean to say. I . . . I *admire* what you're doin, is all, I guess."

"You do? Well, thank you."

"It must take a . . . lot of courage to come down here like this. You must be scared."

"Well . . ." he said, seeming to falter. He looked away. "Not a lot," he blustered. She could see clearly then how frightened he was.

She reached out and touched him on the forearm. "Well, you ought to be. You better be careful. What you're doin is dangerous."

"All right," he said, softly. Then he cut his eyes back at her. He seemed to shake himself, to stand straighter. "You really think it's so dangerous?" He grinned. His accent was clipped, short. It sounded strange and out of place. He smiled at her. His eyes were blue, but darker than her own. She faltered a bit. She thought, for a moment, that he was condescending to her, and it made her mad; she looked at his face, at the grin there, and he seemed almost immature, almost on the level with the ninth-grade boys who had been horsing around Ramsey's a little while ago. He seemed both superior and silly at the same time.

"I really mean what I'm saying," she said, frowning. "I'm not like most of the people in this town. I'm really not. And I'm almost as old as you are, too."

"Oh. Okay," he said.

"I heard there was gonna be a demonstration," she said, and he looked startled.

"Where'd you hear that?" he said.

"Around."

"You heard it talked around?"

"Yeah. Around school and all. At Maud's Cafe," she said. "Everybody in town hates what you're doing, Paul. But I'm for you. I'm with you."

He stared at her, a curious look in his eyes.

"You . . . well, who are you? You live here all your life?" he said.

"Yeah. Born here. I'll prob'ly die here, to tell you the truth. I hate it here, if you really want to know."

"Well, you're gettin out," he said.

"Huh?"

"Middlebury."

"Oh. Yeah." She looked up at him. A warm flush seemed to spread over her, touching her skin beneath her clothes. She smiled. "Maybe I'll join your demonstration. You need some white people?"

"Are you jokin me?" he said.

"No. Maybe. No, not really. I don't know about the demonstration, though. I mean, like I go to Maud's all the time with my folks. Everybody goes there after church on Sunday, you know?" She wondered if what she was saying sounded silly. She would just try to be herself. He was looking steadily at her.

"If you're serious, we may be able to use you," he said.

"Use me?" That sounded strange to her.

"Well, that's just . . . a way of putting it." He smiled down at her. They stood there for a minute.

"Maybe you could tell me about Yale and all," she said. "I'm curious about . . . you know, Eastern schools and all. I've never lived outside Alabama."

"Maybe I . . . can do that," he said. He looked at his watch again. "Look, I gotta go." He didn't move. "So. See you around, then, okay? Ellen."

"Yeah. Okay."

He patted her on the shoulder. Then he was gone out the door. Mrs. Ramsey was shaking her head, muttering to herself. She had gathered all the sticky Coke glasses from the back and was washing them in soapy water. Ellen watched Lacy walk slowly up to the front. Ellen's pulse was still skipping, her blood hot.

"I can't believe you did that," Lacy said. Her expression was locked halfway between a laugh and a frown. She had a napkin wrapped tightly around her finger, and her navy-blue skirt hung awkwardly on her lanky frame. "You're weird, Ellen," she said. "Weird."

Ellen hugged her books to her breasts, looking out at the street where the boy had gone. She still felt tingly, drawn to him, excited by the danger and by his long, lean body.

"He's not like any boys around here," Ellen said.

"No," Lacy said, "he's not. That's for sure. God, I don't see what you see in him."

"I don't . . ." Ellen stopped, looking at Lacy. She did seem like a stranger, or rather someone who had somehow turned into someone else. There was such a gap, such a distance, between them. Ellen felt as though she had moved away from her and all the others in Hammond, stealthily, like a prowler in the night.

Chapter Four

꒰ ꒱

I T WAS A WARM DAY FOR EARLY FEBRUARY; THE SUN WAS BRIGHT IN the street, and Mac could see several people sitting on benches in the park across the way. The scene seemed peaceful; Mac rubbed his itching eyelids and sighed. He leaned back, and his swivel chair squeaked. His stomach was sour and uncomfortable. The scene was peaceful, but the day was not. This was the day that Mac had long dreaded: the day of the planned demonstration. He had no idea what to expect, but every time he closed his eyes, he saw violent red flashes of fire and blood, and Carleton Byrd informing him, with his limp eyelids, that he had royally fucked up any chances of Gulf International ever coming to Hammond. He was not going to let that happen. *No way.*

He had slept poorly, waking with a start in the dark early morning. He was wide awake immediately, and he knew at the moment of waking that he would not be able to go back to sleep. The pale green luminous hands on the alarm clock showed ten minutes to four. Belinda snored away on the other side of the king-sized bed, and Mac got carefully out of bed, being gentle with the covers. It made Belinda very angry if she sensed he was pulling the cover too much to his side. Even if he did it in his sleep. She had said that people *should* be blamed for things that they do in their sleep, since it's usually even *more* something that they really want to do, because it's their subconscious doing it. Mac padded into the bathroom and ran some cold water; he cupped his hand and drank. Then he stood over the toilet, dangling, waiting for the water to come. He needed to pee badly, but more and more lately he had had trouble; he worried as he waited. Finally, the stream came, unsteady, jerky, with some going onto the tile beside the toilet. He shook his head. If Belinda got her bare foot in it, she would complain. *Let her.*

He found his old brown bathrobe and went down the hallway, past the closed doors of his son's and daughter's bedrooms, down the stairs to the kitchen. He liked the spaciousness of their house, and recently he had decided that he wanted to buy an old one, one of the old antebellum mansions in town, and fix it up. A house just like the one they had sold when they got married. A house with history, with pedigree. *What was wrong with that?* But Belinda would have no part of an old house. ("I lived in a drafty old house all my life," she had said. "Good riddance to that. Now I want me a newer one still!") So he had shut up about it. He put on the lights and filled the kettle with water from the spigot. He got out his favorite mug, white with ROLL TIDE written on it in red letters. It was a big, oversized mug, and he dumped two spoons of instant coffee in along with three spoons of sugar.

He sat down at the table. He had had a lot of trouble going to sleep the night before, and he had had to work hard to keep the demonstration out of his mind. He thought he remembered dreaming fitfully about it, but he couldn't remember any details very clearly. There was a bird, like an eagle, with pools of blood for eyes, he remembered that much. Oh, and a nurse in a white uniform who kept saying to him, "It ain't fur to the spur." He shook his head. He didn't know how it all fit, but he knew that it was still on his mind when he awoke. He was worried. His plan (he didn't know, maybe it was just a fantasy) was this: He would do everything he could to keep any kind of racial trouble down until Gulf International had made its commitment and come in and started building the plant. That included coddling the nigger Long, going along with him as far as he could go, and then arresting him quietly when he broke the law. On the other hand, he had to somehow keep Rooster and his boys quiet by letting them know that he and the Citizens Council was doing everything they could to frustrate the communist nigger movement from taking over the town. If he could balance those two, they could get through this temporary mess; the niggers would get tired of all this agitation and such, and things would get back to normal. The world would once again be like it used to be, except that he would be drinking bourbon and water with senators and maybe even Governor Patterson, his feet propped on the stone fireplace out at Shady Grove Plantation, taking his ease with other men like himself. He imagined that those men were watching him now, too. Even old Thomas Jonathan himself, saying, "Take care of this for us, Mac. Earn your way. Then we'll welcome you."

.~.~.~.

He had gone in for a trim yesterday afternoon, just to test the atmosphere in Rooster's barbershop, and it had alarmed him.

"We'll be there, yeah," Rooster had said. "We'll plan us a little welcomin committee!"

"What you mean?" Mac had said. He had sat there in the chair, smelling the hair tonic and the powder, the clippers buzzing and whining behind his ear, the sheet too tight and uncomfortable around his neck. He could feel the cold metal of the safety pin pressing into the side of his neck.

"Just that. That's all. We'll be there to welcome em."

"Looks to me like the best way is to just ignore em," Mac said. "Lester Sparks'll be there. Maud has been warned; she knows they're comin. No reason for anybody else to even be there."

"Got to eat your dinner somewhere," Rooster said. "Maud serves a good dinner." His eyes had glowed dully.

Looking at him, Mac knew why he feared him, feared what he represented, so much. He was the leader of an almost invisible empire, a network of men that probably included some of the policemen on Lester's force and certainly had the sympathies of most of the white people in the area. It was almost as though the Klan was carrying out silently and furtively in the dark of night the thoughts and desires of the citizens of Hammond. Almost as though they were the *real* police force, the *actual* government. If Rooster took a notion, people would start to die. Vanish. There would be no trace, but everyone would know. Gulf International would know. Mac didn't think Carleton Byrd had just meant out-and-out riots. Any kind of trouble. Racial trouble.

"Who'r you talkin bout gonna be there?" Mac asked curiously, his voice thin and nervous.

"Oh, just me and some of the boys. We'll line up down the street, watch em go by. Like the Mardi Gras. Ha!"

"Rooster, I don't think that's a good idea. You stay away from there," Mac warned.

"Shit. You think they gonna get away with stuff like that?"

"No, they ain't," Mac said. "Let Lester handle it."

"Maybe he'll handle it fine," Rooster had said. "Then again, maybe he won't."

. ~.~.~.

The kettle whistled, and Mac got up and poured his cup of coffee. He got milk out of the refrigerator and added a little. Then he sat back down, cupping his hands around the mug. The little pecan-wood table and chairs that Belinda had bought for the breakfast nook were spindly, and he didn't especially like the frilly, white-with-red-polka-dot curtains in the kitchen, either. The whole house was like that, like a picture in *Better Homes and Gardens* magazine. There was no place to just sit down and be comfortable. Even the furniture in the den was chosen more for its looks than for comfort. "His" chair was a brown corduroy deal with a matching footstool that he could only sit in in one position. By the end of one TV show, he was cramped, and his legs would be going to sleep. They had built and moved into the house in '57, and Belinda still thought of it as too new to really live in and use and get a little dirty. The payments on it were a crime. Mac sipped the coffee. Every time he had a quiet moment, he started thinking about the money: the payments on Lacy's Ford, and Dudley's Volkswagen, and the out-of-sight insurance premiums he paid for them to be able to drive their own cars, and Belinda's Cadillac that she tooled around in and could never get parked quite right. It had a balloon note coming due in three months. He had the money to pay it, of course, but it still made him edgy. He always needed more money. Sometimes he wondered at what point he would stop worrying about it, be able to relax and enjoy it. When he finally got that invitation to the Shady Grove Deer Drive? He was well on the way to finding out. Unless something went wrong with the paper mill and all his plans for the houses. It was beyond his comprehension to be broke; but it was always possible. Sometimes, it seemed to him more than a mere possibility. His stomach fluttered, and he belched.

"Shit," he muttered.

. ~.~.~.

This was it. Finally, Paul watched Joe Mancini, standing nonchalantly at the front of the Sunday school room. He was going over

exactly what they were to do when they got inside Maud's Cafe, how
they were to behave, what they could expect.

"The important thing is to keep your cool. They're not gonna serve
us. We just sit there. No matter what they do, what kind of insults they
come up with to throw at us, we don't respond. Okay? You got that?"
Joe was looking at Nathaniel Pierson and Mark Price when he said
that. The young teacher had a woman's stocking tied around his head,
in imitation of Nate, and he wore a tight T-shirt under his light denim
jacket. In addition to the two of them there were Eldon Long and his
daughter, Sally, and an elderly black man named Ruston Sinclair.
There had been plenty of others who wanted to be in on this first sit-in,
but Joe and Paul had carefully limited it, selecting the participants
carefully. They wanted to start out slowly and not have a riot their first
time out. They really had no idea what to expect in Hammond. After
all, it was not Greensboro.

Paul looked at Nate Pierson, the man's dark eyes steady on Joe,
his hand gripped into a fist on the surface of the long worktable
around which they all sat. He had wanted to go on this thing, had
told Joe he was going, even though they would not have picked him
because he seemed too angry and volatile. And Sally Long had spoken up for him, too, so they had asked both him and his friend
Price, thinking that Mark's presence would keep Pierson calm. Nate
sat very still, his tense body like a coiled spring; Paul could see the
muscles in his legs, beneath the tight faded blue jeans, and his stillness seemed about to explode into motion. Paul felt his own body
tighten with anticipation and nervousness. As Paul was looking at
him, the boy looked up, and their eyes locked for a moment, and
then Paul looked quickly away. Paul did not know what to make of
Nate, and something about him, something seething and threatening, frightened him. His eyes were bloodshot and strained like those
of a wounded animal, and when he looked at Paul, it made him feel
vaguely guilty and anxious. Paul had never known anyone quite like
Nathaniel Pierson before.

"We break the law, and we get ourselves arrested," Paul was droning
on, "and that's the point of it. But the only—the only—law we break
is the 'white only' law—we have to remember that. We don't give em
any other reason at all to arrest us. Any questions?" They had been
over it several times. This was a last-minute run-through, just as the
two boys had been taught in Washington to do it.

Paul looked around at the others, wondering if they were as scared
as he was. Long was hard to read with his serious, preacherly de-

meanor. Long's daughter seemed at ease, slouched in the chair, a bored, defiant look on her face. Seeing her, Paul thought of the girl he had met in the drugstore, Ellen Brewster. The two girls were about the same age. Both from Hammond, but from different worlds, Negro and white. He had thought of the Brewster girl often since that day in the drugstore. There was something about her that reminded him of Molly, the way she held her head when she looked up at him, the way light glinted in her blue eyes. And their talk that day had to be the most pleasurable thing that had happened to him since he'd come to this hellhole, and he savored it. Lying on the mattress, unable to fall asleep at night, homesick and frightened, he remembered the way she looked at him and what she had said about his courage, and he felt better.

He had come very close, last night, to packing it in and heading back North. He had lain awake, feeling as though his life were totally out of control. He imagined the kinds of dangerous men he had heard about, waiting out there for him, breathing the same dark air that he now inhaled. And he thought of these colored people, their culture more alien to him than he could ever have imagined, their slow, lazy way of talking and their constant, surprising bursts of laughter in the face of their hopelessness. Laughter and song.

As he lay in the dark, two things had restrained him, kept him from getting dressed and going and telling Joe that he was leaving. They were both images of faces: his father's, and what he would say when Paul came crawling home from Alabama. And the girl's face, Ellen Brewster's, the look in her eyes when she had talked to him. As long as there were people like that here . . .

•~•~•~•

"Who's hungry?" Joe grinned, and there was some nervous, hesitant chuckling and scraping of chairs as they all stood. Paul could see the determined look in Nate Pierson's eyes. At that moment, Paul was glad after all that the boy was with them. He felt a strange mixture of fear and respect for him; he could see that they were all, to varying degrees, drawn to Nathaniel, to his physical strength and his air of single-mindedness. Paul took a deep breath; standing, his legs felt weak and tingling, and he had to force them into a walking motion toward the door, as though he were wading in hip-deep water. There was brittle, anxious laughter. Someone accidentally kicked a metal spinning top that a child had left on the floor, and it clattered into the corner, causing everyone to fall silent. Long stood at the door, looking at them, his eyes playing over each one in turn. He held his hand above his head, and they all stopped in their tracks. Paul watched the preacher close his eyes and bow his head.

"Dear Lord," he intoned, "be with us all on this day. Look down upon us and give us strength to do Your will. In the name of your blessed Son, Jesus Christ. Amen." Long's voice cracked slightly on the "Amen."

⸫⸱⸺⸱⸺⸱⸺⸱

Lester Sparks, the Hammond chief of police, stopped by Mac's office; they were going to walk over together. The word had spread like wildfire; everybody in town knew this was the day. Lester was a big man, and his belly protruded over his thick leather belt, from which hung handcuffs and a pistol and a nightstick. He jangled when he walked. He wore a uniform, khaki with navy-blue trim; for years he had worn a ten-gallon hat, but lately he had started sporting a Smokey-the-Bear hat like those favored by Al Lingo's newly outfitted Alabama State Troopers, who until recently had been called the Highway Patrol. Lester had seven deputies working for him, four on days and three on nights, and he had been after Mac to hire more. "Hammond is havin a crime wave," he had announced to Mac, and Mac had said, "Well, I ain't noticed it. Folks here go out and leave their doors unlocked. What crime wave?" "Just you wait," Lester had said. He liked to chew on a matchstick, and it always sat just in the corner of his mouth. Mac wondered if he had seen that in some picture show and copied it.

They walked down Washington Street together, toward Maud's. It was like a bright, sunny spring day. They passed the pool room, and Andy Wheatly and Red Kershaw were standing in the doorway. The sunlight glinted on Red's bushy orange-red hair.

"Arrest them niggers, Sheriff," Andy Wheatly said. "What they up to, anyhow?"

"Nothin to worry about, Andy," Lester Sparks said.

"Shit," Red Kershaw said.

They passed the barber shop, with its little red-and-white candy-striped pole. It was dark inside, and there was a hand-lettered sign on the door: CLOSED, BE BACK AFTER DINNER.

"Rooster's plannin somethin, I know he is," Mac said.

"Prob'ly save the taxpayers money if he is," Lester said.

"Now listen here," Mac said. "You remember what I told you. We do this by the goddam book. I don't want any funny business. I don't want any violence. That's playin right into their hands. You got all your men there?"

"Roger. Ricky and Dave'r inside, the rest of em on the street. Don't worry none."

"Jesus Christ," Mac muttered. " 'Don't worry none?' " The winter sun was actually hot. His neck was sweating under his tight collar. He had worn a wool suit. He felt that he was walking automatically. He had made this stroll ten thousand times, but it seemed brand-new and threatening now. "Shit, it's turned summertime in February," he said.

"Blackberry winter," Lester said.

"What?"

"We'll have us a cold snap, right round Easter. Always do. Blackberry winter."

Lester's pale gray eyes were darting about. Mac followed his eyes; he could see several people along the sidewalk in front of the café. He saw Rooster and one of the man's cohorts, Bobby Lee McElroy; his pulse rate quickened, his stomach tightened.

"Yessir, always have a cold snap round Easter," Lester repeated.

"Goddammit, I can do without the weather forecast," Mac snapped.

"Sorry," Lester said, "just passin the time of day."

There were more people gathered than Mac had at first realized. Across the street, in front of Scales's Dry Goods, people were lined up as though to watch the Homecoming Parade. There was a festive atmosphere, just like a parade; people were laughing and joking and jostling for position. "What the shit they expect to see?" Mac said. "Just a bunch of niggers actin up, is all."

"Say it's historical," Lester said.

"Huh?"

"It's historical, they say."

"Who says?"

"The niggers. They say history is bein made."

"Shit. Only thing bein made is a bunch of fools." Mac stood at the door of the café, looking around. He was not sure. Everything that happened was history, wasn't it? *What's wrong with me?* He nodded to Rooster. "Rooster," he said.

"Evenin, Mayor," Rooster said. He grinned. Mac moved over close to him.

"I want you to let Lester and his men handle this. I don't want any funny business. You hear, now?"

"Yessir, Mayor," Rooster said.

"If they need any help, they'll ask for it."

"Now don't I know that?" Rooster grinned. He looked as though he knew a secret. Mac went through the front door, and Lester Sparks came in behind him. His stomach growled as he smelled the noon cooking smells inside. Maud was standing behind the cash register. She glared at him, angry, and Mac could see the two policemen behind the counter. Maud's waitress, Alda Mae Woods, was sitting at a table near the front. There were no customers. Empty tables sat on the shiny black-and-white tiled floor.

"Goddammit, this is costin me money," Maud said. She had fiery red hair that shook as she jerked her head back and forth. Her lipstick was a crimson slash across her face, and her cheeks were rouged like autumn winesap apples. "They's a law against this," she said.

"Against what?" Mac said. *Just keep her calm.*

"What them niggers are doin," she said.

"They ain't done nothin yet," Mac said.

"Well, then, goddammit, Mac, where the hell are my customers? Tell me that."

"Nobody stopped em from comin in here," Mac said. He knew how silly that was.

"Them goddam niggers stopped em," Maud said. "And if you don't do somethin about it, I will." She turned to Lester. "And I want my goddam gun back, Lester," she said. Ricky Wiggins, over behind the counter, held up Maud's huge pistol that she usually kept behind the counter, under the cash register. Everybody knew it was there.

"You'll get it back, Maud," Lester said.

Mac sat down at a table and motioned for Lester to join him. "I'll have the meat loaf," he said, "crowder peas, lima beans, and mashed potatoes. And bring some extra corn-bread muffins."

"Yessir," Alda Mae Woods said. She never wrote anything down, but she never made a mistake.

"Fried chicken. I want a breast, now," Lester said. "Peas and potatoes. Bring me some salad. Thousand Island."

"Ice tea?" she said.

"Right." She disappeared into the kitchen. Ricky Wiggins and Dave Gatlin slouched behind the counter. They wore the same khaki uniforms with blue trim. They both looked nervous and anxious. They were young, practically just out of high school. They had both gone to the new Police Academy over in Montgomery for six weeks; Mac had been pleased to be able to send them over there. They were the first Hammond policemen to get any kind of training.

"Y'all git you a cheeseburger while we wait, if you want to," Lester said to them.

"Hell, what's wrong with fried chicken?" Ricky Wiggins grinned.

"All right. Git you whatever you want."

"I want em arrested, is what *I* want," Maud said. "I ain't puttin up with no shit, Mac," she said.

"We got to feel this out, Maud," Mac said.

" '*Feel* it out?' What the hell you talkin about?"

"If we treat this right, then we can nip it in the bud. These things can get outta hand. Look at what happened up in Greensboro. Those folks just sat and sat at them lunch counters."

"I ain't studyin any Greensboro," Maud said.

Just as Alda Mae brought the laden plates out of the kitchen, a hush suddenly settled over the crowd outside; Mac had really not even been conscious of the buzzing until it abruptly ceased.

"Well, they're here," Lester Sparks said.

"This is it," Ricky Wiggins said.

"This is my goddam café," Maud said.

"And all you got to do is just act that way," Mac said, his skin tingling and his breathing shallow. "You make the rules in here. You're inside of the law. Don't worry about it."

The plate-glass door was pushed open, and Eldon Long walked in. He stopped and looked around. He saw Mac sitting there, and Lester Sparks; he looked at Maud, then at the policemen behind the counter. The dark, wiry civil rights worker came in behind him, looking cocky. He stood there, the expression on his face suggesting he smelled something distasteful. Alda Mae set the plates in front of Mac and Lester. Mac picked up a fork and took a bite of crowder peas. He sat chewing. The room was still and quiet, the only movement the slow grinding motion of Mac's jaw. Long looked stiff and uncomfortable in his black suit. He came on into the room and sat at a table, and the fellow, what was his name, Joe Mancini, joined him. The others filed in. A teenaged girl about his daughter's age, dressed like a beatnik, and two young boys, both with what looked like women's stockings tied around their heads. He thought he recognized one of them as Mark Price, a young teacher over at the colored high school. He made a mental note. Price had just, in effect, resigned his job with the Hammond school system. The other white boy followed, Paul Siegel was his name, Mac remembered, and he was with an old nigger man, Ruston Sinclair. What the hell was *he* doing here? The younger people looked defiant and mad. They occupied three tables, their chairs scraping on the tile as they sat down. They all sat there. They all looked at Mac. Maud walked around behind the counter.

"Y'all see that?" she said. She was pointing to a sign that said: WE RESERVE THE RIGHT TO REFUSE SERVICE TO ANYONE. Nobody answered her. "Well?" she said. "Can't one of you read?" She stood there glaring at them. She had on a bright blue dress and a blue ribbon in her hair, over her left ear.

"We all see it," Mancini said.

"Yeah, but can you read it?"

"We can read it. It's unconstitutional," he said.

"I ain't studyin any constitution," Maud said. "We don't serve niggers in here."

"We don't want a nigger," the young girl said, "we want a hamburger."

They all laughed nervously. Except for Mac and Maud and Lester Sparks. The two young policemen poked each other in the ribs and shifted back and forth on the balls of their feet, grinning, until they saw Lester's face. Then their faces sobered, and they stood still, almost at attention.

"Who are you, Judy Canova?" Maud said.

There was a long silence. Mac could almost hear all their breathing.

"We'd like to order now," Eldon Long said.

"I don't care what you'd like," Maud said.

The door opened. Mac looked over that way and frowned, his heart seeming to skip a beat as Rooster came in with his friend Bobby Lee. They walked over, Rooster rocking back and forth with his heavy-footed, clumsy gait, and stood against the wall, their arms folded over their chests. Rooster had on a light blue windbreaker and a necktie; he hardly ever wore a necktie. Lester sat there holding his piece of fried chicken. He gestured with it.

"You people are in violation of the law," he said, "and I would advise you to leave peaceably. Maybe you just made a mistake."

"This is no mistake," the young girl said. There was something about her that looked like Long, the same bone structure in the face, something. "We came in here to eat lunch. And we'd like to order it." Hadn't Long told Mac that he had a daughter? Mac decided that that was who it was.

"The kitchen's closed," Maud said.

"What are they eatin, then?" the girl said. "We'll have whatever they're havin."

"That's the last of it. The kitchen's all outta food. You can sit here till hell freezes over, and you won't git nothin to eat here," Maud said.

"May I ask why you are refusing us service?" It was Mancini.

"Cause you're with them niggers, and this is a white-only restaurant, that's why," Maud said. "Any other questions?"

"You refuse to serve them because of the color of their skin?" Mancini said.

"That's right," Maud said. "You got the picture, sport?"

"That's the way we do things down here, boy," Rooster said. Everybody looked at him. Mac was alarmed that he had spoken. *Here it comes.*

"Rooster," Mac said, "just—"

"Who are you?" Mancini said to Rooster. Mac could hear his smart-ass dago tone. *Jesus Christ! Shut the hell up!*

"That's none a' your business. You're the one in the wrong place. You don't know what's good for you, boy," Rooster said.

There was a long, tense silence in the room. Mac could see the bulge of a pistol under Bobby Lee's red jacket. He knew that Rooster would be armed, too. He felt downright nervous now. They were within an inch of losing control. He looked over at Lester. *Take the chance. Move.* "Arrest em," he said.

"Now?" Lester said.

"Yes, fuckin now," Mac whispered tightly out of the corner of his mouth.

Lester stood up. "I'm afraid," he said, "that if you people don't leave peaceably, I'm gonna have to put you under arrest."

"What charge?" Eldon Long asked.

Lester looked at Mac, and Mac nodded. "Trespassin," he said.

"This is a public restaurant," Long said.

"It's privately owned. She don't have to serve somebody with red hair if she don't want to. She can refuse service to folks from below the Bogue, if she wants to." He was referring to a creek that ran through the middle of the county. Nobody said anything. "Don't y'all wanna move along, peaceably like?"

"Arrest em," Mac said.

"Let em sit there," Rooster said. "Let em rot in them chairs."

"Rooster, this ain't any business of yours," Mac snapped. Rooster looked at him, his eyes thin and flashing, and Mac looked away, hating himself for doing it.

"Goddammit, Mac," Rooster went on. "This is the business of every white man everwhere. I can't believe you said that. Nossir."

"Just let Lester handle it," Mac said. Mac had been holding his fork, along with his breath, and he laid it down, afraid it was shaking, letting out his breath with a long sigh. It came out almost like a moan. Nobody looked at him.

Rooster moved away from the wall, his wooden leg making a dull, uneven thump on the tile floor. He stood behind Long's chair, grinning.

"Rooster," Mac said, hearing the shaking of his own voice.

Rooster rubbed his knuckle on Long's head. Mac could see Long's face, impassive, his eyes looking straight ahead. He didn't move his head, and Rooster rubbed his knuckle in his hair again. Mac squinted at them, pretty well knowing what would happen now.

"Nappy," Rooster said. "Full of straightener, but it's still nappy. Like a ape's." Nobody said anything. Long didn't move, didn't even acknowledge that Rooster was touching him. Mac was astonished.

"Ain't that right?" Rooster said to Mancini. Mancini opened his mouth.

"Don't answer him." It was Long's calm voice. "Don't say a word."

"What, boy?" Rooster said.

There was another long silence.

"We're ready to order now," Long continued in the same tone.

"Don't you understand, nigger?" Rooster said.

"Rooster," Mac said, quickly, "why don't you let Lester handle this."

Lester moved forward. "Boys," he said, and the two young policemen came out from behind the counter.

"Shit," Rooster snorted, and he gave Long's head a push from behind. Long gripped the edge of the table. Mac could see anger, rage, on his face, but he sat very still. Long looked at the girl and shook his head. The girl had a thin film of tears in her eyes. The two young colored men looked wound as tight as a clock spring; their eyes were full of hatred, and, Mac felt, danger. He shuddered. One of the young men stood up; he wore a stained T-shirt and ragged blue jeans, and the muscles in his dark arms rippled. His eyes were wide, almost panicked.

"Nathaniel, sit down," Long said.

"Goddam cracker," Nathaniel said.

"What'd you say, boy?" Rooster said. "What'd he say, Bobby Lee?"

"Whut'd you say, boy?" Bobby Lee echoed. He patted the gun under his jacket. "You know what this is, boy?"

"Wait!" Mac's heart was racing; he realized that he was sweating under the suit. "Sit down," he said, "everybody sit down."

Nobody moved. Maud stood behind the counter, watching them. Mac could see Alda Mae and a black face, one of the cooks, peeping through the kitchen door at the scene. It was quiet. "Arrest em," Mac said.

Lester moved forward toward them. "Git outta the way, Rooster." Long was going to let them arrest them. He wasn't going to fight back. *Now if Rooster—*

"Goddammit," Rooster said. But he backed up, moving awkwardly, his face contorted. "They better watch it," he said. "You boy," he said, pointing at Mancini, "you better git your ass on back to wherever you come from."

"I'll handle this," Lester said.

"See that you do," Rooster sneered. "We don't need their kind around here. You better watch yourself, boy."

"That's enough," Lester said.

"Whose side are you on, anyhow?" Rooster aid. "Goddammit, Mac!"

Mac jumped in then. "He's arrestin em, Rooster. What more do you want?" He motioned to Lester to get on with it.

"Well, we'll find out, won't we?" Rooster growled. His cramped, gimpy walk moved him back to where he had been standing earlier. He leaned back against the wall. "A nigger don't speak to me that way and git away with it," he muttered.

"Yeah," Bobby Lee said.

"All right," Lester said to them, "y'all are under arrest. Now what I'd like to do is have you all just walk peaceable to the jailhouse. All right?"

"You're askin *us?*" Long said.

"I can git the cars and haul you there three by three, but I'd just soon have you walk. Ain't but three blocks."

"A parade, like the Mardi Gras," Rooster said, and he and Bobby Lee laughed.

Long stood up. Slowly, one by one, the others stood. Ruston Sinclair looked scared to death. There were tiny beads of sweat on the blond boy's upper lip, and his eyes were wide. Mancini wore his cocky grin. The three younger coloreds looked sullen and angry. Mac looked on with amazement at how docile they were. Why, they didn't have their hearts in it at all. This was going to be a piece of cake.

"All right," Lester said, "let's go."

Lester led the way, the two young policemen brought up the rear, and Mac fell in with them; Rooster and Bobby Lee and Maud watched them go. Outside, the sunlight was so bright it blinded Mac momentarily, and he blinked several times, hearing the buzzing of the crowd and then the cheers and shouts. Mac looked around. There must have been several hundred people gathered to watch them march toward the jail. Mac saw his wife, Belinda; she was standing next to O. B. Brewster's wife, Martha, in the doorway of Scales's Dry Goods. Belinda waved, laughing, and Mac lifted his hand in greeting. He could not force himself to smile, even though deep down he felt relief. As they moved on down the street, Mac saw O.B., standing aside, leaning against a lamp pole. He watched them go by, his face flat and expressionless. Mac nodded to him, and O.B. did not return the nod; Mac didn't know if he'd seen it or not. Most of the crowd seemed relaxed, in a jovial, holiday mood. They laughed and pointed. But Mac noticed several more of Rooster's buddies, men he knew to be Klansmen, dotted about in the crowd. Even though Lester was in control and the niggers hadn't fought back, Mac still felt a vague anxiety, a dread. He kept walking, Lester now setting a quick pace. His stomach rumbled and growled, and he thought of the plate full of food, sitting back there on the table getting cold. Alda Mae was probably right now scraping it into the garbage. The winter afternoon sun beat on his head with almost the fierceness of late spring.

Another one of Lester's deputies, Ronnie Young, stood next to the front door of the tiny redbrick jailhouse. It was behind city hall, and it contained two cramped offices in the front and six small cells in the back.

"Like I been sayin, we need a bigger jail," Lester said.

Mac just shook his head.

All of those arrested but Long filed down the little dim hallway into the cells, and Mac could hear the doors clanging shut. Long stood at a little wooden desk in the front, Lester writing down all their names on a yellow legal pad. Long stared at Mac, his eyes watery and red-rimmed.

"Well, we won, didn't we?" Mac said. "That didn't do anybody a speck of good, did it?"

"Nobody won," Long said, "this time."

"I don't know what you expect to accomplish," Mac said.

"Evil is doomed in this world, Mr. McClellon," he said. "You broke the law, not me," said Mac, feeling vindicated, with the assurance of knowing that he had done the right thing. Carleton Byrd couldn't question that.

"Maybe this'll get in the papers. The law can be changed. It *will* be changed," Long said. His bloodshot eyes were steady on Mac.

The look on Long's face made an icy cold creep up Mac's veins, and he shivered. Long's calm disturbed and frightened him. The man looked as though he welcomed being put in the jail. Mac sighed and turned away, moving back outside into the sunshine.

People had followed them, gathering on the lawn around city hall, and as they craned their necks, looking at the jail, Mac held up his hands.

"There ain't anything else to see," he said. "Y'all might as well go on home."

People began to disperse, laughing and talking among themselves. They seemed to think it was some kind of lark, but Mac had a hollow, hot ball in the pit of his chest. If he had felt nervousness and fear early this morning, what he felt now was a nameless, faceless foreboding that there was too much that he didn't understand, couldn't grasp. Meanwhile, the image of Rooster rubbing his knuckle in Long's hair remained vivid. *Why the hell couldn't everybody just let well enough alone?* Lester came out the front door.

"Well," he said, "they're arrested. You still want me just to let em set there, not book em nor nothin?"

"Right. Just let em cool off."

"How long you wanna hold em?"

"Just let em sit there, Lester," Mac said, shortly. "Let's see what happens. Did you see any reporters there?"

"Reporters? From the newspaper?"

"Yes, from the goddam newspaper!" Mac snapped. "Where the hell else do reporters come from?!"

"Naw," Lester said, "not that I noticed. You see any?"

"No, I didn't," Mac said.

"You know," Lester said, "if we have to arrest many more, ain't gonna be any place to put em."

"Why would we need to arrest any more?" Mac said.

"You can't tell what the niggers might be up to," Lester said. "Can you?"

Mac didn't answer.

"It's crowded in there," Lester said.

"We can take some of em down to the county jail if we have to," Mac said.

"Well, like I say, we could use a new jail."

"Shut the fuck up," Mac said. He had avoided the violence, and yet he couldn't understand why he still felt terrible, almost physically sick with worry.

.~.~.~.

O.B., Martha, and Ellen sat at their kitchen table, eating a supper of pork chops and canned green beans. O.B. cut his chop with a chipped bone-handled steak knife, part of a set that they'd gotten as a present when they were married, of which only four remained. The pork chop was thin and cooked dry, and the beans were almost tasteless. Martha had simply dumped them in a boiler and heated them on the stove. It was the kind of thing that had once made O.B. angry; now he felt nothing but thin disgust as he sprinkled pepper on his beans. They ate in silence. Martha wore a blue long-sleeved blouse that was buttoned crookedly up the front; she had been taking a nap when O.B. had gotten home from work, and she had had to rustle around with the supper. He knew that she had been taking nips from her bourbon bottle in the kitchen while he sat up front watching the television news.

"I thought it was funny," Martha said. "You should've seen Mac's face!" She giggled.

"I did," O.B. said. He had been strangely moved, but now he laughed softly. Glimpsing Eldon's eyes, he had seen something old and familiar there, a determination, a strength. As he had stood there in the crowd, he had remembered the hundreds of meals he had eaten with Eldon and the man's parents, Blount and Punchy, in their cabin, when they had been children, and now here Eldon was, risking his safety for the right to eat in a white restaurant. There did seem to him to be something useless and silly about it.

"What was so funny about it?" Ellen spoke up. Martha cut her eyes at her, putting down her fork.

"I don't like that tone," she said.

"Excuse me!" Ellen said sarcastically.

"All right!" Martha said darkly. Then she looked around. She seemed to brighten. "It was just funny. I've always thought niggers were funny."

"I was just askin," Ellen said. "They got put in jail? Sally?"

"Yep," O.B. said.

"I heard that. But I didn't believe it. Sally?" Ellen chewed, shaking her head; her hair was tied back in a short ponytail, and she wore one of his old gray sweatshirts, one that Martha had fussed at her in the past for wearing. It wasn't ladylike.

"Sally and Eldon, and those two white boys from the North, and these two boys Nathaniel Pierson and Mark Price. Somebody said

Mark Price teaches over at the colored high school, but he looks like a teenager," O.B. said. "And, oh yeah, old Ruston Sinclair. He farms down in the Flatwoods." O.B. was surprised that he felt a nervous excitement about it. He wondered what he would have done, had he been Mac. How would he have handled it differently? Maybe he *could* have been able to sit down and work something out without carting people off to jail. He did not know. But he was bothered, troubled at the thought of Eldon and the others sitting in the old jail.

"Ruston *Sinclair?*" Martha said. "Was that who that was? His wife used to work for the Harrises. For years. I'll be."

"You'll be what?" Ellen said. Martha sat there, staring at Ellen for a moment.

"You never let up, do you?" she said.

"What do you mean?" Ellen said.

"You give me such a hard time. For no reason."

"No mothers and daughters get along." Ellen shrugged, moving the food around on her plate with her fork.

"Belinda and Lacy do. She was telling me just this—"

"No, they don't," Ellen said.

"They most certainly—"

"Mrs. McClellon might *think* they do, but you ought to hear Lacy's version of it."

"Well . . ." Martha said, as O.B. sighed. He was tired of their fighting. "Belinda said that they do lots of things together."

"Well, they don't," Ellen said.

Martha poked at her food. Her thick dark hair was matted at the side of her head where she had been sleeping, and her eyes were puffy. O.B. chewed the dry pork chop. There was a knock on the back door, and they all looked up. It was dark; anyone coming to the house would be knocking at the front, or ringing the bell. They all looked toward the door.

"Who in the world could that be?" Martha wondered.

O.B. got up and went to the door and opened it. He stood there a moment, not saying anything. Cora Long stood on the steps. O.B. felt his eyes widen, his pulse quicken. He could sense her warmth, just looking at her. She wore a yellow housedress with a gray sweater over her shoulders, and as she just stood there, their eyes locked; then Cora looked away. The sight of her, at the back door, took O.B. back almost twelve years. A *maid. Coming to the back door every morning.*

"Who is it?" Martha said.

"It . . . it's Cora," O.B. said.

"Who?"

"Cora Long. Come in," he said, stepping back, and Cora came into the brightly lighted kitchen. He tried to be casual, but he could tell that Cora felt it, too, felt the electricity, and he didn't want Martha or Ellen to see it. Cora stopped just inside the door. She looked around the room, then at Martha and Ellen at the table. Martha was looking at her with narrowed eyes.

"Sally got arrested, Daddy said," Ellen said.

"Yeah, she did," Cora replied. O.B. realized that he was staring at her. He glanced over at Martha and saw that she was observing him, her eyes narrow slits as she looked from him to Cora and back. He hoped that she had not been drinking a great deal. It was hard to tell.

"What do you want?" he blurted. Cora's dark eyes wavered, and she glanced at him and then away, at the wall, at the dark window over the sink.

"I'm sorry to bother you, but I didn't know who else to come to. I think they gonna need a lawyer, to bail em out or whatever. I went down there, talked to Mr. Sparks, and he wouldn't tell me a thing. He just laughed and told me they was just arrested for bein in the wrong place at the wrong time. He wouldn't let me talk to em."

"I don't know what you expect us to do about it," Martha said sharply.

"Eldon doesn't have a lawyer?" O.B. said.

"No," Cora said.

"Looks like he woulda lined up a lawyer, doin all . . . . this, you know?" He thought of Sparks and Mac, the power structure, the men who ran things, thought of them lined up like a wall against Eldon. He knew what it was like, going up against Mac.

"Well, if he did, I don't know about it. I called up Mr. Morris, he's the only lawyer I know, cause I remember what he did when we bought that house and with the church, too. I tried to explain to him what I wanted, but he hung up in my face. So I figured wasn't any use in callin another one. I thought . . . well, that you might know what to do."

"O.B. is not a lawyer," Martha said.

"Martha, she knows I'm not a lawyer," he said.

"I was just remindin her. I don't know what she wants."

"Mama!" Ellen said, "she just told you. Sally and Eldon are in jail!"

"Well, then they musta done somethin to get em there, far as I'm concerned," Martha said. "They looked right proud of themselves, to tell you the truth."

Cora said, "I was hopin maybe you could call somebody. Or go with me to see—"

"No. No way," Martha said.

"Martha—" O.B. said. He felt a surge of dismay. She would make it as difficult as possible.

Martha's voice was raised now. "No way you're leavin this house. Leavin us with . . . all this goin on."

O.B. looked steadily at her; he felt the old wrath stirring inside him. Then he looked back at Cora, who took a step back toward the door. *Her eyes.* Old longings crept into the back of his consciousness. *Her hands.* She stood with her hands clasped in front of her breasts, holding the old gray sweater—it looked like it was an old one of Eldon's that she had just thrown on—holding it tightly before her, like a shield.

"All what goin on?" O.B. said.

"I'm afraid. There's talk, all over town. The niggers . . ." She stopped, looking at Cora out of the corner of her eye. She took a deep breath. "All right. I'll say it. It's *niggers* that would act like that! I've heard. Nobody's safe anymore, not even in their own house!"

"Oh, for God's sake," O.B. said.

"That's right, go ahead," Martha said. "Take her side!"

O.B. could see Ellen watching them, her eyes curious. She had been a little girl when it had happened, but you never knew what children saw and heard and remembered. And there had been loud fights and crying. O.B. could see the glint of tears beginning in Martha's eyes now, but they seemed to be tears of anger. He did not know how much Ellen could see, could understand.

"Goddammit, Martha!" he said. "I never said I was going down there. Just take it easy, will you?"

"I shouldn't be puttin this off on you, I—" Cora said, wringing her hands.

"Eldon's on some kind of a jag," O.B. said. He realized he was making an attempt to lighten the moment. "He even wants me to run for mayor."

"*Daddy!*" Ellen said. "You?"

"Forget I said that," O.B. said. He hadn't intended to even tell Ellen about it. *Did he really have to blurt that out?* Ellen just stared at him, her face open and astonished. O.B. looked away. His head throbbed.

"But you? He wants you to run for mayor?" Ellen said.

"We talked about it. What's so goddam funny about that?"

"I didn't say it was funny," Ellen said. "I was just shocked. I can't imagine you—"

"Well *I* think it's funny," Martha said. "Ha, ha, ha!"

O.B. stood flat-footed, half hearing their voices. Old memories drifted, floated in his mind. *Her hands.* He knew that if he did what was good for him, he would stay there with Martha, send Cora on downtown by herself. Even lend her his truck if she had walked. He knew also, at the same time, that he was not going to do what he *should* do, that he would go with her. The idea of being with her, for just a little while, excited him, awakened in him the old feelings of sweetness and desire and secret evil. He was fearful and excited, but he told himself that he was simply going to drive her downtown to get Eldon out of jail. That was all.

He made a move toward the door.

"Oh, no! You're not gonna go off and leave us here alone!" Martha was standing now behind the table. Their cold supper dishes were scattered about, ignored.

"I need to go with her," O.B. said.

"Why?"

"There may be . . . papers to sign, something. She's a colored woman, alone, Martha. For God's sake."

"I don't mean to put y'all out," Cora said.

"The hell you don't!" Martha screamed. Her eyes were wide, flashing with anger; Ellen still sat at the table, looking confused.

"Martha, don't!" he said. He was afraid of what she might say. He would not have put it past Martha to tell Ellen all about it, after they were gone, but he knew he would take that chance.

"Why do you have to drive her? Why can't she go in her own car?" Martha said, her voice shrieking now.

"I . . ." Cora's eyes were wide, frightened. "I walked," she said.

"*Walked!*" Martha looked from one to the other, her eyes flashing. "Walked? You . . . walked?"

"I'll only be a little while," O.B. said.

"All right, then! Go! Leave us here!" Martha slumped back in the chair, her arms falling on the table. She began to cry. "Just get out of here! Now! If a bunch of niggers are more important than your own wife and daughter . . ."

"I can go by myself," Cora said.

"No!" Martha said bitterly. "He wants to go with you! You can see that, can't you?"

O.B. put his hands on Martha's shoulders. She sniffed, looking up at him through tear-filled eyes, her mascara blotted on her cheek. "You've been drinkin, Martha," he said, "go to bed."

"I ain't been drinkin *enough*," she said.

"Can I come?" Ellen said.

"No," O.B. said. "You stay with your mother. Take care of her."

"I don't need anybody takin care of me," Martha said, with the same bitterness.

"I'll be back in a few minutes. This . . . your mother . . . this is just an overreaction. A few minutes," he said.

Martha turned away, staring at the wall. Ellen looked at him strangely, and he hurried Cora out the door, his hand just gently touching her back, and the back door rattled to behind them. Outside, in the darkness, he gripped her arm and guided her around the house, toward his pickup truck parked at the curb.

Cora felt a vague alarm, but she watched in silence as O.B. pulled the truck off the pavement at the turnaround at the end of the street. He shut off the engine, then the lights. A pale half-moon hung over the swamps across the river; it sparkled gently on the surface of the river, far below them.

"What you doin?" she asked. He sat in shadow, against the door of the cab.

"I just want to talk a minute," O.B. said.

"Suppose somebody was to come along here? You crazy O.B. Besides—"

"Nobody's comin along. You can duck down if they do."

"Fine," she said sarcastically, "I can duck down." She knew her voice had a hard edge. She was already uncomfortable coming to him for help, but she had told herself that she had nobody else to turn to. She had panicked, thinking of Sally and Eldon in jail. But sitting in the darkened cab, this close to O.B., reminded her too much of fifteen years ago, when they had . . . *Why did I do this?*

He seemed to be peering at her. She tried to make out his face in the dimness of the moonlight. She could feel his presence in the heat of her blood, a youthful heat from her distant past. *I should not have come. I should have known better.*

"What's the matter?" he said.

"Eldon and Sally are in jail, and you ask me what's the matter? You goin parkin with a married colored lady, and you ask me what's the matter?"

"We're not 'parkin.' I just wanted to talk to you. Where the hell else we gonna talk?"

"Maybe we don't need to talk." They sat in silence for a few moments. She still nursed resentment and hurt at the icy way Martha had acted. *What can I expect? Unlike Eldon, she is not capable of forgiving.* Cora could see the lights of a tugboat, upriver, coming around the bend, just south of where the Tombigbee River intersected with the wide Tuscaloosa, the spotlights playing from side to side, on the low trees of the swamp and then on the chalky bluffs on the town side. In just a few minutes, they would begin to hear it, the faint liquid chugging of the engines. A Birmingham-to-Mobile run. Cora couldn't see the barges on the black surface of the river. She could just barely make out the lighted cabin in the distance.

"Cora . . ." he began.

"What?"

"Listen . . . I've wanted to see you."

"No," she said. She could tell that he was staring at her. She heard it in his voice. She held her breath. Old feelings jarred her, stirring and growing slowly within her. She felt her body stiffen. She could hear a car going by up on Commissioners Street, and then the night was silent again. "You can't start that again, O.B."

"Why not?"

"Because it was a long time ago. It's forgotten."

"No, it's not forgotten," he said. *No, it is not forgotten.*

⋅⌣⋅⌣⋅⌣⋅

One afternoon, on a clear day in spring, when she had been working for them a little over a year, O.B. had come into the kitchen where she was. Often she would see O.B. looking at her in a longing way, and she admitted to herself that she enjoyed getting back at him, seeing him remembering what had passed between them, because not a day passed that she did not think, still painfully, about the humiliation he had caused her. On that day a little two-ring circus had come to town, and Martha had taken Ellen. Sally, hearing Ellen talk about it, had begged them, and Eldon had taken her, too, to sit in the colored section at one end of the tent.

"What are you doin home from work?" she had asked, and he had not answered. They had not been alone together since they had been teenagers, in the country, and the fact of their aloneness hung in the air between them. She remembered awkwardly putting down the dish she was washing and drying her hands on the rough dish towel, looking shyly at him as he stared at her. She felt her lingering anger at him melting away. *Eldon, this is your fault. This is your doing.* Eldon had wanted her to take the job. Eldon—still so much younger in mind than she, she thought—had insisted that he had forgiven O.B., that what had happened between her and O.B. when they were children was now completely absolved by God. He had stared at her in a detached, otherworldly way, with what she had thought was the glint of challenge in his eyes, almost as though he was testing her, as though he somehow *had* to put her through some sort of trial by fire. Now, precisely at the moment O.B. came into the kitchen, she realized that she, too, had known all the time that it was a trial, had been sure all along that this moment would come. And that she would fail.

She stood looking at his tall, lean body, the slight stooping way he held his neck. She stared into his blue eyes, remembering the abandon and the passion. She knew that she loved Eldon, with a warm depth that sometimes brought tears to her eyes when she pondered it, but she did not experience with him the wild flame of desire that she had known with O.B. She knew it was a sin, but she could not forget it. God put it there; it had been constantly before her every day since she was seventeen, and she could not forget the way O.B. had made her feel, the wholeness and completeness that had been theirs.

He reached out and touched her, and she looked down at his hand, pale against the darkness of her arm. Everything, all the old feelings and longings, came flooding back. Those years ago, he had made her feel different, filling her with hope for more than she knew she had any right to expect. He had transplanted her, for what seemed now only a brief moment, out of that dreary life in that leaning, patched cabin on old Mr. Hubbard's place, and what they had had together had glowed with what had seemed to her a purifying fire. In that moment in the kitchen, as he touched her, she forgot how much he had hurt her, remembered only the happiness, the innocent joy of their youth.

She had let him lead her up the hall to the front bedroom, and they had removed their clothes in silence, without speaking, both breathing in short, ragged gasps, both, she knew, remembering the long-ago feel of each other's bodies, and they were together quickly and tenderly and then violently. And she had known immediately afterward with a clarity as pure as their passion, that she could not continue it. She could not hurt Eldon anymore. She had already hurt him, and she had to confess it to him, to put herself right with God and with herself. She had quit the job the next day, knowing in her heart that she would never give in to that dark desire again. And she and Eldon had cried together, in the night, and they had prayed for days, and he had forgiven her. And she did not doubt him. She knew that those youthful, sunlit years were gone. She knew, now that she and O.B. were adults with families of their own, that their passion was a dark sin that marked her soul. God will forgive you, Eldon had said. I forgive you and I love you, he had said, the tears streaming from his eyes.

．～～～．

"**W**ell, I've forgot it," Cora said. "I love Eldon. I love my family."

"I love mine, too," he said. "But I can't stop remembering. I've tried, but I can't."

"Don't, O.B. We been through this—"

"I know it. But I can't help it."

"That last time like to killed Eldon, O.B. I ain't gonna let it happen again. So crank up and let's go."

"I love you, Cora," he said. The words hung in the air between them. She could barely make out his blue eyes, steady on her.

"That's ridiculous," she said quickly, "that's your gonads talkin."

"No, it's not," he said. "I think about us all the time, the way it was for us, and—"

She felt suddenly faint, dizzy, as though she couldn't get her breath. She shook her head to clear it. "You can't live in the past," she said. "That was a long time ago. Things are different, they've changed. We were foolish, O.B." She wanted him to see the truth of what she was saying; she realized she was chewing the knuckle of her right hand. . . .

．～～～．

It seemed to O.B. that the night was suspended in a vacuum, that they were all alone for a moment in the world. The tenderness and the longing he was feeling he had never felt with any other woman. For years he had not believed it was possible that a white man could love a colored woman in that way; it was against everything he had been raised to believe. He had accepted that it was nothing but sex, assumed that it had to be. Possibly that's all it was in the beginning, and in the brief renewal, twelve years ago, after they were both married and with children. Now, as he watched her silhouette framed in the side window, he knew her well enough to know that she felt the same way he did. It was dark and forbidden, sensual and dangerous, and yet it was light and freedom and sweetness, too.

She smelled faintly of a jasmine perfume that he had almost forgotten, a slim, delicate sweetness on the chilly night air, and it took him back to their days of youth, scenes flooding his memory like fragile fragments of a dream remembered . . .

.~.~.~.

She came along the narrow, sandy road that wound along the creek, eating a pale red plum, holding others in her hand, and they watched her from back in the plum bushes growing along the bank. In the sunlight, O.B. could see the juice of the plum running from the corners of her mouth, and he licked his lips, spying on her. Ants crawled on their forearms, and they nudged one another, stifling their laughter, holding still against the ants. They both wore identical patched and faded overalls, with no shirts and no shoes, O.B. burned nut brown by the summer sun, Eldon black as pitch, his damp, sweating skin shiny in the afternoon sunlight. She stopped, hearing them in the bushes.

"What dat?" she said, and they laughed, their breath coming in little gusts. She stood in the sunlight, shading her eyes to peek back into the bushes. She wore a loose cotton dress, made from flower sacking, faded lavender with tiny pink and green flowers all over it, and it seemed to cling to her youthful body at the breasts and the hips. It came to midthigh, and her long, mahogany legs tapered to her small bare feet in the sandy roadway. They had hidden and watched her naked in the creek, watched her splashing her plump breasts with the clear, cool water, straining to catch a glimpse of the curly black hair down there. They had been watching her all summer. Eldon had said that she knew they were watching her, but O.B. had said no, that couldn't be. No girl, even a nigger girl, would let boys watch her buck naked.

"What dat in there?" she said again.

"Old cane-cutter rabbit," Eldon said.

"Black rabbit and a white rabbit," she said. "White rabbit like a sweet bunny."

"Gimme them plums," O.B. said, making his voice as deep as he could. "I want them plums."

"Come git em, white rabbit," she said. She threw back her head and laughed, wiping her mouth with the back of her hand. O.B. could see the afternoon sunlight glinting on the long line of her throat, on the narrow white ribbons tied in her short-cropped hair.

They struggled out of the bushes, brushing at the ants on their arms and legs.

"Y'all nasty," she said. "How long y'all been in them bushes?"
"Long enough," Eldon said.
"Gimme them plums," O.B. said. His tongue felt thick in his
mouth when he looked at her.
"All right," she said. As she put one in his outstretched hand, her
fingernail bit sharply into his palm like a fiery coal that ignited his
blood. He looked into her almond-shaped, flashing dark eyes, and they
were sassy, laughing, inviting.

As small children, they had been a threesome, inseparable, together,
unaware. All three of their fathers were sharecroppers, on the same
huge cotton and dairy plantation, O.B.'s father functioning more as
manager of one of the dairy barns. That was the only thing that set
their families apart, that and the fact that the house the Brewsters lived
in was bigger, newer, better furnished then the wooden shanties where
Cora's and Eldon's families lived. It was a system, a class structure,
that they never thought to question, any more than they would have
questioned the fairness of Old Man and Mrs. Hubbard living as they
did in a house that would have made ten of one of theirs.

It was a childhood of long summers, of fishing in the creeks and the
river and the farm ponds on the Hubbard place, of picking plums and
blackberries, of riding mules and baiting yearling bulls. They all did
their share of before-daylight milking, of chopping and then picking
cotton, the three of them together, laughing and flopping atop the piles
of raw cotton in the wagons to ride back from the fields.

And they grew up together, swimming together, becoming more
and more aware of the changes taking place in their bodies, more
aware of who they were.

Dust motes drifted lazily in the rays of sunlight slanting through the
cracks between the rough wood boards of the old barn. The loft was
dim, piled high with hay, the bales stacked to the rafters, and more of
it, loose, piled under the eaves. It was hot, the air musty with the
smells of the hay, the raw smell of manure from the barnyard, the
odors of motor oil and harness and mules. Cora climbed up the ladder
ahead of him, and he looked up at her, squinting at where her legs
disappeared in darkness under the cotton skirt, and she looked down at
him and grinned, shaking her head.

"What you lookin at, white boy?" she said.

He felt awkward, tingly with excitement and anticipation. He was tongue-tied, unable to answer her. They reached the loft level and swung out, dropping one by one onto the loose hay. She giggled and kicked her long bare legs in the air, her laughter echoing hollowly in the barn, off the tin roof that they both knew would be hot to the touch. The skirt rode up her thighs, bunched at her waist. She made no effort to cover herself, and he stared. He had been on a hard since they had started the climb, and now it was almost painful, straining, pressing against the rough cloth of his overalls.

"Can I . . . touch you?" he asked, his voice thick, choked.

She lay back, the skirt of her dress around her waist. He could see the dark nipples of her breasts pressing against the cloth. The curly black hair crowded the valley between her legs.

"Yes," she said, softly. "You can touch me."

He rubbed her, and she moaned. She helped him with the buttons of his overalls, and they fell away from his lean, young body, whiter around the middle where the summer sun could not reach. Her fingernails scratched leisurely, aimlessly, across his chest, circling his nipples, pecking playfully at them. Then she held him in her hand and stroked, and he watched openmouthed: her deep tan hand, its pale amber fingernails, its white palm wrapped tightly around his dick. His blood was like liquid fire in his veins.

"You want to put it in the honey box?" she whispered.

"Yes, oh, yes," he moaned. And she pulled him on top of her, guiding him, gently teaching him. She cried out, as though in pain, and he hesitated, but she told him with her hands to keep moving, and she cried out again, and this time he knew it was with pleasure, and he felt his own pleasure coming, like an electric jolt from his groin, and he cried out himself. And afterward, they had lain there, in the musky heat, his head on her belly, not talking, looking into the now more level sunrays, her hand playing softly and aimlessly through his hair.

⋅∾⋅∾⋅∾⋅

Winter, now, on the hard-packed dirt of the basketball court behind North Macon County Training School, where Eldon and Cora went to school. He and Eldon had walked from Boligee Store, under the heavy gray sky, carrying the worn and slick basketball that he had gotten for Christmas; they had been talking of hunting and had gone to the store for cold drinks, their hands fishing in the icy water of the cooler and pulling out long Nehi grapes, jostling each other, and they had found themselves facing a large metal sign on the wall of the store, a picture of Paulette Goddard, stretched out in a bathing costume, holding an RC Cola. RC, BEST BY TASTE TEST the sign said. Paulette Goddard's legs were bare, long and white, and her breasts were rounded, exaggerated by the costume. The two boys had stood there looking at it, silently; O.B. had been aware that Eldon had been waiting to say something, but only empty, ungainly silence had passed between them.

"That white lady looked good," Eldon said to him later, at the deserted basketball court.

"Yeah," O.B. had said. He felt strange, uneasy. Eldon just looked at him. O.B. felt a vague, nameless guilt that he did not understand.

Eldon, his denim coat hanging loosely on his frame, which was growing more thin and gangly, elbowed him sharply, grabbing the ball and dribbling, bumping him suddenly, pivoting and shooting at the netless iron rim, the ball grazing the old wooden backboard and darting through the rim.

"H," Eldon said. They played "horse" all the time.

"I wasn't ready."

Eldon threw the ball to him, with force; they were standing close, and the ball jammed into O.B.'s belly, almost knocking the breath out of him.

"H!" Eldon said, again. "Your go."

"Goddammit," O.B. said. He started to dribble. Eldon stole the ball deftly, pivoted away from him, jumped and shot, the ball cleanly falling through the hoop.

"O!" Eldon said. "You asshole white son of a bitch!"

"What!" O.B. said. He grunted, grabbing the ball. "Nigger shit-ass." He dribbled and shot, the ball bouncing off the rim with a dull, metallic clank, then Eldon rebounded and shot.

"R!" he said. He glared at O.B.

"What the hell's wrong with you?" O.B. said. He had feared the look in Eldon's eyes, the anger somehow tempered with pain.

"You don't like me lookin at that white lady, do you?" Eldon said. "But it's all right for you to . . . to . . ."

"What?" O.B. said. A cold, hollow dread had gripped him. Cora! It was Cora!

"Nigger can't look at a white lady, can he?" Eldon had said. "But a white man . . ."

Suddenly, Eldon was on him, twisting O.B.'s arm in a hammerlock until pain shot through his shoulder. "Goddammit," O.B. panted through his teeth, struggling, gradually getting out of the hold, then grabbing Eldon. Now both their breaths made cloudy steam in the raw air. They went down in the dirt, grunting, rolling over and over, first one on top then the other, gasping and whimpering with the effort. They wrestled for what seemed like hours, until they were both exhausted, their breath coming in short pants; O.B. remembered the searing feeling of the bitter-cold air in his lungs as they lay there, side by side, the afternoon growing darker and colder, until their breathing gradually returned to normal. Eldon suddenly put his hand flat in the dirt, in front of O.B.'s face. He picked it up, leaving a handprint in the fine dust that covered the court. He nodded to O.B. "Go ahead," he said.

O.B. placed his hand over the print, covering it, blotting it out completely.

"My hand littler than your'n, but it's blacker than your'n," Eldon had said.

O.B. had somehow heard the message there, known what Eldon was saying, even though he could not have put it into words. O.B.'s father had recently fussed at him for spending so much time with niggers. And Eldon had become a nigger. Whatever that was.

·~·~·

And then, inevitably, had come the last time for him and Cora. It was early spring, and they were in the old fishing shack, on a canvas bunk against the wall, looking out through the glassless windows at the pale green new growth. Cora had put her dress back on. O.B. was moody and quiet. He had started going to the new high school in town then, and he was going out for the high school baseball team. For some time, he had been noticing Martha Crocker, a girl in his class; she had thick black hair and large, full breasts. He had grown tall and lean, and the girls flirted with him, the town girls who walked to school in groups, giggling, and who occasionally drove their parents' automobiles around. He had grown self-conscious of his overalls, horrified that sometimes they would have flecks of cow manure on the legs from his early morning milking chores before he caught the creaky old yellow bus down on the highway. So he had talked his mother into ordering him new pants, corduroy and khaki, from the Sears and Roebuck Catalogue; these new pants he kept cleaned and pressed, and changed into them just before catching the bus, and out of when he got home before his afternoon chores. He'd paid for them himself, dime by dime, out of money he earned on weekends setting fence posts for Mr. Hubbard, who owned the plantation his father farmed shares

on. His mother and father teased him about how fastidiously he cared
for them, ironing them himself on the back porch of their little white
farmhouse.

O.B. and Cora sat there for a while in silence, the only sound the
occasional chirping of a bird. "We got to stop," he said to her, feeling
his pulse throbbing in his ear. The air was heavy between them. She
didn't answer. It was as though she had known what he was going to
say. "It ain't right," he said.

He felt clumsy, inadequate for something like this. She sat there,
leaning against the wall, her long legs stretched out in front of her.
She had on a dark blue dress, buttoned up the front; the material was
rough and coarse, the dress plain and unadorned. O.B. thought of
the little pleated skirts, the soft sweaters, that the town girls, the white
girls, wore.

"I mean," he said, "it was all right, I reckon, when we were little.
But . . ." He stopped. He wished she would say something. "The
Bible says . . ."

"I don't care bout the Bible," she said. Her voice sounded weary,
older than her years. She seemed to have gotten so much older than
him. As though the years had affected her differently, he thought, as
he looked carefully at her. He still thought she was beautiful, with high
Indian cheekbones, skin like the soft, pungent crust of fresh-baked
bread. She had taught him all he knew of love, but he knew now that
he had to move on.

"I mean, it was all right as a *substitute*, you know? I need to be with
my own kind. It ain't right."

She stared out the window.

"Well, say somethin," he said.

"A *substitute?*" she said.

"Yeah. You know. I mean, you need to be with your people, too.
Colored. You know. It was like a game."

"A game?"

"Like we were just playin around. Like children will do. We were
a substitute for each other not havin a person, you know, of our own
kind. We ain't children anymore, Cora." He had rehearsed this, lying
on the clammy sheet in his room, hearing the night sounds out the
window, the crickets and the tree frogs and the distant, lonely owls.

"You right bout that," she said. She sighed. Her chores, he knew,
were caring for her younger brothers and sisters. There was a house
full. "But you wrong about me not havin somebody," she said.

"Huh?" he said. A stab of jealousy already, even before she said it.

"I got me a nigger man," she said. She stood up and walked over to the window. His eyes followed the way the dress slid on her curves, and his own young body throbbed for her with a dry, searing pain. He was not sure; he was bewildered, unsettled. He had done plenty of soul-searching about this, and he had been sure he was doing the right thing. But now he could not bear to think of her with anyone else. *What had he expected?*

"Well," he said, "that's good. Who?"

"Somebody," she said.

"Well, good. That's . . . more natural. That's . . ." His voice sounded weak and false to him. He did not want her to know how he was feeling. He couldn't let her know. He was desperate about who it was, but he didn't have the nerve to ask her again. *Eldon!* He looked at her, trying to pierce her outwardly cool facade with his eyes. *Her own kind!*

She turned around and fixed him with her eyes, her slanted, almond eyes. They seemed to smolder in her face now, with a heat that boiled up from deep inside; she was framed by the window, the spring sunlight behind her brushing on the delicate new leaves. "What you mean to say," she said, "is that fuckin me was just like beatin your meat."

It was like a blow to the gut, making him suck in his breath.

"No!" he said. "That's not what—"

"Unnatural. All right." She stared at him. He shifted uneasily on the bunk, his brain raging. "You a white man," she said. "I know that. I know how white people think."

"It's not what you think," he said quickly. "I'm not sayin that!"

"Maybe you ain't sayin it. But that's what you mean. I'm just a nigger. All right to fuck, but that's all." Her voice was quick, cutting and angry now.

"There's nothin else for us to do, Cora," he said, and his own voice sounded shrill and whiny in his ears. "It ain't my fault."

She stood with her hands behind her. He could hear a lone bird chirping outside, down along the edge of the Bogue.

"We could go up North," she said.

"*What?*" He was astonished, astounded. His mouth hung open.

"To Detroit, or Washington. It don't matter up there. Colored and white marry one another up there."

"*Marry!*" It was as though she were speaking in another language.

"You know what that word means, don't you?" The sunlight was suddenly brighter outside, her face more in shadow. He looked down at his black brogans, on the rough planks of the cabin floor. The word seemed to hang there, in front of his face.

"I ain't near to thinkin about marryin, Cora," he said. "I got my baseball. School."

"*Baseball!*"

He looked up. "We can't *marry*, Cora!" he said. "It ain't right! A white man and . . ."

"A nigger?"

"Colored! The Bible . . ." He stuttered. He stopped speaking. He took a deep breath, his mind betraying him with blankness. "I never led you to believe . . . well, I never said anything about *marryin*, for God's sake." He wanted to break and run, flee the cabin and the woods.

"No," she said, "you didn't." Her voice was firm, controlled.

"You knew all along that . . . that . . ." he stammered.

"Yes," she said, "I did."

"Goddammit, Cora," he said, "I can't change the way the world is! It ain't my fault that it's the way it is! Shit!" He was shocked to feel the sting of tears behind his eyes. He did not know why they were there.

"It's all right," she said. She moved toward him, easily and fluidly, sitting beside him. She put her arm around his shoulders. He could smell her body, her cool, dry skin, the faint, sharp scent of lye soap. He had started to cry, and she had cried, too, holding him, her sobs like thunder in his ears. And he had not understood why they were crying, was not to know for many years.

.~.~.~.

"**C**ora," he said, in the darkness of the truck cab, "why did Eldon come to see me?"

"Huh?"

"Why did he come to see me and try to talk me into runnin against Mac McClellon?" He was thinking about Eldon, sitting across his desk from him, in his stiff suit.

"God, O.B., I don't know. He's insane with all this movement stuff. He *believes* in it. He thinks he's gonna . . ."—her voice fell off— ". . . make a difference."

"Don't *you* believe in it?" He was trying to make out her face in the dim moonlight. He was curious about her feelings. She was still a mystery to him. Years of mystery.

"God, I don't know. All that talk about justice, and freedom, and all that. It's hard for me to understand those words. But they're important to *him*. So they're important to me. I reckon I'm still tryin to figure out what I believe."

"Freedom?" he said. "Freedom's important to anybody." He thought of Eldon, his earnestness, his seriousness. *My hand littler than your'n, and blacker than your'n!* She was silent for a moment. Softly, in the distance, he heard the faint, rhythmic chugging of a tugboat rounding the bend south of where the Tombigbee intersected the Tuscaloosa.

"I just ain't got time for it," she said. He heard the same weariness, the same fatigue, he had heard in her voice before. "I'm just tryin to live," she said. "It scares me. All this has started, and it's like a snowball. It can get *too* big."

He reached for the key.

"O.B.?" she said. He looked at her. "You ain't gonna try to be the mayor of Hammond, are you?"

"No," he said. "I don't know." He turned the key in the ignition, and the engine kicked into life. "I never thought about it before," he said. He didn't know what he might do.

Chapter Five

~❧~

MAC McCLELLON WAS IN ONE OF THE CRAMPED LITTLE FRONT offices, drinking a cup of coffee with Lester Sparks. "But why won't you let her see him?" O.B. said.

"Orders," Sparks said. His bulk filled the narrow straight chair he sat in. It was his office, but Mac was sitting behind his desk. There was nothing on the walls but a calendar.

"Lester was under strict orders not to talk to anybody, and not let the niggers talk to anybody," Mac said. "Hell, they ain't booked on anything. We just lettin em cool their heels."

"You scared her," O.B. said to Sparks.

"Hell," Mac said, "don't hurt to put the fear of God in em from time to time." He sipped his coffee from a wax paper cup. He leaned back in the chair and propped one foot on an opened drawer. His coat was across the back of the chair, and he had his collar loosened, his tie hanging down his front. O.B. had not talked to him in a while, since the meeting.

Suddenly, the door opened, and Lyman Wells stood there. He was a lawyer, and he wore a pinstriped suit with a vest. O.B. could see his Phi Beta Kappa key hanging from a gold chain in front. Mac sat looking up at him, his eyes narrow slits.

"Lyman, you started workin for the N Double A C P or somethin?"

"No, Mac," Lyman said. "I'm available to anybody got the money to pay me."

"Niggers?"

"Yeah," Lyman said. He lived in a big house out near where Mac lived. O.B. remembered he was a graduate of Vanderbilt Law School, and he could feel Mac's resentment, his dislike of the man, hovering in the air like smoke.

Mac snorted and looked away. Then he looked back at O.B. "What's your interest in all this, O.B.?"

O.B. felt suddenly on guard. He felt almost guilty. "I've known Eldon Long all my life," O.B. said. "His wife asked me to help. I was obliged to."

"Uh-huh," Mac said. "Where's she?"

"Out in the truck. What'll I tell her, then?"

"Well, they been in, let's see . . ." he looked at his watch. "They been in there a little over nine hours now. I reckon we can let em go. Lester, go turn em loose." Lester got up and hitched up his pants and went down the narrow hallway toward the back.

"No charges?" Wells said. There was silence in the little office. "I guess I'll just head on home then."

"Yeah," Mac said. "I'm surprised you got time to come down here anyway, what with goin to the Shady Grove Deer Drive and all that." O.B. and Lyman Wells looked at Mac, whose eyes seemed to glitter. What was he talking about? O.B. wondered. The Shady Grove Deer Drive was in November! All this had upset him, that was clear to see, O.B. decided as Mac leaned over and spit into a metal trash can. His hands were shaking, and he was glaring at Lyman as though he wanted to leap up and hit him.

" 'Night, now," Wells said. The front doorway scraped to behind him.

"What the hell you think that stuck-up son of a bitch has got goin for himself now?" Mac said.

O.B. was peering down the dim hallway. He didn't know why Lyman had come, and he didn't care. "I don't know, Mac. Lester told Cora Long that—she couldn't see her husband—"

"Shit. He was woofin her."

O.B. shrugged. He had never liked Mac very much, but they were longtime "friends." He had known Mac since he had started school, and he had always been a bully. O.B. had known that Mac came from the same kind of family background as his; if there was much difference it was that Mac's parents were even poorer than his. So they had grown up together, playing sports together, and when O.B. had begun to excel, Mac had always been there on the team, a constant, brooding presence, O.B. sensing his resentment. He remembered that Mac had, several times when they were still in high school, tried to date Martha after she started going with O.B. Ever since they were boys, it had been clear to O.B. that Mac didn't really like him. That he was jealous of him. Something.

Now he watched as Mac put the cup on the little desk and stood up, pulling the blind aside to look out the window, toward the street. He was looking at O.B.'s truck, parked under a streetlight at the corner. Cora sat in the truck, her face turned toward the jail. Mac looked back at O.B. "So what's your big interest in all this, O.B.?" Mac said.

"I told you," O.B. snapped. He caught his breath, pushing the anger back. "I told you," he said, more calmly. He could tell that under his forced-calm exterior, Mac was on edge about what had happened. He remembered the way he had looked, strolling along that afternoon.

"You did tell me, didn't you?" Mac said. His voice was thin, suspicious.

Eldon, carrying his suit coat over his arm, his shirt open at the collar, came up the hallway, followed by the others. He smiled at O.B., then at Mac. His face was calm, serene. There was an aura of satisfaction about him.

"Cora's out in my truck," O.B. said. He carefully observed Eldon's eyes; they wavered for just a tiny instant. Maybe the man's smile froze for a fraction of a second. *What can he read in me? Smell in me?* "You want me to run y'all home?"

"No, that's okay," Eldon said. "It's a nice night. We'll walk. We'll all of us walk," he said. He said it as though walking held some special significance to him.

He went on out, and the others filed out after him. O.B. nodded to Sally; she did not return his nod but looked at him with flat, impassive eyes. Except for Eldon, they all looked lifeless, not nearly so chipper as they'd looked earlier, walking along the street in the sunlight. *Maybe nine hours in jail will do that to anybody.* He could see only fear in their eyes, whereas earlier there had at least been defiance with the fear. Lester nodded to Mac and followed them out, the door scraping to behind him.

"Maybe they've learned em a lesson," Mac said.

"I wouldn't count on it," O.B. said.

Mac sat back down. He put his hands behind his head, peering at O.B. out of narrow slits of eyes. Mac had always been chunky, and his face was getting fuller year by year, his belly expanding against his belt. He just sat there, looking at O.B., his jaw working as though he had gum in his mouth, a slow, rolling motion.

"Sometimes a man gets a hankerin after chocolate nookie," he said, after a minute.

O.B. felt a flash of anger. "Just helpin her out, Mac," he said tightly. He could tell that Mac didn't believe him. "She used to work for us."

"Seems like I remember that," Mac said.

"Me and Eldon go way back," O.B. said.

"Now I know that, too," Mac said. "It ain't any of my business, a' course. I don't know what O.B. Brewster does in the dark."

"That's right," O.B. said. His anger was growing. This was the same old Mac, full of bluster and jokes at somebody's else's expense, but it wouldn't do to get mad at Mac and show it. O.B. thought that as mayor, Mac was a powerful man, though he had never been completely clear on what he did as mayor. He was curious about it now, after Eldon's request. But this was not the time. O.B. made as if to go.

"Sit down, why don'tcha?" Mac said.

"I got to go. Martha's at home, waitin for me."

"Yeah. How *is* Martha?" O.B. thought that his concern was genuine, but he could tell he was curious, too. Ever since the PTA meeting, the town had been gossiping, whispering about her. O.B. could see it, even if Martha was blind to it. O.B. appreciated Mac's concern, but at the same time he resented it.

"She's fine," he said. He moved toward the door.

"Listen, O.B., no sense beatin around the bush," Mac said, and O.B. paused, hearing almost a note of desperation in Mac's voice. Mac went on, "I'm lookin to you to use your . . . *influence* in the nigger community to keep down all this business."

"I got to go, Mac," O.B. said. He was beginning to feel trapped, the way he had felt the night of the meeting.

"Wait, now. It's just that people got to stick together. Pull their load." He picked up the cup and looked at it, then tossed it into a metal trash can in the corner. He seemed suddenly nervous, looking at O.B. with eyes that were almost pleading. "Let me remind you, O.B., that Gulf International ain't gonna build that paper mill if the niggers get outta hand around here. Now I've been told that by higher-ups in the company. It ain't just speculation on my part. It's a fact—"

"So? I'm in the farm-implement business. I—"

"Goddammit, O.B. I'm talkin about the economy of this whole area! You! You're a goddam businessman. And you got a big note comin due at Planters and Merchants, too, let me remind you."

O.B. felt a sudden sense of genuine alarm as he fully comprehended what Mac was saying. *So that was it!* "But we talked about refinancin that thing, Mac," he said. "You said that would be no problem." His voice had taken on a higher, stricken quality that he did not like to hear in himself.

"Right," Mac said. "No problem durin good times. In times of, well, economic depression so to speak, it might well be a problem. With Gulf International comin in, I can make all kinds of deals. Lookin to the future, you understand. That's the way the money business works. But without them, O.B. . . . well, frankly, the future don't look so good. I couldn't go out on a limb."

O.B. stood looking at him. He could feel his heartbeat in his ears.

"You tellin me you can't refinance it, Mac? Goddam. When's it due?"

"Well, I ain't got my papers in front of me, O.B. Sometime this summer. Early fall, maybe. What's it matter?"

O.B.'s mouth was dry. He had worried and fretted about his business ever since he had fired Rusty Jackson; Ernest and Clyde were so slow that jobs piled up, and they stayed behind, so that O.B. had been going back into the shop, breaking out his old worn work clothes to work alongside them, initially taking pleasure in the way the familiar tools fit his hand, but that left no one up front to figure, and give estimates, and try to sell the tractors, disk harrows, and hay-balers that provided the solid, substantial income. At least working back in the shop had hidden him briefly away from the angry farmers who came in to complain about how long it was taking to get their equipment fixed. Until they found him back there.

Mac went on in his almost begging voice, and O.B. noticed that he was sweating. "You got nigger customers, O.B. You know em. Hell, you grew up with Eldon Long, and he's the ringleader of the whole mess. You could talk to him. What we need is to get them two meddlesome Yankee college students on outta here, get the niggers to just calm down and realize what side of their bread the butter's on, you know? They can't get along without white people. Hell, ninety percent of em don't want this. Some of em come to me, told me all the plans for all this shit this afternoon. They don't want to go to school with white people. You know that, O.B. You talk to em. Hell." Mac seemed to be rattling on distractedly, nervously, his uneasiness scaring O.B. more than if Mac had appeared in control.

"You said we could refinance it, Mac," O.B. said. He felt weak. Failure settled over him like a cloud.

"And I ain't said we couldn't," Mac said. "I don't know how to figure you, O.B.," he went on.

"Whattaya mean?" O.B. said weakly.

"Well, Lacy comes home and tells me that Ellen's goin around all over the high school tryin to talk up support for the niggers. And for those outside agitators. Got all the young folks upset. It's agitation talk, O.B. And she must be gettin it somewhere. I'm concerned about you, an old friend like you. Why, our daughters practically grew up together. Almost like sisters." Mac paused. "Hell, I remember Ellen as a little girl, playin dolls with Lacy out in the backyard. In that playhouse. You remember that playhouse I built her? That time? Hell, O.B., I worry—"

"You don't think I—" O.B. stopped. He was surprised by what Mac was telling him. He had not known that Ellen was doing that.

"I tell you, O.B. I don't know what to think anymore," Mac was saying. There was a warmth in his voice now, the supplication even more intense. "We go back a long way, O.B., so let me tell you somethin. This is war, boy. What them niggers are doin is bad news, it's communism is what it is, and the lines are gettin drawn. Now you're a businessman. You're an American capitalist, right? That's all I'm sayin. If that paper mill don't come in here, all our asses have had it. You think the bank won't have to foreclose, collect what's due it? I ain't runnin a charity. That's just the way it is."

"Well, I understand that, Mac," O.B. said, his own voice stronger now, looking at Mac.

"And you better understand this, too." Mac's energy seemed to come back, as though fed by O.B.'s. "If Long and those niggers keep on the way they goin, the Ku Klux Klan is gonna git in on it, and then it'll be Katy-Bar-the-Door! I can't hold *them* fuckers down. They're crazy. Rooster was hanging out up there at Maud's this afternoon, him and Bobby Lee McElroy, both of em carry'n guns. Scared the piss out of me. I didn't know what the hell they might do. I tell you, O.B., if we have all them riots and such shit as that around here, we can kiss that paper mill good-bye. You and every goddam businessman in this area better realize that."

O.B. sat down then. He pushed the worry about his business from his mind as he thought of Martha, at the kitchen table, the inky, blotted mascara on her cheek. "I got to go," he said, but he didn't move. The little office was very quiet. O.B. wondered where Lester Sparks had gone to. Then he remembered Eldon, sitting across the desk from him that afternoon, his agitation, his flashing eyes as he asked O.B. to run for mayor. He looked at Mac. He thought of the arrest earlier, the Negroes going into Maud's, the senselessness of it all. "Maybe you ought to just call in the FBI, let em take over," O.B. said, his voice constricted.

"What?" Mac peered at O.B., disbelief on his face.

"Well, shit, Mac, it'd solve the problem with the paper mill, wouldn't it? Maybe it'd solve a lot of—"

"I can't believe you're sittin there sayin that, O.B. My God!" Mac said. "You call that maintainin the status quo? Why, the federal government— Hell, they're worse than the niggers!"

"It ain't right," O.B. cut in, feeling his arms and legs tense.

"What? What 'ain't right'?" Mac said.

"All this. Everything. I don't know."

Mac sat looking at him, tiny beads of perspiration lining his upper lip. "I tell you," he said, his voice taut, "maybe a little chocolate pussy'll turn a man's head, and then—"

O.B. stood up, the anger surging within him like a flash fire. Mac leaned back in the desk chair, his eyes jumping about. "Wait now, wait," he said. "I was *jokin*, O.B., for God's sake," he said.

"Well, I don't like the joke," O.B. said. His arms were trembling. Mac looked away, then back at him.

"Awww, hell, O.B., sit down," he said. O.B., remembering the note coming due, did as he was told. "Listen," Mac said, "no hard feelins? I mean, this is just business, all right?"

"All right," O.B. said, his voice tight.

Mac spoke rapidly now. "All I want you to do, O.B., is use your influence as a white man. Everybody knows you, and they like you. You can rally the white folks around you. Even most of Rooster's boys look up to you, you fuckin jock!" He winked, but it was a dry, humorless wink, and his smile was forced and disappeared almost immediately. "And this is the most important part. I want you to get next to Eldon. Talk to him. *Influence* him. Open his goddam eyes, for Christ's sake. And talk to other niggers. That old man today? Ruston Sinclair? He's a farmer, you know him. What the hell business did he have bein there? Huh? Talk some sense into their heads."

"I can't do that, Mac," O.B. said. He tried to speak firmly, but his voice rang hollow in his ears. It was as though someone else were speaking.

"What the hell you mean, you can't do it? Goddammit, O.B. Are you a white man or what?"

"Yeah. I am," O.B. said. He felt very tired, unable to think clearly. "But I got no influence over Eldon Long. We . . . we're not . . . I can't." He could not—would not even if he could—explain his relationship to Eldon to Mac McClellon.

Mac shook his head, speaking slowly, in a drawl. "Somethin's got you screwed up, O.B. This ain't the man I know." He paused, looked away, then back at O.B. "Now I know that you got a tough-ass situation at home and all that. And I don't mean to poke my nose in your personal affairs. But I know your *business*, your finances and all, and . . . well, O.B., you ain't in good shape. You ain't in good shape any way you cut it."

O.B. sat there. His anxiety was like bile in his throat now. He tried to keep his outer self calm, but he knew that Mac could see his distress. "I don't see why you want *me* to do this, Mac," he said.

"Because you're a hero in this town. Or you were, once upon a time."

"Will you stop that shit? I ain't no hero. Other people always thought more of my ball playin than I ever did. You know better than that, Mac. I never really made it. I never had the chance. . . ." His voice trailed off.

"All right. They just *thought* you were a hero, then. Whatever. But that's why you gotta do this. I'm puttin it to you straight." He paused. "Please," he said. "I'm askin you, please."

"No," O.B. said, "I can't do it." He said it with weariness, with resignation.

Mac seemed to swell behind the desk. He looked around, as though for someone for support, maybe Lester Sparks, and then he took a deep breath, his stubby fingers clasped tightly together on the desk before him. "You got no choice, O.B.," Mac said, his voice shaking. "You got no choice. You'll do it, or you're a broke man, O.B. I'm tellin it to you like it is."

O.B. realized that his fingers were gripping the edge of the seat of the wooden chair he was sitting in, and his legs were rigid. Mac leaned back in the chair. He folded his arms across his stout chest and stared levelly and steadily at O.B. across the desk.

.~.~.~.

Paul still thought he could smell the damp, clammy air of the jail in his clothes and in his hair, even after two days. He had been terrified of the dungeonlike quality of the small brick jailhouse, the tiny cells with open, seatless toilets, their bowls rust-stained and full of dark, brackish water. The hours in there had seemed an eternity, but Mancini had smoked endless cigarettes and chattered with self-confidence. *He is as frightened as I am*, Paul had kept telling himself. Paul had not wanted the Negroes, especially Nate Pierson, to know how scared he was, and he had kept his cool fairly well. The fellow called Rooster had scared him the most, with his calm air of menace, the glint in his snakelike eyes, the way he shuffled on what looked like an old-fashioned peg leg.

Now Paul sat behind a desk in an upstairs Sunday school room, making notes on what they would talk about in his citizenship class that afternoon. He and Mancini had targeted the movie theater with its segregated balcony and the lunchroom at the bus station downtown as the next locations for sit-ins. And they were making tentative plans for a boycott of local merchants, too, but that would be very complicated. Right now he felt discouraged. He had been excited about going to Maud's, but now it seemed that it had been useless, an exercise in futility. What had they accomplished? He had lain awake worrying that all they had done was put the white power structure, and people like that Rooster fellow, on notice, given them fair warning so that they could get their defenses in order. And he had no doubt that there would be opposition, much stronger opposition than they had encountered at Maud's. It was almost as though Mr. McClellon and his police chief had felt that if they allowed his group to sit in for a while at Maud's, then he and Mancini and Long would be satisfied and pull back, accepting it as some sort of victory. McClellon was sadly mistaken if he did. They had not been served, of course. *Had I expected us to be?* He did not know what he had expected. He now could remember only sketchily what had been in his mind as they walked that gauntlet of people who watched them in sullen silence as they moved down the sidewalk toward the café. *What must they think of me?* he remembered wondering, and he recalled realizing, as he stealthily glanced at the sparse crowd of spectators, that he was looking for the girl, Ellen Brewster.

Consciously now—downtown, wherever he found himself—he looked for the girl from the drugstore. She had taken on a kind of warm glow in his memory, and whenever discussions got heated and tense, as they were getting now, he found himself thinking of her as an escape. Things were not moving fast enough for Nate and Mark Price and Sally Long, and they were constantly badgering him and Joe about it. Mr. Long, on the other hand, was cautious, almost tentative at times, and there was visible friction developing between those two factions. Then there were the more conservative Negroes, a group that Paul utterly failed to understand, who seemed to resent his presence, looking at him as suspiciously and, sometimes, as resentfully as their white neighbors. There were times when all these elements, together with the whites and their threats, filled his mind to bursting, and he felt himself growing so tense that he thought he would scream. At those times, he would think of Ellen, about the way her dark hair curled about her ears and the way she held her schoolbooks to her breasts and it would calm him. She *did* remind him of Molly, and it seemed remarkable that he had somehow met her, off here in this alien land.

Sitting in the empty classroom now, feeling tired and hungry, he closed his eyes and visualized her image, her dancing eyes, her warm smile. He had begun to think of her constantly. He would be her mentor. She had opened the way with what she had said to him, and he would open her eyes to all the injustice in this world. She would be his link to this closed white society. And yet . . . he instinctively resisted telling Mancini about her. They had been warned about getting involved with *any* young girls, especially the black ones. But in none of the workshops had this exact scenario been played for him. He would be careful. Anyway, she had probably just been flirting. It was probably all some put-up, some dare made by the tall girl who kept watching them from the back of the drugstore. He had been a fool over girls before.

Paul sat very still. He was suddenly uneasy, afraid. Maybe his father was right. Maybe that—girls—was the real reason he was down here. He shook his head. *No.*

Eldon drove slowly down a deserted, Sunday-quiet Washington Street, past Maud's Cafe with its little bright red neon sign. The lunch crowd had come and gone, and the street was empty, and Eldon found himself driving along the route they had taken from Maud's to the jail. The sense of accomplishment, of satisfaction, that he had taken immediately after their arrest was now gone, and he felt tired and defeated. And even in the jail cell, he had known that the others had not had the same sense of satisfaction that he'd had. They had been angry, bitter, full of hatred; he had seen their energy being drained, dissipated by the dark emotions. His sermon that morning had been based on the Gospel of John: "In my Father's house are many mansions." He had pleaded for tolerance, warned against reverse racism and the destructiveness of hate. The congregation, mostly older people and children, had listened passively, as though his passion were irrelevant to them. Sally had been there, in the front row; but none of her friends. She had stared into her lap through most of it. After Sunday dinner, fried chicken and mashed potatoes, Sally had gotten up abruptly, shoving her chair away from the table. She had already changed into the faded denim that she wore almost constantly now.

"Where you goin?" he had said.

"Over to the Youngbloods'," she said. She had stood there, slouched to the side, looking at him. "We gonna hang out," she had said. A hollow, persistent ache nagged at him when he thought of her with Nathaniel. The way they all hung out over there, with the white boys. Her expression said, You brought them here. You started this.

"I don't want you hangin round over there," he had said. "I'm not talkin bout the white boys. Some of those other people are full of hate, of—"

"Daddy!" she had said, moisture flecking her eyes. He wanted to go on, but he stopped, held it in. She looked defiantly at him and slammed the door behind her.

After she was gone, Cora had just sat there looking at him, a curious scowl on her face. He had not given her any opening, asked her what she was thinking. He had excused himself and gone into the living room and picked up the Sunday paper. After a while, he had heard the sounds of her washing dishes in the kitchen.

When he had left the house, he had intended to go and see O.B. He wanted to pressure him, have it out with him over what he wanted him to do. It bothered him that he seemed drawn to the man, and he drove around, avoiding going there. He passed the tall Confederate statue and turned up Main Street toward the river. The day was overcast, gray, winter hanging on, reluctant to give way to spring. He knew the gloominess of the sky affected his mood. He had been depressed since the day of the sit-in (as he now knew to call it), anxious, uneasy about the fact that the town had slipped right back into its everyday patterns, totally unaffected by what they had done, ignoring it completely, as though it had not happened at all. ("Be patient," Mancini had said to him. "These things are a long, slow process. Greensboro's a big town.

It's gonna make the news. Down here you never seem to be makin any progress. But you are. You just have to believe that.")

He turned over and drove up Commissioners Street, past O.B.'s house. His truck was parked at the curb, but Martha's car was gone. He continued on, driving slowly, past the white-only Community House, the white-only swimming pool, down to the river landing. This part of town was called Gritney; Eldon knew that the name came from the name of a steamboat that used to stop there regularly, in the last century, a boat called *The Gretna*, a boat that put on minstrel shows on the deck, shows called "Silas Green, from New Orleens!" The Silas Green shows still came around, but by truck now, used to be once a year, now less frequently; there were layers of posters for them on the sides of the buildings down on Strawberry Street. They were Negroes in blackface, playing to an audience of white and colored, separated by a wall of canvas down the middle of the tent. Young girls in skimpy, gaudy costumes and old men named Rastus who wore funny hats and tripped over their own feet. Eldon cringed, thinking of the shows. He had told his congregation to stop wasting their money, but they flocked to them nonetheless.

Eldon stopped the car for a moment, gripping the wheel as he looked out over the wide Tombigbee River, the water dull and cola-colored in the muted winter light. He decided that he had to go and see O.B., especially since it appeared that Martha, and maybe even his daughter, were out, so that he and O.B. might go at it alone. He knew his feelings toward O.B. were complicated and that he did not completely understand them or trust them totally. *What do I want from him? His approval? Lord, help me.*

He had been both pleased and alarmed when his old friend had brought Cora to the jail. Pleased that O.B. had been there for her, and yet frightened. It brought back too much of the past. But it was almost as though O.B. had made a gesture, taken sides against Mac and the power structure. And Eldon felt a vague desperation now, an urgent sense that they must get on to the next stage, whatever that was. And to get to the white community, O.B. was his only real link.

When they had been boys, Eldon had thought that it had been as painful as anything that life could hold to know that O.B. was regularly making love to the girl that he, Eldon, was growing to love. Eldon had already known that God was calling him, and the day he had told Cora that he was planning to give his life over totally to God was the same day she had told him, holding him close, that she was his and no one else's, that it was over with O.B., that it had been nothing but some kind of child's game anyway. And Eldon had forgiven them, in his heart. But a few years after they were living in town and Eldon was starting to preach at several little churches scattered around, Cora had gone to work as a maid for O.B.'s wife, in O.B.'s house, and then the pain was worse, so fiercely worse. He had insisted on it. He knew now that he had so desperately wanted to believe that any attraction between Cora and O.B. had vanished with his earlier absolution of them.

Today, from this long perspective, it seemed almost unbelievable to him that he could have done that, but they had been in dire need of the money; Sally was a toddler, barely out of diapers, and that simply was what colored women did; there were no other jobs but teaching, and Cora had had no education beyond the little training school down in the Flatwoods. It had been a mistake, a dumb, foolish, terrible mistake, considering what had happened to his mother, the awful, terrible humiliation of having his wife work as a domestic in a white man's house. And his inchoate, never-expressed worry had been justified. Cora and O.B. did again fall prey to lust. At first he had hated O.B., blaming him entirely. But then he could not be that dishonest with himself, or with God. Cora had been just as much to blame. He had not known if he could survive the bitterness and the agony, the burning hurt, but he somehow had. After months of anger and suffering, he had forgiven them both again. He loved Cora, and he knew that she loved him. And he loved O.B., almost like a brother, one who had somehow been forced to live at great distance, or even, somehow, in another time. In spite of the distance, there was something in their shared history that connected, that made contact, and he knew, in his heart, that he trusted O.B., while he did not trust any other white man whom he knew.

He parked at the curb, behind O.B.'s pickup truck. There was a cinder driveway that went between the yellow brick house and a board-and-wire fence that was heavy with dark, dormant honeysuckle vines, but it was too narrow for a car without scraping the honeysuckle. Eldon's shoes crunched on the cinders, dumped, he knew, from the coal stoves in O.B.'s house, knew because that's the way he paved his own driveway, with the ashes from the stoves and fireplaces of his neighbors. He went around to the back, where a huge, leafless old fig tree, its branches as thick as a man's leg and growing level with the ground, dominated the yard. An empty chicken yard took up the very back, with several spindly peach trees growing there, the wire fence across the back covered with more honeysuckle and wild privet. Eldon knocked. He heard stirring inside, then O.B. opened the door. He stood there looking at Eldon's face. Eldon felt warm, heated air drifting toward him.

"I want to talk to you," Eldon said.

"All right," O.B. said, stepping back, opening the door wider. Eldon came into the kitchen; newspapers were scattered about over the kitchen table, as though O.B. had just been reading them. The color-splashed funnies were piled on top. "You want some coffee?"

"No, thank you," Eldon said. He stood feeling awkward, clumsy. He did not understand what it was about O.B. that always made him feel that way initially. "Are we alone?" he said.

O.B. cocked his eye at him. A smile seemed to flicker across his face for a brief moment. "Yeah. Martha and Ellen went over to Meridian, to Martha's mama's. We're alone."

Eldon sat down at the kitchen table. He waited. O.B. sat down across from him. "A Coke or somethin?" O.B. said.

"No, nothin," Eldon said. "Have you given much thought to what we talked about?"

"What's that?" O.B. said. "Me bein responsible for slavery and everything else from the beginning of time?"

Eldon smiled. "No. The mayor's race."

O.B.'s face seemed to cloud. He folded his arms across his chest. "Eldon, just since I came down there to bail you outta jail, I've lost some customers. A. C. Logan, from out at Gallion? He heard about it, made a point of comin by and tellin me that I couldn't count on his business anymore, or his brother's either. That's two of my biggest accounts. Just for bringin Cora down there. Whattaya think would happen if I tried to run against Mac? I wouldn't have any business left."

"You'd have black business," Eldon said.

"People are already callin me a nigger-lover around town. It's got Martha all upset. Folks have even been ugly to Ellen. All she's doin is tellin people to be decent, and they make fun of her."

Eldon thought he heard a radio playing somewhere in the house. He was not surprised at what O.B. was saying, and he appreciated the man's position, even felt compassion for him, but he couldn't let him get away with it. "What are you sayin, O.B.?" he said.

"I want no part of it. I got no business messin around with anything like that, Eldon."

O.B. wore an old gray sweatshirt. HHS was stenciled faintly across the front, and under that, in smaller, faded, barely discernible letters, was BASEBALL. He sat stiffly in the chair, holding his lean neck at an odd angle, a pose that Eldon remembered from when they were boys: O.B. looked as though he could barely abide sitting down, was just on the verge of leaping up, of bursting into motion. Anything that required stillness, Eldon knew, prompted this pose: the baiting of a hook, or the forced immobility in the woods, hearing the turkey's low gobble, the turkey getting slowly closer, so slowly that it was maddening. So maddening that they had more than once given in to the temptation to scream, or shoot into the air, hearing the heavy bird crashing away through the undergrowth in its panic. If either one of their fathers had known they had done that, spooking off a rare and valuable turkey for the table, they would have been beaten; but on those few occasions when they had done it, they had laughed together until they cried.

"That's what you are," Eldon said.

O.B. looked up, a puzzled look on his face. "What?" he said.

"A nigger-lover." The word hung between them, like smoke in an airless room.

"Don't start that, Eldon," O.B. said. O.B.'s blue eyes looked so innocent that Eldon felt a sudden fury.

His anger led him right back into the trap: He saw them, Cora and O.B., clearly, together, their naked bodies locked in hot embrace, their movements jerky and frantic, the image so clear that it blinded him. *Get a grip. Get a grip now. I have forgiven.* He swallowed.

"Okay. All right," he said, his voice more controlled. "Listen. You got to understand." He breathed deeply. "What's happenin now. I want to talk about that. We talkin about the most important thing you or me are gonna know about in this lifetime."

"Come on, Eldon," O.B. said. He tossed his head impatiently.

"No, wait. I'm sorry about what I said about . . . you know, nigger-lovin. You're right. That's in the past." He sat there a minute, looking at O.B. The sudden sense of rage was gone, with numbness in its place. He felt himself smiling slightly. *I have forgiven.* "God's been real patient with me about that, O.B. He'll be real patient with you, too. You don't know how important this is. Whatever you do, whichever way you go, affects it. You see?"

"No, I don't," O.B. said. "I can't win any mayor's race, Eldon. That's foolish. I got no money or anything."

"It doesn't take money. All you got to have is your name on the ballot."

"Shit," O.B. said.

"People all over the country will look at us and say that's the way to do it. It won't be easy, but it'll be bloodless. People like Rooster

Wembley won't have the law on their side. The power'll shift, O.B. Decent people'll have the power." He could not understand why O.B. couldn't see it as clearly as he did.

"I can't win it, Eldon. Can't you understand that?"

"Miracles happen if you make em. We can do it." Eldon leaned back, crossing his arms over his chest. Some of his energy had returned.

"Dammit, Eldon! You talkin about pie in the sky. Nothin's gonna ever change the way people are. You can't just decide the way somethin ought to be and go out and pronounce it that way. Shit. Even *I* know that, and I ain't even been off to preacher school."

"Don't say anything about that!" Eldon's fury seemed to hit him again like a sudden burst of light. "You got no right to throw off on that!" Eldon knew that O.B. knew about how he had gone off to the little seminary in Nashville, the one run by the *white* Southern Baptist Church, for *coloreds*, where he had spent eighteen months stoking the furnace, washing dishes, and waiting tables in the dining hall, poring over the ragged, secondhand books into the night, while Cora had worked as a cook in the cafeteria of U. S. Smith High School and later as a teacher's aide. All this was right after the disaster of Cora's trying to work for them. It had been torture to leave her, but he had to trust. When he had come home, qualified now to take over the congregation of the Mount Sinai AME Zion Church, it had become Cora's turn. She had gone to Selma University for two years, studying into the night after working in the school's laundry when she wasn't in class to take an associate's degree in math that certified her to teach at the high school. No white man could throw off on how he and his wife had struggled to better themselves. Not even O.B. "I won't have that, O.B.," Eldon said levelly.

"All right. I'm sorry. I didn't mean anything by that," O.B. said.

Eldon thought his apology was genuine, and he tried to relax again, shaking his head, looking at O.B. *Like a brother, from another, brighter, time.* "I'm hurtin, O.B.," he said. His voice was thin. O.B. was looking at him peculiarly. "I'm hurtin for Sally. And I'm hurtin for Ellen."

"Ellen? What's she got to do with this?"

"She's the future, O.B. I'm hurtin for all the young people that got to inherit this world that you and me and all the rest of em fucked up." He realized that he was on the verge of tears; he was confused and panicked by the roller coaster of his emotions. He could not let O.B. see him cry. He would never let a white man see him cry. Any man.

"You're crazy, Eldon," O.B. said. "All this is gettin to you too much."

"What! How could it get to me 'too much'?" He sat up straight, his fists clenching on the table.

"Calm down," O.B. said. "Okay. But this is *your* fight, not mine."

"No. It's yours, too. It's more yours than mine. All this bigotry is hurtin your people more than it's hurtin mine," Eldon said.

O.B. snorted.

"You'll see," Eldon said. "All the hate will eat you up."

"Come on, Eldon," O.B. said.

Eldon swallowed. His throat felt tight. He had to trust O.B. "God didn't create this world for hate, O.B. He created it for love. Hate won't win. It can't."

"I don't hate anybody—"

"Let me ask you this," Eldon said, interrupting. "If Jesus was to come down here today, right now, to Hammond, Alabama, and walk amongst us, whose side you think He'd be on? Huh? Would he walk with us? Huh? Or with Rooster Wembley and Mac McClellon?"

O.B. paused. "I don't see what Jesus has got to do with it, Eldon," he said.

Eldon laughed harshly. "You don't? You don't?" he said, feeling incredulous.

"Hell no, I don't," O.B. said. "God created the world like it is. He created Rooster Wembley, too, didn't he?"

"*Satan* created Rooster Wembley," Eldon said, although he had to laugh at the very idea.

"Shit." O.B. grinned. "All right. I don't want to argue with you. You're the expert on Satan and God and all."

"No," Eldon said, suddenly weary, "I'm not an expert on anything, but I do know you owe me somethin, O.B."

The softness in O.B.'s eyes faded, and they became hard. "I said don't start—"

"No! All right." Eldon paused. The room was very quiet except for that radio playing somewhere in the house. "I've forgiven it, you and her. But I can't forget it. It ties us together. Like those blood oaths we took as boys."

"Playin Indian. That was just—"

"It was our blood. Both red, if you remember." *A brighter time.* "The same color. And we both loved the same woman." *White skin, brown skin.*

"Loved? Loved?" O.B. echoed, his face contorted with fury.

"You *loved* Cora. I know you did!" Eldon said.

"No! I never loved her. Get outta here!" O.B. was almost shouting. His fists were clenched on the table.

Eldon felt the flames of his own rage now. He held his jaw rigid, his arms tense, his hands clasped in his lap.

"You tellin me you never loved her?" Eldon said thinly. He forced the words between his lips.

"I'm tellin you it ain't any of your goddam business," O.B. said.

Eldon stood up slowly. His breath was coming in short gasps, and he rested his knuckles on the table, calming himself, controlling his breathing.

O.B. said, "Get outta my goddam house."

Eldon stared at him. "All right," he panted. "All right. I'll get out of your fuckin white man's house." He got control of his breathing, looking down at O.B. "Blood brothers," he said, tightly. "But I'll tell you this. God wants this, O.B. Jesus is on our side, and He wants you converted. God is gonna deliver His people out of bondage; He's sayin 'Let My people go!' And *you're* part of His plan!" He stood breathing evenly. "And we got a lot that ain't finished between *us*, O.B. And we're gonna have to settle it. One way or the other. Sooner or later." The words seemed to hang there in the heated air of the kitchen. Eldon turned and moved blindly toward the door, pushing it open, stepping out into the damp, raw winter cold.

PART 2

SPRING

Chapter Six

ᴇᴥᴥ

ELLEN KNEW THAT IF SHE WENT DOWNTOWN ENOUGH, SOONER OR later she would see Paul again. The weather had turned warmer, the trees leafing out, flowers appearing in yards and in the planters in the public square. She was sitting on a green iron-and-wood bench that sat near the center of the park, near the fountain, a position that gave her a good view of Washington Street where it intersected with Walnut, an intersection that anyone downtown was likely to pass. She had seen him walk by one day earlier with the other one, Joe Mancini, but she had been too shy to approach him, and she had been disgusted with herself. It had made her depressed for several days that she had missed that opportunity, although she'd marveled at the ease with which the boys had walked around town; she was frightened for them, certain that they were in great danger, and she fantasized about rescuing Paul somehow, intervening with the police or whoever might be after them, the Ku Klux Klan or whoever. She had seen Paul only that once since she had talked to him in the drugstore, and she wondered if he even remembered who she was, even remembered her name. She wondered if he ever thought about her.

She was certain that she was falling in love with him, if love meant thinking of someone all the time, letting that one person become what you thought of when you went to bed at night and when you woke up in the morning. He represented another world to her, as though he had been sent to save her from this town and from her mother. The other boys she had known, had dated, had seemed like mere children next to this man who had the courage to leave the safety of his home to come to this part of the country that must have been strange to him and put himself at risk. She longed to share that idealism with him, thinking that it would give meaning to her life.

She never shared all these feelings with Lacy or any of the other girls; but she had found herself defending the boys when her friends talked about them, when they were mouthing and repeating things about Negroes that she knew they heard from their parents. Ellen would argue with them, and they would cut her off; Dudley McClellon had nicknamed her "Ellen Luther Coon."

Ellen had never really dated much. She had gone through the junior high school parties, the walks around the block in the dark, slow-dancing in the dimly lighted basements of friends. She had been turned off by the sweaty pawing and kissing, and she had gotten a reputation early on that she wouldn't do as much as the other girls, and the impression had stuck to her. Everybody else had gone steady, but she never had, and her mother had asked her why many times. When her mother was drinking, she acted as though the fact that Ellen had never gone steady was a personal affront to her. "What did I do?" she would say, staring at Ellen. "It's just not natural not to have boy-friends," she would say.

Ellen had been content to go to occasional movies with the girl-friends of her youth, but she'd had to gradually stop inviting them to her house because of her mother's drinking, and she had found herself without any close friends at all, except for Lacy, and their relationship had grown more and more superficial. Ellen had become a serious student, which isolated her more at school. The others seemed to resent her good grades. To make up for her lack of friends, she'd learned to be alone, and her mother thought *that* was weird, too. Ellen spent a lot of time reading, borrowing books from the library and buying paperbacks of the classics in the drugstore. Her mother eyed them suspiciously. "Paperbacks are dirty books," she had said once, but Ellen had found her refuge in them. The characters there were more interesting, more worldly, than her acquaintances, who were mostly interested in drinking and sex.

Not that she had anything against sex. There had in fact been one boy, from down at Ashville, a slightly older boy, who had had his own car. They had dated for a while and had become very physical quickly; she was surprised that it had happened so easily and naturally, and Ellen had been secretly proud of herself. They never went anywhere but the Grove Drive-in Theater or parking along the river, soon making love regularly, until she had finally backed off, frightened that the lovemaking had come before the love had; and when the love hadn't come, there hadn't seemed to her much reason to continue.

"You broke up with him?" her mother had said incredulously. "Good heavens, Ellen! Why?"

"Well . . . he . . . you know." She had blushed.

"He wanted to go all the way?" her mother asked. "Okay, then." In spite of her mother's misunderstanding—hadn't it always been like that?—it had made Ellen feel very good to have that secret from her mother, to have this private knowledge that her mother's drinking could never touch.

She saw Paul coming out of Ramsey's Drug Store, a package of cigarettes in his hand, and she was suddenly alert, her body poised on the bench. He stopped on the corner, opening the package. She watched him put a cigarette between his lips and light it. He had on faded jeans and a blue denim shirt with the sleeves rolled up past his elbows. He flipped the match into the gutter, and she watched him exhale, a cloud of white smoke rising over his head and picking up the sunlight; he stood smoking, looking up and down the street, like someone idly passing time. She got up, smoothing her skirt and inspecting her blouse, and went along the sidewalk to the corner. He saw her from across the street and smiled. When the light changed, he strolled across to where she was standing.

"Hello there, Ellen Brewster," he said. *He remembered her name!* He was looking down at her, smiling. Ellen shaded her eyes from the high sun.

"How have you been?" she asked.

"Well," he said, "all right, I guess. Been in jail since I saw you last." He laughed. "I guess you knew about that. Everybody knows about that."

"I heard about it. I didn't see it. I was in school." She thought to herself that that sounded stupid. "I mean . . ." Anything she could think of to say would just make it worse. He would laugh at her.

"Beautiful," he said, waving his arm, indicating the air, the newly leaved trees in the park. He drew on the cigarette inhaling deeply. "Wonderful weather," he said. He took a tentative step into the park, and she moved aside, then in step beside him. She could tell that he wanted to walk with her. She was certain that he wasn't just patronizing her.

"Aren't you," she began, after a few steps, "aren't you afraid to walk around town like this?"

"A little," he said. "But you got to live." He grinned. "You got to have butts."

"Doesn't anybody bother you?"

"I don't walk by the pool hall," he said. "People, you know, say things, look at me funny. But I'm used to that by now." He drew on the cigarette and looked down at her. "Aren't you afraid to be walking *with* me?"

"Oh, no," she said. "I don't give a damn." She looked away, at the fountain, the goldfish pond. She looked back at him. His blond hair was ragged at the back of his neck; he needed a haircut. "No," she said seriously, "I don't."

He glanced at her out of the corner of his eye, and she noticed that his eyes played briefly over her breasts. He sat down on the edge of the concrete goldfish pond.

"Hey, listen," he said, "wasn't it your dad that came down and got us out of jail?"

"Yeah," she said.

"Well, that's great. I mean, we really appreciated that. He must be a nice guy."

The way he said, "guy," his clipped, snappy way of talking, intrigued her.

"He is," she said.

"Maybe I can meet him sometime," he said. "Tell him how grateful I am."

"Maybe you can," she said. Her heart seemed to jump in her chest. *Meet her father.* "What . . . what's your major?" she said.

"Huh?"

"In college. Whattaya studyin?"

"Oh. English," he said.

"*English? I* want to major in English. I love literature."

"Really? Who do ya read?"

"Oh, everybody. Hemingway. William Faulkner—"

"You read William Faulkner?"

"Of course," she said. She squinted in the sunlight, trying to see his face clearly.

"Does everybody in the South read Faulkner?" He laughed.

"No," she said, not getting the joke if there was one. "Nobody, practically. He . . . he's hard to understand," she added earnestly.

"Yes, that's true. At least at the beginning. I had to read *Absalom, Absalom* my freshman year and found it hard going. But I like Faulkner now. So. You're going to . . . Middlebury, right?" He grinned at her.

"Yeah," she said. "I hope to. I'm waiting to hear about scholarships." She sat down next to him, feeling more relaxed, more confident. "You . . . live with the Youngbloods?"

"Yeah!" He laughed. "They're some kinda people, you know? I mean, you never would expect to find people like them in a little burg like this, you know?"

"Everybody thinks they're strange," she said.

"No kidding?!" he said. He laughed again, easily, his light hair falling loosely over his forehead. His teeth were even and white in the spring sunlight.

"How old are you?" She realized she had blurted out the question, and she felt her cheeks start to redden. "If you don't mind . . . you know . . ."

"No, that's okay. Twenty-one," he said. "How old are you? No, wait. Let me guess. Ahhh, seventeen?"

"Yes," she said. "Not hard to guess, huh? I'll be eighteen in five months."

"Sweet seventeen and never been kissed," he said.

"Don't count on it." She laughed, at ease with him now, as at ease as she'd felt the first time she'd talked with him in the drugstore that day. All her friends had said they would have nothing to do with "those people." "He's a Jew, Ellen," Lacy had said, wrinkling her nose. That meant nothing to Ellen. She suspected it really meant nothing to Lacy, either. He was looking levelly at her. He took a last draw from the cigarette and ground it out beneath the heel of his heavy boot. He leaned back, peering at her, a questioning, inquisitive look in his eyes.

"Maybe . . ." he said, "maybe you'd like to come over to the Youngbloods' sometime. You know. Lots of kids hang out over there, and—"

"Sally Long?" she said.

"You know Sally Long?" he said. Her heart sank. He did not remember what she had told him. He had not been listening to her at all. "Hey, okay, I remember now," he said, "Yeah. Sally hangs out over there. She goes with this guy, Nate Pierson. We just sit around, you know . . . play some music? You know?"

"I don't know if I should," she said.

"Yeah. Well, I'd understand, of course. Anyway, it's no big deal. I just thought maybe . . ."

"Well," she said, feeling the boldness return, "maybe I will. When?"

"Oh, I dunno," he said. "Anytime. Afternoons. We teach classes in the mornings and sometimes at night. Yeah."

"Well, I will," she said, "I definitely will."

"I'm walking," he said, "you want to walk over there now? With me?"

Ellen felt a prickling tingle run up her spine, a kind of forbidden thrill, and she shivered. She knew it was dangerous, and bold, and foolhardy. She knew her parents would disapprove. She thought of her father, then pushed the thought from her mind.

"Sure," she said. "Let's go."

⋅∾⋅∾⋅∾⋅

They cut through back streets, down Jackson by the Presbyterian church, then down Ashe Street. Paul kept walking too fast for her; he would speed up and then slow down. She had thought that they would stroll more leisurely, but she realized that he was nervous, that he wanted to get off the streets. His legs were long, and she could barely keep up with him. Just when Ashe Street moved into Frogbottom, the Negro section, they veered up Maple Street, a raggedly paved, narrow street full of potholes that curved around to the east, a street lined with deep limerock ditches. Green slimy water flowed in the bottom of the ditches, and they smelled raw and damp. Paul walked more slowly now: the houses were old, some very large, shabby old Victorian houses with porches around three sides, some small brick cottages with rusty screen porches and overgrown yards and cracked sidewalks.

Carl and Melody Youngblood lived in the largest of the houses, three stories with wide covered porches at the first two levels. The house was painted a faded, dull crimson and fronted by a sagging black wrought-iron fence and a sandy, grassless yard totally shaded by a huge magnolia tree. It was a once-proud house that must have at one time dominated the then-thriving neighborhood in which it sat. Ellen could see hundreds of creamy new buds on the giant magnolia, buds that would be, in midsummer, milky white blossoms as large as ladies' hats.

The iron gate scraped shrilly on the buckled sidewalk; some of the heavy branches of the magnolia sloped down almost to the ground, and the thick green leaves blotted out the afternoon sun, so that the yard was gloomy and dim.

"That's quite a tree," she said. She felt nervous, apprehensive, and she knew that her voice gave her away.

"Yeah," he said.

They went up the wide steps and across the porch. Floorboards squeaked under their feet. Over the ornate front door was a stained-glass fanlight, intact, a peacock with its motley colored tail fanned out. Ellen paused, admiring it. It was clean, polished, free of the spiderwebs that clung to the corners in the other windows. Paul pushed open the door, and they entered a wide, empty hallway, with stained and torn wallpaper, which led them to a big, sunny kitchen across the back of the house. A little girl, about two years old, was sitting in a high chair in the middle of the room. She wore a cloth diaper and nothing else.

"Paul," someone said. And as Ellen turned, the voice said, "Oh!" A woman stood there, and Ellen knew who she was, having seen her around. She was Melody Youngblood, Carl's wife, the little girl's mother. Her hair was blond and long, hanging straight down her back. She wore an old pair of overalls over a dingy T-shirt and had a bandanna tied around her head. Her feet were bare. "Who's your friend?" she asked Paul.

"This is Ellen Brewster," Paul said. "This is Melody," he told Ellen. The woman just looked at Ellen, her face blank and expressionless. The house had the cold, damp feel of poverty, making Ellen shiver. She was repulsed by the gloom of the wasted house and yet moved by it, too, and felt her heart going out to these people. Coming from upstairs, Ellen heard music playing, soft guitars, then a high, lilting woman's voice.

"Who's around?" Paul said.

"I dunno," Melody Youngblood said.

Paul led Ellen out of the room, taking her hand. It was the first time he had held her hand, and his touch was cool and exciting, like a mild electric shock. and she tried not to show her reaction. They went up the central stairway; about every other step creaked as they stepped on them, and Paul grinned at her. "This is a neat old house," he said. "It's sturdy, but it doesn't sound like it, does it?" They went up the second flight, to the third floor, and the music grew louder. Ellen could tell now that the music was coming from a record player, a good one, probably a stereo. "The circle of light . . . the clouds of the night . . ." sang the high voice. "We are the believers . . . we are the believers . . ."

Paul rapped on the doorframe with his knuckles. They looked into the room. There were several gray-and-white-striped mattresses on the floor, against the walls, which were covered with bright, flowered wallpaper. The music was loud in the room, and Ellen smelled a strong odor, a pungent, spicy odor like the incense she had smelled visiting the Episcopal church, and the air in the room seemed smoky. A Negro boy was sitting on one of the mattresses, facing them; he wore jeans and no shirt, and his body was muscular; his skin looked glossy and polished in the light from the overhead lamp and the windows, which were closed but without blinds or curtains. He wore what looked like a nylon stocking around his head. He seemed, to Ellen, to be wearing it defiantly. She suddenly felt unwanted, a stranger.

The boy's eyes seemed wide and brooding.

"How you doin, man?" Paul offered.

The boy did not answer.

Ellen, looking nervously around, saw Sally, sitting on another mattress, leaning against the wall. She was staring at her, holding a wilted-looking cigarette in front of her face.

"What the hell you doin, Ellen?" Sally said, her voice harsh, cutting through the music. "What you doin bringin her here?"

"Sally?" Ellen felt awkward, out of place. The room seemed so bizarre to her, so like something in a dream.

"Shit," Sally said. She shrugged. She took a long draw on the cigarette, then held her head back, holding her breath, and it dawned on Ellen as she gaped at Sally that they were smoking marijuana. She had read about it and heard about it, and now she was horrified, frightened to be in the room with the threatening strangeness of it all.

"Paul, I don't—" she said.

"All right," he said.

Sally, smirking, let the smoke out in a gush as Paul and Ellen hesitated in the doorway.

"If it ain't little Ellen," Sally said, standing up. "What's a little white girl like you doin down here?" She went over to the stereo that was sitting on the floor, speakers propped in the corners, and lowered the volume. She wore skintight dirty-looking jeans and a wrinkled green cotton blouse. Her tightly curled hair hung over her face. She stood there, smiling crookedly at them, holding the cigarette in front of her, with three fingers.

"I just . . . came down here with Paul," Ellen said. Her voice was tense, trembling.

"Paul, huh?" she said. "Well. You want a hit off this stick?"

"No, thank you," Ellen said quickly, awkwardly.

"Who the hell this girl?" the boy said. "Goddam, Paul. What you doin?"

"She's okay," Paul said. "Don't worry about it."

"Shit, man," he said. "She a town white girl. What the fuck?"

"Hey—" Paul said.

"She a spy, man," the boy said. "She down here spyin!"

"No!" Ellen surprised herself with the way she spoke up. The music droned on softly in the room, all of them looking at her. "I'm not a spy! Don't say that." She tried to make her voice firm, afraid she was showing her terror. *Why didn't Paul do something?"*

"Honkie," the boy said, mumbling under his breath. "Fuckin cracker."

"Okay then." Ellen turned toward Paul. She had been glad, at first, to see Sally, but now she wanted to leave as quickly as possible.

"Wait." Sally stepped closer to Ellen. The scent in the room was stifling, heady. "What you want with us?" she demanded, narrowing her eyes.

"Nothin," Ellen said. She wanted only to get out of the room now, out of the house. Why had she ever come? "I asked Paul if he knew you; he said he did." Her voice shook.

"What you want to see me for?" Sally said. "You ain't wanted to see me in ten years."

"I just thought . . . I don't know." Ellen blinked her eyes, her hands gripped tightly at her sides. She looked around the room. She knew she was in another world from the one where she spent her days, and yet she knew she was right here in Hammond. She had heard her friends talk about how all the Negroes who were out making trouble used illegal drugs, but she had not believed it. "I don't know why I wanted to see you," she said, "I just did." Her eyes stung with tears from the smoke in the room and from her fear and sorrow for Sally.

Sally was staring at her. "There's somethin in me that really hates you," she said, turning away. "I don't need this shit."

Ellen's mouth was dry, and her knees felt weak. Images of herself and Sally, as little girls, rushed into her mind. Suddenly, with great clarity, she remembered the long afternoons when she had known that her mother was drinking, shut away in her room with the curtains closed. The terror and the fear she had felt. And Cora was there, her strong arms, her smell like lye soap, and Sally, the only friend she had had before she started to school, their constant make-believe, playing, growing together like sisters. An innocent love as deep as sisters. And then it had stopped; as abruptly and savagely as a sudden death. They had moved into their separate worlds. *But not this far!*

Paul just stood there beside her, not saying anything. Sally turned slowly back around. Her dark eyes were steady on Ellen's face; her hair, oily and dirty, hung limp as Sally tossed her head, tossing the hair defiantly, a crooked grin on her lips. "We gonna burn your white ass." Her voice was barely above a whisper. "White man show me a whip, I show him my fist. I can't stand it anymore."

"Yeah," the boy said from the mattress. "Yeah." He spoke rhythmically. "Tell em we gonna get em. Tell em that. Tell em all the colored preachers and the colored teachers, they gonna boycott. They gonna be nice and polite. Say, Sorry, Mister Charlie, we ain't gonna buy from yore store no more! But us! Us is young niggers. Us is young, ignorant niggers; We gonna burn. Burn their house down. Tell em that." The woman on the record player was singing, now, "Will the circle . . . be unbroken . . . by and by . . . Lord by and by . . ."—an old hymn that Ellen knew, had heard all her life. The boy's rhythmical voice kept time with the music. "You tell em, girl. You tell em, girl."

"Yeah," Sally said. "Pass the word mongst the rich white folks."

"I didn't come down here to spy," Ellen insisted, her words sounding thin and hollow in her ears. What they said was terrible and hideous, so alarming that she could not grasp it.

"What'd you come down here for, then?" Sally said.

Ellen felt dizzy with panic and confusion. She felt Paul's hand on her arm. It seemed to her that Sally's eyes were burning into her skin. It was as though Sally was both the little girl she had once played with and a dangerous, threatening stranger, and it was too much for her. She turned, almost blindly stumbling from the room, holding onto the rail as she started down the steps. Her shoes slipped on the worn carpet, and she stumbled but held on, regaining her balance. She heard Paul call her name, and she paused at the second landing to get her breath.

"Wait a minute," Paul said, behind her, "I'm sorry. I'm really sorry that happened. I—"

"It's okay," she said. She could hardly breathe. Her words echoed in the musty emptiness of the stairwell.

"I shouldn't've brought you here," he said.

"Yes. I'm glad you did." She tried to steady her breathing. She looked at Paul, read the concern in his eyes, and she was grateful. "I'm glad you did." She paused. "You must think I . . ."

"That's okay," he said. He put his arm across her shoulders. After a minute, they started down the stairs to the first floor. The other one,

Joe Mancini, was standing in the hallway, watching them come down. His eyes were dark, his hair long and curly over his collar.

"What's going on?" he said.

"Nothing," Paul said.

Mancini looked suspiciously at Ellen. He eyed Paul. "We better talk," he said.

"Okay, okay," Paul said, over his shoulder, as they went out the front door, the heavy old door scraping behind them. They stood on the shaded porch, in the dim gray light, the sun lower in the sky, the afternoon fading fast.

"What did he mean?" Ellen said.

"Oh, nothing. Nothing. Don't worry about it." His forehead was creased, but he looked down at her and smiled. She hugged her arms against her sides. The heat of the day was gone, and the spring night would be cool. Her body still trembled, whether from the chill or from her confrontation upstairs she did not know. "Can you get home okay?" he asked.

"Oh, sure," she said. "I can cut across the back way." She made herself sound confident.

Then she felt a warmth from him, standing so near. She was confused, worried about Sally, about what Sally had said to her, and she was perplexed by the strange house, the drugs. She wondered if *he* used them. She wondered what he thought of what had happened. She realized that she did not know him, did not know him at all, as he put his hands gently on her shoulders, then leaned down and kissed her forehead, just at the hairline. He smelled clean, faintly of cloves.

"You better go," he said.

She went down the cracked and uneven sidewalk, her mind reeling in what seemed to her a thousand directions. The western sky was pink and golden, ablaze. She walked into it, walking home.

·~·~·~·

It was the first evening warm enough to sit outside, and Eldon moved two folding metal-and-wooden chairs into the front yard. Cora was sitting across from him, looking at the last light in the western sky; she had said that she was very tired. She had changed into a pair of black wool slacks and a light blue sweater; Eldon wore his suit pants and his white shirt, open at the collar. They sat in the middle of the small yard, on one of the only patches of grass; the rest of the yard was sandy dirt littered with pieces of limerock.

At a church meeting earlier in the week, they had discussed a boycott, the two white boys spelling out the procedure, and he knew that it had upset Cora and some of the others. It was dangerous, and they were inviting retaliation, Cora had said. There had been rumors, talk on the street, that word had gotten out about their plans, and the nameless, faceless Klan had let it be known that it would do something to show its opposition.

"The classes are goin well," he said, but she did not answer him. "We got twenty-eight people all together. Startin next month, we'll have sixteen young people at the church."

She sighed. He wanted her to be interested in what he was saying. He was determined to interest her. He wanted her to see that the talk on the street was all bluster, that they had a systematic, civilized plan that they were committed to following.

"Sally's gonna teach the children's class," he said.

"Sally?" She looked away, turning her face from him. She seemed distant, resigned, unwilling to express what she was feeling. Eldon could hear a television playing next door. The Johnsons were watching *To Tell the Truth*, their windows open to the spring evening. He heard a burst of laughter, then faint, tinny voices.

"Yeah, Sally," he said. "She's been trained by Joe and Paul."

"I bet," Cora said bitterly.

"Whattaya mean by that?" he said.

She stared at the sky. "Nothin," she said. Then she looked at him, her eyes drawn, strained. "I'm just tired."

"I don't think—" he began.

"I'm sorry," Cora said. "Just tired, Eldon. And frightened. I'm scared for Sally, for you. For everybody."

He did not answer. Her distance made him feel fragile, lonely. He needed her.

"Don't mind me," she said softly, "okay? It's . . . easy to get discouraged."

"Yeah," he said. "Okay." He swallowed. She had been so moody lately. He could see her profile in the dusk, gazing at the faint western sky, as though she were a million miles away. He missed her, desperately. She always got tired in the spring, as the end of the school year approached. He followed her gaze; one lone, flat cloud barely reflected the last of the sunlight, a faint, barely perceptible glow on the cloud's underbelly. Gazing at the sky, he felt relatively content; things were going well, and O.B.—He looked at Cora, then back at the sunset. He realized that it had become a struggle of wills between him and O.B. He was going to win that one, too. But now he thought with pleasure of the classes, the gradual, spreading awareness among his people of what they had to do. The rumors of Klan activity made it more imperative that they move, that they continue their drive. They would start the boycott and go ahead with the plan to integrate the picture show. He turned away from the sunset, toward town, and only slowly became aware of another glow, almost like an imitation of the faded sun, an orange-yellow flicker. He stared at it impassively for a few seconds before he realized it was fire. He stood up quickly. It was coming from the direction of the church, three blocks away, and he felt his pulse begin to rush. "What's that?" he said sharply.

"What?" she said, lazily, distractedly, at first, and then, hearing his tone, she stood up and looked that way. "My God," she said.

"Fire," he said. "Somethin's on fire!"

They stood there for a moment, in shocked silence. *The church!*

"Call the fire department," he said, moving quickly through the gate, jumping the ditch into the street.

"Wait a minute, Eldon!" he heard her call, but he was running, his shoes pounding on the roadway. He could see several people running toward the glow, which he could now clearly see was in front of the church, and as he rounded the corner, he could see it, outlined against a big elm tree that grew next to the church, a large cross, flaming and sputtering. As he neared it, he could smell gasoline and hear the crackling of the flames. His run faded to a jog, his breath panting in his throat. A small group of people, their silhouettes still and unmoving now in the dusk, lit by the glow of the flames, stood in the street looking raptly at the cross. He jogged up to them, and they stood in silence, watching as the flames began to die down. A four-by-six board about six feet long formed the crosspiece, mounted on a tall creosote pole with what looked like baling wire. The pole was stuck into a neatly dug hole in the churchyard, Eldon realized, as a piece of flaming cloth, burlap, it appeared, broke from the cross and fell to the lawn. They watched it sputter and then go dark. A slight breeze had come up, fluttering the ragged black pieces of burned cloth that hung from the charred cross, and the small group stood as though hypnotized by the movement of the dying flames.

Gradually, Eldon began to hear a siren. He listened. It was not the fire siren, but a police car. It grew louder, and in a few moments a city police car, its blue lights flashing, rounded the corner, going too fast. It slammed on its brakes, sliding on the loose limerock, scattering the group as it came to rest, rocking slightly, in the middle of the street. Its siren whimpered and was silent, but the bright blue lights continued to flash round and round, on the nearby houses and trees, on the front of the church, on the smoldering cross.

The young policeman Ricky Wiggins got out of the car, looking around at the people silently watching him, and spotted Eldon at the edge of the road.

"Well, Reverend," he said, "what we got here?"

Eldon started to speak, but his voice caught in his throat. His indignation was overwhelming, choking him like the smoke and fumes from the cross.

"A cross," he said, his voice forced, hoarse. "Somebody burned a cross here."

"Sho appears like that, don't it?" Wiggins said. He jumped the ditch, his pistol flapping on his hip, and stood looking up at the cross, chewing on the inside of his lip. Then he kicked the base of the cross with the toe of his boot, and several black shreds fluttered to the ground. "It's a big son of a bitch, too, ain't it?" he said. He jumped back across the ditch and leaned against the hood of the police car; the headlights sprayed across into the yard of the church, and the blue lights spun around rhythmically. Eldon felt the beginnings of a tight headache, as he squinted against the uneven light flashes. The air was acrid. Eldon could taste the burned gasoline at the back of his throat. The taste of fear, of death, he thought.

"Now," Wiggins said, "who saw what?"

Nobody said anything.

"Anybody see anything?" Eldon said. Silence. He swallowed. His fury and anger had ebbed like the cross's flames, his fire inside smothered now by a blanket of fear, settling over him like heavy, damp fog. He saw Edna Blanks standing across the street, her broad face expressionless, her gray dress like a tent in the dimness. "Edna?" he said.

"I ain't seen nothin for sure," she said. "Don't hafta see nothin for sure."

"What's that?" Wiggins said. "What she say?"

"I think she means we all know who did this," Eldon said. His voice was shrill. Wiggins stared at him.

"That right? Well, then you better tell me, cause you know more than I do."

"It's the Klan, Mr. Wiggins," a voice said from back in the shadows. Eldon recognized the voice of old Clem Watson.

"The what? The Klan?"

"Yassuh, sho nuff," Watson aid.

"The Ku Klux Klan?" Wiggins said. "Jesus. Ain't no such animal."

"Ain't no animal," Edna Blanks said. "Cept it's white and walks on two legs."

"Now, Auntie," Wiggins said, "the Klan is a old wives' tale. Ever' body knows that."

"Ain't no old wives' tale burned that cross," Edna said.

Wiggins stood looking at the cross, his hands on his hips, chewing his lip.

Eldon's rage gave way to hollow frustration. "Call it what you want to," Eldon said, "but surely you pretty well know who burned that cross. It's a threat, to our lives, our safety. It's—"

"It's a prank," Wiggins said. "Like them teenagers always paintin the hat on the Confederate monument soldier bright red. It ain't anything to worry about. But we'll find out—"

"Nothin to worry about?" Eldon said. His voice was tight, almost squeaking. He felt the frustrated anger of years beginning to boil within him again.

"Now don't get yourself upset, Reverend," Wiggins said. Sarcasm dripped from the title. "Like I say, we'll find out who done it, sooner or later." He walked around to the side of his car and opened the door. He stood there a minute, looking at Eldon. "We'll get a street crew down here tomorrow mornin, take it down and get rid of it. Y'all go on home and forget about it. Look on it as a prank, like Halloween."

"A prank?" Eldon said. "This is not a prank!" He was fighting back the helpless rage, trying to stay calm.

"You leave it to us, all right?" Wiggins said. He paused a moment, looking at Eldon, his policeman's cap perched on his head at a jaunty angle.

"This is not a prank, Mr. Wiggins," Eldon said, "and I want it investigated for what it is. It threatens the lives of the people of this community, it—"

"Whoa, now," Wiggins said, holding up his hands. "I'll tell em." He got in the car and slammed the door, the motor roared, and he scratched off down the street, turning the corner, the white car almost fishtailing on the limerock and gravel, the blue lights still flashing.

When the sound of the car died away, the group stood there in the quiet. Eldon could not see the cross now, only smell it, its rancid aftersmell lingering in his nostrils. Like the smell of hell itself, he imagined. It was a message, as clear and precise as if it had been written in stone: Stop! Now! They all knew it, and knew who had sent it. The Klan was as palpable as the very air that they breathed, was just as much a part of the fabric of the town as that air.

Eldon turned away, breathing deeply in the cool spring evening, trying to clear his lungs of the taint; following his lead, the others all moved silently away, back toward their homes, their unspoken fear as tangible as the gathering darkness around them. None of them needed any words. Eldon shivered slightly, his thin arms suddenly chilly under the single layer of his shirt. They would not be intimidated, he vowed. They would go ahead, and he would lead them. Anger pounded within him, his rage and his horror battling for his soul as he walked, nodding silently in the darkening night air.

.~.~.~.

McClellon's secretary looked at Eldon out of slightly amused eyes. She was standing behind her desk, on the thickly carpeted second floor of the bank, as though she had no idea how to behave around him. He had gone there first thing the next day, intending to push McClellon into doing something about the burned cross and the threat that it implied. Eldon knew he had to turn the incident to his advantage, trap McClellon into admitting that he had had something to do with it, but he also had to be careful. He had studied McClellon for years and knew him to be a sly man; and he knew better than to make any white man mad. He had to appeal to any sense of decency McClellon might have, without making him mad, because once a white man like McClellon was angry at a nigger, that would be it.

"All right. I'll see if he's in," the secretary said, disappearing into McClellon's office. Eldon heard whispering inside. After a minute, she reappeared. "Mr. McClellon said to come in," she sniffed, her nose in the air.

He went past her into McClellon's office, where the mayor was sitting behind his desk, in his shirtsleeves. The windows were open, and a gentle spring breeze ruffled the papers cluttering his desk. Eldon could see the pale green trees of the park across the street, shifting about in the mild breeze, the spring sunlight glittering on the new leaves. McClellon's office smelled faintly of hair oil, of shaving lotion. The street noises were muffled and sleepy. Mac was frowning. Eldon sat down. The morning was already warm, and Eldon's suit felt heavy. What was McClellon thinking? *He knows what I want.* How is he going to treat an angry black man in his fancy bank office? A memory came to mind of Mac as a boy, strutting down the street with his friends, taking up the entire sidewalk, forcing anyone coming toward them into the gutter. Eldon shook off the recollection. They were no longer children. Surely, Mac would respond to reason.

"Well?" Mac's face was passive, a blank.

"I want to know if you've found out who burned the cro—"

"I ain't the police chief, Long," Mac said.

Eldon saw then that Mac would simply bluff and bluster. He hesitated only slightly. "But you're the mayor. I want those people brought to justice."

"What people you talkin bout?"

"The people who burned the cross!" Eldon said. He knew there was exasperation in his voice. He knew that he would do better being calm, businesslike. It was okay to show his anger, but it had to be controlled. He took a deep breath.

Mac leaned back in his chair, holding a ballpoint pen between his fingers. "I tell you, Long," he said, "niggers have been known to pull shit like that theirselves, you know."

"What?!" He was not sure he had heard him right.

"Pull a cross-burnin like that, for sympathy. To git attention, all that."

"I can assure you that—"

"All right! But you got to admit it's a possibility. We got to look at all the angles."

Eldon was shocked. But then he should have known. "Mr. McClellon, I can't believe that you'd—"

"Well, you better just goddam believe it!" Mac said. He sat stiff in his chair, glaring at Eldon, his eyes bulging slightly. "Now," he said, "what did you want to talk to me about?"

Eldon said nothing. He had come up against something thick and solid and seemingly as immovable as the white chalk bluffs along the river. He looked at the man's narrow slits of eyes, his heavy jowls. His shirt collar seemed to fit too tightly around his neck, and the large knot of his blue-and-red striped tie jutted sharply. Eldon clasped his hands in front of him, to keep them from shaking, he realized.

"Well?" McClellon said.

"Mr. McClellon," Eldon began again. "Last night, when the cross was burned, why did a *police* car answer the call? Why not the fire truck?"

"I don't know, Long. Maybe sometime they send a police car to . . . check it out or somethin. How do I know?"

"It was almost like they already knew what was there. That there wasn't really a fire." He felt calmer now. Maybe they could discuss it rationally. "I know a fire alarm was called in. I talked to the person who called it in. I know . . ." Eldon stopped. He was arrested in midsentence by the expression of mild amusement on McClellon's face.

McClellon leaned back, tossing the pen onto the desk. "You know what, Long?" he said, after a minute. "You gettin paranoid, you know that?" He just sat looking steadily at Eldon. "I don't usually git involved in stuff like this, to tell you the truth. But Lester Sparks did tell me that the *first* call that come in said there was a cross burnin in front of the AME Zion Church. So the police dispatcher knew that already, see? The dispatcher said the call was from a . . . person of the colored persuasion. So she sent Wiggins around there, and that's what he found."

"What happened to the cross?" Eldon said.

"Say what?"

"The cross. It was gone this morning. What'd you do with it?"

"Thowed it on the junk heap, I reckon."

"What about fingerprints?" Eldon said.

McClellon laughed. "You can't get any fingerprints offa somethin like that. Been burned and all. Besides, what would you do with em if you got em? You don't really have a crime here—"

"No crime? It's no crime to burn a cross in front—?" Eldon's voice rose, tight with tension and disbelief.

"Hold on! Now wait just minute. It ain't *right*, now. I'll grant you that. Defacing property, I reckon. That's a crime, kinda, I guess. Then again, they didn't exactly harm your church property none. But listen." He looked at Eldon, slowly blinking his eyes. "This is what's peculiar. It hadn't been dark more'n half an hour when the thing burned. And it was set with a posthole digger. Now you can't tell me that somebody didn't see somebody out there diggin that hole, or heard em, as many folks as live around there. It being suppertime and all, everybody home from work. Somebody woulda had to bring it in there on a truck—"

"Edna Blanks did see a truck. A pickup, right before she saw it burnin. And she said there were men working along that ditch late that afternoon. She thought they were city workers, working on the water lines or somethin."

"Well, they prob'ly were."

"White men, she said. Three of em. She didn't know em. Said a couple of em looked kind of familiar, but she didn't know em. They coulda dug the hole right then. Nobody woulda paid any attention. And then they would have just driven up there with the cross, just after dark, and placed it and lighted it. Edna saw em drive away."

"You mean they drove all over town with a twenty-foot cross on their truck?" McClellon laughed, a low chortle, snorting under his breath.

"It was dark," Eldon said.

"It hadn't been dark that long," Mac said.

"Long enough," Eldon said. He felt his energy draining; he was arguing with the man, and there was no winning. McClellon leaned back in his fine desk chair, picked up the pen again, rolled it between his fingers. Eldon could feel his hard wooden chair, uncomfortable on his thin buttocks. He could sense the man's scheming, his conniving, smell it like the acrid odor of the cross the night before.

"Did Edna see em set the cross and set fire to it?" McClellon asked.

"No," Eldon said. "She only remembered seein a pickup drivin off sometime before it flamed up."

"Or it was just passin by on the street. Not 'drivin off.' There's lots of pickups around, Eldon," McClellon said.

"They are tryin to scare us," Eldon said. "Tryin to make us stop."

"Stop what?" McClellon said. Eldon watched McClellon's face. The man was sweating, but his eyes were impassive. He heard a car horn blowing down in the street, then it was quiet again.

"Stop what we're gonna do next," Eldon said.

"And what the hell is that?" McClellon said.

"Surely you've heard about the boycott, Mr. McClellon," Eldon said, and McClellon waved his pudgy hand in the air, as though at an annoying fly. It was clear that the threat did not surprise him.

"Look, Long," McClellon said, "I don't know why you're comin to me with this."

"Who else am I gonna go to with it?" Eldon said. "You think they'll stop with cross-burnin? I know the danger we face."

McClellon looked uncomfortable as Eldon said that. Eldon watched him carefully. He seemed suddenly vulnerable, frightened himself at the mention of more violence. The white man ran his finger around under his collar. He was perspiring freely. He coughed.

"Who's this 'they' you keep talkin about?" he said.

"Come on, Mr. McClellon," Eldon said, sensing a weakness. "You know as well as I do. You know the Klan is behind stuff like that." Was McClellon scared of them, too? But he was a part of them, wasn't he? All the white men were part of the same thing. Nevertheless, from the way McClellon's eyes wavered, Eldon had a strong sense then that he had truly struck a nerve.

"I don't know any such a thing about any Klan," McClellon said, toward the open window. "Sure, there are hotheaded boys around. You can't talk to some of em. But they're all bark. Hell, you start all this marchin around and sitting down in white cafés, you can expect some of that stuff. They got to be heard, too. You keep that shit up, and . . ." He turned back around, looking at Eldon. "And they won't stop at cross-burnin, nosiree. Any more of that demonstration shit, and I'll be keepin you locked in the jailhouse for your own protection."

"Mr. McClellon, my people will be free. It will happen, because it is God's will. Do you understand what I am saying?"

"I hear you," McClellon said, a slight smile on his face.

"No matter that you and your kind—"

"Now hold on!"

"All right," Eldon said. He stopped. He had to be careful. "We are on the side of right, Mr. McClellon. And someday all the world will know that. God wants us to do this, you see. And to start, I want the cross-burnin investigated," Eldon said. "They are trying to scare us off, to thwart the will of God." He looked steadily at McClellon, who did not blink. Then he said, "I can always call the FBI myself."

"Yep," Mac said. He pointed. "There's the phone. I'll pay for the call." His voice seemed to shake slightly, as though he wasn't sure that Eldon wouldn't take him up on it, but then he grinned stiffly. "They'll listen to you, and they'll ask you questions, and they'll fill out the papers, and two, three years from now maybe they'll send some asshole in here to ask questions and sniff around. Maybe." His voice was tight, constricted. "It's not their jurisdiction, you see. See, they not gonna step on the boys in Montgomery's toes. And the boys in Montgomery not gonna step on our toes. It just don't work that way, Long. We got a perfectly good police department here, paid for out of good taxpayer money, and we can keep the peace around here without any interference from the federal government." The rigid, set grin faded slowly from McClellon's face, replaced by a look of smug self-satisfaction. Eldon knew that he was right. Mancini had used almost the same words. Eldon felt helplessness, the almost physical pain of frustration, and he willed it away.

"Mr. McClellon." He took a deep breath, calling on all his strength. "We are not going to halt the demonstrations. We will keep on." McClellon's face darkened in a frown. "In the past month," Eldon went on, "at least seventy-five black people have attempted to register to vote, and they have been humiliated, harassed, and otherwise mistreated. Only six of the seventy-five or so have been registered. I want you to know that if this kind of thing—"

"The county registrar—"

"*This kind* . . . of thing continues, we will instigate a boycott, a full boycott of all white-run businesses in this town. No Negro will trade at any business run by a white man, including this bank."

McClellon's face registered no surprise. He had heard all about it, of course. "You can't do that," he said.

"Oh, yes, we can," Eldon said.

"You can't survive doin that. That's . . . ridiculous."

"It's not ridiculous. It's goin to happen. Then, we—"

"Now wait a minute—"

"I'm not finished, Mr. McClellon," Eldon said. Mac glowered at him, his face a dull red. "There are several 'white only' establishments around town that we plan to test," he said.

"Which ones?"

"Never mind that now." Eldon felt that he still had an advantage somehow and was determined to hold on to it. "We—"

"Whattaya mean, test?" McClellon said. "Test what?"

"The law. Jim Crow. The laws are wrong, Mr. McClellon, and we—"

"But they're the law, goddammit!" McClellon said. "I'm tellin you, Long. You goin to jail, boy." He worked his mouth, a slow, grinding motion; the line of his jaw seemed rigid, his teeth clenched. His entire body seemed to tremble slightly as his hands lay on the desk between them; his fingers had tufts of coarse black hair on the backs of the first joints. "You're crazy. You break the law, you go to jail. You want to go to prison? Is that what you want? Workin on a road gang, bustin rocks in the sun? Shit. A fancy preacher like you? Why're you in this?"

"I told you," Eldon said.

"What?"

"Freedom," Eldon said, watching the man's face.

"Freedom? Goddammit man, this is America. You're free. Everybody's free!" McClellon shook his head. He was sweating more now, alarm flashing in his eyes. "No. Listen. It don't make sense. You pull this shit, it gits in the paper, gits on the news, gits all blown up, outta proportion, you know how they are."

So that was it. That's what frightened him.

"Who?" Eldon was almost toying with the mayor now.

"Who what?" Mac said, squinting.

"Who are they? You said I know how they—"

"The goddamn *news*. Don't fuck with me, Long," Mac said, and Eldon felt a sense of confidence, of hope. He had to fight a sudden, insane, giddy impulse to laugh. *So that was it! McClellon wanted to stop the demonstrations so that the paper company wouldn't renege on its promise to build the mill.* McClellon's face was crimson as he took deep breaths, trying to settle himself down. *I could just make one phone call, tell them. But they were white, too, and what would that get us? No, going on with the demonstrations would accomplish our purpose, and if the mill doesn't come in, so be it.*

What, Eldon asked himself, had he actually expected from the man? Had he really thought that McClellon would immediately agree to investigate? Admit that he knew anything? Or had Eldon really only been after this heady sense of suddenly having the superior position? Maybe that *was* what he wanted, what he *needed* now, simply to win one small point from McClellon. He eased backward in the chair; he felt some of the tension going out of his arms and legs, as though he had transferred it to the white man across the desk. He smiled.

"Listen here," McClellon said softly, still facing the window. "Listen, now. I want to tell you this again." Eldon leaned forward. McClellon turned to face him, studying him shrewdly. "I can arrange it so you'll never have to worry about money again. If you want, it can be just a big cash settlement—you name the amount, I'll git it, within reason, 'a course—and all you got to do is agree to stop all this nonsense. At least until Gulf International gets in here. Then we can all look to the future together."

"No," Eldon said. "No deal." He felt clean in the face of this, above it.

"Wait now," McClellon said. "Hear me out—"

"No, Mr. McClellon," Eldon said. "We are goin forward with our campaign. We won't stop until this entire society is integrated, and there are no color barriers left."

"God, man! That's not gonna ever happen! Don't you realize that? All you're gonna do is git innocent people hurt. Can't you see that?"

Eldon sat there calmly. A balm had settled over him, a serenity that he had not expected. He could see droplets of sweat on McClellon's forehead and upper lip. When he spoke, his voice was relaxed, free of the tightness. "I pray that nobody will be hurt, Mr. McClellon. But I fear that they will, before all this is over. I remind you that it's your duty to keep the peace. We trust you to do that."

McClellon sat behind the desk, his face tightened into a grimace. His shoulders were hunched, and he seemed to be looking up at Eldon. Eldon was remembering his reading of Ghandi in the workshops he had attended in Montgomery, the sermons he had listened to.

He felt exhilarated, as though he had somehow, at least momentarily, transferred the pain of years to this white man. "And," Eldon said, McClellon's slitted eyes steady on him, "when it is all over, we'll love you. We'll forgive you."

McClellon's eyes widened slightly. There was a long moment of silence, nothing but the muted street noises in the distance, and then McClellon seemed to tense even more, his body like a tightly coiled iron spring. When he spoke, his lips barely moved.

"Git the fuck out of my office," he said.

Eldon stood up, fighting the temptation to smile. A wave of uncertainty drifted at the back of his mind, but he pushed it away, fastening on the triumphant moment, however brief and insignificant it might prove to be, as he went out past the girl, his nostrils picking up the heavy, almost funereal scent of her perfume. It seemed to him that his walk had a spring in it, an energy, a lightness, and he smiled to himself now as he went down the stairs and through the lobby, toward the big glass double doors and the sunlit street beyond.

Chapter Seven

◥◤

AS MAC DROVE HOME FROM WORK THAT EVENING, HE WAS STILL thinking about Long's threat, the boycott. Long was proving to be a little more than Mac had bargained for. He was smart. Mac had underestimated him, thought that he could scare him with the threat of jail, or, if that failed, buy him off. But now he knew that wasn't going to work. Long had a tough streak. He had gone around for years looking meek and skinny and small, slightly ridiculous in his stiff, poorly fitting suits, so serious that you never saw him laughing and joking and carrying on like all the other niggers. Now Mac thought of him as wily, calculating, and clever behind those red-rimmed, blood-shot eyes. The man had never looked Mac directly in the eye before today, and when he had, the effect had been powerful. He had looked like a man who meant business, and if he did, with this boycott, the results would be chaos. The white folks in Hammond simply wouldn't sit still for it. There would be trouble. The arrests at Maud's had merited one small paragraph in *The Tuscaloosa News* that someone had called in, nothing else as far as Mac knew, and the cross-burning hadn't attracted any reporters either, so there was no way that Gulf International knew anything about any of what had gone down so far. Mac had called down there, just in case, asking Carleton Byrd some routine questions that Byrd had seemed impatient with. Evidently, the executive had heard nothing.

The motor in Mac's Buick purred soothingly as he turned down his street, a street that always made him feel warm and welcome. He could see the trees budding and leafing out, the bright green of the new grass on the still brown-streaked lawns that by mid-May would be solid deep green and thick. The late afternoon sunlight was soft, the air mild. At this time of year, the midday sun hinted of the furnace blast of summer to come, but the mornings and the evenings were still fresh, comfortable. Belinda would have the windows open. She would have his bourbon and water already poured, sitting in the freezer, and his paper would be folded on the table next to his chair in the den. It was nice to be waited on like that, but he knew he would not be able to get comfortable in that chair, no matter how many times he shifted around. Tonight more than ever.

He pulled into the driveway; everybody was home. All their cars were there, all looking hastily parked. Belinda's Cadillac was pulled only halfway into the three-car garage, and Dudley's Volkswagen was parked mostly on the lawn. Lacy's Ford was in the garage, the top put halfway back up, as though she had gotten that far and then decided to quit and go inside. He had told her that morning that it was too early in the year to be putting the top down. Mac muttered under his breath, thinking that none of them really appreciated what they had, except maybe Belinda. As he glided slowly into his slot in the garage, he bumped Dudley's archery set and knocked it over; the big bull's-eye target, packed tightly with pressed straw, rolled back out of the garage and onto the lawn, where it rolled in a circle for a moment and then fell flat. "Shit," Mac muttered.

If they had had to live in the kind of poverty he'd grown up in, they'd appreciate what they had. He thought about the succession of whitewashed frame houses with rusty screens and rotting stoops out in Shortleaf, a part of town that all the other young people in town made fun of. He remembered his first car, a 1931 Ford pickup that had been wrecked twice before he got it. *Jesus God.*

He dropped his coat onto the sofa in the living room, heading straight back to the kitchen. Melvinie, their cook, was standing at the stove, stirring peas in a boiler. Steam drifted lazily above the pot.

"Evenin, Mr. McClellon." She was frowning, but then she was always frowning, and had been for the fifteen years she had worked for them. Today her dark face made him think of Long, his eyes, steady and confident on him across the expanse of his desk that afternoon, as if he'd just treed Jesus! Melvinie was about sixty, as wide as she was tall. She wore a loose gray cotton dress, and she had a pair of his old corduroy bedroom slippers on her feet. She complained all the time about her corns.

"How you doin, Vi?" he said.

"All right," she said, "so far."

"What's for supper?" he said.

The kitchen was warm, stuffy, full of cooking smells, and he realized he was very hungry. "Ros beef," she said, almost a mutter.

He found his drink in the freezer. The heavy glass tumbler misted over when he took it out, and he sipped it. He loosened his tie and tugged it off. He heard Belinda calling him.

"Okay," he yelled. She was on the sunporch. He went back through the living room, dropping his tie onto the coat on the way. Belinda was sitting at a card table she had set up in the corner, writing on her little cream-colored folded notepaper with her initials engraved on it. She wrote notes inviting other women to play bridge, and she wrote notes thanking them for coming to play and for inviting her to their games. Women right there in town. Women whom she talked to on the phone practically every day. Mac thought it was wasted energy, but she thought it was important. "What?" he asked, standing looking around the bright room, the afternoon sunlight slanting and reflecting on the black-and-white tile floor.

"Lyman Wells called. Wants you to call him," she said.

His nerves, already frayed, just about snapped. "What the hell did he want?"

"I don't know, Mac. I didn't ask him. He just said to please return his call."

"When?"

"Anytime you can, I guess," she said. She had not stopped writing. She wore a white dress, fresh and pressed. He knew that she had played golf that day, at the country club. She bathed in the afternoon and dressed before supper. Except that she called it dinner. She was thin, getting too thin, he thought, and she had tiny wrinkles around the corners of her eyes and her mouth. She was almost flat-chested, and her hips were narrow and lean. Her blond hair was carefully styled and brushed. *Don't hold your breath, Mr. Fancy Pants Vanderbilt Nigger-Lover. It'll be a cold day in hell before I return any call of yours.*

He took a slug of his drink as he went back through the house to the den, finding the paper, *The Birmingham News*, folded next to his chair. He sat down and looked at the front page, his eyes skimming the headlines without really reading them. He took a long drink of his bourbon and water. *What the hell does that bastard want?* Mac knew he was somehow tied up with those civil wrongs workers, and it pained him to think about it. Lyman Wells was the perfect example of the kind of snob who kept Mac out of the Shady Grove Hunt Club. And here he was, acting like a nigger-lawyer. Mac sat the drink on the end table next to his chair and rubbed his temples. Then he picked it up and drained it. He would go and fix himself another.

.•~~~•.

Although they had been trying for years to teach Melvinie to cook the roast beef rare, it always came out overdone. ("She does it on purpose," Belinda said. "I know she does!") Dudley sat opposite Mac, and Lacy and her mother faced each other across the middle of the table. They sat eating in silence, their forks scraping on the plates.

"Well, did everybody have a good day, or what?" Mac said. He had had three stiff bourbons, and he felt more relaxed, his blood warmed. The tensions were pushed to the back of his mind.

Dudley frowned. He looked down at his plate, then back up at Mac. He had a row of dull red blemishes along the line of his jaw. He had them all the time now. Mac couldn't imagine where he'd gotten them from, unless it was chocolate. He and Belinda had never had a pimple in their lives. He watched Dudley pick up his fork and shovel mashed potatoes into his mouth; that's all he was eating, leaving the peas and meat on his plate.

"Eat your peas, Dudley," Mac said. "No wonder you've got—"

"For God's sake, Mac!" Belinda said.

They ate in silence for a few moments. *Foot in his mouth again. About the goddamn pimples. Well, somebody's got to tell him.*

Mac said, calmly, "I was gonna say no wonder you're not growin. You know, the football team and all."

"Yeah!" Dudley said sarcastically.

"Drop it, Dad," Lacy said, and Mac cut his eyes at her. He sat there, holding his fork. If he had used that tone with *his* father . . . He forked a piece of the roast beef into his mouth and chewed.

"Well?" he said. "What happened at school today?"

"Nothin," Lacy said.

He looked at his wife. She looked crisp and fresh.

"You play golf, honey?" he said.

"Yes. With Clara Witherspoon."

"Who won?" he said. He chuckled.

"We didn't keep score," Belinda said.

"You didn't keep score?" He frowned. "What's the point then?" Belinda sighed. "Just for the exercise," she said.

They ate for a while in stony silence. It seemed ridiculous to him that someone would play a game without keeping score. Finally, the quiet, the scraping of the forks on the plates, got on his nerves.

"Is somethin wrong?" he said. They all three looked up at him, their faces open, quizzical.

"What?" Dudley said. "What'd I do?"

"I just want to know if there is something wrong in this family," Mac said.

They all stared at him.

"Why no," Belinda said. He looked at the three sets of eyes, all fixed on his face, then pushed his plate away from him.

Forget it. Forget trying to have a decent, pleasant meal in this family.

"What's for dessert?" he asked.

"Lemon pie," Belinda said evenly. "Melvinie made it this morning."

"Hot dog," Dudley said, and Mac could see him groping with his foot for the button under the carpet beneath the table that would ring the bell back in the kitchen and signal Melvinie to bring in the dessert. He heard the bell ring, *ding-dong*, as though it were right there in the room with them. He thought it was silly to have the bell, but Belinda's mother had had one, and Belinda had to have one, too, though Mac would just as soon have yelled to Melvinie through the swinging door.

"I know some gossip," Lacy said.

"Lacy, I don't think—" Belinda said.

"No, really, it's about those civil rights workers, you know?"

A sudden alarm went off in Mac's head. He felt his stomach burn as he remembered Long's face that afternoon, the threat of the boycott. Long somehow had him by the short hairs, he thought, remembering Gulf International. A bubble of burning gas moved up his throat, and he swallowed.

"Well," Belinda said.

"You know the two white boys that'r livin with the Youngbloods? Well—"

"Shhhhhh," Belinda said, her finger at her lips, as Melvinie came through the door with the pie. It was already sliced into pieces, and she put it in front of Belinda. They all sat there, quietly watching her get four plates from the sideboard, along with the wide silver cake knife,

and put them on the table. There was no sound but Melvinie's bus-
tling, the snuffling of the slippers on the carpet, until she went back
into the kitchen, and the door swung to behind her with a swish.
Belinda started serving the pie onto the plates. Her thin hand arched
delicately on the gleaming silver knife.

"Go on," she said, handing Lacy the first plate.

"Anyway," Lacy said, spooning the pie into her mouth.

"Don't talk with your mouth full," Belinda interrupted.

"Anyway," Lacy went on, chewing, "you know the blond one? He's
right good-lookin. Paul Siegel is his name. Anyhow, Ellen Brewster's
goin out with him."

Mac had started on his pie, but now he looked up quickly from his
plate, not sure he had heard right. Belinda sat in stunned silence,
gaping at Lacy, her mouth hanging open.

"Say what?" Mac said. A sudden image of a flaming cross jumped
into Mac's mind. He shook his head .

Lacy looked from him to her mother. Her eyes darted to the tabletop
as she squirmed in her seat. She looked guilty, sheepish. "Did I hear
you right?" Mac demanded. Lacy was already tan from sunbathing in
the backyard on weekends, but now he thought he could see deeper
color creeping up her long, lean neck.

"Well, yeah," she said, petulantly. "Ellen's goin out with that boy."

"How do you know that?" Belinda said.

"Because she told me," Lacy said. "And I saw em. I saw em walkin
along the riverbank. And she asked me . . . she asked me . . ."

"What? What did she ask you?" Belinda said. Her eyes were narrow,
and she was sitting erect, stiff in her chair.

"If she could use my car sometime, maybe," Lacy said. She looked
up. Her eyes were clouded, shifty.

"Are you makin this up, Lacy?" Mac said. He was surprised, curious. This was a complication he had not foreseen.

"No! Cross my heart!"

"Well," Belinda said. Her lips made a straight, thin line across her
face. Mac put his fork down. He could not believe what he was
hearing. *The little Brewster girl? Who used to hang out over here
sometimes? O. B. Brewster's daughter?*

"Wow," Dudley said.

"Dudley, you are excused," Belinda said, snapping.

"But—"

"Leave the table, please, Dudley," she said. "Now. This doesn't
concern you."

Dudley stood up, scowling. He had finished his pie, and he took another piece, defiantly, with broad gestures, but nobody said anything. He went out toward the front of the house, grumbling, holding the slice of pie in his hand; Mac thought one of the words he heard him say was "shit."

"Dudley!" he said, but the boy was gone.

They sat there for a few moments. The room was quiet. Lacy looked up, her eyes darting from one to the other. Then she looked back down at her plate. Her shoulders were slumped, her neck bent.

"Does her mother know about this?" Belinda said.

Lacy said nothing. Mac could see the color in her neck. His mind wandered to O.B. Mac found himself feeling sorry for the man.

"Lacy! Does Martha Brewster know about this?" Belinda replied sharply.

"No," Lacy said, barely above a whisper.

"She's doing this behind her parents' backs then?"

"Yes," Lacy whispered.

"Little Ellen Brewster?" He shook his head, incredulously, still not fully taking it in. It seemed to him that this amounted to the next-worst thing to hearing that your daughter was going out with a nigger. Poor old O.B. This might take some of the gumption out of him. Poor, poor bastard.

"I might have known!" Belinda snapped, looking at Mac, her eyes flashing darkly. "Go to your room, Lacy," she said. Lacy just sat there, her shoulders slumped. "You are excused, young lady," she said.

Mac watched Lacy stand up, tall, taller than her mother; she wore khaki Bermuda shorts and a green blouse. Her long legs flopped awkwardly as she left the dining room. He heard her footsteps on the stairs, going upward, toward her room.

Mac picked up his fork. He doodled aimlessly with the pie remaining on his plate. Belinda sat staring at the center of the table, her hands folded in her lap on the large linen napkin. He sneaked a couple of looks at her.

After what seemed to him minutes and minutes of silence, she said, "You've got to tell them."

"Say what?"

"Inform them. Tell O.B. and Martha." She looked at him. Her eyes seemed more relaxed now.

"Me?" he said. "*Me* tell em?"

"Don't you have any concern for them? They're old friends, after all."

"Yeah, but . . ." He sat there. The bourbon had worn off, leaving him feeling weary. He could not bear the thought of being the one to tell O.B. what his daughter was up to. He had thought he would spend the evening dozing in front of the television. "Tomorrow then—"

"No, Mac," she said. "You better tell em tonight." She picked up the napkin and placed it carefully beside her plate. She looked at him, her eyes sparkling, a barely restrained smile on her thin lips. *She's enjoying this* Mac thought, shocked. "Wouldn't *you* want to be told something like that?" she pressed him. "Immediately?"

"I guess so," he admitted. God! In one sense it served O.B. right. He wouldn't use his influence, tell his buddy Long to back off, and now look at what had happened. Maybe knowing this would make O.B. finally take the stand he needed to take. Mac thought of Carleton Byrd, of Gulf International, and he sighed. The base of his neck ached dully. His supper felt sour in his stomach. He watched his wife look away, then stand, smoothing her dress, her bracelets tinkling like tiny wind chimes on her thin arms.

***

Mac parked in front of O.B.'s little brick house on Commissioners Street, behind Martha Brewster's old Ford with the dented fender. He remembered hearing how she'd backed into a post in the A & P parking lot; some of the girls at the bank had said that she was drinking when she did it. He sat there for a moment, after he shut off his lights, looking at the house. He knew that it was bigger than it looked from the street; the front was only two rooms wide, half of the front a brick screen porch with a wide, curving concrete arch and a three-step cement stoop. Mac remembered the interior as being long, with a hallway and several rooms on each side, stacked like a shotgun house. Funny he remembered so much. He had not been here in years. He got out, slamming the sturdy door of the Buick, and went up the cracked sidewalk, dead brown grass cramming the crevices.

He couldn't understand a man settling for as little as this, he thought, looking around. O.B. had always seemed to be one step ahead of him when they were growing up. They had never been close friends, but it had sometimes seemed that way because they always seemed to be the two competing for the recognition, the popularity, and the honors always seemed to come effortlessly to O.B. Whereas he, Mac, had had to struggle for everything he got. He remembered youth baseball, when he and the others were laboring just to learn to hit and throw, and it was like O.B. had been born being good at it. And later, with the girls. Mac had envied O.B., the way the girls flocked around him. The ease with which he grabbed the head cheerleader. A girl Mac had had designs on, too. And O.B. signing that pro contract, even playing in the majors. The way the town looked up to him. He *was* a hero, though he seemed to be too dense to know it, to take advantage of it. He came from pure white trash, and look how high he had managed to climb. And now look at him. O.B. was a puzzle to him. Well, this news ought to take him down another notch, but he immediately felt guilty for thinking that way.

He knocked on the door, and after a moment, heard movement in the living room. The front door opened a few inches. Martha Brewster stood there, holding a yellow bathrobe together at her throat. She just looked at him, her eyes vague, opaque.

"Is O.B. here, Martha?" he said.

"Yeah," she said. She stepped back, opening the door wider. He stood there uneasily, feeling self-conscious. Her thick dark hair was fluffed out, as though she had just brushed it. Whenever he saw her now, he could see the suggestion of the high school beauty she once had been. He looked past her into the room, taking a tentative step inside. The living room was crowded with furniture, newspapers cluttering the sofa against the wall. He thought he got a whiff of bourbon, but that could have been left from his own before-supper drinks.

"Let me go get him," she said, backing toward the hallway. "He's fixin supper."

Jesus. It was after eight o'clock. What kinda man fixed supper in his own house that late?

After she had gone into the hallway, he moved some newspapers and sat down on the sofa, studying the cramped room. A black-and-white television set in a dark wooden cabinet sat in the corner, playing, its sound off; something was wrong with the horizontal hold, and the picture rolled over and over. He watched it. It seemed to stick for a few seconds every fifth roll. A western was on. It looked like *The Rifleman.* He and his family had had a color set for almost a year now, one of the first in town. Everybody said that once you watched color, there was no going back to black-and-white. Mac agreed, watching the pale picture stick and roll.

O.B. came into the room then, wiping his hands on a dish towel. He wore an old white dress shirt, tucked crookedly into his baggy khaki pants, both the shirt and the pants streaked with old grease stains, faint from washing. Mac felt suddenly like an intruder, like an outsider who had happened on a family at a time of grief. O.B. was looking at him questioningly, his eyes wide.

"Mac," he said, nodding. "Anything the matter?"

"Oh, no," Mac said, and then realized that something was very much the matter, that that was why he was here. "I mean . . . well, yeah. Sit down, O.B."

"What is it, Mac? Somethin's happened to Ellen."

"Well. Is she here?" He felt nervous, suddenly frightened at what O.B. might do when he found out.

"No," O.B. said. There was a silence, O.B. looking at him. "She's over at Julie Deaver's house. Studyin. Why? What the hell is it, Mac?"

"Would you mind turnin that off?" Mac gestured toward the flopping television. "The thing's givin me a headache, flippin over like that." He was stalling for time.

"Okay," O.B. said. He switched off the set and then sat down in a chair across from Mac, folding the dish towel and placing it on the edge of the coffee table between them. Mac felt unsure about what to say. He had actually been more surprised than horrified at Lacy's news, and he had not felt nearly so indignant as Belinda had. Now he felt meddlesome.

"Is this about the White Citizens Council?" O.B. said.

"The *Citizens* Council," he said, "not *White*. No. It's not." The literature and brochures that they'd sent Mac had said to correct that every time he heard it. He was tired of doing it. Besides, he didn't see why it couldn't just be "White," for all he cared. Might as well be honest about it. "No, actually," he said. "I tell ya, O.B., Belinda and me are not ones to meddle in other folks' affairs, you know? But we felt like you and Martha ought to know."

O.B. continued to stare at him. "Know what?" he said.

"Well," Mac said. He coughed, shifting on the couch, feeling like a complete fool. God, he resented Belinda's making him come over here on this errand!

"Know what, goddammit?" O.B. said.

"Well," he said, "Lacy just happened to mention, while we were eatin supper, just let it slip out . . . well, that Ellen was goin out with one of those young men, college boys, you know, from the North that'r down here." He shook his head. "They call theirselves civil rights workers. Civil wrongs would be more like it."

"Ellen?" O.B. said.

"Yeah." He looked at the coffee table. The words tumbled out of his mouth. "Paul Siegel is his name. He's a Jew. I've met him, of course. Long, your buddy the nigger preacher, introduced him to me." *Yeah. His buddy.* He thought of Long, in his office that afternoon, the look in his eyes. The boycott. O.B. either couldn't or wouldn't talk him out

of it. But this was not the time to mention *that*. "Now I tell you, O.B.,
I couldn't believe it, and I had my doubts, but Lacy swears it's the
truth. She said that y'all didn't know anything about it. And Belinda
said that . . . well, us bein old friends and all, I ought to come over
here and tell you about it. I mean, if it was Lacy, God forbid, I'd sure
as hell want to know. I can tell you that."

Not wanting to look at O.B., he stared at the surface of the coffee
table, which was covered with a layer of glass, underneath which were
family snapshots. He saw several of Ellen and of O.B., and among the
yellowed ones, with black-and-white checked borders, was one of a
lady in an old-fashioned bathing suit, standing in front of what looked
like a model T. "You understand why I'm here, I hope," he forced
himself to continue, "I tell you, slippin around like that is serious
business. The thing to do is nip it in the bud. Let her know what's
what." He stopped. O.B. seemed to be staring at the blank, cold
television screen. "I don't mean to tell you how to raise your daughter,
O.B. Ha! It sounded like it, didn't it?" He felt like a total fool.

"You know this for a fact? This is not just some rumor shit?" O.B.'s
voice was firm, steady.

"Yeah. I don't think it's a rumor. Lacy—"

"How long? How long this been goin on?" O.B. said.

"Well now, I don't know . . . how long, or anything like that. I
mean, they ain't been here but two, three months. I don't know." He
looked at the coffee table, at the woman in front of the Model T. She
looked vaguely familiar to him. "I don't know," he said, again, patting
his knees. "Well . . ." he said, sighing heavily. He wanted to get out
of here, but he didn't feel that he could just up and leave so quickly
after dropping such a bomb on his old friend. He tried to think of
something to say. He felt a sense of vague unease, as though this might
have something to do with Gulf International and his plans, but that
was ridiculous. It was just that crazy Eldon Long, bringing those young
boys in here. He stood up. O.B. was just sitting quietly. Mac felt sorry
for him, but almost angry at him at the same time. Why didn't he say
something?

"I . . . I reckon I better go," Mac said, edging toward the door.

"All right," O.B. said.

He stood there in the doorway for a few seconds, not knowing what
he expected. Did he want O.B. to say "Thank you" or what? He stood
there awkwardly, nodding his head. There was a sense of incompletion
about all this, as though it were the beginning of something too complex for him to take in. He kept thinking of Long's eyes, steady on him,
threatening him with a confidence he'd never seen in a nigger before,

and he thought of Carleton Byrd and his condescending, patronizing smile, holding his Marlboro as though it were delicate and breakable, looking at him with pale eyes as though he could see into his very soul and knew every secret he had.

"I'll say good night," Mac said.

"Good night," O.B. said.

·~·~·~·

O.B. sat in the darkened living room. He looked at his watch, a Timex waterproof with luminous hands that Ellen had given him for Christmas: It showed ten-fifteen. He knew that she would be home soon. She was never out past ten-thirty on a school night, rarely past ten. He would have to confront her. He dreaded it. He had always hated disciplining her.

"She's with that goddamn Jew," Martha had said, crying, after Mac had left. She had listened to everything from the hallway.

"How do you know?" O.B. had said.

"She just is, she just is," she'd insisted. She had stood fidgeting, as though her hands had minds of their own, breathing heavily.

She started back toward the kitchen, and he had said, sharply, "Where you goin, Martha?"

She had not answered, and he had walked back there and found her tossing back a shot, using a heavy glass jigger that she used for that purpose. She poured another. She looked at him, her eyes swimming, her body swaying slightly. Then she tossed it back, coughing and squinting her eyes, her hands holding the edge of the kitchen counter. He watched her numbly.

"I'm goin to bed," she murmured. "I need my sleep. Goddam."

She turned and went out of the room. He knew that she would fall across the bed and be asleep immediately. He heard her bump the wall in the hallway, heard the door to their bedroom rattle.

Now he sat in the living room, one lamp burning low in the corner, waiting for his daughter. He thought about Martha, snoring on the bed, her face pressed against the pillow, her mouth open. She had gone only two weeks without taking a drink before this last time; on the wagon for only two weeks. During this last drinking jag, she had taken to wetting the bed occasionally, something that she had done once before. He remembered being awakened by the warm, almost hot liquid, the smell harsh and ammoniac, practically making him gag, and he would get up, leaving her there, stripping off his pajamas and leaving them on the floor, padding quietly through the dark house to the front bedroom to sleep alone in the old wooden poster bed that she had bought at an estate auction. They had never mentioned it when it happened; by the time he came home the next afternoon for his midday meal, the sheets would be washed and hanging on the line in the chicken yard out back, with fresh sheets on the bed, everything far more tidy than it would be on normal days when nothing had happened. This time, since he was already sleeping in the front room, she had let it go for several days until he smelled it. He had brought it up, and she had shamefacedly changed the sheets and washed them.

He looked at his watch. Ten-seventeen.

He stretched his long legs out in front of him, his old baseball knee aching dully. He was tired, and when he was tired, his knee stiffened, giving him pain as though to remind him of his shortened, aborted career. He'd come to think of it as a sign from God, a badge that he would be required to wear as he aged and moved further and further away from those days. He remembered the day he'd cracked the knee-cap, tearing the ligaments, as vividly as though it had only just happened. There'd been the smell of the grass, and the dust on the base path, the feel of the coarse wool uniform damp and pungent with his own sweat. A hot July afternoon, in Yankee Stadium. Yankee Stadium! The one he'd heard about on the radio, that lived in legends. He remembered how a routine slide into third base became, somehow, awkward; how, he didn't know although he had gone over it in detail, in his mind, thousands of times over the years. Perhaps it had been a lapse in concentration, something in the half-empty stands that caught his eye; or maybe he'd become distracted worrying about the score (which was 6 to 3, in favor of the Yankees, against the White Sox, in the eighth inning. Sure, they could have used an insurance run, but they were not desperate for it). Whatever it was, it had caused him to hit the red dirt just slightly off, so that his knee buckled under him, his hip hitting not quite flat enough, and he had felt the sharp, wrenching pain and gritted his teeth, hearing the umpire: "SARRRRFE!" He had been slow before that, but not too slow for a catcher, and he had told himself he could still do it, even slowed down a little more. He had played the entire next season in the minors, in rehabilitation, hitting .289 and catching every day for the Mobile Bears, but in constant pain, soaking his knee in diathermy for hours, and the next year he had had to move aside for a boy named Bruce Sanderson, a youngster. They let him catch front ends of doubleheaders, and night games before day games, and play some first base, and he had known the handwriting on the wall when he saw it.

His manager in Double A, in Mobile, a grizzled old-timer named

Gerald Reed, who had been a shortstop with the Yankees back in the late twenties, had told him he could probably play on with a minor-league contract for years, but O.B. had said no. He could not put Martha back through that, the dark apartments and the long absences. She had been bitterly disappointed, but they had had no choice, no place else to go. They had come home to Hammond. *If I had had the guts, maybe we could have gone somewhere else. I failed her.* She never got over it. *I failed everybody, because I had the chance, and I didn't make it.*

The *Hammond Times* had interviewed him and done a story on him when he had signed, and the paper interviewed him and did a story on him when he came home. Since then, he had been asked to speak to every Rotary and Kiwanis club and every high school athletic banquet in West Central Alabama, and he had forced himself to accept some of the invitations, and the talks had been agony for him; he had felt tongue-tied and dull, but they always told him he was wonderful. Especially the mothers at the athletic banquets. He did not believe it. On those occasions, young boys always asked him for his autograph, and that embarrassed him. He would look shyly at their parents, who would beam back at him and sometimes wink. After Pearl Harbor, when the United States declared war, he was found to be 4-F because of the knee, and he had spent the war in civil defense, patrolling the streets during the mock air raids staged by planes from Craig Field over at Selma. He had coached some American Legion ball for a while and helped out some at the high school, but he had not enjoyed it; his heart was not in it. Later, when Little League, and then Babe Ruth League, came to Hammond, they had asked him to head it up. Begged him to, practically. But he had pleaded too little time, knowing he couldn't bear being that close to the sounds of the bats, the smell of the grass. He had preferred, up to now, to just dream, to deal with it in memory. He took some pleasure when little boys still pointed him out to each other, and a team at each level bore the label BREWSTER TRACTOR on the backs of their uniforms. He went out occasionally to watch them play, but up until now he had refused to coach them. Until this spring. And now it looked as though things were becoming so hopelessly complicated he would be denied even that pleasure, that release.

The front door opened, and Ellen came in, holding a couple of schoolbooks and a ring notebook over her chest, walking gingerly, being careful not to make any noise. She closed the door gently, twisting the key in the lock. She turned around, dropped the books on the sofa, looked at the lamp in the corner. She froze for an instant.

"Daddy?" she said. "Oh. I didn't see you there. You still up?" He didn't answer. "What are you doin sittin in the dark?"

"Sit down," he said. "I want to talk to you." His tone was harsher than he meant for it to be, but the whole situation filled him with dread, and so hurt him to the quick that he could barely stand to think about it.

She didn't say anything, standing still, poised as though arrested in midmotion. Her face was in shadow, and he couldn't see her eyes. Then she sat on the edge of the sofa. He got up and turned up the lamp, then sat back down and looked at her. She smiled tentatively. He was very tired, and he was having trouble sorting out his feelings. All he could think of was how beautiful she was, with her dark hair pulled back from her face, her sky-blue eyes matching the blue sweater draped over her shoulders, the arms hanging loose and limp, the sweater fastened with a gold clasp at the base of her neck. Her lips were still the lips of the child, and yet ripe, like a woman's, and her legs were getting longer, more shapely. She had on no makeup, and her legs were bare, her feet plunged into scuffed penny loafers without socks. She looked at him expectantly, her face as open as a child's, but also with what he could see, could recognize, was just a hint, just a tiny suggestion, of a woman's subterfuge. He had seen it so often on her mother's face and on the faces of other women. It was a look that was infuriating, a self-satisfied, silent admission of something that women seemed to think he somehow needed, but that he did not, in reality, care to know. But now he *did* want to know. He wanted to know her secret, to take that secret away from her, wipe it roughly from her being. She would not give herself to some man she hardly even knew, some man distant from him; she would not leave him, even in spirit. She was his daughter.

"Have you been seeing a boy behind our backs?" he said.

She stared at him, her smile fading. "Seeing?"

"Seeing, dating, whatever you call it," he pressured her, his voice almost hoarse. "Goin out with him. You know what I mean. Just tell me yes or no."

She sat back on the sofa, crossing her legs. She was trying to look casual, but he could see the tenseness in her body. She seemed frightened, and he thought her face had paled.

"Dating, no," she said. "Seeing, maybe yes."

"Whattaya mean, maybe? Don't lie to me, Ellen."

"I'm not lying to you! I'm not." She took a deep breath. "You couldn't call it datin." She sat looking at him. He thought he could see her lips tremble. "Who told you about it?" she said. Her voice was high, barely controlled, and her clenched lips shook, barely perceptibly.

The backs of his eyes stung with tears of frustrated anger. The worst thing was the violation of trust. They had always been good friends, together through the worst times. He cared less about what she had done than that she had done it behind his back. "What have you been up to?" he pleaded. "You might as well tell me."

"Daddy . . ." she said. He waited. She looked away, then back at him. "I . . ."

"What?" he said.

"I . . . I love him," she said softly.

"*What?* Who? Don't be silly! Love who?" The sadness lightened. This could be handled. He felt in control, reasonably certain now that this was schoolgirl business, that she would make a 180-degree change by morning. "Tell me what's happened, Ellen," he said. She didn't answer him, didn't move.

"Were you with him tonight?" he said.

"No," she said.

"You were studying? Where?"

"Julie's," she said, softly.

"Are you lying?"

"Daddy! No!"

The anger that he had felt was giving way to distress, to an intense, cold fear of losing her. He had known it would happen someday, but not like this! He couldn't lose her like this! "How long have you been seein this boy?"

"Just . . . a few times." She looked at him, her eyes wide and full of tears now. "Just to talk."

"To talk? What the hell do you talk about?" He knew that his anger and fear were in his voice; he fought to control it.

"Just . . . things."

"Things! Goddammit, Ellen," he said. "I won't have you doin that, I won't have it, do you hear me?"

"Yessir," she said. She looked at the rug, then she looked up at him, her eyes flashing. "I *hear* you," she said. They stared at one another.

He wanted to punish her, restrict her in some way. He didn't know what to say next, was afraid of what he might say. She was sniffling, but her eyes remained steady on him as she sat straight, her head up.

"Those boys have no business here," he said. "They're troublemakers. Here today, gone tomorrow. Listen to what I'm tellin you."

"Yessir."

"Ellen . . ." He stopped. "You're so young, Ellen. So goddam young." He narrowed his eyes, squinting at her, trying to see her clearly. She was so like her mother had once been, even if she did not know it, would never have guessed it, and would have been insulted if he had told her. He wanted her to remain the way she was now. He did not want what happened to Martha to happen to Ellen; he could recall so clearly Martha's freshness, her beautiful energy as a cheerleader. He did not want what happened to everybody to happen to Ellen. He wanted her to remain innocent and happy. He wanted to protect her, from herself, from the world.

"Nothing's happened, if that's what you mean," she said.

"I don't want to know that," he said quickly. "I can't stand to hear about that. Just . . . stay away from him. From now on."

"Daddy, I . . ."

"I forbid you to ever see him again, Ellen. I mean it."

"But I . . ."

"You don't know what love is, Ellen," he said. "You're too young. You don't *love* this boy. Now I don't want to hear any more about it." That would settle it. He knew that she would not defy a direct command like that. He could still see the pain and desperation in her eyes but would handle that later, after the boy was gone, after all this was settled down. Time would pass.

"How can you say that?" she said, her voice trembling.

"I'm older than you are, Ellen. I've been around a long time. I *know* what love is." An almost overwhelming sadness came over him. He felt old and tired. His mouth was dry, and his eyes were stinging faintly again. He swallowed, blinking back the tears, straining to see her. He would not lose her, he thought. *I will not lose you.*

"Go to bed now," he said. "School tomorrow."

"Daddy . . ."

He glanced at her.

"I love you, Daddy," she said. She stood up, looking almost defiant.

"I love you, too, punkin," he said.

He watched her go out of the room, her shoulders rounded now, her back looking narrow and small. She was holding herself as erect as she could; he knew that she had to salvage some pride. His knee pained him, aching and stiff. He filled his lungs with air and let it out slowly, a long, pensive sigh. Eventually, this would be forgotten; it would be history. He felt exhausted, drained. He thought of Martha, sound asleep, and of the raw, sickening smell of liquor on her breath. He would force her to go to the Alcoholics Anonymous meeting; he would take her to the one in Tuscaloosa if he had to. He thought of Ellen again, going to bed, and his heart ached as he pictured the ratty old teddy bear Talky that she still slept with. He remembered the day he had taken her into V. J. Elmore's, when she was just three, and had let her pick it out. She had stood there, looking solemnly and seriously at all the stuffed animals, until she had finally chosen a plump little brown bear with a twisted, off-center face and a nose that didn't seem to go with the rest of him, hugging the bear to her thin chest. He had asked her why that one. "This one needs takin care of," she had said.

He felt the tears again, thinking of her as a child, certain that he had saved her.

Ellen woke up with the first orange sunlight. Her window was open several inches, and a cold, morning breeze drifted across the bed. The air was fresh, like spring water, and she could hear birds chattering in the fig tree in the backyard as she snuggled under the blanket, closing her eyes against the early light. Her first thought of the day was, as usual, of Paul, a comforting thought that was abruptly replaced by the sudden, shattering memory of last night, with her father. She squinted her eyes tightly, her teeth biting the knuckle of her clenched fist as the images of the scene washed over her, draining her of warmth, making her almost physically ill. She had felt unclean, caught in a lie, ashamed, and yet she had been proud, too, proud that she had acted on her own, that she had done nothing with Paul to be ashamed of. She *knew* him, and he was good and honest and idealistic, all the things she wanted to be, all the things that she knew that she was. She had often lain in the bed, early on the spring mornings, imagining what it would be like to go back North with him, to be his lover, to live in an apartment near a college. She could visualize the long line of his lean neck, his shoulders, his narrow hips in the tight jeans. What would it be like? To make love to him. To marry him. He could take her away, spirit her to excitement and to intellectual worlds of books and literature. He could love her and protect her. She had known, of course, that she was wrong to see him, to go for walks with him, to sit on the river bluff for so long, talking—wrong because she was keeping it from her parents, especially her father, who would not understand. She had known he would be angry, had known that he would react exactly as he had. And she had known all along that they were bound to find out, that something like this, no matter how innocent it was, could not be kept secret in Hammond for very long. So she had not really worried about it, knowing that they would discover it sooner or later, and she would deal with that when the time came. And now it was here.

The sense of dread stayed with her all day, was present as she walked home from school that afternoon. The day had been agony. All of her classes, except maybe English, were boring. It seemed to her that most of her classmates had already decided that school was over, that graduation was only a formality now, and that same attitude seemed to have infested most of her teachers. Only Mr. Leach pressed them. They were reading poems about spring, poems that Mr. Leach brought in and read to them, while the boys snickered behind their hands, and the girls looked vacant and restless. This morning he had read them one by a poet named e. e. cummings, called "in just." It was about a little goat-footed balloon man. Mr. Leach had told them that the little man was Pan, a Greek god, and many in the class had groaned. Ellen had her purple mimeographed copy of the poem in her notebook; she planned to show it to Paul.

Paul. She didn't know if she dared even think about him, and in the next moment knew that she had to see him again. She would work something out. She would just have to talk with her parents. She cringed, her throat dry, remembering how she had told her father that she loved Paul, and then tried not to think about her parents. She went back over her day in her mind. Lacy, who had had on a green plaid skirt, like a kilt, fastened with an oversized brass safety pin at the side, had avoided her all day, looking at her strangely every time their paths crossed, but Ellen had acted as though everything were normal. Many of her classmates avoided her now, anyway. They talked about her behind her back, she knew, and some made jokes to her face. "Nigger-lover," they called her. And worse. One boy, Dickson Smith, had sauntered up to her and said, drawling it out, his body slouched obscenely to the side, "You screw who? Up yore gi-gi with a Rotor-Rooter, Yankee's cunt." He had grinned at her, running his tongue over his lips. She had shuddered with revulsion.

Ellen walked along in the warm afternoon sunlight, carrying her sweater. She wondered if her mother was at home. *I might as well get it over with.*

Her mother's black Ford was parked at the curb. Ellen went up the sidewalk, through the screen door. The front door was unlocked, and she opened it, tentatively, cautiously, as though there were a vicious dog on the other side. The house was quiet. She smelled cigarette smoke. She dropped her sweater on the sofa and went down the hall toward the kitchen, pausing in the kitchen door. Her mother sat at the Formica-topped kitchen table, smoking a long, thin cigarette. A package of Pall Malls lay on the table, next to a large white ashtray shaped like a seashell. Written on it, in bright sea-green letters, was FORT WALTON BEACH, FLORIDA, HEART OF THE MIRACLE STRIP.

"You started back smokin again?" Ellen asked.

"What of it?" her mother said. She was dressed at least, and her hair was brushed, but it stuck out wildly around her head. She wore a wrinkled pink cotton blouse, blue jeans that buttoned at the side, and pink terry-cloth bedroom slippers. She had put on too much makeup for afternoon; it was as though she thought she could hide her face, when all she did was highlight it, emphasize the watery, pain-filled eyes and the wrinkles at the corners of her mouth. Her face was getting broader, her features less distinct. "I *like* to smoke," she said.

"You smoke when you drink," Ellen said.

Her mother took a long drag. As she blew the smoke out, she picked bits of tobacco from the tip of her tongue with the fingers that held the cigarette. Her fingernails were long and painted tomato red. She stared at Ellen through the cloud of gray smoke.

"It's no wonder I drink," she said. "I have to drink."

"No, Mama—" Ellen started.

"Shut up! Don't you talk back to me!"

Ellen looked over toward the cabinet where the whiskey was usually kept. Her mother's heavy shot glass sat there; Ellen knew it would smell strongly of raw alcohol. She knew there would be a fifth of whiskey in the cabinet, and she and her father both knew that there would be other bottles, hidden around the house, in the attic and in drawers and closets. Ellen had once found one hidden behind the row of book-club books that her mother had collected years ago, and another time she had found one behind a burlap croker sack out in the coal bin. Her mother would forget where she hid them, and Ellen would find them during her mother's sober periods; the sight of them was terrifying to Ellen because she could never know whether or not they signaled a new drinking binge.

She sat down at the table, across from her mother. The room was stuffy, warm, and the air was stale.

"Where have you been?" her mother said.

"School, where do you think?" Ellen could not keep the sarcasm out of her voice, but she didn't want to provoke her mother.

"I don't know. Maybe you played hookey. With some Jewboy. How do I know?"

"Mama, I'd rather not talk about this when you're drinkin," Ellen said.

"I haven't been drinkin! What makes you think I've been drinkin?"

"I just know, that's all," Ellen said. "I don't care."

"You 'don't care'! Well, then, since you don't care, I'm gonna have a drink." She looked at her watch. "It's almost five o'clock in Atlanta," she chuckled, her laugh dry and mirthless. She looked at Ellen, and the stiff smile faded from her face as she staggered over to the cabinet to get a glass and fill it with ice cubes that she kept in a bowl in the freezing compartment of the refrigerator. She got out a bottle of bourbon and poured it over the ice, then added a splash of water from the faucet over the sink. "Now then," she said, sitting back down at the table.

Ellen's throat felt tight. The dread was back stronger than ever, welling inside her.

"Now then," her mother repeated. "You and I are gonna have a little talk about this boy. This Jew. What's his name?"

"Mama, I—"

"*What's his name?*"

"*Paul!*" she didn't want to fight with her mother. "His name is Paul," she said more calmly.

"Paul what," her mother said.

"Siegel," Ellen said. "I don't want to talk about this. Daddy—"

"I'm a woman, Ellen," she said. "I know what you're up to. Don't think I don't."

"What do you mean?" Ellen said.

"I mean, I know you've been . . . all the way with this boy."

"No, Mama—"

"Sleepin with him, whatever you call it now. I can tell. I can tell by lookin at you. You have the look of a whore about you—"

"Mama!" The word had hit her in the face like cold water. Her own mother! She felt indignant, righteous, angry. "You're wrong!" she said. "Oh, boy, are you ever wrong!" Her voice was quivering.

"Don't lie about it! Everybody in town knows all about it. Ellen Brewster, a slut. I didn't raise you that way, Ellen, I didn't—"

"You're drunk, Mama!" She threw the word at her, like an insult. "You don't know what you're sayin. I told Daddy—"

"I don't give a damn what you told your daddy! You can twist him around your little finger! I've watched it, I've watched it for years: 'Daddy's little girl!' It sickens my stomach!"

"Mama, how can you say that?" She could feel herself beginning to cry, but she gripped her fists in her lap, willing herself not to. She did not know how much of what her mother had said was the whiskey talking, but she still felt hurt and angry, deeply wounded that her mother, even if drunk, would say such things to her.

"How could you do this to me, Ellen?" Her mother's voice cracked then, her face withering up like a piece of rotting fruit. Ellen could see tears standing in her eyes, beginning to spill over onto her cheeks. "It's an affront to me! I know you're doin it just to get at me. You and your daddy both want to ruin me in this town. I grew up here, Ellen, but I wanted to leave, too. But we had to come home! Now, I have friends here. I've made a life here. Your daddy has no ambition, he doesn't care." She stopped, gulping the drink, her eyes going vague. "We could be society. But he won't. He failed! Failed! He couldn't make it in baseball, so he came crawling home—"

"He got hurt!" Ellen said.

"Yes, he got hurt! Hurt! Hurt! Hurt! He doesn't care anything about anything but that goddam shop! Certainly not me! And now you! How could you do it?"

"Paul's nice!" Ellen blurted. "He's a decent human bein! He cares about people, and things, and . . . and . . . You don't know! You don't know him!" She felt the words tumbling out on top of each other. "He doesn't have to be down here—"

"No! You're right. He's got no business down here! He's a Jew troublemaker. They're all over the place now, Ellen! Have some sense about you, for God's sake!"

"I do," Ellen almost screamed. "I do have sense! I . . ." She caught herself and stopped.

"You *what?*" her mother said. The room was silent. "You what, Ellen?"

"I *believe* in what he's doin," she said.

Her mother tossed her head, her mouth turned down in a sneer. "You don't understand it. What do you know about it? It's communist, Ellen, and you don't even know it. It's evil. You don't believe in anything but the hormones runnin wild in your body. It's nothin but lust! Don't tell me! Don't try to cover up lust with some talk about *believin!* There's only one kind of believin, and that's in God!"

Ellen stood up.

"Sit down! Sit down, young lady," her mother said.

"No," Ellen said.

"I said *sit down!* And I mean it!"

"No!" Ellen said. "I won't! I won't sit here and have you say these things to me. You . . . you're drunk, and mean! You make me hate you!" Ellen's legs were trembling, and for a moment she felt dizzy, light-headed.

"I know you hate me, Ellen," her mother said. "But I don't *make* you hate me." Her voice was leaden, weary. "You hate me because you are a little bitch. You are just like your father. You don't know about your father. Someday you will. Someday you'll know the truth about him."

"I *know* the truth about him! Don't say anything about my daddy!"

"The truth!" Her mother chuckled, shaking her head. "I could tell you. Someday I will!"

"Shut up! You don't know anything! You old hag!" Ellen's throat hurt from the screaming. She wiped her nose with the back of her hand. She was shaking, panicked. She felt closed in, trapped. She turned to leave.

"Where are you goin?!?" her mother said, quickly, desperately.

"Out!" Ellen said. She walked through the door and up the hallway toward the front of the house, hearing her mother calling her name, a weak and mournful, plaintive sound. The screen door slammed to behind her, and she was outside, in the sunlight, on the front sidewalk. She blinked her brimming, burning eyes in the brightness, feeling the warmth of the afternoon sun on her bare arms. She walked deliberately down the sidewalk, turning north, toward the river, toward Cedar Street, which cut across the edge of Frogbottom, intersecting with Maple, where the Youngblood house and Paul waited for her.

.~.~.~.

She stood on the dim porch that was shaded by the giant magnolia tree. There was a metal pull-bell handle next to the door, and she pulled it, listening, but she heard no sound from back in the house. She knocked on the heavy door, feeling shy and apprehensive. The walk had calmed her some, but the confrontation with her mother had exhausted her, and her arm trembled slightly as she raised it to knock. She heard stirring inside, and, after a few seconds, the door was pulled open. Carl Youngblood stood there, looking down at her. She was startled, by his size and by his appearance. His dark black hair was bushy and curly, and his black beard grew down to the middle of his massive chest. A gold earring dangled from his left ear, a circle with some kind of strange symbol inside. She found herself staring at the earring.

"Yes?" he said, his voice deep and rumbling, making her jump, until she saw he was smiling at her.

"I . . . I came to see Paul," she said.

"Come on in," the man said. He opened the door wider. "He ain't here but ought to be back soon." He laughed, his laughter booming and echoing in the wide, empty, high-ceilinged hallway. "It's almost suppertime, so he'll be here soon. Never seen Paul miss a meal."

She followed him down the hall to the kitchen. The air in the house smelled of cooking odors. Melody Youngblood, dressed exactly as she had been the other time Ellen had been in the house, was standing at a tiny white stove, frying hamburger patties in a black cast-iron skillet. She looked up, nodding to Ellen. None of the appliances and furniture seemed to go with the house, Ellen thought. The tiny three-eye gas stove was dwarfed by the huge kitchen. Its floor slanted slightly, covered with an oddly shaped piece of green linoleum. Carl Youngblood sat down at the table, a rickety, rusted metal table covered with bright yellow Formica, a table very much like the one in her own kitchen at home.

"You want some coffee or somethin?" His voice, though deep, was gentle, with a soft, boyish quality.

"No, thank you," she said. "My name is Ellen Brewster." She felt nervous. She did not know how these people did things, but she remembered that Paul had introduced her to the woman before.

"Oh," the man said. "Carl Youngblood." He stood up and stuck out his hand. It seemed to her an oddly courtly gesture; she was not used to shaking hands with men at all. It felt strange. "And that's Melody over there, cookin up the dog meat."

"The what?" Ellen said.

"Dog meat. Ain't that what they say around town? The Youngbloods eat dog meat. Don't let your dog wander into their yard—they'll catch him and eat him!" He grinned.

"Oh. Yeah." She blushed. She had heard some weird stories about them, but not that one. She nodded to Melody. "Yes, we've met," Ellen said. "Well . . ."

"Sit down, why don'tcha," Carl Youngblood said. "He oughtta be here any second."

Ellen sat down in the nearest chair, a wooden folding chair, the kind you found in church social rooms. Just as she sat down, she sensed more than heard a stirring behind her, in the doorway, and she turned, expecting to see Paul, but it was Sally Long who stood there. She was looking coolly at Ellen, her eyes wide and relaxed. Her hair limply framed her face. Sally just stood there, looking levelly at Ellen, and Ellen, remembering the last time she had seen her, looked away, not knowing what to say.

"Hello, Ellen," Sally said. A slight smile played at her thin lips.

Ellen smiled tentatively. Sally seemed completely changed from the last time here in this house, and it was confusing.

"Sally? How are you?" Ellen said.

"All right. What you doin here?"

"Well . . ." Ellen stood up. "Actually, I came to talk to Paul Siegel," she said.

"You did?" Sally looked around the room, and Ellen followed her eyes. Melody Youngblood was using a wooden-handled spatula to put the hamburgers on a platter with paper napkins on it. The room smelled heavily of hot grease. Ellen looked back at Sally, and Sally seemed to be contemplating her thoughtfully, a slight frown on her face.

"Why don't we go in here and talk?" Sally said, and she went down the hall. As Ellen followed her, she glanced back at Carl Youngblood; he was slouching in his chair at the table, reading a paperback book; he seemed to have tuned her out completely.

She and Sally went into what must have once been an elegant front parlor. The floor was hardwood, but the wide planks were dull and unpolished. There was a coal fireplace, and she could smell the rancid, acrid odor of old fires lingering in the air of the room. The fireplace looked as though someone had been burning garbage in it. There were several plastic chairs. Sally sat down, watching Ellen do the same, regarding her shrewdly, the faint smile still on her face.

"What's with Paul?" she said.

"Huh?" Ellen said.

"I said, what's this business with Paul Siegel?"

"Well . . ."

"You're playin with fire, Ellen," Sally said. "Do you know what you're gettin into?"

"Wait a minute. I'm no more a 'little girl,' than you are," Ellen said.

"Oh, God, you don't know," Sally said. "You don't know nothin." She sat there, contemplating Ellen, who shifted in the hard plastic chair. Ellen felt agitated, nervous and uncomfortable. "You don't know anything about life," Sally went on. "About that boy. I can read it in your eyes, Ellen. I know you. When I saw you that day, it was like all the years had dropped away, you know? Like we was friends again, like it used to be, and all that time just vanished, went away. It made me sad. And it made me mad as hell."

"At me?" Ellen said.

"Yeah, at you. At everybody." She sat back in the stiff chair. "What

makes me madder'n anything is for somebody to feel sorry for me,"
Sally said. "I could take bein spit on, looked and talked through like I
wasn't even there, patted on the head like I was the most darlin little
pickaninny you ever saw. I could even take stayin in my place. But I
couldn't take that pity. No m'am. No way."

"Me?" Ellen was genuinely bewildered. She didn't understand what
Sally was saying.

"Yeah. You. When you were a little girl, and you first learned that
I was a nigger and you were white. You don't even remember, but I
do. When your daddy told us we couldn't go to the park and play
anymore, and we both knew it was because of me. My own mother
could take *you*, but not me! Not a nigger. And you knew. Somethin
so deep down inside you it was like your own heart knew, like you was
born with it." She paused. "I saw the same look in your eyes that day
you came down here with Paul."

"We were little. We were just . . . who we were."

"I know that. I know you couldn't help it."

"And you were mad anyway?"

"Mad as hell. Hated you. Some part of me still does."

"But I couldn't—"

"I said I know you couldn't help it. What you felt was evil. My
daddy would call it sin. I just call it white-man shit."

Ellen stared at Sally, feeling flustered. Her tongue seemed frozen to
the roof of her mouth.

"Now. This white boy," Sally said. "He's a here-today, gone-
tomorrow type of fellow. His stay down here is just temporary." Her
dark eyes narrowed, steady on Ellen. "You don't strike me as the
fuck-and-run type. But how do I know? I mean, we *used* to be close,
but that was so long ago we don't really know each other, do we? And
maybe we weren't even close back then, because I was a little nigger gal
whose mammy worked for the white lady. And you was the white
lady's daughter, wearin pretty little dresses and all."

"I didn't!"

"Pretty'r'n mine. Mine made outta flour sackin. I don't wear no
flour sackin no more." Her dark eyes burned into Ellen, making her
shift uneasily. Sally looked alien, foreign to any of Ellen's experience,
and there was something in her eyes, something that struck Ellen as
dark and mysterious from some old time far away from Hammond and
the two girls sitting in the parlor of an old house that, however ram-
shackle it now was, could have been, probably was, built by people
whose family had owned slaves.

Ellen was slowly aware that Sally was looking past her, over her shoulder toward the door, and she turned. Paul was standing there. He smiled. She stood up. *I am doing it. I have made the irrevocable decision. God help me.* Thoughts of her father nagged at her, but she pushed them away, looking at Paul, his blue eyes dancing. He stood in the doorway, one arm propped on the doorframe; his tight jeans hung low on his hips, and he had on a blue denim shirt with the sleeves and the collar ripped off so that it fit him like a tight vest.

"Hi," he said.

"Hi," she said.

Sally got up and sauntered toward Paul. As she passed him, going into the hallway, she butted him in the stomach with her shoulder, and he doubled over, laughing, grunting, and Sally giggled. Ellen watched them, smiling self-consciously, feeling gawky and ungraceful. Paul punched Sally lightly, playfully, on the shoulder, and she went on down the hall toward the kitchen, laughing. Paul came into room.

"You come to see me?" he said, taking a seat. "What's happenin?"

"My folks found out," she said. She paused. "About us."

"Us?" he said. "Oh. Well." He seemed to be chewing on the inside of his lip. "What'd they say?"

"Daddy had a fit. They told me I couldn't see you again. Ever."

He made the slight chewing motion, gazing past her, into space. His eyes seemed distracted. "But you came anyway," he said, after a minute. "That could be dangerous."

"I know it," she said.

"Maybe you shouldn't hang around down here. I don't want you to get in any trouble."

"No," she said. "They won't do anything. They'll just pitch a fit. My mother . . ." She paused.

"Yeah. You told me," he said. "Listen. Sit down," he said. She sat back down in the chair. "Everybody says . . . Well, Sally"—he jerked his head toward the back of the house—"and Joe Mancini, you know Joe? Well, he's sort of in charge of this whole . . . mission thing. Joe says I can't get involved with somebody who's . . . well, on the other side, you know? Sally says it's dangerous. She says it could get somebody killed."

"I don't know about that," Ellen said, "that seems a bit extreme, to me. Killed?"

"That's what they say."

"Naw," she said. He sat perched in the chair, his elbow on his knee, his chin in his hand. "I mean," she said, "I guess there's some danger. Just you bein down here. But . . . well, I don't know."

"Listen, Ellen," he said, leaning forward. His blue eyes were steady on her, and she felt herself being drawn toward them, almost physically. "Things are gonna get rough around here. This is gonna be a wild summer. All kinds of things are gonna happen."

"What things?" she said.

"Well," he said. He looked around, cocking his ear. She heard the front door close. "Hey, listen. You wanna go for a walk?" he said. They both stood up. Joe Mancini was suddenly there, looking at them. Paul took Ellen's arm, guiding her out the door, past Joe and toward the front door.

"Paul!" Mancini said.

"I'll be back in a minute. Don't worry about it." His voice was irritated, harsh.

Outside, they walked down toward the river, down to the end of Maple Street, toward a cow pasture. They didn't speak until they got to the end of the street, a turnaround, a barbed-wire fence. Paul propped his foot on the fence, carefully placing the sole of his heavy boot between the twisted barbs. A couple of scrawny cows stood in the field, on the green, new grass, looking blandly and impassively at them, slowly chewing their cuds. There were clumps of Cherokee roses and new honeysuckle, only budding now, growing along the fencerow.

"For one thing," he said, as though they had not even been interrupted, "there's a boycott planned. For right away. It's gonna be pretty bad, I think."

"A what?"

"Boycott. All the black people are gonna quit tradin at white-owned stores. All over town. Period." He looked at her out of the corner of his eye. "Your father," he said. "I remember him coming down to the jail that time. I know he's a nice guy. But he's gonna lose all his black business."

"No," she said. "He has good colored customers. He always has had good—"

"No, Ellen, he won't when this starts. He'll lose em."

"But that's over half his business. A lot over half. He'll go broke."

"I don't know if it'll be that bad. But he'll get hurt. Probably hurt bad. A lot of people will. There's gonna be some bad feelins around here. And there'll be demonstrations, at the movie theater and the bus station. Things could get very sticky."

"Why are you tellin me all this?" she said.

"Because," he said. "Because *I* don't think we ought to be seeing each other. I mean . . ."

"What?"

"Well . . ."

"Don't you like me?" she said. She moved closer to him. She felt bold, reckless. Something told her that she had to move now. "Because I like *you*. Very much." She was standing close to him. She could feel the heat of his body, smell his masculine scents. "Look at me, Paul," she said, and he turned to face her. She reached out and touched his bare shoulder, where the sleeve was torn away, touched it lightly with the tips of her fingers. She breathed deeply, looking into his eyes, and he reached out and pulled her to him. He kissed her then, a kiss that started out tentatively, and then grew fiery, and she melted toward him, pushing closer and closer, trying to lose herself in him, excited by his tongue, his hands on her back. The kiss was long, but he stopped suddenly, pushing her away.

"What's the matter?" she said. "Paul?" She was panting. "I want to go back to your room with you, Paul."

"We can't," he said.

"Why not?" She reached out, clasping his arm, but he wouldn't look at her.

"Joe, and everybody," he said. "I . . . I'm scared, if you want to know the truth."

"It's all right," she said. "Come on."

They began to walk back toward the house. Excitement, something forbidden, stung the base of her spine. She walked close to him, her arm entwined with his. She could hear his breathing, his boots on the uneven pavement. As they approached the house, she saw, down the street, a blue pickup truck parked at the curb. It was a battered old Ford, and inside, she could see two men, sitting, looking their way. She noticed them because they were white men, one of them with bright red hair, in this mostly black neighborhood, and they were sitting very still; they were vaguely familiar to Ellen, but they were like all grown people—people her parents' age—people whom she noticed around town but never really saw. As she and Paul went up the walk to the front door, she was too excited to pay the two men in the truck any attention at all.

Chapter Eight

O.B. WAS STANDING OUTSIDE THE SHOP IN THE MORNING
sunshine when he saw the large U-Haul truck going by
on Highway 80. He looked for it every morning about this time. Since
the boycott had been under way, the truck arrived from Montgomery
every morning, loaded mostly with foodstuffs, groceries and milk and
soft drinks; another one came from Selma every afternoon, loaded with
clothing and some more groceries. He knew that they unloaded the
trucks and distributed the food and clothes at the Mount Sinai church,
Eldon's church; most all the Negroes went there to do their daily
"shopping," and the A & P and the downtown stores seemed eerily
empty and quiet.

The boycott was beginning its fourth week now, and O.B. knew
beyond doubt that he was not going to be able to survive it. He could
not go another month. O.B.'s business had dropped off sharply, and he
was worried. He had *no* Negro business now, and since the Logan
brothers had dropped him and several other white farmers had followed suit, he calculated that his business was down by considerably
more than two thirds. He was already hurting bad, and when he
thought about the note coming due at Planters and Merchants Bank,
he shuddered. Everyone kept saying that the thing would end soon,

that the Negroes would buckle under, with no place to get their equipment repaired, but they showed no sign of it, at least where his place was concerned. The weather was beginning to get very hot some days, and O.B. had heard that tempers around town were getting short. He had no idea what he was going to do. He felt caught squarely in the middle.

He could barely allow himself to think about Martha and her drinking, or Ellen and the boy. The whole family had fought about the boy, and he had forbidden Ellen to see him over and over again, but he now suspected that she was defying him, seeing him anyway. He could tell, because he knew her so well, and it was difficult for her to lie convincingly to him. He didn't know if Martha suspected the truth about Ellen and the boy or not.

He swallowed, blinking in the bright sunlight. He wouldn't think about that. He had to concentrate on the bank loan. That was something that he had to confront right away. He narrowed his eyes, idly watching the sparse traffic going by on the highway, remembering, when he had decided to build the new addition to the shop, to expand his business, when he had gone in to talk to Mac about the loan. It had seemed a much bigger step than his slowly acquiring the business over the years. O.B. had been shaky, nervous, but Mac had acted casual, nonchalant, as though he loaned eleven thousand dollars to somebody every hour. Maybe he did. He had seemed eager to let O.B. have the money, as accommodating as he could be.

"What I'd recommend, O.B.," he'd said, "is that you get the loan for, say, two years. Just a straight loan, at a lower interest rate, and go ahead and add to your shop, do your expansion and all, then, after you see what kinda new business you're gonna be doin and all, when the note comes due, well, we'll refinance it then, for however long you need to, and set it up on a monthly payment plan. All right? By then you'll know how long you'll need and what kinda monthly payments we're talkin about. Whatever's best for you, that you can handle all right. You don't even have to pay the interest on these first two years, we'll just accumulate it and include it when we refinance, spread it out after your business grows, which it will. This is a good business decision on your part, O.B. You been a little tin-walled shop for years; now you gonna have a *business!*" Mac blinked at him. "Sound all right to you?"

O.B. had just looked at him across the desk. He was very nervous, and the discussion of that much money made him more so. But he trusted Mac; he had no choice. This was the kind of thing he had not anticipated years ago, when he had decided to go into business for himself. He had no flair for the money side of it. He had worked on farm implements his whole life up to then, except for baseball, and it seemed natural to him to do it for a living after he could no longer support himself playing ball. He had seen no reason at the time to just hire himself out as a mechanic to someone else; he had wanted the freedom of his own business. Certainly, Martha had wanted that. He had rented the building at first, hiring one other mechanic, and soon Martha was urging him to buy it, to build up his business. It had seemed simple, then. There were lots of mechanics looking for work and willing to take what he could give them, and he got the shop dirt-cheap, six thousand dollars for the building and the lot along the highway. He hadn't taken as much pleasure in being the boss as he had thought he would, or as Martha expected him to. Then, two years ago, she had urged him to expand. How much she had nagged him, pushed him into it all, he couldn't say, but he knew she had always wanted the country club and a new house, and this was the only way to one day get it for her.

"Yeah," he had said to Mac. "Sounds fine. In two years, I'll know better where I stand."

Mac had shoved the note across his wide desk, along with a long black ballpoint desk pen, little check marks at the beginning of every line requiring O.B.'s signature. Mac had smiled at him. "Relax, O.B.," he had said, "I don't lend money to businesses I think are gonna fail."

Now it was almost time for the note to come due. Mac had already balked at the idea of refinancing it. O.B. thought of his dwindling bank account, the grudging dollars that went for food. The boycott. There were already a couple of stores in town that relied heavily on Negro business that were about to fold: Grant's Store out in Shortleaf and Scales's Dry Goods. *What was Mac up to?* One thing was the White Citizens Council. Mac had wanted him on the board. And now he wanted him to talk to Eldon, to get him to slow down, back off on the boycott and the demonstrations. But Eldon wanted him, too, wanted him to run for mayor. Both seemed to want to control him, to make him into something that he wasn't.

·~·~·~·

O.B. went back inside the front of the shop and told Paulette that he was going out into the country. He had to go and see his folks, even though he did not have the money to give them that he knew they would be expecting. He was tempted to skip the visit, but he needed to see them. O.B. had been an only child, and there was no one else to look in on them. He didn't see much of them, since they and Martha didn't much get along, and his mother and father had gotten very old and feeble and seemed to care even less now about his life in town than they ever had. When his father had gotten too old to farm, Mr. Hubbard had allowed them to stay on in the little clapboard house, where they existed on their tiny garden, their few chickens, their small checks that they got from Social Security and his father's pension from World War I, and the little extra that O.B. could scrape together at the end of each month. Several hundred dollars a year. Ellen occasionally borrowed his pickup or his mother's car and drove out to see them, but they didn't seem to enjoy visitors. O.B. had bought them a used television set, and they watched that all day long.

He drove along in the brilliant sunshine, the motor of his pickup humming; he turned south, toward the Flatwoods. He drummed his fingers against the steering wheel, feeling the warm vinyl of the seat against his back, and tried to relax, but too much was happening. He worried about Ellen, but, to tell the truth, there was something in him that admired her spunk. He had tried to talk with Martha about that, but it was impossible. He had always tried to raise Ellen to have a mind of her own, and it looked like she was having it. O.B. just prayed that whatever Ellen was doing, had gotten herself into, she wouldn't be hurt by it. He worried that she was already into sex with the boy. And he knew that what the boy was doing was dangerous, and if anything happened, it might involve Ellen, too. He could hardly bear to contemplate it, but he didn't know what he could do, short of locking her up.

O.B. sighed, looking out at the fields along the highway, some of them already turned, smooth black loam ribboned in new rows. It was planting time, and some of the fields he passed lay fallow, scrubby, with last year's spindly cotton plants withered and dead from the winter still standing in uneven and decaying rows. He passed fields of new green alfalfa and then pastures with grazing dairy cattle. The land stretched away toward the south and west, as flat as a griddle, the horizon dotted with clumps of trees. Then he came to the broad pine forests, tall, thick trees all the same height, covering the land for several square miles like a layer of water, as flat across the top as a lake. These were the woods that had given the area its name. The highway went through the crowded, thick trees as straight as a plumbline until the woods ended abruptly in more fields and pastures, the occasional farmhouse sitting back from the road, nestling next to its barns and outbuildings and windmills.

As he drove along, O.B. thought about all he was faced with. He knew he had to try and sort out all his options. He felt desperate every time he thought about the loan at the bank, confused about Mac's attitude toward it. He didn't think he could bring himself to go and *beg* Mac, plead with him. On the other hand, there was no way in the world he could get the money to pay off the loan. He was actually *losing* money now, and if he had to lay off his mechanics and his parts man, he might as well shut down his shop, a business that he had put all his energies into for what seemed now like most of his life. Lately, in the last couple of days, he had allowed himself to seriously consider Eldon's suggestion about running for mayor. Eldon had called him up the other morning and asked him how he was doing, and O.B. had been evasive until Eldon had bluntly come right out and told him that if O.B. agreed to run, he, Eldon, would see to it that the boycott was lifted from O.B.'s business.

O.B. knew he could trust Eldon to do just that; he would get practically *all* the Negro business in the area, because there was nowhere else for them to go. That might isolate him more as a white person, cost his family something in the town, but it would save his business, at least keep him going for a while. He could at least pay the interest for the past two years and then reborrow it, or something. Sure, he would have to deal with his mechanics because they might not like working for what a lot of people would call a "nigger-lover," but with Rusty now long gone, he didn't think that would be too big a problem. Of course, if they were working exclusively for Negroes, there was always the possibility they might just quit, but where were *they* going to go? Everybody's business was down. Everybody had to eat.

He knew he would need cash for Ellen's college next year. It would be a lot, even if she just went to Livingston and lived at home, but she wanted to live in a dormitory, and he could understand that. He wanted to be able to afford it, to let her do what she wanted to do. The boy, Paul, would be gone back North by then, and O.B. would have his daughter back, so he wanted to be able to give her her college studies, the way she wanted. It all came down to money. As he approached his parents' little house, the reason for his visit out here nagged him, depressed him. He hated to tell them that he couldn't give them the money he usually gave them every month, but he just did not have it. They would not understand. Why *shouldn't* he run for mayor if he wanted to? He quavered, thinking of the actual getting out and running for it. Making speeches. Would he have to do that?

He pulled the pickup to a stop in the sandy yard of his folks' house. There was a sagging white picket fence, in need of paint, across the middle of the yard, and behind it was scrubby grass, green now in patches, and several peach trees in bloom. He got out and went through the familiar gate, held to by an old rusty plowshare on a chain, the chain rattling in the early afternoon quiet. The sound of the chain seemed to transport him into another time, distant and pure, as he saw his mother standing behind the screen door, in a light blue apron that came down almost to her shoetops, holding a dish towel. She wore a blue bandanna tied around her thinning dark gray hair.

It had been months since he had seen them, but all she said, as he walked up the dirt pathway, was:

"You et dinner yet?"

"No," he said, coming up on the porch. She was wiping her hands with the cloth.

"Corn bread and buttermilk'll have to do." She pushed open the patched screen door, and, as he stepped inside, he bent down, hugging her lightly, pressing his cheek against the side of her head. She put her hands on his shoulders, just barely squeezing. "Yer daddy's back here," she said. "He's been down in his back."

He went through the living room, with its wide plank floors, glancing at the familiar family pictures on the walls, through the dining room with its round wooden table that his father had made forty years ago, and into the long, large kitchen that ran all across the back of the house. They lived back here. Two armchairs sat facing the old television set at one end of the room. His father, wearing crisp blue overalls, was watching television. He looked up. Sparse gray whiskers covered his chin, and his eyes, blue like O.B.'s, looked cloudy, fading toward gray.

"Odell." He smiled at O.B. "We watchin *The World Turns.*" He looked back at the set. They watched *As The World Turns* every day when they finished their lunch. They talked about the people on there as though they were neighbors; whenever O.B. saw them, they wanted to tell him what Lisa and Dr. Hughes had been up to, as though he normally watched it, too. They called it their "story." They wouldn't miss it. "We got to watch our story," they would say.

The show was ending. His mother stood by the set, waiting until the closing music faded and a commercial for intensified Tide came on, and she switched it off.

"You can watch it," O.B. said.

"Naw, Odell," his father said. "Hell, you don't come out here more'n once a month. We can talk."

"How y'all been doin?" O.B. said.

"Not good atall," the old man said. "Back's troublin me." He had been a big man once, but now he was thin and wiry. He reminded O.B. of the dried, dead cotton stalks that he had seen driving out here. His lower arms, his wrists, looked fragile and brittle.

"You daddy's been puttin his hand up on the screen for Oral Roberts," his mother said.

"Beats anything I ever saw," the old man said. "You ever watched that? Them people git up and walk, throw they crutches away. I figured it couldn't hurt none." The old man sat stiffly in the chair, his feet in faded green corduroy bedroom slippers flat on the floor. He peered at O.B. with his liquid eyes. "What you come out here for, Odell?" he said. "You want the money back, don'tcha?" His father and mother were the only people who still called him by his first name. It reminded him of being a child.

"No," O.B. said, thinking that his father could read him by just looking at him. "I don't want the money back. What makes you—"

"You look like you want somethin. Well, we ain't got nothin." The old man cackled, a dry, rasping laugh. "We—"

"Papa," the old woman said, "he come to visit. Hush."

She pulled up the corner of a tablecloth, revealing their few leftovers from lunch, and cut him a large wedge of corn bread; she brought it to him on a saucer, with a huge jelly glass. "We got sweet milk or buttermilk," she said.

"Buttermilk," O.B. said, his mouth watering. Martha wouldn't allow buttermilk in the house. She couldn't stand to look at it, just like she wouldn't cook turnip greens because they stank up the house. He crumbled the corn bread into the glass; it smelled sweet and fresh. His mother brought a pitcher, and he poured the thick buttermilk over the corn bread. She had brought him a long teaspoon, and he began to eat the cold mush, and with the first taste he was instantly transported back to his childhood. He looked at his mother and father through misted eyes, feeling a sudden, surprisingly intense sadness, a sadness that they were old, that he never saw them anymore even though they were only twenty minutes away. He chewed, sighing.

"Well, why'd you come out here, then?" his father asked, after a minute.

"To see you. Just to visit," O.B. said. He spooned the corn bread into his mouth, and they watched him eat. He dreaded telling them, even though he could tell they already knew. They knew about the boycott, everything. He knew then that what he wanted was reassurance. Warmth.

"How're Martha and Ellen?" his mother asked.

"Just fine," he lied. "This is good." He smacked his lips.

"She don't hardly feed you," his mother said.

"You must want somethin," the old man said. He sat in the same position, as though he were paralyzed. As he stared at O.B., his eyes suddenly turned inward, became almost bitter. He seemed like a shriveled, selfish child; as though he begrudged O.B. the bread and milk he was eating. "I hurt all the time, Son. Nobody cares," he said, his voice trembling, but then his mood seemed to change abruptly. He cackled again, his eyes suddenly merry. "We seen about the niggers on the television. What are they doin, Son?" He slapped his knee.

"Actin up, for sure," O.B. said. His mother stood there, watching him eat, ready to bring him anything he wanted. Her little birdlike eyes darted from his hands to his face, eagerly watching him, taking an almost childlike satisfaction in his enjoyment of the food. He frowned slightly, and his mother's expression responded.

"What's the matter, Son?" she said.

"Well," he said. "You know about the boycott, don't you?"

"We heard," she said.

"Old nigger Buddy Webb? You remember him?" his father said. "We hear he's plowin with a mule."

"Buddy Ed Webb?" O.B. said.

"Yeah, over there other side of Hubbard's place. Tractor's broke down, and he won't even git it fixed cause he's doin this here boy-cott thing you hear about. Beats all."

"Well," O.B. said. He paused. He was thinking of the old man. Suddenly, he said, "To tell you the truth, I'm thinkin of runnin for mayor."

"Doin what?" the old man said. "I don't follow."

"Of Hammond. You know, mayor."

His father looked at his mother. He seemed to shrug, and they looked back at him, their faces blank, expressionless now. *Why did I come out here? I could have done this with a phone call.* He felt suddenly helpless, trapped. They were not like his parents, the people who had raised him. He did not know them at all. He had forgotten that. He had a sudden longing to put his face in his mother's lap, to

let her rub his hair with her thin, cool hands and comfort him the way
she had done when he was a child.

"Politics?" the old man said.

"Why you gonna do that, Son?" his mother said.

"I . . . I don't know," O.B. said. "I don't know if I am. It's probably
a . . . bad idea. I don't know." They watched him chewing. "I'm goin
broke, Daddy," he said.

They both stared at him, plainly not comprehending.

"This boycott, it's killin me for sure. I'm losin money." He tried to
make it matter-of-fact, but his voice quivered. "I can't give you any
money this month." They just looked at him. "Maybe not next month
either. I . . . I've got to do *somethin*. I can't just stand by and watch
everything fall apart. Everything I've worked for. Martha and Ellen
don't know how bad it is, but I got a big note comin due at the bank;
I might have to lay off some mechanics. It's . . . bad." He sighed. "So
I've got to do somethin. Maybe runnin for mayor, being the mayor
. . ." He let his voice trail off. He didn't want to tell them if he did
agree to do it, the boycott would be lifted from him, that he would be
the only white man the Negroes would trade with; it seemed to him
like admitting that he was selling out to the other side, and that
troubled him.

"It's gonna take up the money you give us, ain't it?" the old man
said. He was looking at him shrewdly, as though he had figured it out
and now understood the reason for the visit.

"Yes," O.B. said. "That's what I said. I don't have it, and I can't
borrow it. Do you understand?"

"How . . . how we gonna live?" his mother said.

"Maybe . . . it'll get better," he said. "That's what I'm telling you."
He stopped. "And then I can help you again. Maybe next month.
Anyway, if you hear about it, that's what I'll be doing. Running for
mayor." He looked at them, and they just looked back like children.
"I just wanted . . . to tell you about it. You know?" Why had he
come? They could not understand, even if he could find the words to
describe the dilemma he was in, not that he even understood it himself. All he wanted was to be left alone, to live his life the way he had
planned it. He had had enough disappointments, but they had not yet
made him bitter. That ought to be good enough. His mother and
father were inspecting him intently, their faces curious, inquiring. To
them, he had gone off to town and become successful. He had been a
ball player. He had lived in the big city for a while, played in the big
leagues. He lived in a brick house. He owned a business. He gave

them money. They were simple people, and he longed for just that. That's what he wanted. Simplicity. That's what baseball, the clean baselines, the white ball, had been to him. He peered intently at his father. The old man was broken, childlike and dependent. He would go to his grave unhappy, confused and mystified by life. His father's toothless lips trembled again. O.B. could not hold back the tears that burned his eyes.

"What's the matter, Son?" his mother said, alarmed.

"Nothin," O.B. said quickly. "Listen, I . . ." He wiped his eyes with the back of his hand. The room seemed to hold all the hours of his life, year after year of going off to school, of planting and harvesting, of Christmases celebrated and summers lived; the old wallpaper seemed to have absorbed the days and seasons of cooking and sleeping, the sense and feel of his home. He was separated from that now, apart. He realized that he had wanted them to give him advice, tell him to do it, to run for mayor, solve his problems. Be his parents. They did not understand him now; maybe they never had.

Then the old man said, "The niggers don't wanna be niggers anymore, do they, Odell?"

O.B. looked up. "That's right," he said, startled. The old man had hit it on the head, and O.B. was stunned by his insight.

"I've known old Buddy Webb for sixty years," his father continued, his eyes watering. "He a good man. The niggers is funny, all right. But they good people. Ain't nothing Buddy Webb wouldn't do for you. Now that's a fact."

O.B. set the empty glass on the table. He remembered the day back in the winter when Buddy Ed had come to his shop, and O.B. had had to intercede between him and Rusty Jackson. And it hit him then, like a sudden, startling bolt from a cloudless sky, that it was true that there was nothing Buddy Ed wouldn't do for another man, black or white, and O.B. believed in that, too, had always lived his life according to that simple commandment, because it was "Love thy neighbor," that's what his father was saying about Buddy Ed. It was astonishingly simple. After all, wasn't that what a man's life was all about? Wasn't that the basic rule that made everything else make sense? He thought of Eldon, his pleading eyes. He sat looking at his father, knowing that he had never loved him more intensely than he did now. He stood up. He knew, now, the real reason he was running for mayor. He was filled with a sudden resolve. "I just wanted to stop by," he said. "I had some business out this way."

"Come again," his mother said. "Come whenever you can."

His father said nothing. He nodded his head toward the television, and O.B.'s mother stood up and made a gesture toward turning it back on. "All right," O.B. said. "Good-bye then." He hugged his mother again, lightly, exactly as they had hugged at the front door. He stuck out his hand to his father, who took it, his father's touch as dry and cool and light as paper.

~~~·

Buddy Ed Webb had a small farm adjoining Mr. Hubbard's property, and from the highway, O.B. could see, in his front field, rows of yellowish-brown cornstalks leaning at odd lifeless angles. O.B. turned his truck onto the narrow dirt road that ran up to Buddy Ed's cabin; the truck rattled and bounced over the rusty cattle gap. The road was two tire tracks between the rows of dead corn, and he came out into the yard of the cabin and stopped next to a well, with a creaking wooden windmill turning slowly and erratically in the barely perceptible afternoon breezes. A little Negro child, about three years old, sat in the sandy yard, playing with a tablespoon in the sand. Beyond the house and barn, O.B. could see Buddy Ed, plowing in a field with a mule-drawn plow. His tractor, with a new disk harrow that he had bought from O.B. a little over a year ago, sat in front of the barn. The child, wearing miniature faded overalls was watching O.B. with large brown eyes as he got out of the truck.

"I just wanna see your granddaddy," O.B. said. He saw a Negro woman, tall and thin, in a plain green dress, looking at him from the screenless door of the shack. It was unpainted, with a rusty tin roof, maybe five rooms. O.B. could see the privy out back, and he could already smell it in the afternoon heat. "Evenin," O.B. said.

"Evenin," the Negro woman said. He knew she was Buddy Ed's daughter.

"I wanna see Buddy Ed," O.B. said. "I'm Mr. Brewster."

"He down to de field," she said.

O.B. nodded. He walked around the house, squinting in the sunlight as he went down a path that wound by the barn and the mule lot, down toward the field where he could see Buddy Ed, walking behind the plow, moving slowly behind the plodding, droopy-eared mule. He could smell the hay from the barn, the droppings in the lot, and he smiled. He needed to get out here from time to time. Stay more in touch with who he was. He briefly remembered, for a moment, the image of his folks in their narrow kitchen—their earnest, questioning expressions—and he let the wistful feeling of sadness flow through him as he trudged between the slim, graceful willow trees, plum bushes, and fragile creeping blackberry vines that lined the sandy walkway. He stopped by the sagging barbed-wire fence. A quart jar of ice water sat in the shade of a plum bush, next to it the remains of Buddy Ed's dinner, corn bread and molasses in a metal lard bucket. Ants had found it and were crawling up the side of the pail. Buddy Ed made the turn at the end of the field. O.B. could tell from the old man's appearance that he had already spotted him, and he stopped the mule in the middle of the field, looping the cotton rope reins over the handles of the plow. The mule stood as still as a statue. Buddy Ed shuffled toward him, a slow, rolling gate over the already turned ground. He wore rubber boots and overalls over a heavy wool shirt. His shoulders were stooped, and his hair was silvery white in the spring sunlight.

When he came up to the fence, Buddy Ed smiled at him, his one tooth glistening in his mouth. His dark, smooth face was beaded with sweat. His breath was shallow, pained, and his mouth was contorted behind the smile.

"It's gonna take you a long time, plowin with that old mule," O.B. said, and Buddy Ed shook his head.

"Sho is," he said, almost gasping.

O.B. looked at him in the silence, the only sound the old man's labored breathing.

"Your tractor's broke down again, ain't it?" O.B. said. "I can make that good for you."

"Nawsuh," the old Negro said. He looked away, at the rolling fields, his breathing easier now. "I do jest fine with the mule."

"What about that cornfield? You can't do without your corn this year. What you gonna feed the mule?"

"I gits to it," Buddy Ed said. He propped his boot on the lowest strand of the fence. "We help each other out," he said. He looked at O.B. out of the corner of his eye.

"I'll send somebody out here, fix that tractor," O.B. said. "I owe that to you. It won't be Rusty this time. I guarantee my work, Buddy Ed. I'll send somebody out tomorrow mornin—"

"No, suh, Mister O.B.," he said. "I don't reckon you better. Not nothin against *you*, now." He took out a dingy, wrinkled handkerchief and wiped his face. "They tell us what to do at the church, and I can't go against that." He looked around at the field, the rich black soil. O.B. could smell the rank, pungent dampness of the loam. "I done plowed with a mule for near bout forty years. Ain't had a tractor but six. Reckon I can make out."

O.B. picked up the cold water jar; droplets of moisture clung to the icy glass, and he handed it to Buddy Ed. The old Negro opened it and drank deeply, his head back, his Adam's apple bobbing in his neck as he drank. He screwed the lid back on and handed it back to O.B.

"I thank you," he said, and he took a step back, almost stumbling in the loose soil. His heavy rubber boots seemed oversized, clumsy.

"I won't tell anybody," O.B. said, almost pleadingly. "We'll fix it, and nobody would know."

"*I'd know*," Buddy Ed said. He stood there in the sunlight, looking levelly at O.B.. "We do all right," he said, "we make out. That little baby in the yard?" he said.

"Yeah," O.B. said. "That your grandchild?"

"Sho is," Buddy Ed said. "She ain't gonna hafta go through this, see. Cause we is going through it, now. She ain't gonna hafta be no nigger. If all I got to do is plow with a mule to make that happen, then git outta my way. I plow that mule till he drop!"

O.B. stood looking at the old man. He had known Buddy Ed all his life, since he was a child, growing up down the road. Buddy Ed had always seemed passive, subdued, easily manipulated, but now his resolve seemed firm. Then O.B. remembered another time, years ago, when Buddy Ed, arm-wrestling behind Boligee Store, took on all comers. He was a younger man then, stronger, and O.B. and Eldon had watched him defeat his challengers, one after the other. Now O.B. thought of his own father, his pale eyes grown weary and heavy.

"I got to git back to work now," Buddy Ed said. "I thank you kindly for comin out here, Mister O.B." O.B. thought of the day he had intervened between the old man and Rusty Jackson. He felt a strange sense of pride for Buddy Ed, a mixture of sadness and satisfaction that he did not fully understand.

"Yeah, all right." O.B. watched the old man trudge back across the field, where the sleeping mule stood in its worn makeshift harness, in front of the old hand plow, like a picture in a magazine, something out of some old time now long past. The plow's handles would be worn smooth, O.B. knew. He could almost palpably feel them from this distance; he could experience again in his own memory those handles worn as smooth as glass by the old man's hands and the years.

Then Buddy Ed stopped. He stood very still, stooped just slightly, his hands at his waist, staring at the ground.

"Buddy Ed?" O.B. said. The old man did not move. O.B. climbed the fence then, his hand on top of a fence post, his legs swinging over in a gesture as familiar as walking itself; then he was moving rapidly toward the old man, his shoes sinking into the freshly turned, clodded earth, catching up to him, inspecting him closely in the spring sunlight. "Buddy Ed?" he said again.

"I all right," the old man said, looking at him from his watery eyes. "I . . ." He stood very still. "I just tired, I reckon."

O.B. felt as though he were propelled from behind, shoved by some force that was larger and more powerful than he was, toward the plow. He grabbed the handle, unlooped the frayed cotton ropes, and flicked them across the sleeping mule's rump, seeing the drooping ears lurch suddenly forward with the mule's automatic, instinctual first step. O.B. felt, then saw, the single blade bite into the dark earth. He steadied the plow, feeling the tugging strain at his shoulders, having to step quickly and awkwardly in the furrow until he adapted to the rhythm, following the slow, steady pull of the mule, hearing the soft metallic jingle and squeaking of the ancient harness. He and the mule were one then, and as he piloted the plow toward the fence at the end of the field their progress was laggard, slow-gaited. O.B. felt the sunlight beating on his shoulders. He looked back, squinting, at Buddy Ed. The old man was smiling at him, his head tilted back, his one tooth glinting. O.B. felt a surge of energy then, an almost youthful burst of power. *This old man is my neighbor and has been my neighbor since before I ever heard the word! Our sweat has fallen on the same soil; the same fierce sun has beaten down on both our heads. I can plow his field; we can plow his field together!* It was what his father had meant. "He would do anything for you." This was the cardinal rule that might make some sense out of how a man is to conduct himself in the world. It was the only reason to do anything. O.B. had known it all along, had known it in his heart when he and Eldon and Cora were young, and he had lost it somewhere.

No, he had not lost it. *I have never lost it.* The black earth turned smoothly on each side of the shiny blade. *I am not too far removed from this soil that I can't feel its message again, in my legs and in my heart.* The loamy earth was damp, and it smelled fecund and rich, fertile as life itself. Tears misted his eyes, one droplet spilling down his cheek, but he could not wipe his face because he held to the handles of the plow, and anyway he did not need to see, because he was following the mule's firm, steadfast progress toward the end of the row, toward Eldon and his youth.

O. B. parked his truck on Ashe Street, near Eldon's church. He had made up his mind: He was going to accept Eldon's offer and agree to run for mayor against Mac. The overcast sky was gray and leaden, and he sat there for a moment, looking down the narrow street with its limerock drainage ditches. Most of the small houses had tar-paper siding; some were fairly new, with brick veneer, and some were sagging, unpainted shanties that must have dated back seventy-five years, in disrepair but still occupied. The truck window was down, and O.B. could smell the raw sewage; there were still parts of Frogbottom that had not been connected to the town sewage system, and there were backyard privies and chicken yards. Some people down here kept goats and pigs, and even an occasional cow, crammed into a narrow and cramped backyard. He could smell open cooking fires and hog slop.

The church, with its whitewashed brick and white steeple, looked as out of place as if some giant had picked it up in some neat suburb somewhere and then plopped it down here among these shanties. Its front windows were blue-and-yellow colored glass. It was a spacious church, with a two-story building across the back built of unpainted brick, as though the Sunday school part had been added later. A sign stood in the patchy yard, next to a flagpole. The sign read MT. SINAI AME ZION CHURCH, *Rev. Eldon Long, Pastor, Welcome.* There were smaller letters at the bottom of the sign that O.B. could not make out; it looked like a schedule, times for services. He got out of the truck, slamming the door. A U.S. flag hung limply from the pole in the damp, rain-threatening air. O.B. looked up and down the quiet street. A large U-Haul truck was pulled into the churchyard, its back end gaping open as though it had just disgorged its contents. There was no one around.

O.B. took a deep breath. He felt as though he were going to humble himself before Eldon, to somehow admit defeat. The feeling made him uneasy, apprehensive. He went up a sidewalk, around the side of the church, to the Sunday school building. He tried the door; it was open, and he went inside. He was in a little front hallway; there was a poster on the wall, a large picture of a heavyset black woman, her hair piled on top of her head in a tight bun, her eyes burning into the room. O.B. had no idea who she might be. A door on the right was open, and he looked in. Eldon was sitting behind a desk in a crowded little office. He had obviously heard the door open, and he was leaning out, peering around the door. When O.B. looked in, their eyes met

and locked. Neither man said anything for a moment. The look in
Eldon's eyes was tentative, curious. Then Eldon cleared his throat.

"O.B.," he said.

"Eldon."

O.B. moved into the office. It was about the size of his own. A
window, open a crack, looked out onto dark green and thick privet
hedge. A cool, damp breeze wafted in, smelling of spring. There was
a glass-front bookcase against the wall opposite the window, crammed
with books, mostly worn paperbacks. Eldon had been writing on a
yellow legal pad, and it lay on the desk, a pencil across it. Eldon's lean
hands rested on the edge of the desk. His white shirt was rolled up his
forearms, his dark, narrow tie neatly knotted at the collar. His suit coat
hung on a rack in the corner. His eyes were steady on O.B. as he sat
down in the visitor's chair across the desk. O.B. could see his large,
framed diploma on the wall behind him; it was written in Latin, and
O.B. looked at it for a moment, then looked back at Eldon. There was
a slight, tentative smile now in Eldon's eyes.

"To what do I owe this visit?" Eldon leaned back in his chair, his
smile awkward.

O.B. felt ill at ease. "How long is this gonna go on?" he said.

"How long is what?"

"Don't play dumb with me, Eldon. How long is it gonna go on?"

"As long as it takes. Are you an emissary from Mr. McClellon?"
Eldon asked.

"No," O.B. said quickly.

"Sooner or later he's gonna have to talk turkey with us," Eldon said.
"Ever since the incident at Maud's, he's been, well, reticent about it."
He picked up the pencil and doodled on the bottom of the yellow page.
O.B. knew that he was waiting for him to get to the point, that he
would make O.B. bring it up.

"Maybe he thinks he can wait you out," O.B. said. "I can't."

Eldon's eyes snapped up. O.B. looked away, out the window at the
stiff, broad leaves of the privet.

"People are bein ruined," O.B. said. "I'm . . . hurtin bad. I don't
know if I'm gonna make it." Long said nothing. His eyes were steady.
"There are Negro farmers all over, Eldon, who are sufferin because of
this. I've seen em. I stopped in to see Buddy Ed Webb. His tractor's
broken down; he won't let me fix it. Which means he can't get it fixed.
He's been trying to get his crop in the ground with a plow and a mule.
And he ain't the only one. What about them?"

"What *about* them?" Eldon's eyes seemed to waver slightly. He looked down at his pad. "Nobody's doin anything they don't want to do, O.B. I know that's hard for you to understand. It's hard for any white man to understand."

"I could at least help the farmers out," O.B. said.

"They wouldn't trade with you. Surely you found that out?"

"Yeah, I did," O.B. said.

"You might find one or two who don't care. I understand there are some of my people who are shoppin the supermarkets in town right now. That can't be helped. But most . . . well, they're committed to this. And they'll get more committed in the future. Believe me."

"Committed to what?" O.B. said.

"To our movement," Eldon said. "Get used to that word. Movement." He smiled. "You people don't understand that we're gonna change the world. Startin right here in places like Hammond, Alabama. You won't take us seriously until it's all done!"

"I take you seriously, all right," O.B. said. "I don't have any choice." His body was tense, and he wished that Eldon wouldn't smile like that. He wanted to tell him about his insights at Buddy Ed's place, but he was afraid Eldon would laugh at him. "I'm takin seriously people like Buddy Ed Webb. He can't put food on his table, Eldon. His family's gonna starve. Or go on welfare."

"None of my people are gonna starve," Eldon said defensively. "They have strong bellies. They know how to go to sleep hungry. They know how to sacrifice and do without, because they've done it for so long. Most of em have lived their whole lives off of white folks' leavins. They're tired of it, but it's made em strong."

O.B. looked fixedly at Eldon. He knew the truth of what Eldon was saying, but his reaction to it was confusing to him.

" 'Course," Eldon said, "like I told you, if you want to help those people, all you got to do is agree to run for mayor against Mac, and I'll call off the boycott of your place. I'll say the word, and it'll be lifted. You'll have all the black business in West Alabama. You'll have all the business you can handle." He sat staring at O.B.

It was as though he were reading O.B.'s mind. And O.B. had expected it; he was not surprised. "That's what I wanted to talk to you about," O.B. said. "I'm . . . I'm thinkin of doin it." Long said nothing. "It makes me feel like a fool. I'll probably never get any white business again. . . ." He saw the satisfaction in Eldon's eyes and stopped. He wanted to tell him that he had changed his mind, was on his side, but was he? He didn't like everything his people were trying to do. But it was important to him for Eldon to believe that it was strictly a business decision. He grinned nervously. Eldon grinned back at him. "But if it'll get me out of this, in the short run—"

"In the long run, too, O.B. You'll be on the right side—"

"Get this straight, Eldon!" he said, harshly, not grinning now. "I ain't on any side." *Was that weakness that I felt out in Buddy Ed's field? No!* "I look on this as strictly business. I got to send Ellen to college. I got notes to pay off. I need to do business, so we're making a kind of deal here. I don't want anybody gettin the idea that you're sponsoring me, or that I'm on your damn side or anything like that. We got to get that understood. I don't want you havin a goddam thing to do with my race for the mayor."

"But we'll support you. We'll—"

"Do it quietly, then. Look, I ain't gonna beat Mac. Both of us know that."

"I *don't* know that," Eldon said.

"Anyhow. People are gonna put two and two together enough. They're gonna want to know why I'm not bein boycotted anymore and everybody else is." He knew that he would be even more isolated, alienated, in the town than he was now.

"You don't have to advertise it," Eldon said.

"In this town? Everybody'll know."

Eldon was peering at him, an almost amused, curious look on his face. "What happened to the coaching?"

"Huh?" O.B. said.

"The baseball? The, you know, coaching and all? Can you still do all that?"

O.B. realized with a shock that he had not thought of that in days, that he had almost totally forgotten something that only just recently was as important to him as anything he could think of. The season would be here soon; the big leagues were already cranking up to get started. He knew now that running for mayor was as important to him as the baseball, but he didn't want Eldon to know how he was feeling.

"There's only so much time," he said. "I may have to put that one on the back burner."

The room was silent. The two men looked into each other's eyes. "Tell me this," Eldon said, "other than your business, of course, why are you gonna run? I mean, is that the only reason?"

"Whattaya mean?" O.B. said. *Can he read my mind?*

"I mean," Eldon said, "you're not like most white men. For one reason."

O.B. felt uneasy, and he shifted in the chair. "I don't know what you're talkin about," he said.

"Stay away from Cora, O.B.," Eldon said. His eyes were hot, full of intensity. "I knew you as a boy. I knew you well. None of us change that much. You can't have her now any more than you could then."

"I haven't seen her since that night I brought her to the jail. I told you—"

"And I can tell that you ain't doin this just to save your business. You ain't one to let anybody pressure you into anything. I know you, you got other reasons. And I hope they're the right ones."

O.B. just sat there. He didn't know what to say. After a minute, he said, "What do I do now?"

"Huh?" Eldon said.

"About runnin. For mayor." It still sounded silly in his ears.

"You go down to city hall, get these qualifyin papers to fill out. You'll have to pay a fee. I checked on it. It's a hundred dollars. Just enough to keep pore whites and niggers from qualifyin. Convenient. You got that much, don't you? To spare?"

"Not to spare. But I reckon I can part with it."

"Here," Eldon said. He took a roll of bills from his pocket and counted out five wrinkled twenty-dollar bills. He shoved them across the desk.

"Where does that come from?" O.B. said, pointing to the roll.

"Let's just say from points north. There ain't as much here as it looks like. But this is a legitimate expense of the movement—"

"Wait a minute!" O.B. said. "No. I don't want that. I'll pay it myself."

"Suit yourself, O.B." Eldon folded the bills and put them back into his pocket.

O.B. started to speak, then paused. Eldon's smile flickered and left his face. "Somethin else on your mind, O.B.?"

"Yeah. Do you know this boy Siegel?" Eldon didn't say anything for a moment. " 'Course you do," O.B. went on quickly. "He works with you. All that. Well . . ."

"Why do you want to know?" Eldon said.

"Well, Ellen . . . you know my Ellen?" Eldon nodded. "She's been . . . well, seein him. Goin around with him some. And I wanted to know what you thought of him."

Eldon's eyes were wide, registering with surprise. "Ellen?" he said. "And Paul? How did they . . . I mean, where'd they get together?"

"On the street, in the drugstore, I don't know," O.B. said, waving his hand. "Anyhow, she . . . likes him a lot. It's somethin of a problem." His stomach felt clammy and cold.

"Why?" Eldon said.

" 'Why'?" O.B. shook his head. "Look, I'm sorry I brought it up. I just thought you might be able to tell me somethin about the boy, that's all."

"He's a very nice young man," Eldon said. "Truly now, I like him. All the young people like him a lot. He goes to Yale, I think."

"Yeah," O.B. said. *Yale. And he is from the North.* He represented a world that O.B. knew nothing about at all.

"He is as passionate about the movement as I am, if that's possible," Eldon said, his voice rising. "He's Jewish, so he knows somethin about discrimination. He's down here riskin his life for somethin he believes in. That ought to qualify him for bein seen with your daughter."

O.B. was beginning to seethe, hearing Eldon's tone, the near mockery in his voice. He didn't know what he had expected when he'd asked about the boy. He should have known that Eldon would not give him a straight answer. As he sat there blinking, he realized that he was wanting Eldon to convince him that the boy was harmless. What could Eldon tell him about that? He tried to swallow down his anger, taking deep breaths, and he heard a gentle rain begin to whisper on the bushes outside the window. He remembered that he had left his truck window down.

"You'll call off the boycott for my place, then?" he said.

"As good as done," Eldon said.

O.B. stood up. Eldon, behind his desk, looked back at him with the same faintly amused look in his eyes.

"You act like you've won something," O.B. said.

"Who? Me?" Eldon leaned back, locking his fingers behind his head. "Maybe," he said. "We'll see. We'll see."

O.B. felt a muted shiver run up his spine. He was not at all sure what he was letting himself in for, and he was frightened, but he did not want Eldon to see that. He remembered the day he reported to his first pro team, signed right out of high school, the Dothan Stars in the Class D Alabama-Florida League. He had ridden the Greyhound bus, going directly to the stadium, the season already in full swing when he graduated from high school. He recalled the dingy, dim dressing room, the damp concrete floor and the leaky showers, the stinking toilets. The older men on the team—including the manager, a fat old man named Art Sweeny who reeked of raw whiskey—had sneered at him, looked at him as though he were something disgusting, and they had laughed at the strange mixture of excitement and terror that he felt and couldn't hide. He knew now that they had felt it before, too, when they were young and fresh. But he had not known that then. That same look was in Eldon's eyes. You will find out, he seemed to be warning O.B. You will see what it's like.

O.B. tried to gather himself. *I will show you,* he thought. *I will be more up for this than you suspect.* He smiled. "All right," he said.

.~·~·~.

Mac had a tiny mayor's office, really little more than a desk in a closet, on the second floor at city hall. The county registrar, the county health nurse, and the police department took up most of the first floor, and the second floor was given over to city government, the largest office being that of the city clerk, a slightly effeminate little man named Reuben Thrash. Thrash did all the paper work, kept things running. Mac used his own little office more for socializing than anything else. Any serious business, such as conferences with visiting industry leaders and politicians, he conducted out of his spacious office at the bank.

City hall was in a whitewashed stone building, built in 1827. It had been, at various times, the town's first Presbyterian church, a hospital during the Civil War, a boarding-house that sat right in the town square, and the town library, which had moved to a new building right behind it in 1950, when the old building had been renovated again into city hall. The town's garden clubs kept the shrubs and flowers in the front a showplace; on this early summer morning, it was a blaze of color, with pink and white azaleas, red and yellow tulips, golden-orange daylilies, and God knew what all else. Mac stood there admiring the flowers for a long time. He thought, in spite of everything people could invent to disrupt their lives—boycotts, fights, demonstrations, cross-burnings—the flowers go right on blooming.

He went through the heavy glass front doors and up the stone stairs to the second floor. It was cool in the old building, the air smelling of ink and paper and, thinly, of the rubbing alcohol from the county health nurse's office that always made Mac think of shot day in elementary school. He went into the outer office of the city clerk, nodding and smiling at the girl who worked there, a skinny girl just out of high school, with mouse-colored hair. Mac could never remember her name. She smiled shyly at him, not lifting her fingers from her typewriter, which rattled and chattered away. He stuck his head in Reuben Thrash's office. Reuben wore a bright yellow hand-painted tie; he had proudly showed it to Mac on several occasions, telling him it was a gift from his niece. Reuben was married to a large, masculine woman named Clara, and they lived in a little house on Pettus Street. He dyed his hair coal black, so dark that it looked like a wig. He looked up from his desk, seeing Mac, and started to laugh. He always had a joke for Mac, usually a "nigger joke," and he always laughed loudly at his own jokes.

"Sheriff over in Mississippi?" he said, suppressing a giggle. "Sheriff and his boys fish a dead nigger out of the river. He's got heavy steel chains wrapped around and around him, all over him, lots of chains. Sheriff stands there lookin at the dead nigger. Finally, he says, 'Ain't that just like a nigger? Steal more chains than he can swim with?' " Reuben guffawed, and Mac chuckled politely. He was finding nigger jokes less and less funny these days.

He turned from Reuben's office, thinking to sit behind his own little desk for a while and shuffle through the mail that came for him here, and he found himself face to face with O.B. Brewster. O.B. looked startled to see him there. He shuffled his feet and grinned lopsidedly at Mac. Mac was surprised, too; not startled, but surprised.

"O.B., how you doin?" Mac said.

"All right." O.B. was looking around him. He seemed nervous. What was he up to? Mac wondered.

"You come to see Reuben?" Mac said. "Or me?"

"Well, I don't know," O.B. said. Mac looked questioningly at him. He waited. *Probably got that damn loan on his mind.*

When it seemed that O.B. was not going to go on, Mac said, "Listen. You git that stuff straightened out?" O.B. said nothing. "You know. That I came over to your house about?"

"Yeah," O.B. said.

"Well . . ." Mac said, "good." He waited. "What can I help you with?"

"Well," O.B. said, clearing his throat, "is this where I pick up the papers to qualify for runnin for mayor?"

"What?" Mac was sure he had not heard him right.

"I need to pay my fee, to get the papers and all. To run for mayor."

Mac was stunned, as though O.B. had blindsided him with a sucker punch.

"I'm gonna run for mayor," O.B. repeated. "Against you."

Mac laughed hollowly. "You . . . ? Awww, now . . ." He grinned expectantly. "Is this a joke?"

"No," O.B. said. "I'm gonna run for mayor against you, Mac. It's a free country, ain't it?"

"No," Mac said. He caught himself. *What the hell was he saying?* "Sure it is," he said. "You're gonna run for mayor?"

"Yes," O.B. said.

As the full realization of what O.B. was saying hit him, Mac experienced an involuntary, sharp intake of breath, and then he let it out, slowly. *Be calm. This is nothing to be alarmed about. Careful. Be calm.* His shock was gradually giving way to white-hot anger.

"Goddammit, man!" He was aware that the little secretary was watching them, but he couldn't restrain himself. "What is this? You don't do somethin like this! It's just a . . . just a *formality*. Runnin and all! You're gonna . . . muddy everything up!"

"I need to do this, Mac," O.B. said.

Mac searched his face, thinking that O.B. was a maddening person, always had been. He'd never really been a team player when they were boys. He always had to be *the* star! Mac took a deep breath, trying to calm himself. *Think.* After all, O.B. didn't stand a chance of beating him. He had been mayor for eight years. Everybody knew him. Still . . . he blinked. Everybody knew O.B., too.

"Well, shit!" Mac said. He could see the little secretary, as still as a mouse, watching them. "This pisses me off, O.B. I just got to tell you that. I mean . . ." He looked around the room. Reuben Thrash had come to the door of his office. He was standing there, his face open, wearing his startled expression above his wide, garish tie. "Reuben," Mac said, "you ain't gonna believe this. O.B. here wants qualifying papers to run for public office. Mayor. Can you believe that?" Mac laughed; it was forced and dry. Reuben smiled a painful, strained grin.

"You want me to give em to him?" he said.

"Of course! Of course! Give em to him. This ain't the goddam Soviet Union!" Mac felt himself losing control, as though a motor were racing full throttle in his chest. Reuben and the girl were looking at him with shocked faces. "This boy here? He used to come to school with cowshit on his pants, and now he wants to run for mayor. We used to call him Cowshit! Back in grammar school. Here comes old Cowshit Brewster—"

"Mac!" O.B. said. "There's no reason—"

"Cowshit Brewster!" Mac stopped. The room seemed suddenly very silent. In the distance, Mac could hear the murmur of traffic on Washington Street, the muted, distant blowing of a car horn. All three of them were looking at him now. He breathed deeply. "I tell you what," he said, as softly and as calmly as he could muster, "I tell you,

O.B., why don't we go across the hall here to my office and discuss this?"

"All right," O.B. said. "But there's nothin to discuss."

·~·~·~·

It *was* irrevocable. O.B. would not change his mind now. It was like a vow, a commitment, one that he could not deny. He felt reckless, endangered, but the danger somehow exhilarated him, even though he shuddered when he allowed himself to think of the risk to his family, to his place in the community. What was happening here had to do with a way of life, with cherished traditions. Those things had been fought over before, and would be again. But just knowing that he was running, that he had made the decision, filled him with a tingling such as he had experienced, years ago, in the on-deck circle before his first trip to the plate in a game. He wanted, he *needed*, to beat Mac. *And he would.*

But as he followed Mac across the hall, that heady sense of confidence fled, and O.B.'s chest felt leaden and cold. *No. He would not win the race.* Mac held his future in his hands, and O.B. had no doubts at all that Mac would put him out of business in a minute, destroy him forever in Hammond. O.B. felt both lonely and foolhardy, then, until he thought of Buddy Ed Webb, remembering the expression on the old man's face, the set of his shoulders as he watched O.B. behind his plow. O.B. swallowed, looking at the back of Mac's head, grateful at that moment that he was not looking into his eyes. Somewhere in all this there was a right and a wrong, but he did not know what they were. And then, the almost unbearable image of Cora came to mind. Her eyes, her hands, lean and soft, the palms the same color as his, their fingers intermingling, her fingernails, as sharp as tiny knives, scratching him, the nails amber, with faint half-moons of dim lavender stark against his pale skin.

He followed Mac into the tiny, cramped office. As quickly as a heartbeat, he now felt invulnerable, strong, thinking of Eldon's red-rimmed eyes, their heat, their passion. O.B.'s place in the community. What of it? What had the community ever done for him? A sense of responsibility, of assurance, swept over him then. A responsibility to something larger than the town, his family even, something vast that he was now beginning to see clearly and to understand. He could not know for sure if he was doing the right thing or not, but that did not matter to him. He knew, suddenly, with a clarity like blinding light, that he would somehow survive, that Ellen would, that they all would.

There was only one chair, so both men stood. Mac leaned against the windowsill; the window looked out onto a little deserted courtyard between city hall and the library and the jail. Mac would take care of this in a hurry. He would talk some sense into O.B., explain again to him about Gulf International, about what being a mayor was all about. O.B. didn't have the equipment for the job.

"Okay," Mac said, "okay, but I just can't figure this." O.B. was leaning against the doorjamb, his arms folded across his chest. "Unless it's got somethin to do with the niggers. With your old buddy Long. I can't see how you'd still be friends with that black bastard, if that's what it is. *You* tell *me*, O.B. I want to know."

"About that bank note comin due—" O.B. said.

"Wait! We ain't in the bank now." *I knew it!* "Don't change the subject." Mac was looking closely at O.B., still angry and confused as to how to proceed.

"All right," O.B. said. His pale blue eyes seemed calm, almost passive. His short-sleeved shirt was tight across his shoulders, and his arms were muscular, lightly downed with fine black hairs that didn't seem to go with his blond hair.

"I asked you to talk to Long," Mac said. "To talk some sense into his nappy head. But you wouldn't do it. And now you seem to be hookin up with this nigger business—"

"Not really, I—"

"That's what it looks like to me," Mac said. "Any white man would have to see that. Any white man—"

"Will you let me explain it to you?" O.B. said.

"Okay." Mac took a deep breath. "Okay, go ahead."

"Like I said that night at the White Citizens Council meetin, I got a lot of nigger customers. I been dealin with niggers all my life. Now I'm goin broke, Mac. I'm about to lose everything. I got that note comin due at your bank." O.B. paused to swallow, and Mac could see the tight tendons in his neck; he detected tiny beads of sweat on O.B.'s upper lip and forehead. He wasn't as cool as he was trying to look. Mac felt a little better. "All I want is to keep doin business. That's all."

"But what I don't understand is you runnin for mayor," Mac said. "What the hell has that got to do with it?"

"The niggers think that as long as you're the mayor, in charge, then things won't change. You won't call in the federal authorities to look into the voter registration business. You won't protect em when they sit down in white restaurants—"

"I reckon *you* will? Goddammit, O.B., are you a white man or what?"

"I don't know. I got a lot of nigger friends, Mac. I was out at Buddy Ed Webb's farm not long ago; he's plowin with a *mule*. I don't know. That old nigger . . . he's . . . brave or somethin, this whole thing, all these colored people, I—"

"That old nigger is a goddamn fool!" Mac said. "What about your white friends?" He arranged a shrewd expression on his face.

"I don't know. I'm confused."

"You sure as hell are!"

"All I want to do is get out from under this note. If I can make enough to pay my mechanics, keep em on, get through this and pay the interest on that loan—"

"Interest?"

"Yeah. And refinance it. You said—"

"Things have changed," Mac said. *Go ahead. Lower the boom right now!* "Never mind what I said. That note comes due in September. I hope you've put enough aside or you make enough over the summer to pay it off." Mac watched the expression on O.B.'s face. He was trying for his own poker face. He was bluffing, but he didn't know whether or not O.B. knew it. O.B. was incredibly naïve about business. He might really think that Mac would foreclose on his business for the, what was it? Ten, eleven thousand or so. That was peanuts. And he sure as hell didn't want to own Brewster Tractor company.

"I suppose, what you're tellin me," Mac said, sensing that he now had an advantage, "is that if you replace me as mayor, then the niggers will trade with you and you'll stay in business, and you'll in turn let em take over everything and then proceed to mongrelize the races. Is that right? I don't know what in the world has got into you, O.B. My spies tell me that the niggers are not only gonna continue this goddam insane boycott, they're gonna start right away tryin to integrate the picture show. Now I want to warn you, good buddy. There are a lot of folks around here that are just plain pissed off about all this. People are breakin the law, and they're gonna be treated like the common criminals they are. And you can just pass this bit of information along to your nigger friends. The governor has authorized all the municipal officers in the state to deputize civilians, if the need arises, to help the police. And I'll do it in a minute."

He glared at O.B., but the man showed no emotion. Mac sat on the edge of the desk, folding his arms across his chest the way O.B. was still holding his. His confidence was coming back. There was no way O.B. could beat him in a race for mayor. He smiled slightly. "I am committed, O.B., to preventin all that demonstratin and such bullshit in this town. Some of us . . . businessmen . . . stand to make a lot of money when Gulf International comes in. I . . ." He faltered again. He did not know what O.B. knew about all that. He could not remember what he had told him that night at the jail. He was beginning to wonder just *whom* he had told *what*. "I suggest, O.B., that you go back to your nigger friends and tell em to back off. Tell Long that he better just reconsider trying to sit on the main floor of that picture show."

He rocked on the desk, inspecting O.B.'s expressionless face. "You know, I told you way back at the jailhouse that night, remember? That I just didn't know what to think about you. I oughtta known then. What with Ellen and this boy and all—"

"Leave Ellen out of this," O.B. said abruptly.

"All right, all right." Mac held his hands up palm out toward O.B.. "I'm just levelin with you, O.B. You know people around here don't take kindly to certain kinds of behavior, and nigger-lovin is one of em. I don't have to explain that to you. People from other parts don't understand the way we do things down here, but, by God, people who live here do, and that makes it worse for you. You're gittin yourself in a heap of trouble, buddy boy." His voice was now edged with anger again. When he allowed himself to think about what O.B. was doing, he was incensed.

"All right, Mac," O.B. said. His lips were a tight, thin line. His eyes seemed to turn a shade darker, smoldering. His voice came out choked but firm, making Mac sit up straight, trying to comprehend what he detected there. "Maybe I'm just tired," O.B. said. "Maybe I just don't like all this shit. I try to tell you about Buddy Ed Webb, and you act like he's a . . . monkey or somethin. Goddammit. I'm tired of that. I'm tired of what you say about . . . Negroes. I—"

"Yeah," Mac said. "And I saw that good-lookin Cora Long in your pickup that night."

"You son of a bitch!" O.B. took a step forward, clenching his fists.

"Wait now," Mac said, suddenly alarmed. He stood up, too, sliding his rear end off the edge of the desk. "Hold on! I didn't mean nothin by that. I was just *kiddin* you, for God's sake. Can't you even take a joke anymore?" He cocked his head to the side, peering at O.B. O.B.'s breathing was deep and regular, but his eyes seemed full of something like agony; Mac was completely alert to it now. He backed up until his rear touched the windowsill, then refolded his arms across his chest.

O.B. looked wound as tight as a watch spring, and Mac didn't know what he might do. "I didn't mean nothin by that. Why don'tcha sit down there. Take my chair. You look tight as a drum." He could feel sweat running down his neck, under his collar. His light seersucker coat was clinging to his body. "There's a lot of money to be made with the paper mill comin in," he blurted.

"I don't give a shit about that," O.B. said.

"Well, you better start giving a shit about it," Mac said. "That note comin due, all that." The way O.B. was looking at him kept him uneasy and agitated. There was an obsession in the man's eyes that he did not understand. "You got an obligation to the white folks in this town. Don't forget that. You're a leader in this community, even though you don't wanna be, even though you try ever which way you can to get out of it. You still are. You can't just flush that responsibility down the commode, you can't."

"That's not what I'm doin," O.B. said, thinking: Here is that word again. "Maybe this *is* my *responsibility*. I'm beginnin to understand some things. Finally."

"Well, good," Mac said. "Maybe you'll come to your senses, then, save us all a lot of trouble, and drop this runnin-for-mayor shit." Mac felt a tiny spark of hope.

"Not a chance," O.B. interrupted. "Not a chance."

Shit. "It's foolish on your part. You don't stand a prayer of beatin me. And you just better remember that note."

"You threatenin me?" O.B. said.

"I'm givin you some good financial advice."

O.B. put his hands in his pockets. Mac could hear the change jiggling in his pocket.

"I'll remember that." O.B. turned to go.

"You better," Mac said to his back. O.B. moved toward the door. Mac watched O.B. going back into the city clerk's office. To get the papers! Mac realized that he had been almost holding his breath, and he let it out in a long, slow sigh as he sat heavily in the old surplus swivel chair. He was weak with hurt, anger, and confusion. O.B. had lost his mind; there was no reasoning with him. Life was getting too goddam complicated for anybody. "Shit," he muttered, under his breath.

．～．～．

One night almost a week later, O.B. and Ellen were sitting at the kitchen table. The house was quiet, the only sound moths thumping against the dark windowpanes and Ellen's yellow pencil, scratching on her paper. She was doing her homework, and O.B. was reading the paper. Martha was in bed. She had been drunk when he had gotten home from work, and she had yelled at him about his getting and filing the qualifying papers. She had heard about it downtown. She had accused him of shaming her before the white community. O.B. had been too tired to fight with her, and Martha had finally staggered off to bed. When Ellen had come in, she had seemed relieved that her mother was not up. O.B. held the paper in front of his face, squinting around it, watching her write, the way the tip of her tongue peeked from the corner of her mouth as she concentrated. He heard the soft scratch of the pencil.

Then there was another sound, which he did not immediately identify. Slowly, he realized that someone was knocking on the front door, a rough banging. A fist, not knuckles. Then the doorbell rang. The bell was in the kitchen, and it was loud, and they both jumped, looking at each other. It rang again, the knocking persisting, steady and loud. He stood up. Ellen was looking questioningly at him, gripping the pencil. He went up the hallway to the living room. The banging was louder, and he jerked open the door. Rooster Wembley stood there, his fist poised in the air. He grinned at O.B. O.B. could see, behind him on the porch, two men standing. He switched on the porch light. They were Bobby Lee McElroy and Red Kershaw. The unshaded porch light glinted on Kershaw's shock of bright orangish-red hair. O.B. looked at Rooster, who was grinning.

"Yeah?" he said. "Whattaya want?"

"Well, shit," Rooster said, "that ain't no way to greet nobody."

"You don't have to tear the goddam door down," O.B. said. He saw Rooster's eyes drift past his shoulder, and he knew that Ellen had come into the living room. "What can I do for you, Rooster?" He nodded to Red and Bobby. They stood there self-consciously, looking uncomfortable.

"Well, B. O. Oyster! Can we come in a minute?" Rooster's grin was mirthless. "Or you want to talk out here?"

O.B. stepped back, and Rooster came on into the living room, his wooden leg clomping on the hardwood floor. The other two men eased through the door, closing it behind them, then looking at their feet as though they were afraid of tracking something inside. They all three looked at Ellen and nodded. "Evenin," Rooster said, touching the brim of his straw hat. He did not take it off.

"What's goin on?" O.B. said.

"Maybe the little lady might not want to be in on this," Rooster said. O.B. glanced over at Ellen. She stood inside the door, holding the notebook she had been working in in front of her.

"What?" O.B. said, "in on what?" He sensed the threat in the old barber.

"Well," Rooster said. "All right." He paused thoughtfully. "We're a delegation representin some segments of the population of Hammond. And we have been appointed, so to speak, to come over here and tell you that you got no business runnin for mayor, or anything else, in this town. So we want you to forget it, forget them ideas, and just sit tight."

"Mac send you over here?" O.B. said.

"Nooo, now. He wouldn't do nothin like that. Mac don't even know about this." Rooster's smile was a smirk. Bobby Lee and Red were watching them, their eyes narrowed. Red ran a beer joint across the river in Green County. O.B. had heard that there was gambling in the back room. He had heard that all of them sometimes played in a game upstairs over Andy Wheatly's pool room. He didn't know what Bobby Lee was doing for a living now. They were both sorry; they reminded O.B. of men who would drift through jobs at his place, the type who was always late, always smelling of whiskey by Friday. O.B. looked back at Rooster.

"Sit down, why don't y'all," he said. He didn't like them standing, alert and ready, in his living room.

"They'll stand," Rooster said, sitting down on the couch. He looked at the pictures under the glass on the coffee table, nodding his head, smiling.

O.B. felt disquieted, nervous. He looked steadily at Rooster. "Who are . . . these people you talkin about?" O.B. said.

"Oh, just some citizens." Rooster leaned back against the couch, stretching his good leg out before him, under the table. He pushed the hat up on his head. The sweatband of the hat was stained and yellowed, and O.B. could see thin strings of gray hair sticking to the sides of Rooster's head. His sharp chin jutted toward O.B. "I don't think you've quite thought this out very thoroughly," he said. He grinned the mirthless grin again. "There's a . . . well, a certain order to the way things is done. Now we got us a good mayor in this town. The times right now . . . well, we all know what's goin on. We figure white people got to stick together. No sense wastin time and energy havin two white men run against one another, is it?" He waited. O.B. did not answer. Rooster looked shrewdly at him, his yellowish eyes squinted.

"Tell you what, O.B. If Eldon Long wants somebody to run for mayor, let him git a nigger."

"I'm not doin this for Eldon Long," O.B. said quickly. He heard the slight quaver in his voice, and he tried to swallow it away. He could not let these little, slimy men get the better of him.

"Yeah?" Rooster said. "The word's already gone out. Niggers can trade with Brewster Tractor Company now, but nobody else. And the Brewster of Brewster Tractor Company is runnin for mayor against the most popular mayor Hammond has ever had, a man who's gonna bring prosperity, and peace, too, goddammit—pardon me, little lady—to us. And Mac ain't gonna take any shit—" He paused. "Little lady, you sure you want to hear all this? Cause I'm so . . . emotional about it, I just can't hardly control myself."

"She can stay," O.B. said, thinking he could always tell her to leave if things got out of hand. Meanwhile, he wanted her here as an ally. For moral support.

"All right. He ain't gonna take any . . . crap off these niggers, and they know it. Maybe they want somebody they can push around, but that don't sound like the O. B. Brewster I know, that I've cut his hair since he was a boy. Ole B. O. Oyster! Nosirree-bob." He cut his twinkling, merry eyes at Ellen. Then he looked back at O.B. "But, hell, maybe he's done already made a deal with em, or somethin. I don't know nothin bout dealin with niggers. I never cut a nigger's hair, wouldn't know how to start. I don't have no wire cutters in my shop." Bobby Lee sniggered. "I don't talk nigger language. But I hear you do. I hear you and this Long nigger growed up together down in the Flatwoods. That right?"

"We knew each other when we were children, yeah," O.B. said. "We grew up together. Yeah," he said, more firmly. "That's right."

"Folks are sayin that you're a nigger-lover, O.B. Now I don't cotton to callin folks names, specially folks I've known all they lives. Lots of folks round here love darkies, nothin wrong with that. But we all know what nigger-lover means. These are strange times. It's like the Civil War that my granddaddy fought in, all over again. You got to be careful. You don't want to be doin nothin that's gonna hurt the white folks' cause. And you're about to do that, O.B." He sat there looking levelly at O.B., making him shift in his chair. He was tired, so tired that he was having trouble focusing on what Rooster was saying, and he was feeling the anger rising in him again, a kind of impatient vexation that this man was in his house saying these things to him. "All I want you to do is give me your word that you're droppin out of this thing, and stayin out of the way. Whatever these niggers do now, they gonna meet with solid resistance. Somebody might get bad hurt. You don't want to be in the middle of it. How about it?"

O.B. clasped his hands in front of him. His instinct to survive this was strong now; he could feel it inside his chest. He cleared his throat. "No," he said.

"Huh?" Rooster said. "Did I hear you right?"

"You heard me," O.B. said. "I told you. I'm runnin for me. I got a right to do that. I got just as much right as Mac McClellon. I—"

"He's the goddam mayor, O.B.," Rooster said.

"I got a right to run if I want to. Now get outta my house." He said it though a cold, icy fear was rising within him. These men were small and fearful, weak-minded, but there was never any telling what they might do.

"What?" Rooster said. "What?" He let out a long sigh. "Lordamercy. You boys hear this? Jesus."

"Daddy!" Ellen's voice sounded full of panic, hysteria.

He turned to her. "You go on to your room, Ellen."

"No." She stood firm in the doorway, breathing deeply, but her eyes seemed deceptively calm and steady. He knew her so well that he sensed more than saw the trembling in her lips.

"Go on to your room, Ellen," he repeated. "I can handle these people. They don't mean any harm." He said it sarcastically. The room was silent for a moment.

Rooster sighed deeply. "You makin a big mistake, O.B." He dragged himself slowly to his feet. "I thought maybe I could talk some sense into your head. You don't know what you messin with here, boy." He tested the false leg, grunting. "Reason I asked this little lady to leave in the first place, O.B., is that I wanted to tell you. We keep a watch on what's goin on. We got a surveillance on the Youngblood place, where them agitators are stayin. Your daughter's name appears on the log quite a few times. Now, I don't know what the hell to make of that—"

"It has nothin to do with anything," O.B. said roughly, his white-hot anger growing even more intense.

"Oh now, oh now," Rooster said. "Maybe it does. Maybe it don't. I reckon you know all about it. You don't seem surprised none."

A fear, a sudden terror for Ellen, her vulnerability, flashed into his consciousness. "She and Sally . . . Long . . ." He hesitated, knowing how bad it sounded when he was saying it. ". . . they were friends when they were little. They . . ." *Don't drag her into this any more! It's not fair!*

"Lordamercy. Now you sho got a nigger-lovin family, O.B. But lemme tell you, it wasn't no Sally Long that she was visitin. Nosirree. It was that Jew agitator Siegel. But don't let me be jumpin to no conclusions here. I can't keep up with these young people no more. What with all their goddam nigger music and everything, Little Richard and what not. You ever see a picture of *him*? I ask you, what *is* that? Lord. I got a niece lives up in Birmingham, she's crazy about Elvis. Now if he ain't a white nigger, I don't know what is! Beats all. There's a nigger in *his* mama's woodpile somewhere, sure as shootin." He shook his head, sighing and grinning. Then his grin faded, and his copper eyes were flat, lifeless, level on O.B. "It comes at you from everywhere, O.B. You can't get away from it. It's comin to a showdown, and you just better make goddam sure you wind up on the right side. I'd sure as hell hate to see a good ole boy like you git his ass rapped upside a tree somewhere. Or driftin to the bottom of the quarry with concrete blocks for bedroom slippers. It can happen."

O.B. took a step forward, and all three of the other men tensed. They were frozen, poised, waiting.

"Daddy," Ellen whispered behind him.

"You're threatenin me, you bastard," O.B. said thinly, hating Rooster with a fury he didn't know if he could control.

"No now," Rooster said. "I'm just giving you some good advice. People git real mad. You mess with their way of life, they git downright pissed off."

"I ain't scared of you and your Ku Klux Klan," O.B. said. He knew he was being foolhardy, but he couldn't help himself. He wanted to push Rooster's face in. Bobby Lee and Red stood awkwardly, their eyes worried and confused; they were almost harmless until somebody pointed their guns for them, and O.B. could see that they did not know what to do. They had not said a word during the entire visit.

"Yeah, well," Rooster said. "They can be some bad asses, whoever they are. Under them sheets. It ain't any of *my* Klan. Don't know nothin about that." He grinned at O.B. "Me and some of my friends now, you heard? We gonna be deputized. Yessir. Ole Ked and Mobby McMee there. Next time there's any trouble, we gonna have us a citizens' posse. To help out the police." He winked. "I know old Mac and Lester figure they want us where they can keep an eye on us, I can see right through em, but that's all right with me." He winked at O.B. again. "You could be a part of that, O.B. We'd welcome you. You better give all this some thought. I'd advise you to think right hard on it." He was moving toward the door, the wooden leg thumping on the floor.

Red and Bobby Lee followed him out. Rooster looked back through the open door. "Think right hard on it, ya hear?" he said. The door closed, and O.B. stood there. In a few seconds, he heard the screen porch door's rattling slam, and he did not move until he heard the sound of a motor starting, coughing and revving, pulling away from the curb, and then silence. O.B. felt hollow, light-headed. He realized that he had been holding his breath, and he let it out in a long sigh, then turned to Ellen. She stood in the doorway, clutching the notebook in front of her chest. Her eyes were wide, rimmed with tears. Her lips were trembling openly now.

"Daddy, I . . ." she said, her voice a dry whisper.

"Don't worry," he said, his own voice sounding hoarse in his ears.

"What he said . . ." she said, "what he said about . . ."

"They're evil, dirty people," he said. "Don't pay any attention to what he said. Go to bed." His weariness seemed to be dragging him down toward the floor.

"Good night," Ellen said softly, and she went quietly down the hall to her room.

O.B. stood in the silent room. Gradually, in the quiet, he heard a sound, coming from behind the closed bathroom door. Martha. He had not known she was up. She must have been listening in the hallway, through the fog of her mind. It sounded as though Martha were coughing, and he moved slowly to the hall door, hearing her in the bathroom, and he realized she was vomiting. He felt his own fear rising in his stomach like bile as he stood there, his shaking hands thrust deeply into his pockets.

PART 3

SUMMER

Chapter Nine

THE SWEAT WAS TRICKLING DOWN ELDON'S NECK, UNDER HIS COL-
lar. He could feel the afternoon sun beating down relentlessly on
his head. His scalp tingled with anticipation; he had heard rumors that
the white people knew all about the planned march on the picture
show, and he expected them to be waiting for them. He had heard that
the word had leaked, probably from some of the older, more conservative of his people, the ones who still worked in the white kitchens,
cleaned the white toilets. He had no idea what to expect, but he was
prepared for the worst. What could happen? They could be arrested
again, even roughed up. But there was a limit. He knew now that Mac
McClellon didn't want anything getting into the papers or on the
television news. Maybe they would just calmly go in and watch the
picture together on the main floor. How sweet and beautiful that
would be. Eldon sighed.

They moved steadily up the street, around the corner, a line of
them, led by Joe Mancini and Sally at the front; Eldon was bringing
up the rear. There were an even dozen of them, the boy Paul laughing
and joking in the middle of the line, Edna Blanks in a blue dress like
a tent, Nathaniel Pierson in his bulging T-shirt, looking out from
behind his angry scowl, several other youngsters, and a few older

people. Most of them looked scared and nervous, walking along in tense silence. It would go according to plan. Eldon knew it would, felt confident that they had covered everything in the classes. *Lord, be with us!* The threat, the fear of bloodshed, of needless pain, hovered over them. *It's my imagination. It's my worst fear. These white people are . . . What are they? They are victims, too. Lord, help us remember that.*

As they turned the corner onto Washington Street, Eldon, squinting against the sun, could see the crowd up ahead, lining the street across from the Dauphin Theater. In spite of what he had heard, he was shocked at their number; there must have been several hundred people. He heard a murmur go up, cries of "There they come," and he could see Lester Sparks and Henry Davis, who owned the theater, standing under the marquee that overhung the sidewalk. DAUPHIN, it said in tiny, closely packed white light bulbs. The letters underneath spelled out *Wackiest Ship in the Army*. 3:00, 7:30. It was a Monday matinee, which was, according to Mancini, the lightest crowd of the week, the time least likely to provoke violence. "There's usually no more than twenty there," he had said, "hardly anybody in the balcony."

The box office sat to the side, under the overhanging marquee, and the white-only side opened onto the pavement in front of the main lobby. The side marked COLORED was a small window, opening onto a narrow alley that went along the brick wall of the theater to a side door, where there was a tiny, cramped lobby with stairs leading up to the colored balcony. The group slowed, forming a line. Henry Davis, the owner of the theater, was frowning as they moved under the marquee, but Lester Sparks was grinning, his eyes searching the line, finally resting on Eldon's face. He nodded, in what looked like a friendly greeting, but Eldon could see the angry steel glint in his eyes.

"Go home, niggers!" somebody shouted from across the street, and there was laughter. The white people were behind a row of sawhorses that the police had probably set up. "Whew! Stinks around here!" someone else, a girl, yelled. Everyone stood, eyes straight ahead. Eldon knew that they were focusing their concentration, running the instructions from their classes through their heads. He saw Joe Mancini step up to the window and buy a ticket. The girl in the booth, pretty, with dark hair, kept looking over Joe's shoulder at Mr. Davis as she punched out the ticket. It clacked out of the little brass-topped machine, and Joe tore it off. Sally stepped up to the window. As Eldon watched her, his pulse fluttered lightly, quickly; he could feel the sweat clinging to his face.

"Colored is round to the side," the girl said.

"One adult, please," Sally said.

The girl was looking at Mr. Davis and at Lester Sparks. They stood there, watching.

"I said, colored is round there," the girl said. She grinned self-consciously. The crowd was hushed, watching from across the street.

"I just want one adult ticket, to see the picture," Sally said. Eldon could hear the edge of anger in her voice. *Let her be calm, Lord, let her be calm.*

Mr. Davis stepped up to her. He was a short man, about Eldon's age, a little, thin man not much taller than Sally, and he looked nervous. His lips twitched; his hands were clasped across his chest. "I'm sorry," he said, his voice a high squeak, "but you gotta buy your ticket round there." He smiled tensely. "You been doin it since you was a little girl. Maybe you done forgot." He nodded his head.

"I ain't forgot," Sally said.

She waited at the window. Everyone stood there, quietly now, in the afternoon heat. Eldon could see heat waves shimmering off the pavement of Washington Street. There were no cars. They must have blocked off the street. The white people across the way watched, somehow looking eager, many with cocky grins on their faces. Eldon saw O.B. back in the crowd, watching intently, and he saw Rooster Wembley and two other white men standing in the doorway of V. J. Elmore's Store, across the way. He knew them to be Red Kershaw and Bobby Lee McElroy. McElroy had been with Rooster the day of the sit-in at Maud's. Eldon was alarmed. They held long, heavy-looking sticks. He had heard that Lester Sparks had deputized some men in anticipation of trouble. He let his eyes play over the crowd, and then he saw other men, too, with sticks. Eldon was shocked. They were ax handles, shiny new wooden ax handles. Surely, nobody would *use* those things. Surely, Mac McClellon and Lester Sparks wouldn't . . . He began to sweat more freely. He saw Joe Mancini whispering calmly to Sally. The line stood there patiently, sweating in the sun.

Then Sally moved around to the colored window, and the girl swiveled in her chair and sold Sally a ticket. Eldon watched the line move up, his people buying tickets at their usual window, then stepping back, waiting, holding the tickets in front of them. Paul bought his at the white-only window. Eldon stepped up, the girl looking at him with amused contempt, shoving the ticket across to him, taking his dollar and giving him back change. ADULTS 70 CENTS, CHILDREN 35 CENTS, the sign said. They all had their tickets now, and Joe called them into a group. "You know what to do now," he said calmly, looking at each one of them. He gave a nod. They moved as a group toward the front lobby, under the marquee. Eldon's blood fluttered and danced in his veins; his whole body was alive with anticipation. But Lester Sparks seemed to know exactly what they were doing. He stood in front of the glass doors, his arms folded across his chest. The young cop Ricky Wiggins stood next to him, in front of the other set of doors, looking scared and nervous. Eldon noticed that he had started to grow a mustache. It looked wispy and thin, almost as if his upper lip were soiled.

"Where the hell you think you goin?" Sparks said.

"We're goin in to see the movie," Joe Mancini said. Eldon edged himself closer to the front. He could see that Sparks was searching for him with his eyes. Their eyes locked.

"Long, what the hell is this?" Sparks said.

"We've bought tickets, Mr. Sparks, and now we want to all go in together and watch the picture. On the main floor."

"Well, you can't," Sparks said. "You bought tickets for the balcony. That's where you sit." Eldon said nothing; they all just stood there, patiently. But Eldon knew that all their hearts were beating rapidly, all their pulses racing as fast as his. He wiped the sweat from his brow. The handkerchief felt soft and cool on his face. He carried his suit coat over his arm, and he could feel the cloth of his shirt sticking to his arm under the coat. "I can let these two Yankee white boys in on this floor," Sparks said, "though I'd like to put em under the jail. But you coloreds go around to the side like you always have, and I don't want no trouble."

"It's the same price either place," Eldon said. "We're going in here. We're going to sit together. We're not sittin in that balcony again."

"Now, Eldon," Sparks sighed. "Don't make this hard for me. You gonna wind up right back in that jail again."

"For simply buyin a ticket and goin to a picture show?" Eldon said. "We are children of God, Mr. Sparks. We are doing this for justice and our dignity as people and citizens! This is America."

"It might be America, but it's Alabama, too," Sparks said. "You know what the law says, Eldon. I'm sworn to uphold it. And all my men."

Eldon was standing next to Nathaniel Pierson. He could hear the boy breathing, almost jerking the air into his nostrils; he could sense the tenseness, the rage, in Nathaniel's body, feel the heat as he glanced at him. The boy's muscles beneath the T-shirt looked hard and rigid. His body was poised, uneasily balanced, as he shifted his weight back and forth on the balls of his feet. He saw that Sally stood with her hand resting on Nathaniel's forearm. Eldon took a deep breath.

"The time has come! You can no longer corrupt the will of God, Mr. Sparks! We're goin in," he said.

"No, you ain't."

Eldon could see the lobby behind Sparks, through the glass doors, looking dim and cool. There was a sign on the glass, just at Sparks's head, an ice cube with white frost clinging to it underneath the letters AIR CONDITIONED. COOL INSIDE. Eldon had been walking by on the street before, just as the doors were pushed open, and felt the rush of cold, damp air into the muggy afternoon, carrying with it the belly-tightening aroma of fresh popcorn. He'd looked into the spacious lobby with its carpet and sofas and ashtrays on stands, a sanctum where none of his people, except those few who worked there cleaning up, had ever been, could ever even go. He swallowed. He took a step forward.

"Please move aside, Mr. Sparks," he said. "The picture gonna start in a minute."

There were two sets of doors, Sparks before one and Wiggins before the other, and they moved forward as a group. Eldon saw panic and confusion in Wiggins's eyes. The young police officer suddenly moved to the side, his hand on his pistol, looking frantically at Sparks, and Sparks said:

"Goddammit, Wiggins! Just stand fast. They ain't gonna—"

But Nathaniel and Sally, followed by Mancini, were pushing through the door; the group melted to the left, leaving Sparks sputtering in front of the door.

"Stop!" he said. "I order you to stop!" The group pressed forward. Eldon could hear confusion, movement, some shouting behind him. The sound of heavy boots, scraping, then pounding the hot concrete. "In the name of the law!" Sparks shouted. *Lord, be with us*, Eldon prayed. *Lord, make his face to shine upon us!*

He heard, then felt, more scrambling behind him, and then he heard a cry of pain. He turned, horror-stricken, as he saw Rooster Wembley and his men wading into their group, swinging the ax handles like baseball bats.

"Rooster! Goddammit!" he heard Sparks shouting angrily, and Eldon screamed, "Get down! Get down! Cover your heads!" He saw some people dropping to their knees and covering their heads with both arms, as they'd been taught, and there was grunting and panic, a whirling chaos of shouts, cries of "Oh, Jesus!" and "Bless the Lord!" A swirling of color, of red and yellow gingham skirts and blue denim shirts. Eldon raised his arms over his head and felt a stinging, fiery blow across his buttocks. He closed his eyes for a moment, and when he opened them, he saw Edna Blanks, directly in front of him, moving her weight with speed and agility, swinging her arms at a lean, skinny man with pasty, clay-colored skin, who brought the ax handle in his hands crashing down onto her head. He heard her grunt, saw the man swing again, the wood glancing off her forehead, the blood spurting down across her face. "Get down, Edna!" Eldon screamed, watching her fling her fists blindly, seeing the man swing the club again, catching her across the mouth as she, stunned, her eyes wide with shock and pain, dropped her arms, looking at Eldon with anger and disbelief. The man swung again, hitting her in the back of the neck, and Eldon could hear a sickening crunch as her heavy body sagged and went down. Eldon followed her to the pavement. He could hear grunting and heavy breathing, the sound of police sirens nearby. *Lord, let them have an ambulance. Let them have an ambulance!*

He looked up, shielding his face, squinting in the harsh afternoon sunlight. The chaos was subsiding. He heard crying, whimpering, and he looked around. Edna lay facedown, as still as a statue, a pool of dark blood forming next to her head. People were looking up, stirring, getting to their feet. Eldon struggled slowly up, the backs of his legs paining him. He looked frantically around, his breath coming in gasps, unable to fully comprehend what had happened. He saw Nathaniel, his head bloody, being led away in handcuffs, with Sally crying, walking along beside him. He saw Paul and Joe, handcuffed together, standing next to the box office, their faces pale and ashen, as though they were about to be sick. Sirens roared, an ambulance came screeching down Washington Street; Edna had been turned over, and her dark, lifeless eyes stared upward toward the sky. *She's dead! Edna's dead.* "She hurt bad," he heard someone say. *Lord, let her live. Lord, let her not be dead!*

᠁᠁

When it had started, O.B. had watched in horror as the men began to wade in with the ax handles. He could not believe it. He had never seen anything like it. He saw the fat schoolteacher defending herself, a woman, against men not in uniform, and without thinking, O.B. had moved forward quickly, only to be stopped by Hoyt Blessing, one of the city policemen. Hoyt had pushed O.B. roughly in the chest. "What the hell you think you're doin?" Blessing had said, holding his pistol in his hand, at his side.

"Look what they're doin, Hoyt!" O.B. said. "Goddammit!"

"Back up, buddy," Hoyt said. "This ain't any of your business."

O.B. stood shifting uneasily. He could hear the cries of pain, see the struggle before him, and he had moved again, drawn toward the struggle as though by a magnet, and Blessing had pushed him again, stronger this time. O.B. had looked into the man's eyes, at the steely glint there, the panic and the fear. Hoyt's face was spotted with droplets of sweat, and his nostrils were pale and bloodless. He was looking at O.B. as though he did not know him. *This man would shoot me! He would kill me in a minute!* O.B. froze, unable to move. *What is happening to these people I have known all my life?*

He restrained himself then, held back the impulse to go to the woman's aid, to the aid of them all. Eldon was in there, and his little daughter, his little girl. Thankfully, the chaos was subsiding now, and O.B. looked around, at the white people standing near him, at the way they looked at him out of the corners of their eyes, then looked away, as though embarrassed by what he had tried to do, or by what they had seen happening in front of them, he did not know which. Bottom line was that they would not look him in the eye. *People I have known all my life!*

He was trembling inside, quivering, and he only dimly heard the sirens, saw, past Hoyt Blessing's bulky body, the people in front of the picture show beginning to look up, to get to their knees and look around, their eyes wide and disbelieving, reflecting a helplessness that O.B. felt and knew now as well. He could see the men, among them Rooster Wembley and Buster Jackson, hefting the ax handles, some of them grinning self-consciously. It was over. *No, it will never be over. It has gone on as long as there were men around to do it, and as long as there are men around, they will keep on doing it.* O.B.'s mouth felt as dry as cotton, and he realized that he was sweating heavily, his shirt soaked through. He stood apart, separate from the others. *I will not be one of them. I will not be one of the men who will allow this.*

He saw Eldon then, standing, his arm around a young girl who O.B. knew must be his daughter. They were all right. Next to them was the tall boy O.B. knew to be Paul Siegel. He was all right, too, and, looking at the scene, O.B. felt a stab of pain like a ax blow to his own chest, and he was afraid that he had whimpered aloud. He looked around. Nobody was paying him any mind now, and he stood there in the harsh, angry sun, his eyes burning, his muscles as tense and as rigid as steel.

·~·~·~·

Paul sat on the narrow cot, his head throbbing. The cells were dimly lighted, smelling of unclean bodies and stale urine. Nathaniel was stretched out on the upper bunk, his eyes closed. The doctor had looked at Nathaniel's head, where he'd taken a blow from Ricky Wiggin's billy club, and had put a bandage over it. The old doctor had laughed, turning to the policeman next to him. Paul knew his name was Dave Gatlin; he and Mancini were learning all the policemen's names.

"If you don't want to hurt a nigger too bad, hit him in the head," the old doctor had said to Gatlin, chuckling. The doctor checked them all out. There were numerous head bumps and skinned knees.

This is it, Paul was thinking. *It has really started now. There will be no stopping us now.*

They were all crammed into the few little cells. Paul was worried about Edna Blanks; she had not looked good. Paul still felt the racing excitement, but it was dulled now with worry over Edna, worry over all of them.

Long was in the next cell, and he was concerned about Edna Blanks, too. Paul had nervously told him not to worry.

"Why not?" Long said.

"Just don't worry. We'll be out soon."

"How you know that? Besides, it's Edna I'm worried about." Long's voice was tense. "And I guess they could keep us in here forever. We got—"

"No, just . . ." Paul had shaken his head. The lawyer would be here soon; it was already set up. There was plenty of inside information that they kept from Long; Mancini insisted on it. But Paul guessed it was for the best. He was willing to go along with that. But when people started getting badly hurt . . . He rubbed his temples with his stiff fingers. He had been stunned and shocked by the intensity of the violence in front of the theater. He had never seen such hatred as he saw in the eyes of some of the men who came after them with the clubs. He was frightened, suspecting that he and Mancini had bungled the whole thing. He took a deep breath in the dank air. *Jesus!* He could see Long in the next cell, his head down, looking tired and drawn. Suddenly, looking at the older man, he realized that this was what it was all about. This was the test, the trial by fire. Though he was scared, he felt his determination growing. The dingy jail did not seem nearly so intimidating as it had the first time, and he stood up and stretched, glancing at Nathaniel stretched out on the upper bunk. The white bandage was startling against his black skin; his eyes gazed steadily at the dark ceiling. *I cannot let them down.* He wondered if Nathaniel knew that Mancini and Sally had been on his case about his relationship with Ellen Brewster, and how it threatened to endanger him, and the cause. Mancini had called him a fool; Sally had laughed bitterly, shaking her head.

"Everything's under control," he said suddenly to Nathaniel, hearing the bluster in his own voice, and the boy just looked at him. *It is in control. I will show them. I have championed these people, and I will not let them down!*

"Smells like niggers in here," a voice said, and Paul could see an old white man who looked drunk, sitting in the last cell at the end. He wore dirty, paint-spotted overalls without a shirt. He was glaring at them. "Goddam, what's goin on?" he said. "Where'd all the niggers come from?" Even from this distance, Paul recognized the harsh, kerosenelike smell of raw moonshine, which he'd been introduced to at the Youngbloods'.

Faintly then, Paul heard someone begin to sing. It was just a whisper, and he couldn't make out the words, until someone else, and then a third voice, joined in. "Ohhhhh, freedom . . . ohhhhh, freedom . . . before I'd be a slave . . ."

"Shut up!" the old man shouted. "Goddammit, cut out that racket!"

". . . I'd be buried in my grave, and go home, to my Lord. . . ." They were all singing now, and Paul began to hum, then sing along, the dull pain in his head softening, fading. He looked up, smiling, feeling warm tears behind his eyes. He tried to see Mancini, a couple of cells down, but he could not see him. A sense of well-being, of almost happiness, flooded his chest. He concentrated on the song, the words of it, pushing the doubts from his mind.

"Stop it! Goddammit!" the drunk yelled.

". . . and go home, to my Lord, and be free!"

Dave Gatlin came in from the office up front. He rattled his club against the bars. "Cut it out!" he said.

"Ohhhh, freedom . . . Ohhhh, freedom . . ." They sang, their voices rising, and Gatlin rattled his club against the cell bars as loudly as he could, and the old man kept screaming, at the top of his lungs.

"Stop this nigger shit!" he yelled. "Stop it!"

". . . and go home, to my Lord, and be free!" Paul sang, knowing now, believing now, that the words were true and were the central, abiding focus of his humble, strong, invincible young life.

.~.~.~.

"Close the door," Mac said. He watched Lester stand up and get the door, and the noise level went down. He could barely hear them singing now, just barely hear old Ted Mack yelling at them. *We have done it now! We have royally fucked up now!* Rooster was leaning against the wall, his arms folded, his wooden leg cocked out at an angle. The late afternoon sun slanted through the narrow, dusty window.

"It was Rusty Jackson that done it," Rooster said. "I told him—"

"I don't care who it was," Mac said. He was so angry he could feel his face flushing. Rooster's yellowish-brown eyes were calm, steady. "I told y'all and told y'all that we couldn't afford no shit like that! Goddammit! There was no sense in knockin that old nigger woman in the head!"

"She's a schoolteacher!" Rooster exclaimed. "She ought to know better! She didn't have no business doin what she was doin—"

"She was defyin a direct order, Mac," Lester said. "She woulda run right over Henry Davis if somebody didn't stop her. In his own place of business."

"I know all that," Mac said. "But all you had to do was arrest her. Like you did them others. She's laying up there in the hospital, and goddammit, she might *die*. You understand that? You think that won't git in all the papers? Hell, it already is, I bet, but if she dies, shit! That goddam Gulf International fellow will be on me like a duck on a june bug if she dies! He'll be down here mad as hell. I'm just waitin for the goddam phone to ring. 'Well, Mr. McClellon, y'all sure fucked it over this time!' Shit."

The two men just looked back at him. He was mad at Lester for talking him into deputizing those men, frustrated at his mistake, furious at himself because he had known all along the idea was nothing but trouble. He had rationalized to himself that if they were deputized, it would keep them on the right side of the law, and they had agreed to turn in their pistols and be issued the "riot sticks," as Lester called them. They had promised, no shotguns. But the niggers had sucked them right into the trap! Cross-burnings and such got no publicity, but something like this! He had been looking right at that redneck Rusty Jackson when he'd lit into the nigger woman. White trash! *No more of this 'deputy' shit!*

They said if she made it through the night, she might live. Mac's throat felt dry; there was an unpleasant, metallic taste in his mouth. He felt responsible. He shifted in the chair.

"I'll tell you this," he said. "If she dies, that dumb asshole Rusty goes on trial for murder!"

"He was just doin his duty," Rooster said. "He was a deputy, he was within—"

"Shut up!" Mac exploded, then took a deep breath, calming himself. He looked at the two men. Rooster had a strange, tentative expression on his face, as though he didn't quite know what to make of being spoken to like that. Mac made his voice as calm as he could. "We got an election comin up," he began.

"Shit!" Rooster interrupted.

"I'm gonna beat O.B., no doubt about that," Mac said quickly, "but the campaign is comin up and all. And we got to remember about Gulf International. It's all tied in together. All we got to do is hold things down until those boys make a commitment. Hopefully, they'll come in and start buildin, and then it'll be too late for em to back out. They backed out on Montgomery, they could do it to us. I know what I'm talkin about. We got to learn from Montgomery's mistakes. We might have to . . ." He stopped, squirming in the chair.

Rooster was looking at him with suspicion. "What?"

"Give a little," Mac said. He did not look at the old man. "Just a little."

"To the niggers? You crazy?" Rooster said.

"Just talk to em. Give in a little bit. I don't know," he said irritably.

"Give in a little how, Mac?" Lester said.

"I don't know," Mac reflected, feeling helpless. "Make em think we're takin em seriously. I been thinkin of seatin Long on the Citizens Council . . ." His voice trailed off.

"The *White* Citizens Council?" Sparks said.

"We got to make some gesture to em," Mac tried to reason, "to keep em quiet, keep things under control."

"I'll tell you one goddam thing." Rooster's voice was ominous in Mac's ears. The distant singing had died out, and the room was very quiet, the only sound the purr of the window air conditioner. "If they keep on goin into white-only cafés and such, tryin to sit where they ain't supposed to in the picture show, ain't supposed to *by law*, then by God somethin bad's really gonna happen to em! Somethin *worse* than already has."

"We'll just keep on throwin em in jail," Mac said. "Till they get so tired of it they—"

"You know, churches can burn down," Rooster cut him off. "Houses been known to burn down, too. It's that goddam nigger church and that nigger preacher where all this stuff's gettin started. He's a trouble-maker. And them goddam little shit-asses from up North. They got no business down here. If you can't send em packin, then maybe some-body else can!"

"Anyhow, you got to take your orders from Lester," Mac went on, trying to change the subject.

"That's right," Lester said. He stood very still, leaning against the wall.

"And that goes for all those boys you recruited. I know most of em are good boys. They're just . . . overeager, is all." Mac was watching Rooster closely, trying to read the expression in his amber eyes. He knew that there was probably no limit to what Rooster might do if he was provoked. "If you gonna be official deputies, then you gotta go along with what Lester and his men say. Now, Rooster"—Mac tried to look stern, confident—"I do appreciate what y'all are doin. I do. The whole town does. The governor himself has gone on record as bein grateful to all citizen volunteers, and I feel the same way. But y'all can't keep on bein deputies unless you fit in with the police. Now it's plain as that. Let's just say it's . . . on hold. In my position, I just can't go along with it right now. I don't want any goddam FBI Justice Department men snoopin around down here, and I don't think you do either. They're a pain in the ass to everybody. You can understand that, can't you?"

"I reckon," Rooster said. "Okay. Maybe we . . . don't need to be deputies, then."

Mac felt himself relax, surprised it was so easy. Relief shot through him like a sedative, though he knew better than to fully trust Rooster. "It's, well, a matter of appearance," he continued. "We got to be careful about how things look, is all. We all feel the same way you do, God knows. Ain't that right, Lester?"

"Yeah, that's right," Lester said.

"I think I'm readin you, Mac." Rooster was standing up straight now, moving his leg around as though it had gone to sleep. He flexed it, scraping it on the floor. "You can count on us to, well, do the right thing as good white folks." He grinned, not saying anything more.

After a minute, Mac said, "What?" *What are we talking about?* he worried. *What's this?*

"We'll see," Rooster said. "I best be gettin on home. The missus probly got supper cookin." He went out, with his rocking gait, and Mac looked at Lester. Lester's face was an impassive mask, the matchstick jutting sharply from the corner of his mouth. *What had just happened?* Mac was so relieved that Rooster had not insisted on remaining a deputy that he was able to push whatever the hell else the man was hinting at out of his mind.

·~·~·~·

Later, near dusk, Lyman Wells came into the little office at the front of the jail. Mac and Lester were drinking bourbon out of paper cups, from a bottle that Lester kept in his desk across the hall. After two drinks, they had toasted their victory, Mac feeling warm and comfortable now, the niggers quiet back there in their cells. He was unsettled by Lyman's sudden appearance. Lyman was wearing a vested suit, a light gray pinstripe, looking cool and crisp in spite of the heat, and he carried an attaché case. He wore large, horn-rimmed glasses, and they looked clean and shiny.

"Mac," Lyman said. "Lester. How y'all doin?"

"Fine," said Mac, surprised to see the lawyer and instantly suspicious. "Want a drink?"

"Naw, don't guess so," Lyman said.

"What can we do for you?" Mac said, eyeing the Ivy League–looking lawyer. He knew Lyman was here again because of the prisoners.

Lester stood up, gesturing to the chair, and Lyman sat down, putting his attaché case on the desk. "What are they charged with?" he asked.

"Disturbin the peace," Lester said, "creatin a public nuisance. We ain't filed any formal charge yet."

"Bail?" Lyman said.

"Up to the judge, I reckon."

"Now wait," Lyman said. "We don't have a felony here—"

"What's your concern with this, Lyman?" Mac asked. An uncertain, dim uneasiness crept into the back of his mind as he pictured Lyman, in his neat, crisp tan hunting clothes, holding a drink of bourbon before the fire at Shady Grove Plantation. *Goddammit, just when you feel like you got something settled down and can relax.* "They call you or what?"

"No," Lyman said. "After the sit-in at Maud's you know? After that, I was contacted by . . . certain organizations, to give them . . . some legal representation in Hammond. That's all."

"Organizations?" Mac said. "What the hell you talkin about?"

Mac's unease was still disturbingly vague, threatening him like a monster outside the door in the dark. He already hated Lyman for what he was, that world he represented, and now here he was representing these niggers! Something was badly out of kilter.

"Well." Lyman leaned back, the cuffs of his shirt showing neatly out of the arms of his jacket. "Surely, you don't think, Mac, that these folks are acting independently, do you? I mean, this is a . . . national movement. Who do you think is footin the bills for the two boys?"

Mac said nothing. He knew who was footing the bills. *What had those boys said? Snick? A bunch of meddlesome, pointy-headed bleeding-heart Yankee liberals!* He looked at Lyman's shifty eyes behind the large glasses.

"Who? Tell me."

"Well, Mac"—Lyman cut his eyes at Lester, then back at Mac—"there is an organization called the Student Nonviolent Coordinating Committee. 'SNCC.' You've heard of it, haven't you?"

"On the news, I think," Mac lied. He glanced at Lester. He didn't want Lester to know that the boys had told him that weeks ago, and it had just slipped right out of his mind.

Lyman chuckled, then he looked serious again. Mac could feel his pulse beating in his ears. The reminder of some sort of outside organization behind what was going on alarmed him anew. *And this prissy, overeducated son of a bitch was a traitor to the cause.* Lyman was the kind of southern priss-ass who had always looked down on Mac, made him feel unclean and crude. With his piano lessons and his studying French or some such. Moving so easily in that world that Mac had to work like holy hell to even get a glimpse into. His very first damn year out of law school, Lyman had been invited to the Shady Grove Deer Drive, and both senators had been there that year! "Snick sent those boys here? What the hell for?"

"To teach classes. To organize the whole thing," Lyman said. "I don't know all the details. I'm just—"

"What the hell do they want?" Mac said.

"You know what the Negroes want, Mac," Lyman said.

"Goddammit," Mac said. "And you're on their side, huh?"

"I'm not on anybody's side," he said, "I'm just an attorney. Part of my job is to see that their rights are protected. Their right to an attorney. Whether or not they're guilty, well, that's—"

"Guilty? Of course, they're guilty." *How could he sit there and—*

"Whatever," Lyman said. "Right now, I'm just authorized to post their bail, handle their court appearance and all. If, like you say, they're guilty, then they'll . . . whatever, pay the fine, spend the time in jail. Whatever." He crossed his legs at the knee, carefully straightening the cloth of his trousers with his fingers.

"They'll spend the fuckin night in jail," Mac said. He could feel his anger beginning to take over, beginning to push his uncertainty away.

"Surely there's no need for—"

"They spend the night in jail. You can take it before the city judge tomorrow."

Lyman stood up. "All right," he said. "If that's the way you want it."

"That's the way it is," Mac said, angry. He was staring at Lyman. The man even wore a goddam Phi Beta Kappa key. His red-and-blue-striped tie was tucked neatly into the vest.

"This is all very complicated," the attorney said, picking up his attaché case. "The word in Washington is . . ." His voice trailed off.

"Is what?" Mac said. "Goddammit, Lyman! What?"

"Well," he said, "things are going to change, Mac, whether you want them to or not. Change can be peaceful, or violent."

"Well, I'll just tell you," Mac said, feeling his face beginning to warm, "I don't know about this change shit, but I'll tell you this. I want it to be peaceful around here; I'm committed to that. Peace and calm, just like it's always been around here, you hear?"

"You might be biting off more than you can chew, Mac," Lyman said.

The son of a bitch. "You just let me worry about that, okay?" Mac said.

"All right," Lyman said. He stood there for a moment. He looked as though he expected Mac or Lester to say something else. When they didn't, he said, "Gentlemen," and he went out the door.

Mac sat behind his desk, not looking at Lester. He could feel his fury coloring his face, and he took several deep breaths, until gradually, his anger subsided, replaced by a foreboding.

"Goddammit!" he said aloud.

～～～～

The next afternoon, Cora sat in the living room, the house quiet and empty without Eldon and Sally. Two oscillating fans hummed softly in the room, turning back and forth, not quite together, so that their movements were out of kilter, out of balance, reflecting the tenseness that tore at her insides. Eldon and Sally and the others had spent the night in jail; Eldon had described for her, after their first trip there, the damp mustiness of the place, and she had slept very little, thinking about Sally and Eldon. And all night, images of Edna, her head in a pool of blood, had flooded her mind; she had seen the whole thing— looking on from a spot half a block away, where a few black people had gathered, suffering the glares of the white people—had seen the pasty-skinned man, his hair like dirty rat's fur, swing the ax handle with both hands, like swinging a baseball bat, and, though she had been too far away to hear the sound that it must have made hitting the back of Edna's neck, she had heard it in her mind, had heard it all night as the scene played over and over in her fitful, waking dreams. And she had seen O.B., too, as he had rushed out, stopped by Hoyt Blessing, seen the way he strained forward as though he would rush the scene and attack the attackers. She had felt a secret thrill. And then she had experienced guilt as she had realized that she was arrested by the image of O.B. and had momentarily forgotten what was actually happening in front of the theater.

The room was warm in spite of the fans. She wore a thin gray dress, and she had her hair cut shorter for the summer. *Where are they?* She felt anxious; she knew they had gone before old man Alston Carmichael, the city judge. She had heard all about it. All of them had been charged with one count of disturbing the peace, and each Negro had been charged with one count of attempted violation of state segregation laws. That same lawyer, Mr. Wells, had been their attorney. Word had spread through Frogbottom that they were free now. She glanced at her watch. Eldon had probably stopped by the church. He had hardly had time to get home, and yet she was anxious.

She heard him on the porch, and he came into the living room, standing very still for a moment, looking at her. He threw his jacket over the back of a chair and sat down on the sofa, his legs splaying out before him. He looked tired, almost to the point of exhaustion, but a smoldering excitement, an exhilaration, shone in his eyes.

"Where's Sally?" she said.

The light in his eyes seemed to flicker for a moment. "She went over to the Youngbloods'. With Nate." He blinked his eyes. "She's all right."

"Good," she said.

"Maybe this'll bring us all together," he said. He smiled.

She was astonished at his mood, his attitude. He seemed somehow energized. "What do you mean?"

"Maybe this'll bring everybody around. All you conservative people. We got to all pull together, and—"

"Eldon! Edna might *die*!"

He didn't answer her for a moment. She could see tears in his eyes;
they were bloodshot, as though from worry and lack of sleep. "Don't
you think I know that?" he asked softly.

"And next time it could be you. Or *Sally!*"

The room was silent, only the whine of the fans. After a long
silence, he said, "I told you people would get hurt. Maybe even killed.
That's the only way we're ever gonna get anywhere—"

"You *want* people killed?"

"No! God, I don't."

"But—"

"I'm as upset over what happened to Edna as anybody. I didn't plan
it that way—nobody did! It's a risk we take! It's the risk we take walkin
down the street every day in this godforsaken place!"

Her anger subsided. In its place was a sudden, cold fear. "We could
leave," she blurted, without even thinking, and he stared at her. *We
could go away, up North, where things are different.* She could not
help seeing O.B. then, in her mind's eye, as he had looked many years
ago, when she had thought that they might really go away together.
Thinking of O.B. now made her feel guilty again, and she looked
quickly away from Eldon's level stare. "We could leave, go to another
part of the country." Her voice lacked conviction now, she knew. "We
don't have to stay here."

"I'm committed to this, Cora," he said slowly. He sighed. His voice
sounded as though he were instructing a child. Even as he spoke, she
was thinking of O.B., *his* voice in the darkness of the pickup cab, the
touch of his hand on her arm. "It's just startin, don't you see? I
couldn't be . . . in any other part of the country. My soul would
always be here."

"Yes," she murmured.

"These people are my people."

She could hear the low whisper of the fans, a buzzing, almost like
insects.

"That jail," he went on, "it was so hot. It's dirty in there, smelly."
He sat slumped on the sofa. "I couldn't sleep. I prayed, and I thought
about Edna, all night long. God!" He put his face in his hands. She
could see his thin shoulders shaking as he wept. She wanted to touch
him, comfort him, but she did not move. She stood up.

"I'll get you some water," she said, and she went down the hall, her
sandals flapping on the linoleum. Thinking of him there, crying,
made her heart swell painfully in her chest, and she was blinking back
her own tears. Damn you, she was thinking, damn all of you. Only

Eldon—or maybe it was all men, she didn't know—thought the world could be just and fair. Yes, even O.B. To him, finally, those years ago, it had all made sense. He was white, and she was a Negro. That's just the way it was. The sheet was balanced; he was being just and fair. She let the water run in the sink until it was cool, then filled a glass. *Damn you. I was born knowing what it takes you goddam men a lifetime to even begin to learn!* Eldon really thought that what he was doing with this movement was going to make a difference. That it would change the hearts of people, white people. She knew better.

She could remember them both as boys, so clearly, Eldon always smaller, skinnier, trying so hard to keep up with O.B., who was tall and athletic and strong, and she knew that it had taken Eldon a long time to figure out that she and O.B. were lovers, and she recalled the betrayal that she saw in his eyes when he finally realized it. It was as though Eldon had simply assumed, since he and she were both colored, that *they* would be the couple. She smiled wryly. *He had been right after all.* But it had been to O.B. that she had been drawn, with an aching and a force that she could not control; his lean arms and legs and his pale blue eyes had filled her with a longing that had consumed her, filled her with fire, and she felt her insides being torn now with that same desire, and it frightened her. *I am no good! I am evil.* She knew that one firm gesture from O.B. would be all it would take, and she knew that he eventually would make that gesture. He had done it before, and she had gone headlong toward the consuming, destructive flame. *I will not do it again! I cannot help myself.* She thought, then, of Eldon, the cold, raging jealousy that sat like a cancer within him. *It would destroy you. It would destroy us all.*

She went back up the hall and into the living room. Eldon looked up at her, his eyes pleading. "You got to understand, Cora," he said.

"Edna might die."

"I know it. I know it." His voice was weak.

"For what?" she went on. "What did you accomplish yesterday? Huh? Was it worth it?"

"Yes," he said. She could see the hurt in his eyes. "It was worth it. We just have to have faith that it was—"

"Was it worth Edna's life?"

"It may be worth a lot of people's lives before it's over. I'm tired, Cora."

"*Your* life? Sally's?" She stood looking down at him. "Eldon, you're too idealistic. You're carried away with all this. It ain't gonna make any difference in the long run. Don't you know that?"

"No!" he said quickly. "I don't know that. Dr. King—"

"Dr. King!" she interrupted. "Dr. King! I'm sick of hearin about Dr. King!"

She could see that she had wounded him. "Don't say that, Cora," he said, an edge of bitter anger in his voice. She backed away.

She made her voice calmer, quieter. "I know this much. I ain't got but one life, and one family. I don't wanna see my baby up there in the hospital. Or dead. Killed by white trash hate!" He was staring at her. "White trash don't make me what I am. What white trash thinks don't matter to me." She was going on rapidly. "You think I care? I laugh at em. We been laughin at em all our lives! Just cause they think we down don't make us down! We—"

"Not all white men," he interrupted, and she knew that he was thinking of O.B., and she stopped speaking. His eyes glowed. His stare was flat and level.

"Don't start that, Eldon." She looked away.

"Look at me," he said. "Look at me."

Their eyes locked. Neither one said anything for a long moment. She could see the pain, the vulnerability, in his look. She knew then, all over again, why she had loved him all these years, why she had wanted to take care of him when she had seen how hurt he had been about her and O.B. And she had felt that need persistently over the years, and it was still strong. The need to do for him, to make him better. *This is really love. This feeling . . .* He took a long, slow drink of the water she had brought him.

"I'm so tired," he said. "So tired." She knew then that he did not have the energy to pursue the way he felt about O.B., but it would never go away. It was a devil that he could not bury.

"Here," she said, putting her hands on his shoulder, turning him, arranging him on the sofa. She unbuttoned his shirt and pulled it loose from his pants, smelling the musty odor of the jail clinging to it. She began to massage his shoulders, feeling the tenseness and rigidity of his neck. But as she kneaded his skin, she felt his body relaxing.

"Ummmm," he said.

She let her hands drift around his neck; she knew her hands were cool against his sweaty body. Her fingers played lightly across his chest, his nipples, and he pressed back against her, and she pushed her breasts against his naked back. Then she brushed her lips lightly along the ridge of his shoulder. She heard his breath quicken, and she responded by squeezing his chest, then letting her hand drift down to his lap, slowly caressing him through his pants.

"Um," she said, "what's that?"

She leaned against him, fighting the image of O.B. that lingered at the edge of her mind. She continued to caress him, her movements becoming swifter, almost frantic, and she felt her own breathing quicken. He turned slightly, then, twisting his head, and she kissed him. He was completely hard now, and she let him lie back on the sofa, moving in front of him and loosening his belt, his zipper, pulling his pants and undershorts down around his ankles.

"Relax," she said softly, gently. "Let me do the work."

She pulled the light dress over her head. She climbed on top of him, straddling him, feeling the sudden silky heat as he entered her. She moved smoothly and rapidly, her breath coming now in gasps and moans. *Goddammit, I love you.* Through her slitted eyes, she could see the muscles in his chest and stomach rippling. She felt him grip her hips, his fingers kneading the flesh of her buttocks, guiding her, fitting his short, jerky movements to hers, beginning to moan himself. She felt the sweat pop out all over her body, then her climax coming, exploding all over her body, and she cried out, soaring, the intensity almost painful. He cried out, too, and then was still. She crouched, not moving for a moment, then stretched out on the couch next to him, fitting her body to his, feeling the film of perspiration that connected them. She closed her eyes, relaxing, feeling sleep coming, knowing, from his breathing, that he was drifting off, too. She began to doze.

"Across Jordan. Across Jordan. I will lay my body down," he said. The words were whispered softly and sleepily against her ear, from far away.

She hugged him. "Go to sleep," she said. She heard his breathing become deep and regular again, felt his muscles slacken against her. He seemed so far away from her. *We have always loved each other. No matter what happens, we must always remember that.*

⦁⦁⦁

Mac hated being put on hold. That was something new that people had come up with to keep you in your place, he thought. He had dreaded talking with Carleton Byrd at the district office of Gulf International in Mobile, and he had put it off, thinking that Byrd would show up in town to check things out, or at least call when he read about all the mess in the newspapers. Mac was nervous and curious about what the paper-mill people would say at this point, and he realized that he could delay no longer; he had to call. Maybe the *Mobile Press Register* hadn't carried the story, but *The Birmingham*

News sure had, a big story with a picture of Edna Blanks wearing a little white straw hat. It had been on the television news, too, and on the AP wire. An AP reporter from Birmingham had called him and asked him if he had a statement. He had been astonished. It was the first time he had ever talked with somebody from the Associated Press, and he had been tongue-tied before he got around to saying that he really had nothing to say.

He heard the phone click. "Carleton Byrd here," he heard, in a clipped, midwestern accent. Byrd managed to sound busy just saying his name; Mac could imagine him sitting in a cool, air-conditioned office overlooking the bay, smoking a Marlboro.

"Mr. Byrd," Mac said, "this is Mac McClellon."

"Oh," the voice said, "yes."

"I wanted to call you—"

"How are you, Mr. Mayor?" Byrd said. "I was going to get back to you soon." *Back to me?* Mac breathed deeply. He turned to look out the window.

"I was just wonderin," Mac said, "if y'all are closer to makin the announcement. See, there's a mayor's race goin on, and, well . . . You said to call you, and I was wonderin . . ."

"As a matter of fact, we are," Byrd said.

"You *are?*" Mac said. *Maybe I won't even have to mention all that other . . .*

"We are ninety-five percent sure, Mr. McClellon," Byrd went on. "Of course, we were disturbed by the business with the colored lady. The one who got hurt? How is she, by the way?"

"Edna Blanks?" Mac said. She was still in the hospital, still in critical condition. "She's gonna be fine. Listen, that was just an isolated incident, Mr. Byrd. Law and order. Don't worry about it. The man was a deputy, just doin his duty. She was . . . trespassin. This is still the sleepy little wonderful town that it's always been." *Go on, keep talking.* "Listen, I need—"

"Let's hope so," Byrd said.

"I need to make some plans," Mac pressed on. "About the announcement and all. I want to have it big doins, you know? Have some of your top-management people up here, call in all the press and all. That kinda thing needs plannin, so we need to know—"

"The only thing that would prevent us from announcing at this point, Mac, is if that sort of thing got out of hand," Byrd said.

"Like I said, it was just an incident. I mean, they're not even very well organized around here," Mac said.

"Who?"

Mac said nothing. How best to answer that? His head began to ache and throb. The niggers seemed fragmented, going off in twenty directions all at once. And yet there was the Snick business. The line buzzed and crackled.

"Who do you mean?" Byrd repeated.

"The colored people. The Kneegrows," Mac said. "We git along here. Everybody likes one another. Every barrel's got a coupla rotten apples in it, though. It's like that all over. That's life," he said. He chuckled. *Ninety-five percent sure!* "We git along good here," he said jovially. *Come on, you smarty-pants asshole!*

"So you told me," Byrd said flatly. "Well, I think our top brass might want some further assurances from you. I told them you would be happy to give them."

"Assurances? Oh. No, you can tell em there'll be no more of that sort of thing—"

"I mean," Byrd said, interrupting, "some assurances that perhaps you'll—you folks in Hammond—will take the lead in . . . well, accommodating the Negroes. Somebody's going to have to do it, after all."

"Do *what?*" Mac said. He felt the bottom begin to drop out of everything as the image of Rooster's face popped into his head. *Accommodate them?* He stared at the deep green of the trees across the street in the park. "What kind of accommodatin you talkin about?"

"Well, Mac." Byrd seemed to emphasize his use of Mac's first name. "That would be up to you. I mean, give them something of whatever it is they want, I would think. Otherwise, how are you going to prevent more trouble?"

"I've got things under control. You can count on that," Mac said, his voice dropping down an octave. He had tried to think of some token, some bone he could throw the niggers, but he knew Long wouldn't buy that. It was unthinkable, outlandish, totally out of the question in their way of life, to allow the niggers to eat in white restaurants and marry white women, but that's what they wanted, and Long had made it clear that he wouldn't stop until he got it. There was no way for Byrd to understand all that. Mac shook his head. He could hear Byrd breathing on the line.

"We're counting on you!" Byrd said. "You want us, we want you, right? So I can give them the assurances?"

"Huh? Oh, yeah. 'Course." *Now what am I saying?*

"Any more trouble, Mac, and they might have to hear it from you for themselves."

"Right. Right," Mac said. He realized that he was perspiring despite the fact that he kept his office almost cold, so that in the humidity of the afternoon, moisture formed on the glass of his windows.

"Excellent!" Byrd said. "Was that all you wanted, Mac? I'm a bit busy this morning."

"Yeah," Mac said.

"Call me anytime, all right?" The phone clicked off. Mac sat holding it for a moment. After a few seconds, he heard a dial tone. He replaced the phone. His sleeves were rolled up his arms, and his collar felt tight and stiff. *They ought to outlaw neckties in the summertime.*

Mac looked out at the park, the Confederate statue barely peeping now over the fully leaved treetops and thought about how he'd tied his future to Gulf International, and to this man Byrd's vague certainties. Mac had heard all his life that this was the way fortunes were made. You got into a position like this, you got inside information, and you acted on it. That's what he had done. He was borrowed to the hilt, he had invested everything he had, everything Belinda's parents had left, *everything*, in the land parcels and those houses, and if they sat vacant for very long, *if they sat vacant forever*, he would be ruined. Far worse than the money, he knew, would be the end of his dream of being one with the men, the senators and the governors, drinking bourbon and water around the fireplace at Shady Grove Plantation. He could not bear to think about that.

The morning had already grown hot, and the city park across the way looked deserted. Mac sat there chewing on his lower lip. Gulf International was 95 percent sure. They *were* coming in. Things were going to work out, Mac told himself. The worst was over. The worst was over.

Chapter Ten

THE TOWN, HER TOWN, WHICH WAS THE ONLY HOME SHE HAD EVER known, always so warm, inviting, now looked alien and forbidding to Ellen. She could see it spread out before her as she crossed the tall river bridge north of town, in Lacy's car, the muddy Tuscaloosa River below her, sparkling in the sunlight, snaking off to the west where it intersected with and formed the wide Tombigbee, which disappeared toward the south, toward Mobile and the Gulf of Mexico. She could see the buildings of downtown, a cluster of three- and four-storied brick squares looking, from here, like children's building blocks, clustered around the thick green of the city square, the park. Streets and houses stretched away toward the south, dotted with trees and shrubs and lush green lawns. Two tall water towers, painted bright silver, glinting in the sun, towered over and dominated the town. On the one closest to her, the Northside Tower, was written, in large black letters: HAMMOND, ALABAMA. CITY OF THE PEOPLE. A thick haze, like a layer of fog, hovered over the treetops, and the town lay baking, parching in the fierce summer sun. She passed a sign that said WELCOME TO HAMMOND, HOME OF TEN THOUSAND HAPPY PEOPLE AND A FEW OLD GROUCHES! reading it through a thin film of tears: she had driven automatically, by rote, all the way home from Tuscaloosa, where she

270

had seen a doctor who had confirmed her suspicions: She was pregnant.

She parked Lacy's car on Washington Street, near Ramsey's Drug Store, leaving the keys under the floor mat. She had smoked five of Lacy's Chesterfields on the drive home, and the pack was almost empty, but she left it like that, over the sun visor, turning away from the drugstore when she got out. Lacy would see the car when she came out. Ellen could not bring herself to go into the drugstore. There was always a crowd there now, with the municipal pool closed—word had gotten out that the Negroes would try to integrate it, and so the city had decided not to open it this summer—and there was nothing much to do, and the last thing in the world she needed was noisy teenagers. And it would pain her even more, now, the way they looked at her.

She was already an almost total outcast with her schoolmates. She had missed a period earlier in the spring, but that was not unusual for her, and then she had missed another one just about the end of school, and she had known the truth immediately, realized that she had been knowing the truth for some time and not admitting it to herself. She had gone through the round of senior parties, even finals week and graduation, which itself had seemed subdued and anticlimactic, in a kind of daze. Her classmates treated her as though they had come to expect that. She had grown depressed, unable to concentrate—thank God her teachers looked at finals for seniors as a mere formality—and her parents had looked at her curiously. "It's graduation," she had heard her mother say to her father. "Surely, she's not still pinin over that boy." "No," her father had said quickly, as Ellen had hurried down the hall, not wanting to overhear any more. She could tell by the way her father looked at her that he knew she was still seeing Paul, but he had not mentioned it, except in the way his eyes always looked hurt. A great deal was passing between them without any words; she knew how much he was suffering, and it pained her deeply. And now this. She could not bear to think of how much it would torment him if he knew she was pregnant. Just the thought of his disappointment was unendurable to her.

She cut across the street and went through the park, under the huge, heavy shade trees, stopping by the goldfish pond, with its fountain bubbling and spewing with water. She stood there awhile; the tiny droplets in the air felt cool on her face, and then she continued on across the park, heading in the direction of the Youngbloods' house. Shimmering waves of afternoon heat rose from the pavement. She didn't pass many people out walking.

She went up the crooked, uneven sidewalk and across the porch, not knocking now, pushing open the heavy door, calling out.

"Melody?" She heard her voice echo in the massive emptiness of the dim, cool old house.

"Ellen?" she heard a voice call from above, and she looked up the staircase, seeing Sally's face peering down at her in the gloom. "Come on up," Sally said. *Thank God. Sally was there.* She took the steps two at a time, hearing the creaking under her shoes. Sally stood in the hallway on the third floor. She had on shorts, blue jeans torn off above the knees, a T-shirt. She was smiling. "What's up, white folks?" she said.

Ellen stopped stock-still. She knew her face must be pale, frightened, because she watched the smile fade from Sally's face, watched her tilt her head and inspect her closely.

"What's wrong?" Sally said.

"I'm pregnant," Ellen said.

The two girls stood there for a moment, Sally's face registering shock, disbelief, and then Ellen felt herself breaking, felt the tears coming, the sobs choking up from her chest. She took a tentative step forward, giving way to the helplessness and terror that flooded her, beginning to sob openly as Sally put her arms around her, held her, her thin arms rigid around her, strong and firm.

The image of her father plagued Ellen's thoughts, his face there before her tightly clenched eyes, his eyes steady on her.

"It's all right," she heard Sally say softly. The girl's arms held her securely. "I know somebody that can take care of this. Don't worry. It's all right."

The sound of Sally's words, her voice droning and solid, were comforting, even though Ellen did not hear, did not comprehend, what she was saying.

⋅〰〰⋅

O.B. was driving his pickup out into the country, down toward the Flatwoods, driving along slowly, getting out of the shop for a while. He had to get away from the town, and all the old longings—things so deep within him that they were a part of his very core—pulled him back toward the country of his youth. He felt better as he drove. It gave him time to think, to clear his mind, to try to assess exactly where he was right now.

One of O.B.'s mechanics—Ernest Benson—had quit him when the boycott was lifted, but he had put the word out and almost immedi-

ately, to his great surprise, hired a new one, a great big man named
Farley Grimes, from over at Coatopa. Farley had played football a
couple of years at Livingston State, and O.B. knew that he was the
type of man who didn't like anyone telling him what to do. O.B.
was glad to have the hulking man in his shop. He didn't know what
else might happen when the word spread about what was going on
with him. So he had two mechanics, and, with the increase in business, they had all the work they could do. It had leveled off now that
planting time was over, but a lot of the farmers used the hot summer
months for routine maintenance, so they were busy. He had a good
parts man, and Paulette was getting better at keeping the books and
sending out the statements. O.B.'s real problem was one he had always had: His customers tended to ignore the monthly statements,
coming in maybe twice a year to pay on what they owed. Still,
enough was coming in to keep him going now; he was paying his
employees and himself, cutting his own take-home salary in half,
and he had put aside some money toward the note coming due at
Mac's bank. His hope was to get far enough ahead that he could pay
the interest and then reborrow the money, at whatever terms Mac
would give him, and then worry about it in the future, when all this
was over. But he knew he wasn't making a lot of progress toward that
short-term goal.

And in the fall he would also be faced with Ellen's college expenses.
She had shown him a letter from the Registrar's Office at Middlebury
College, informing her that she had been admitted as a student in the
fall. And there was the possibility of a scholarship, but she would not
know about that until later. He had been both furious and speechless.
She just chose to ignore the fact that he had told her repeatedly she
could not go up there. She had also applied and been admitted over at
Livingston, where the competition was so much less intense, with a
full tuition scholarship, and he intended to make her take it, but she
still wanted to live in the dormitory, and that would cost money, too.
She had applied for scholarships from the Rotary, Kiwanis, and United
Daughters of the Confederacy, but of course she had been turned
down by all of them. O.B. knew that the town was talking about him
and the boycott, about her and the northern boy. O.B. knew that she
was still seeing Paul, but couldn't bring himself to say anything to her.
Martha seemed oblivious to it, whether through choice or not O.B.
did not know. Her drinking continued, and more and more now, she
stopped even making the effort to get out of bed. He'd just as soon she
stayed there. He was going to force her to go to A.A. as soon as all this

business was over, when Ellen had left home, and they could start fresh.

There had been an article in the *Hammond Times* about his running for mayor, and Malcolm Rodenberry, who ran a little print shop, had called him up and asked him if he wanted cards and posters. O.B. had told him no, not right now. And several people had mentioned it to him, some jokingly, some curiously. He had heard nothing more from Rooster Wembley since that night, and he had not spoken to Mac McClellon. And Eldon had made no more demands on him.

It had not rained in two weeks, and the air was crisp, a dry, searing heat that kept the shop muggy and sultry. When he had left the shop, he had not known exactly where he was going, but now he did know: He was going to see Eldon's parents, Blount and Punchy. He had heard that Punchy had been sick again. And Blount had had his tractor overhauled shortly after the boycott had been lifted. He had told himself, as he turned the pickup south, that he was going to check on the tractor, but he had known almost immediately that he simply wanted to see the two old people, to talk to them. To renew something. He wanted to find out how Blount felt about everything Eldon was doing, and about *his* running for mayor. He had heard that they had just recently registered to vote. (He thought about his own parents, who had never voted in their lives. He remembered his father fuming and snorting about politics, about Big Jim Folsom, but he had never voted.) He wanted to talk with them about all that was going on; after witnessing the awful violence in front of the picture show and dealing with his own sense of frustration, O.B. wanted to find out what they thought about it all.

When he and Eldon were young boys, Blount and Punchy had been almost like a second set of parents for him. Blount was a big man, strong and gentle as a huge black bear, gone paunchy in recent years but still powerful; Punchy was small and wiry and yellow. For over fifty years, she had been the cook in the Hubbard household, and on afternoons like this, still and scorching, he and Eldon had gone to the shady back porch of the big house for tall glasses of lemonade. He had eaten many a meal at their cabin, four rooms with a dog-trot hall down the middle, the walls papered with old newspapers, the house smelling inside of kerosene and musty slept-in quilts and the lingering smells of years and years of wood fires and greasy cooking: fatback and greens, corn bread, and thick, heavy, underdone biscuits that Punchy called "cat heads." O.B. had slept there on occasion, too, until he was about twelve, when his father had simply said no. *No more.* Sleeping, in winter, under piles of quilts, a fire sputtering in the brick fireplace, and in summer on the naked corn-shuck mattress that would sag in the middle, so that the two boys would wake up in the morning crammed together in the center of the bed.

He cut across on the new farm-to-market road that skirted the old Hubbard place. On both sides of the road, straggly rows of Negroes, mostly women and children, wearing wide-brimmed straw hats, were chopping cotton. Some of them stopped their work as he passed, looking up to see who was going by. They waved, lazily, some of them recognizing him, others waving as they would to anyone passing by. He knew that from time to time they would sing, breaking into song almost spontaneously; he remembered the rhythm, the chant, almost as though it were locked in his bones, just as he remembered the smooth feel of the hoe handle in his hands and the feel of the savage sun baking into his hat, scorching the cotton shirt buttoned at the wrists to protect his body from it. The singing would begin with one voice, maybe distant, punctuated with the rhythmical grunts, chop *Uh*, chop *Uh*. "Swing Low . . . sweet char-i-oh . . ." *Uh*. *Uh*. "Comin for to carry me . . . home . . ." *Uh*. "Swing Low . . ." Before long they were all singing. "I . . . *looked* . . . over Jordan and *what* did I see . . . comin for to carry *me* home . . ." It seemed to O.B. now a sweet, simple time, when all he had longed for was a drink from the sweating water jar at the end of the row, all he had to focus on was the hoe blade, chopping the weeds away from the delicate cotton with as smooth a stroke as he would later have in the batter's box. The same comfortable, primary satisfaction.

He turned off the farm-to-market road onto a gravel lane that wound through pastureland, with clumps of grazing cattle. In the shimmering distance, he could see the long, low dairy barn of the Hubbard farm, its weather vanes and air vents on the sloping roof. He came to a section planted in cotton, and sitting near the road, with the fields around it planted almost up to the house, was Blount and Punchy's cabin. He pulled into the cramped dirt yard in front of the little house that they had lived in for over half a century. There was new siding tacked onto the outside, maroon tar paper with a brick design, and all four chimneys had been rebuilt with bright pink bricks. There was a narrow porch across the front with a screen door that opened into the central hallway. White tufts of cotton were stuffed into several small holes in the rusty screen. O.B. got out, slamming the door of his truck, hearing the sound of the slam echo across the silent fields. He stood looking at the house for a moment. Then he walked over and looked around the side, seeing Punchy, in a cane-bottomed chair, dozing in the shade of a chinaberry tree. She wore a long gray dress down to her high-top brogan shoes and a blue bandanna around her head; she looked tiny and frail in the chair, and he walked up to her carefully, not wanting to startle her. He stood there for a moment, and she opened her eyes suddenly, squinting at him in the sunlight. She was holding a cardboard fan in her lap; it had a picture of Jesus praying in the Garden of Gethsemane on the back.

"Mister O.B.," she said. "How you is?"

"How you doin, Punchy?" he said. He leaned down and hugged her. She was light as balsa. She smelled of sunlight and talcum powder.

"You lookin good," she said. "When you seen Eldon?"

"Not too long ago," he said. "I heard you been sick."

"Rheumatiz," she said. "Hurt like a boil. But it gone now. Took me to a doctor over in Selma, he say I'm gonna outlive *him*. He *sho* don't know what he talkin bout, now do he?" She cackled softly.

Her eyes were watery, with tiny red veins clustering around the black pupils. When she laughed, her mouth was almost toothless, her lips and the two upper teeth that she still had stained with snuff. He could see that she held the snuff tin, along with a wrinkled white handkerchief, in one hand and the fan in the other, both resting in her lap.

"Is Blount around?" he said.

"He down to de cow barn," she said. "He be back in a minute. What the time?"

He looked at his watch.

"Almost two," he said.

"He be back shortly," she said. "How your peoples?"

"They all fine," O.B. said. "Mama and Daddy don't get outta the house much. Daddy's back, and all."

"The miseries. Sho nuff." She nodded her head. "You got a girl. Sally's age. Ain't that right?"

"Yeah. Ellen. She's fine, Punchy. Graduated from high school last month."

"Is? Lord." She fanned herself with the cardboard fan. "Is it gonna ever rain, or what, Mister O.B.?" she said.

He looked out past the barn, at the field of waist-high cotton, his eyes playing over the familiar house, and the yard, shaded with mimosa and chinaberry trees, with one large pear tree down near the barn. Over behind the house was their garden; he could see tall tomato plants, weighted down with heavy, ripe tomatoes. She saw him looking at them.

"Take some home," she said. "Blount put em in a sack for you."

"Okay," he said, already tasting them, remembering eating them off the vine still warm from the sun. "I'd like that. His cotton looks good."

"Sho nuff," she said. "Don't forgit them maters, now. More'n us and the birds both can eat. Ain't gone do nothin but rot."

"Okay," he said. He heard a truck door slam around front.

"Dere Blount now," she said as he came around the corner of the cabin, grinning, having seen O.B.'s truck. His stomach hung out over his belt, straining at the buttons on the front of his blue, sweat-stained work shirt. His close-cropped hair was gray.

"Mister Billie," he said, grinning and nodding. He was the only one who ever called him Billie. That was his name, Odell Billie Brewster, on his birth certificate, and O.B. had always hated it. Once, during the short time he was in New York, playing for the Yankees in the summer of 1936, a sportswriter who'd nagged him into telling him what his initials stood for had written a story headlined BATTLING BILLY BREWSTER, and O.B. had been embarrassed. He had never told anyone again. Only his parents called him Odell, and only Blount called him Billie.

"Blount! How you doin, man?" O.B. said.

"Hot enough for you?" Blount said. He was pulling up two more cane-bottomed chairs into the shade. The two men sat down across from each other, Punchy in the middle. She was fanning with the cardboard fan; it moved back and forth rapidly, a flutter. Blount wore knee-high rubber boots, still wet; he must have been hosing out the dairy barn. He was looking at O.B. expectantly, as if he were waiting for him to state the purpose of his visit. Blount would not do much small-talking.

"I hear y'all got registered to vote," O.B. said, and the smile flickered on Blount's face. He seemed embarrassed for a moment.

"Some a' Eldon's doins," he said. "He claim we ought to do it. Say we got a right."

"Yeah," O.B. said. *You do. You do have that right.*

"That boy," Punchy said. She shook her head.

"I . . . I'm glad," O.B. said.

"You is?" Blount looked up at him, openly curious.

"Well," O.B. said, "yeah. Did Eldon tell y'all I'm runnin for mayor of Hammond?"

"Mayor? Sho nuff? Whooooeee. Naw, he ain't told us nothin."

"I am," O.B. said. He waited, to see what they would say, remembering his own parents' reaction when he had told them.

"We sho vote for you, then. Sho nuff."

O.B. smiled. "Y'all can't vote in the city election. Y'all live out here in the county."

"That right? Well, then," Blount said. He shook his head.

"Have y'all heard anybody talkin about it?"

"Bout you? Naw, ain't heard nothin." Blount leaned back in the chair, his knees apart, his large, hamlike hands resting on the knees of his brown cotton pants. "Cept bout all that other stuff. What they tell us at the church. Those white boys from the North come out chere. They tells us to go on and trade with you, after they done tole us not to, ain't more'n seem like a month before. I ain't seen Eldon."

"When have you talked to him?" O.B. said.

"He call on the telephone. We got a telephone now. He say he checkin on us. He busy, I reckon."

"Yeah, he's busy, all right," O.B. said. O.B. sat looking at the two old people. Blount smiled broadly at him. *What did they really think of me, years ago, when we were boys? What do they think of me now?* O.B. realized that he did not know them, hardly knew them at all. He had seen resentment and hatred in the eyes of the Negroes in town, in the flashing eyes of Sally Long, as he had watched the policeman lead her away from the picture show, yanking roughly at her arm. He realized, with a sudden start, how much Sally looked like her grandmother as a young girl. He had seen anger, fury, in the eyes of the muscular Negro boy next to Sally, a frightening, dangerous warning like a ticking time bomb. And Eldon's pleading eyes, full of pain and misery and suffering. Eldon's father's eyes were level on him, sparkling in the afternoon light. What was the joke? O.B. thought. *Is there a joke?* "Eldon is . . . very serious," he said, not knowing exactly what he meant.

"Sho is," Blount said. He laughed, his teeth snaggled. Then his face seemed to relax out of the grin, his jowls heavy, his lips purple and plump. "Sho is," he said again. "Yessuh, Mister Billie, us gine vote. Me and Punchy gine go up dere and put our marks down and vote! What you think of that?"

"I think . . . that's great," O.B. said.

"Sho is," Punchy said.

"Eldon, he say niggers ain't got to stay down," Blount said. "He say one day ain't gonna be no sucha thing as niggers and white folks, say it gonna be like just peoples, like heaven, ain't gonna be no color that nobody would notice. The lion lay down with the lamb, white and colored alike, be like the Garden fore the Fall! Me and Punchy, we ain't gone be round to see it, nosuh. That ain't no matter. Us knows it's comin, Mister Billie. Us knows!"

There was a long silence, and O.B. watched Punchy fan herself with her handkerchief. The two old people sat there staring at him, their eyes full of laughter, laughter through years of pain. Years of a hardscrabble dirt-poor existence.

O.B. stood up. He had found out little directly that he had come out here for, and yet . . . He suspected the old man of some ulterior meaning, something hidden from him. He felt closed off from him. Maybe it had always been there, and O.B. had just not been sensitive to it.

"You ain't got to rush off? You want a dipper of water?" Blount said.

"No, that's okay. Yeah. I got to go."

"We sho vote for you if'n we could, Mister Billie," he said.

"Sho would," Punchy said. Her voice was singsong, like an answering chorus.

"I know you would, don't I?" He grinned at them. He waved. He knew they were watching him walk away, their eyes following him until he went around the corner of the house. He sat behind the wheel of his pickup for a moment, remembering them as vital, young, and strong. As he backed out onto the lane and turned his truck back toward home, he saw them sitting under the chinaberry tree. He would never know what they really thought, what they felt. *Did that fire he saw in Eldon's, in Sally's, eyes lie buried in theirs? Had they hated him for being white, when he was a cocky child?* His truck bounced on the gravel, the orange dust rising behind him and hovering there in the motionless air, just above the earth's surface. O.B. shook his head. He did not know. *I may never know,* he thought.

.~.~.~.

He was still on the farm-to-market road, before he got to the state highway, when he saw the car, vaguely recognizing it, although it took him a moment to realize that it was Eldon's black '55 Chevrolet. O.B. rolled to a stop beside it; it sat beside the road, its two left tires on the chert, the window on the driver's side rolled down. He looked down the road, squinting his eyes in the afternoon sun, and in the distance, through the shimmering heat, he could see a figure beside the road, walking. He went on along the road, watching the figure in the distance grow larger, closer, until he realized that it was not Eldon's lean, wiry figure, but a fuller one, and then he could see the skirt, recognizing who it was. She stood there on the shoulder of the road, waiting for his truck to approach, the dry, dusty rows of cotton stretching away behind her. If she recognized who he was, she gave no sign as the truck rolled to a stop beside her, the tires crunching on the loose surface. She looked at him through the open passenger-side window.

"It just went dead," Cora said, "wouldn't start. Wouldn't even turn over."

"Battery," he said. "When we get back to town, I'll send somebody out."

His engine idled smoothly. She just looked at him through the window. Her eyes, the way she looked in the sunlight, stabbed him like a knife. He looked away from her. The green-leaved cotton plants, looking drooped and wilted in the sun, stretched away to the horizon, the flatness of the land broken only by power poles along the road. O.B. could see a yellowish-gray hawk, sitting on the power line a hundred feet down the road from them.

"Visitin my sister," she said. "She's got those two babies. Lord. It just went dead all of a sudden."

"It needs to get tuned up," O.B. said. "Get in."

She hesitated for the slightest moment. She pulled open the door and climbed in. She wore a thin blue sundress, her shoulders bare. The dress rode up her legs as she settled into the seat, and she pushed it down.

"I'm not dressed for walkin," she said. She wore thin sandals on her strong-looking feet; her feet looked almost as big as a man's, long and lean, creamy coffee-colored. He sat looking at her, her dark eyes, her hair chopped off as short as he'd seen it since they were children.

"What?" she said, after a moment.

"Oh." He realized he had been staring at her and looked away. He knew that she was aware of the effect she had on him. "I've just been visitin Blount and Punchy," he said.

"Really? How they doin?"

"Great," he said.

"I thought about stoppin by. It's so hot. Whew." She fanned herself with her hand.

"I got a jug of water in the back," he said. "Want some? I don't know how cold it is."

"Yeah. I used to walk five miles to Boligee Store and five miles back on a day like this. I can't do it anymore." She smiled; her teeth were even and white, the skin of her face as smooth as carefully polished

fine wood.O.B. got out and rummaged in his carrier just behind the
cab. He had tools there, jumper cables, too, and he thought of going
back and looking under the hood of her car. He could get it started, but
that would mean she'd be long gone from him. . . . There was a piece
of canvas there in the carrier, too, part of an old tent, a blanket, two
flashlights. He told himself that her car trouble was probably a combination of things, that he would send Farley Grimes and one of the
Negro boys out here. He found the thermos, unscrewed the top, and
poured her some water. He handed it to her through the open door of
the truck. She took it, smiling. "Thanks," she said, sipping the water,
looking at him over the thermos top. "It's cool. Tastes like spring
water."

"It's out of the spigot at home," he said. "I put some ice in it
yesterday. I had to drive over to Meridian and get some parts." She
handed him back the top, and he screwed it back on. "I drove around
all over Sumter County, over around Emelle and York, tryin to collect
some." He put the thermos back in the carrier and slammed the top.
He climbed back in behind the wheel. "I collected twelve dollars from
one fellow, thirty from another. That was it."

"It must be hard," she said.

"Yeah. I don't have hardly any white customers left."

She looked away, out the window. He drummed his fingers against
the steering wheel. The sun was hot on the roof of the cab, and the air
inside was growing stuffy. Their closeness was almost painful to him;
that they were out here together almost unbearable.

"How do you feel," he said, "when you come back out here?"

"What you mean?"

"Where you grew up and all. Where we . . ." He paused. "It makes
me feel sad," he said.

"Me, too," she said, not looking at him, her eyes looking pensively
out across the cotton field. His eyes followed hers. He did not want to
look at her now. He didn't have to. He could feel her presence on the
seat beside him, sense the heat of her body, her breath. The hawk
flapped its wings and lifted from the power line, rising slowly into the
air; it began to circle, higher and higher over the field, until it was just
a speck against the bright pale blue of the sky.

"Let's ride around," he said, putting the truck in gear.

"I better get back to town," she said.

"Why?" He looked at her then, and their eyes met.

"All right," she said. He felt a tense excitement as he eased out on
the clutch. He went down the road a half-mile, then turned off on a

dirt road that he knew, which wound around and eventually dead-ended at the river. It went through cotton fields, then pastures, skirting a lake and a swampy area full of willow and catawba trees. He and Eldon and Cora had fished the lake often, gathering worms from the catawba trees as bait, sitting on the grassy bank with cane poles propped in the crotches of Y-shaped limbs that they cut and trimmed and stuck in the soft ground. The memory pictures jolted his mind with their clarity; flat white perch and scarlet-throated bream, wet and glistening in the sun; the light reflecting off the rippling surface of the lake; Cora in her faded and clinging cotton dress. He glanced over at her. She had braced her arm in the open window as they bounced down the dirt road, her eyes watching the road ahead, sitting poised on the seat, her firm and solid legs pressing against the skirt. She seemed to sense him looking at her, and she glanced at him.

"Somebody's gonna see us, O.B.," she said.

"Nobody lives down here," he said.

"Albert Westin," she said.

"We ain't goin that far. We'll stop at the lake."

They bounced and swayed along. The road was sandy, rutted, cut through mainly for cotton wagons, though people back in here had cars and trucks now. There were large dry holes, and the road veered out to the side in spots, around the places that were crusted, dry and caked across the top, but that O.B. knew, three inches below the surface, would be damp black clay that would suck the tires down like quicksand. He went through a gate, bouncing across a rusty, uneven cattle gap, and turned across a field, making his own path now, driving toward the stand of willows and catawbas, and then the lake came into view. O.B. drove up almost to the edge before cutting the engine, and they sat there in silence, neither one of them saying anything for a long time.

Gradually, O.B. became aware of the buzzing and clicking of the cicadas back in the bushes. He glanced over at her. She was looking at him, an open, fearful expression in her eyes.

"We ought not to be out here, O.B.," she said.

He coughed, his throat dry. He could feel the perspiration on his forehead. "I was *meant* to come along and find you there. It was meant to happen."

"No," she said. "You don't believe that."

They sat there looking at each other. He could see a thin film of tears in her eyes, until she looked away, her hand over her eyes, as if to hide what he might be seeing there.

"What's the matter?" he said.

"I don't know. I don't know." She shook her head. "All this that's goin on. With Edna hurt. With everybody. I don't even know Eldon and Sally anymore. It's like they live in a different world. I can't touch em. It scares me."

O.B. didn't say anything for a moment. Looking at her, he could feel his pulse in his ears. "Eldon said . . ." He paused. It made him feel self-conscious and guilty to use his name. "Eldon said that all this was the most important thing that would happen in his and my lifetime. I didn't know what he meant. I still don't. But I'm beginnin to see some things." She was looking levelly at him now, the tears in her eyes glinting like pieces of silver in the sunlight. "I know this," he said. "Things ain't ever gonna be the same again." He looked out across the lake, at the way the sun played on it, ripples visible but tiny. The water sparkled, tiny pinpoints of light moving about the surface like fireflies. "When I come out here, and see Blount and Punchy, I get . . ." He could not find the words. "I get so down." He shook his head. "This doesn't make any sense. I look at Martha, and I can't touch her, either. I can't get inside her, you know? Inside her head and her heart." He spoke haltingly, trying to frame his feelings. "I don't know *her* anymore, either. And it's like I'm holdin on to Ellen, scared she's gonna slip away, too. I'm scared to even look at her . . . scared she won't be there if I do. Does that make sense?"

"Yeah," she said, her voice low, almost hoarse. "I know what you mean."

O.B. nodded. Something was choking him. His throat was parched. He thought of the water in the back and then remembered the way she looked drinking it, looking at him over the rim, her eyes seeming to dance, her eyes that were so changeable, like the surface of the earth with first sun and then clouds moving over it. He looked long at her, the line of her neck, the thin cloth of the dress over her high breasts. He could almost see the dark nipples pushing against the cloth. He could smell the damp heat of her body, tinged with the faint scent of the jasmine. "I love you, Cora," he said.

"Don't say that. I told you—"

"But I do!"

"There's nowhere for it to go, O.B. You told me that a long time ago, remember?" There was bitterness in her voice.

"Maybe I was wrong."

"You can't go back O.B.! Too much has happened. We both got family." She looked steadily at him. "And no matter what anybody says or what happens, you're still a white man and I'm still a nigger."

Her words stung him. "No—"

"Yes! Ain't any way either one of us will ever get that out of our minds. No, thank you. I don't want that again."

"You feel the same way I do, Cora. I can tell you do. Let yourself feel. Let yourself love me—" He felt desperate. Alone.

"I don't love anybody—" she began, and then seemed to catch herself, turning away from him, looking out across the lake.

He opened the truck door, stepping down to the ground. He got the thermos from the back and poured the cap full of water, his hands shaking slightly, and drank deeply, feeling the soothing coolness in his throat. He poured it full again and handed it to her; she took it and drank. He was watching her, his eyes narrowed. He propped his foot on the running board.

"What did you mean before?" he asked.

"What?" She wouldn't look at him as she held the cup in front of her.

"You said you didn't love anybody."

"I . . . I was just . . . sayin that. That's all. Forget it." She still would not look at him as she handed him the cup. She put her hands against the dash, and he could see the tenseness in the backs of her hands, the tenseness of her body concentrated there. "There ain't any future for us, O.B.," she said softly. "And that's all there is, the future. You got to understand that. Eldon . . . he's a good man, a decent man. He believes in the future. He believes. More than anybody else I ever knew, he believes." There was frustration, pain, in her voice.

O.B. tossed the dregs of water onto the ground and screwed the top back on the thermos. As he put it back in the carrier, he saw the blanket, the tarpaulin. He knew that she would not refuse him, because she had come out here with him. He took a deep breath, thinking of her as a girl, and as she was now. Thinking that when he looked into her eyes, he *could* go back, erasing the years, making Blount and Punchy and his own parents young again.

The sun on his head was making him dizzy. He reached into the shadows of the cab, touching her cool, smooth hand, tightening his grip around it. She did not resist, staring back at him, a serene, distant look in her eyes, as though she, too, were somehow transported.

"We're crazy, O.B.," she said hoarsely. "Nothin good can come of this."

He pulled at her arm, and she slid across the seat, stepping outside, blinking in the brightness, and then shading her eyes with her flattened hand. He pulled the tarpaulin from the carrier and spread it on the thick grass, then spread the blanket on top of the tarp. He squinted at her; there was no shade, and the fierce sun beat down on them. She stood there, not moving, for a moment. Then, with the barest, slightest movement of her legs and feet, she shook loose the sandals and stepped out of them. At that tiny, almost intangible gesture, O.B. felt his breath catch in his throat. She bent over, grasping the hem of the sundress, and straightening up, pulled it over her head, dropping it on the grass. She wore no brassiere, and through her thin white panties he could clearly see her thick black patch of pubic hair. Her breasts were rounded, plump, her nipples large and dark and erect. Her breasts rose and fell with her breathing, which was quickened now, as she looked at him, her tongue in the corner of her mouth. He reached for the buttons of his shirt, and she watched him undress. When he was naked, she rolled her panties down her legs and stepped out of them. She lay down on the blanket. She held her arms up to him.

O.B. dropped to his knees beside her, his body aching and burning for her. When he took her in his arms, everything else disappeared, as if they were locked together in a private universe. Together. Alone and safe and secret and sweet.

Chapter Eleven

~⌐⌐~

ELLEN AND PAUL AND SALLY CUT DOWN A CINDER-PAVED ALLEY, walking along in silence, headed for the Stoner Funeral Home. The narrow alley was dim, shaded from the afternoon sun by high back fences covered in thick, fragrant honeysuckle. Ellen had not slept well for a week. She felt drawn and tired. She grasped Paul's hand tightly, feeling his hot, sweating palm. She was frightened and felt as out of control as she'd ever felt in her life.

She had trouble reading Paul's reaction to all this. He had been remorseful, frightened. He had offered to take her away, marry her, telling her over and over that he loved her, but she could not do that to her father. When Sally had told them about Stoner, the abortionist, Paul had come up with the three hundred dollars but had asked them in a strained voice not to mention any of this to Mancini.

"They say there's nothin to it," Sally said. "Like clippin a hang-nail."

"Stop sayin that," Paul said, and she could hear a tremor in his voice.

Ellen shuddered. She wanted to believe that there was nothing to it, but she did not feel it.

"Women go down here and walk out and go back to work. Ain't any problem," Sally said.

They approached the back door of the funeral home, a low, unpainted concrete-block building with a rusty tin roof. Ellen had seen it from the front, with its little red neon sign in the window. STONER'S it said. She felt the sweat running down her neck, her blouse sticking to her back. The man had told Sally to tell Ellen to wear a loose-fitting skirt, and she had worn a cotton pleated one, black with red roses, one that her mother had passed on to her when it no longer fit her in the waist. Sally knocked at the back door. After a few seconds, the door opened, and Abraham Stoner stood there.

He was a large man, with bulging eyes and cheeks. He pushed open the screen door, stepping back to let them into the room, and Ellen saw that he wore a dingy white dress shirt open at the collar. Black pants stretched against his ample stomach. She saw gold rings on his fingers, glinting dully in the naked overhead light bulb that hung from the ceiling. He grinned at her, a gleaming gold tooth in the center of his mouth.

"This the girl?" he said.

"Yeah," Sally said.

He held his hand out stiffly, palm out, toward Paul. "Stop right there, white boy," he said.

"He's with us," Sally said.

"No, he ain't," the man said. "He ain't comin in. He can wait in the alley. But he better stay outta sight." Paul just stood there, looking helpless.

"It's okay," Ellen said, her voice a whisper. Paul stepped back, and Stoner closed the door in his face. Ellen felt alone then, lost.

"This is—" Sally said.

"I don't want to know her name," Stoner said quickly. "I ain't ever seen her before, won't never see her again. When she walks out of here, I ain't never seen her in my life." He looked at the two of them, his eyes flat and emotionless. "Less git this straight. You ain't ever seen me either. You ever tell about this, you dead meat. I won't hesitate to have you hurt bad if you tell. You won't never tell nobody anything again. You understand?"

Ellen's body shivered. "Yes," she said.

"You got the three hundred?" he said.

Ellen had it folded in the pocket of her blouse, three crisp one-hundred-dollar bills. She handed it to the man, who quickly counted it, then looked at her. It was hot and stuffy in the room. There was a heavy smell of alcohol and formaldehyde, like the biology lab at school, and Ellen felt a wave of nausea.

"How far along?" Stoner asked.

"Two . . . two months," Ellen said. Her voice came out thin and reedy as she stared at the metal table in the center of the room. There was a skimpy, flowered bath towel on it, like the kind that sometimes came with soap powder. *This is happening to someone else. I am dreaming this.* She closed her eyes. Images of Paul and their baby hovered behind her eyelids. She heard them talking as though they were in another place, another time.

"Listen here," Stoner was saying, "Yore daddy better not git wind of this. I don't want no preacher come poundin on my door."

"I don't tell him nothin," Sally said.

Ellen's stomach cramped. The air in the room was so stifling that she could hardly breathe. "How . . . how long does it take?" she said.

"Snap," the man said, snapping his fingers in front of her face. "You in a hurry?" Ellen breathed deeply, trying to fill her lungs. She felt dizzy, and her hands were shaking. She looked around the room. There were rubber tubes hanging from the ceiling, a large sink in the corner with metal pans stacked in it. The room opened through an archway into another, larger-looking room, where she could see, sitting on two sawhorses, a gray casket. She felt faint. She had thought about this for a week, imagining what she would see here. She thought of Paul, waiting, scared, and her heart felt swollen in her chest, pressing on her lungs, smothering her.

"Yes," she said softly. "I'm in a hurry."

"I sees a lot of ladies in a hurry." The man chuckled. "They gits in a hurry when they done been stung by the trouser worm! Git up on the table then," he said. "Here." He pulled a chair up next to the table. She stood looking blankly at it. "Step up on that," he said. He grinned. "Most of the folks that lay on that table don't *walk* in here to git up on it." He was chuckling, looking at her with his round, protruding eyes. "Relax, honey lamb. In a few minutes, you gonna be good as new. Ain't nothin to worry about. You might as well laugh about it. You in a hell of a lot better shape than old Miz Sara Polk over there." He jerked his head, indicating the room with the coffin. Ellen shivered. "You ain't got to Te-Te, is you?" he said.

"No," she said.

"Go on, then," he said.

She stepped up onto the chair, Sally helping her, and sat on the metal table, surprised at its coldness, which she could feel through her skirt. She lay down on her back, looking up at coils of black rubber tubes like a nest of snakes above her. Her mind seemed to shift about, from clarity to a fuzzy state, as though she were experiencing something that was happening to someone else. Every time she closed her eyes, she could see Paul, his eyes, the way he looked at her. He would be there for her. He was being strong through this. The tears burned behind her clenched eyes.

"Take them panties off, honey lamb," Stoner said, his voice muted, distant, and she fumbled with them, pulling them down her legs, over her sandals. She felt Sally's hands fold her skirt around her waist. She could see the man, washing his hands in the sink. Then he pulled on a long pair of pink rubber gloves, snapping them against his hands. He fiddled with a tray of silver instruments, like dentists' tools, only longer, larger, and Ellen closed her eyes again. She tried to concentrate on the blackness, the emptiness. "Wait a minute," she heard him say. "You want some aspirin? You can have a drink of shine if you want it." She kept her eyes tightly shut; she seemed to have lost the ability to open them.

"You don't give her a shot or anything?" she heard Sally say.

"She don't need no shot. Maybe some aspirin."

"Ellen? Ellen?" Sally said.

She opened her eyes. Sally held a jelly glass of water and two aspirin in her palm. "Take these, why don'tcha?" Sally's eyes were worried, concerned. Ellen could read her friend's fear. She tried to swallow, but her throat was so dry and painful. She sat up on her elbow, taking the glass, sipping the water. It was tepid. She threw the pills to the back of her throat, gulping some more water. She was at an awkward angle, and some escaped her mouth, running out of the corners. She lay back in the hot, ovenlike room, her body burning, except for her private parts, which felt cool, exposed to the air. She felt the man's rough hands spread her legs, and she shut her eyes again, gripping Sally's hand, her other hand twisted into and tightly holding the rough towel beneath her.

She felt something metallic, like ice, touching her, and she flinched. She sensed his movement, but she felt nothing but the clammy, metallic chill. "Lordy," she heard him say, his voice hollow-sounding, as though coming from far away, "this sho a tight little white pussy."

"Don't talk to her like that, Abe," Sally said, her voice constricted, distant.

Lord, let him hurry. Just let him hurry. Just let it be over with and forgotten. She didn't care what he said. She just wanted it to be over. She felt a stinging, like a pinprick. Then she felt a burning, scalding sensation that seemed to run up her body from her pelvis, making her cry out.

"Hold still now," Stoner muttered. "Wait a minute. Everything's all right." She gripped Sally's hand and the towel. Her body rigid, she tried to control her breathing. The pain was subsiding now, but there was an afterburn. "Hand me them Kleenexes," she heard Stoner say to Sally. She felt him swabbing her, wiping gently. "All right, then," he murmured.

"That's it?" Sally said.

"That's it," Stoner said. Ellen lay with her eyes closed, gazing into a black empty darkness. She relaxed her hands, letting her body slump against the table. *Her baby. Their child!* "Ain't as much fun as gittin it in there, but it's just about as quick, ain't it?" Stoner's voice echoed strangely, as though it were coming from down in a well.

Ellen opened her eyes. The unshaded bulb hanging from the ceiling blinded her for a moment. When she blinked, her eyes were dry and scratchy. She had not cried, she thought. Not once. *I have not cried. My father would be proud of me. My father!* She tried to sit up, propping on her elbow. Sally was staring at her, alarm in her eyes.

"Don't sit up too fast," Stoner said.

"She's white as a sheet!" Sally said. "She ain't got no color atall!"

"Let her alone, she'll be all right," Stoner said. He put his hands in her back, helping her to sit up. Ellen felt giddy, wobbly. "Here," he said, holding out a handful of tissues to her. "Make that a wad, and hold it on your pussy. Help her over to the cot, Sally. Put that wastepaper basket there for her."

"Where?" Sally said.

"Over there," he said, indicating the other room. "There's a cot over there, let her lay down, hold them Kleenexes to her." He looked at Ellen. "If you feel sick, puke in that wastepaper basket. Don't puke on the floor." He turned back to Sally. "You come on in here and git her some ice-cold orange juice. I got some Kotex in here she can wear home." He looked back at Ellen with his bulbous eyes. She felt exhausted, her clothes clinging damply to her all over. "You gone bleed a little, off and on. Ain't nothin to worry about. Be bout like you got your monthlies. You be glad to git em again, won't you?" He chuckled again.

Sally helped her down to the floor; Ellen's legs felt mushy, boneless, and she had to put her arm around Sally's shoulders as she held the tissues against herself, trying to do exactly as the man had told her. They moved clumsily into the dim room, sunlight slanting through dusty windows that opened onto the alley. Ellen avoided looking at the coffin. Sally helped her onto the cot, putting a flat, knotted pillow behind her head. The raw, sweet smell of formaldehyde was even stronger in this room; it seemed suspended in the air, palpable and real, and Ellen had the sensation that it was penetrating her skin, clinging to her pores like a stain. Sally left her, going after the juice, and she lay there, holding the tissues between her legs. She felt oddly at peace now, removed, detached. Gradually, her eyes became more accustomed to the dimness in the narrow little room. The gray metal coffin was sitting on the sawhorses, against the wall, closed. Ellen blinked her eyes. Across from her was another cot. A form. She peered at it in the gloom.

The naked body of an old Negro woman lay there, her eyes open and staring at the ceiling, her thin, toothless mouth twisted into an agonized grin. Ellen felt suspended, stunned, and she stared, mesmerized: The old woman's arms and legs were thin, just fragile sticks, and her ancient breasts were wrinkled, empty pouches, flattened against the ribs of her chest. Her belly was sunken, and Ellen could see the gray, ashlike hair between her legs, matching the tufts that clung tightly to her skull. She's so still, Ellen thought. As still as death.

She felt a wave of nausea, bitter saliva forming in the back of her throat, and she fumbled for the metal trash can. She could smell the sourness of her vomit mixing with the sticky-sweet death smells, the dusty air of the room, and she kept gagging until she was empty, too exhausted to move. She tried to spit, but her mouth was dry again, burning with the bitterness of her own bile. She lay back. She was almost embarrassed that she had vomited in the room with the old woman. She looked across at her. The old woman's eyes, in her wrinkled, prunelike face, stared lifelessly up into the dimness. Ellen thought of sunlight, of flowers, of her own soft bed at home. Of her father. Then she thought of Paul. She felt the tears begin again, and this time, she let go, let the wet sobs rack her body, her tears wetting her hot cheeks as she gripped the rough fabric of the moldly mattress. The image of her father crowded her inner vision as she gave herself over to the crying, surrendering to the dull, heavy sorrow that lay in her breast like death.

Paul waited for them in the alley. He was smoking, and there was a pile of twisted cigarette butts on the gravel at his feet. He was perspiring freely. The air was heavy and humid, full of the smell of earth and flowers; it was liquid, oppressive air, unlike anything he had experienced before, and he wondered if he would ever be the same person again after he left this place. After *they* left . . . If she would go. The desolation and helplessness and paralyzing fear that he felt was like a hollow, cold core at the middle of his being.

He knew that he loved Ellen. He had reached out to her, grasped her like a life jacket in a deadly, stormy sea, and now . . . He knew that he would shrivel up and die if anything happened to her. If it was in any way his fault, he knew that he could not ever live with himself again.

Ellen and Sally came down the cinder alley, and he felt as though he were seeing her after a long absence, after days or months of painful separation. Ellen was walking slowly. Her face was ashen, the color gone from around her nostrils and the corners of her mouth, her hair damp and sticking to her scalp. Her eyes were flat and feverish, faded almost gray.

He held her, feeling her trembling limbs, alarmed by the way she looked. She clung to him, and he felt his legs grow weak; then he pulled himself erect, his arm around her, and they went back down the alley, looking up and down the street before they crossed to Paul's car. Paul saw a red pickup truck, parked a couple of blocks down, that had a strange, familiar look to it, focusing sharply the clammy fear that he lived with every day, but it quickly passed into the fringes of his consciousness as he helped her into the backseat of the Volkswagen.

"What happened?" he said, his voice tight with the panic he felt.

"Whattaya mean, what happened?" Sally said. "What the fuck you expect happened?"

"Did somethin go wrong?"

"No," Ellen said, her voice soft and breathy. "No. I'll be okay."

He got behind the wheel. He looked back at her. He could feel his hands shaking.

"I love you, Paul," Ellen said. Her eyes were pained. He looked nervously around, up and down the street, his eyes flicking past the red pickup. He looked at Sally, then back at Ellen where she lay against the seat. The motor was rumbling and sputtering.

"I love you, too—" he said.

"We got to get outta here," Sally said. "Fore somebody sees us."

He ground the car in gear and moved away from the curb. He loved her, and he would love her forever. *She is going to be all right!* "You sure she's okay?" he asked Sally. Sally nodded. "Where can we let her off? We can't drive right up to her house. Can we?"

"No!" Ellen said. "Around the corner. My mama's sure to be there. I'll just have to take a chance with the neighbors." She was crying.

"Jesus," he said. He pulled the car to the curb, turning around to the seat so that he could see her. "I'm sorry, Ellen, God, I'm sorry." He could feel the tears burning in his eyes. He wanted to protect her, and the thought of being away from her now, when she needed him, was as painful as fire against his skin. He loved Ellen, more than he'd ever loved anyone in his life. And yet he felt himself losing her. It was as though he had found himself down here, in this strange, unsettling world, separated from everything he had ever known, and she had been there for him, she had loved him back, and now everything was conspiring to take her away from him! *No! I will make it up to you!* She was like an angel who had appeared in this hell, and he would rescue her, save her, take her away.

He helped her out of the car. He watched her through a film of tears as she crossed through the yard of the Episcopal church, around behind the parish hall, disappearing through a gap in a hedge covered with honeysuckle, next to an old, sagging chicken yard.

.~.~.~.

Ellen stood in the kitchen, listening for sounds of her mother in the house. Some of her strength had returned, as she brushed at her hair with her fingers and tried to straighten the wrinkles from her blouse and skirt. The smell of the back room of the funeral home still lingered in her nostrils; she imagined that she would smell it for the rest of her life. She wondered if the smell was in her clothes. She wondered how she would get rid of the sanitary napkin. No problem. She was having her period. Her mother wouldn't notice. She never noticed anything when she was drinking, much less what Ellen put into the trash. Ellen stood very still, listening; she could hear the television playing softly in the front of the house. Her mother sometimes left it on while she napped. It was a little after four; there was nothing on but a children's show or two, cartoons; her mother never watched those. She saw her mother's heavy shot glass sitting on the counter, next to the sink. She moved over toward the shot glass, her legs still unsteady, picked it up, and sniffed it. A fresh, raw smell of alcohol. There was a thin, tiny puddle of dark whiskey in the bottom. She put it back exactly where it was. She turned away, thinking that she would go quietly to her room, and saw her mother standing in the doorway, looking at her. Ellen jumped, startled, her blood racing. Her nerves were completely frayed. Her mother was looking at her strangely.

"What's the matter?" her mother said. She wore wrinkled cotton shorts and an old HHS T-shirt of Ellen's.

"Nothin," Ellen said. "You just startled me."

"Are you sick?" her mother said. "You don't look good."

"No," Ellen said. "I'm . . . it's so *hot*. It's hot in here."

"Come on up to the living room," her mother said. They had a window air conditioner there. It was the only room in the house where they had air-conditioning.

The room seemed to tilt back and forth; Ellen felt tiny shooting pains, like electric shocks, in her belly.

"I just need to lie down," she said, "really I do." She moved toward the hallway door, down the hall to her room, past her mother, who watched her anxiously. Her legs felt numb, swollen, as she lay down on her bed on top of the spread and closed her eyes, but the old dead black woman's face leaped at her from the blackness. She lay staring at the ceiling, at the water stain that had looked, ever since she was a tiny girl, like an almost-perfect map of Europe.

***

She did not remember closing her eyes, but she must have slept, because the room was almost dark now, the windows reflecting gray dusk, and her mouth tasted bitter and sour. She could hear no sound in the house. She sat up, and a sudden, piercing pain shot through her abdomen, like a white-hot poker being driven through her. She cried out, muffling the cry at the same time, and she held herself still, as the pain began to throb in rhythm with the beat of her heart. She felt so tired she didn't know if she would be able to sit up farther, even if the pain allowed her to. Slowly, she swung her legs down. She felt the stickiness then, and she smelled the blood. In the dim twilight of the room, she saw with horror that her spread was covered with dark blood; her skirt was sticking to her.

"Mama!" she cried out. "Mama!"

There was no answer. She lay back, sweating profusely, the sweat mingling with the blood. *Where is my mother?*

She heard her door open. Her mother stood there, in the dimness. In the light from the hallway, Ellen could see that she held a glass. "What is it, Ellen?" she said. She switched on the light. Ellen could see the shock on her mother's face. "Ellen!" She dropped the glass, and it shattered, the ice cubes skittering across the floor. "Goddammit, Ellen what is it? What's wrong!" Her image was bleary through Ellen's tears, her vertigo.

"I need to go to the hospital," Ellen said.

⚬⚬⚬

Ellen lay in the high hospital bed, the blinding whiteness of the room hurting her eyes. It seemed to her that she'd drifted in and out of consciousness, and she felt hot and feverish, cool and calm, by turns. The pain was gone; in its place was a hollow numbness. She remembered the drive to the hospital, her mother weaving down the street, pulling into the emergency entrance of the hospital, leaning on the horn; she had been embarrassed, for herself and for her mother. She had listened in a kind of suspended delirium as her mother tried to talk to the nurses, then the doctor. She remembered being rolled down a long corridor, then voices around her and fluorescent light bulbs drifting past over her head.

"Who did this to you, Ellen?" she remembered her mother shrieking, close to hysterics. "I don't know where he is!" she had heard her mother saying. "Somewhere out in the country! Send the police after him!"

Him? Her father? Paul?

Darkness.

"She'll be okay, Mrs. Brewster," she had heard a man's calm voice say. "She's out of danger now."

She closed her eyes.

⚬⚬⚬

She was suddenly aware of someone in the room with her. The glaring, painful overhead light was out, soft yellow light spilling out of the bathroom now, and as she came into awareness, she jumped, her entire body reacting to the presence. It was her mother, her black silhouette, standing before the window, the blinds almost closed. Her mother's voice was a jumbled murmur. *Who is she talking to?* There was no one else in the room. She narrowed her eyes, and she could see the telephone cord, the shape of the phone against her mother's ear. Her mother's voice was harsh, muted and sharp.

"Yes, Lester," she heard her mother say. "It was him. I know it was. He raped her. It had to be rape." There was a long silence. Ellen lay very still, her body rigid and tense. She moved her arm. It was painful, so she lay still. "The son of a bitch. He raped her! He raped my baby!"

There was another silence, as her mother listened, her breathing raspy and frantic. "I don't care. Listen. Rooster Wembley came to our house. He'll know what to do. Goddammit, if the law won't do something, then Rooster will. He'll get that boy, bring him in. Goddammit!"

Ellen closed her eyes. Her mother was drunk. She was crazy. She heard her mother put the phone down. Then she heard her dialing again. She could hear her mother's soft whimperings; her breathing was ragged, coming now in short, tortured gasps. When she spoke into the phone, her voice was shaking.

"Rooster!" Ellen heard her say. "This is Martha Brewster. Yeah. My daughter, Ellen, has been raped by that Jew! She's in the hospital! She . . ." Her mother's voice collapsed into sobs. Ellen lay there, panicked, helpless to move. She felt the tears stinging her eyes. Fear—terror—welled up in her, sweeping her away. *Lord, let me die! Lord, let me die!*

᛫᛫᛫᛫

"**G**od damn you!" Mancini's dark eyes flashed anger. He looked as though he wanted to attack Paul physically. Paul stood silently in the middle of his room. Carl Youngblood had heard from a friend of his, an orderly, about Ellen's being taken to the hospital, and Carl had told Mancini all that had happened. Now Paul didn't know if Joe was madder about his not telling him or about what had actually happened. Paul felt overwhelmed with worry about Ellen. The Youngbloods' house was quiet, and Paul didn't know if anyone was overhearing them.

"I'm sorry," Paul said.

"You knew better," Mancini said, "but goddammit, you couldn't even resist a little snatch, and now look! Just look!"

"It wasn't like that," Paul said weakly. "I love her, Joe."

"Shit!" Mancini snapped.

Paul felt his own anger rising out of his fear. *What have I done?* "You son of a bitch," Paul muttered, "I love her. It was our child. I told her we could go away together—"

"Don't be a goddam fool, Siegel," Mancini sneered. "You get your head turned by the first little slit that walks by—"

"To hell with you, Joe!" Paul clenched his fists. He was bigger than Mancini, taller, and he took a step toward him.

"Don't mess with me, Siegel," Mancini said levelly, standing poised. He was wiry, his body coiled and ready. Paul stood still, the only sound in the room their breathing. Mancini slowly pointed at him, the sneer still on his face. "You have royally fucked up, Siegel. You know how much danger we're in down here, and now our asses are worth about a plug nickel. We're leaving. Pack your things."

"No," Paul said. "I can't leave her."

"Shit! Come to your senses, man!"

"I can't leave her, Joe. You can take my car. But—"

"What the hell do you think you're gonna do for her?"

"I don't know. But I can't run off and leave her. I know that."

Mancini leaned back against the wall. He crossed his arms over his narrow chest. "Do you think they're even gonna let you get close to her, after this? Shit, man."

Paul felt the tears stinging his eyes. He could not help it; he sobbed openly. The heavy, dank air of the old house seemed to cling to him. He knew that Mancini was right, and the thought of not seeing Ellen, of not being with her during this, choked him. He could hardly breathe, thinking of her in the hospital. Mancini just watched him crying. Finally, Paul controlled himself. He was standing with his arms hanging limply at his sides. His breathing grew more regular.

"Okay. Pack your things," Mancini said after a minute. "I'll pull the car around to the backyard. Come on."

"No."

Mancini pushed him in the chest, and Paul took a step back. Mancini stood in front of him, gritting his teeth, and Paul felt hollow with frustration and helplessness. Mancini spoke slowly. "Pack your goddam things, Siegel. Or leave em." Mancini turned to go.

"Wait," Paul said, reaching for him, but Mancini was gone, and Paul stumbled after him. He watched, through the film of tears, Mancini going down the steps in the dim stairwell. "Wait, Joe," he said, hearing his voice echo in the huge old house. His legs felt weak, his arms sapped of all their strength. He was terrified at the idea of Joe leaving him here all alone. *I cannot leave her.* He heard the back door's rattling slam. He took a deep breath and moved slowly down the stairs. *He will have to understand. My life is worth nothing if I leave her.* He stopped in the downstairs hallway. He listened for sounds of Joe in the backyard. The house was silent.

"Joe?" he called out. His voice felt thin and dusty. Mancini did not answer him. There was an eerie hush, too much quiet, and he moved cautiously through the lighted kitchen toward the back door. His heart began to pound in his ears. "Joe?" Silence. His pulse raced. He pulled open the door. He stepped out onto the narrow back porch.

Suddenly, his arms were grabbed from behind, and he was twisted to the side, held stiffly erect, and total fear gripped him like a vise. A figure appeared before him. In the yellow light spilling through the screen, he could see the mask: like a dingy white pillowcase with eyeholes crudely hacked into it. Yellow, animal eyes fixed on him. He could see other men, shadowy white figures in the backyard, one group dragging a limp body across the sandy yard. *Joe!*

"Yessiree-bob," the man behind the mask said, his voice jovial, "it's time we showed these Yankee assholes some real southern hospitality!"

And then Paul felt a sudden, sharp pain in the back of his head, and his eyes became unfocused as he felt his body slumping downward, and then everything went black.

O.B. heard the phone ringing when he opened the front door. He had been out near Gallion, trying to sell an old man a used tractor, and he had not hurried home. He was in no rush to get home these days. He crossed the living room wondering where Martha and Ellen were, the phone ringing insistently. He went into the hall and picked it up.

"Hello?"

"Mr. Brewster?" a male voice said. He did not know the voice.

"Yes." O.B. felt a sudden sense of vague alarm.

"Let me say first that your daughter is all right. Okay? This is Dr. Tucker, at the hospital. Your daughter became ill earlier this evening, and your wife brought her out here. She was . . . well, very ill. I can explain it all to you when you get out here."

"Out there?" O.B. felt disoriented.

"Yes. You'd better come on out here now. Your wife is with your daughter."

"In the hospital?" O.B. was stunned.

"Yessir. She is in the hospital, will be for a few days. Just for observation. We think she's fine. Barrin any more complications, she can go home in a few days."

"A wreck? Was she in a wreck?"

"Nossir. I tell you what. I'll meet you at the emergency entrance, okay? I can fill you in. Dr. Tucker. I don't think we've met. I know who you are. I'll watch for you."

"I'll be there in five minutes," O.B. said.

O.B. could not believe what he was hearing. The doctor had taken him to a small office off the emergency area and told him about Ellen's botched abortion.

"My wife brought her in?" O.B. asked. His voice was high, a remote echo in his ears.

"Yes," the doctor said. He was young, thin, his blond hair cut short in a crew cut; he wore a knit shirt under his white hospital smock. "She got her here. It was . . . —" the doctor shook his head—". . . right heroic, the state she was in. She was hysterical. She had obviously been drinkin a great deal." He leaned back in the metal chair. "Apparently, your daughter had the abortion sometime today. In Tuscaloosa, she said. Of course, she won't tell us where it really happened. Anyhow, sometime this evening, she started to hemorrhage, and when she discovered it, she called her mother, and they came right on out here. She was lucky. Sometimes this sort of thing happens in the middle of the night. When the patient realizes what's happenin, if she ever does, sometimes she's too weak to do anything about it. And she just bleeds to death."

"Goddam," O.B. whispered. "I want to see her."

"Okay. Do you want a minister? Or a priest?"

"Who?" O.B. frowned.

"You know. Your minister?" The doctor cocked his eye at him.

"No," O.B. said.

"All right," the doctor said. "I just wanted you to be prepared. There will be questions from the police. What she's done is illegal." He sat looking steadily at O.B., his eyes deep blue, like blueberries. "And your wife is saying all sorts of allegations and accusations—"

"Accusations?" O.B. was puzzled.

"Yes. You'd best be prepared. She is insisting that your daughter was raped. At times she . . . doesn't seem to be entirely clear on exactly what has happened to the girl. I suspect that she's been drinking heavily. It would seem, for some time."

"I want to see my daughter," O.B. said.

⋅∽∾∿⋅

She lay still, her head back on the pillow. There was an IV in her arm, a thin yellow tube snaking down from a clear glass jar on a stand beside her bed. She breathed regularly, and her dark hair was stuck to her forehead in damp ringlets.

"She's sleepin now," Martha said, "thank God!" She pulled at O.B.'s arm, motioning to the hallway, but he jerked his arm away. He leaned over the bed and kissed Ellen on the forehead, gently. Then he moved toward where the hallway light spilled through the cracked door.

Martha stood in the hallway. She was shaking, her eyes like those of a frightened rabbit, her cheeks streaked with her black mascara, where she had been crying. Her clothes were wrinkled, her skin pale in the harsh white light of the hallway. O.B. felt an intense hatred for her. He blamed her. Whatever had happened it was her fault, it had to be.

"Goddammit," she began. "Lester said—"

"*Lester?*" he said harshly. "What is this? What the hell is goin on, Martha!"

"I don't know. I don't know, O.B." She licked her lips. "You can talk to him. I . . .—" She looked around—"I need to run back home. I need . . ."

He was looking at her steadily, his eyes, he knew, icy, totally without compassion. He felt nothing for her now but a slow, burning anger.

"I need some medicine," she said. "I have to have some medicine."

"All right," he said. His anger was flat and heavy, tinged with disgust. "Go home. Get your medicine."

Her anxious, panic-stricken eyes flicked over his face; her hands worked over and over, massaging whatever she was holding in them, her car keys, a black plastic billfold.

"Don't be like that, O.B.," she pleaded.

"Like what? I said go get your medicine. Are you comin back?"

She looked around, then back at him. She didn't answer.

"Maybe you better not," he said. "Take your medicine and go to bed. I'll stay here for a while."

"Okay," she said.

He watched her go down the hall, the sandals slapping on the tile floor, until she disappeared around a corner. He went back into the room. Ellen still lay in the same position, sleeping deeply. He felt his chest fill so that he could not breathe, with a feeling of love so intense that when the tears came he shook so much that he had to grip the foot of the bed with his hands. His body shuddered and shook with throttled sobs. He had not realized that he could feel such pain, that he had not been there for her. This anguish, this torment that she had suffered, tore at his guts like fire. After a minute, his ragged crying subsided; he wiped his eyes and stood looking at her unblemished profile, her face soft and peaceful, reposed, safe for the moment.

There was a muffled, tentative knocking at the door. He moved over there, wiping his eyes again, and looked out. Lester Sparks, in his navy and khaki uniform, stood awkwardly in the brightly lighted hallway. He looked at O.B. in an apologetic way. He jerked his head. O.B. went outside the door.

"What did she tell you?" O.B. demanded.

"Nothin," Sparks said. "She wouldn't tell me hardly nothin. Said she was pregnant, and she went to Tuscaloosa and got an abortion. She didn't remember the doctor's name, nor where his office was, nothin like that. She wouldn't tell us the boy's name." Sparks looked levelly at O.B., his eyes the color of flint. "Doctor run me out then, told me she had to sleep. She wasn't gonna tell me any more, anyhow." Sparks put his hand on O.B.'s shoulder, turning at the same time to walk down the hall, and O.B. fell in beside him. "Now, Martha," he said, not looking at O.B., "she says Ellen was raped. She had it all figured out. She says it's the outside agitator, the blond one. She told me that the boy raped Ellen, that it had to be rape cause she ain't but seventeen and the boy is a grown man. I happen to know that he's twenty-one, cause Hoyt Blessing stopped that little Kraut car of his and checked his license one afternoon, made notes on his vital statistics. What Martha's got figured out is that the boy done the abortion himself, that him and that other one, Mancini, must be medical students, and they just done it theirselves." He shuddered. "Probably with a coat hanger or somethin."

"Shit." O.B. could not separate the anger from the pain now. He could feel his pulse pounding in his temples as he gripped his hands in front of him.

"I'm just tellin you what she was goin on about," Sparks said quickly. "I figure she'll hit you with it, so I might as well let you hear it from me." They had reached the end of the hallway. Sparks turned O.B. around with his hand on his shoulder, and they walked slowly back down the hall, away from the waiting area. "Now, O.B., I do know that your daughter has been seen with the boy. I'm gonna have to pick him up, question him, find out what he knows. I don't know how you feel about all this, man—"

"Pick him up," O.B. said. The boy was a faceless, haunting figure. She had defied him with the boy, violated their trust, endangered her very life. His *grandchild!* he realized, startled and confused.

"All right. But I tell you, it don't rain but it pours. We got a house fire out in shortleaf and a wreck on Highway Eighty, out toward Gallion. Soon as Ricky and Hoyt and them get back in, we'll go around there and get him. You know he's stayin over there with them beatniks, them Youngbloods." They had reached the door of Ellen's room. They stopped. "That's all I know right now, O.B.," Sparks said. "I sho am sorry about all this. That's a sweet little girl in there."

"Thank you, Lester," O.B. said.

Lester patted him on the shoulder, and O.B. watched him walk down the quiet, deserted hallway. He then slipped noiselessly back into the room. O.B. was besieged by conflicting emotions of anger, sorrow, and love for Ellen. He moved over to the window. A full moon was up, the night clear and cloudless, and moonlight slanted through the blinds and made silver bars across the bed. O.B. sat down in the chair, feeling drained, fatigued, his old knee injury paining him sharply. It was a moment before he realized that Ellen's eyes were open, staring at him, and he stood up.

"Ellen!"

"It's okay," she said. "I'm all right, Daddy." He moved quickly to the bed, taking her hand, holding it. It felt hot and dry, feverish.

"Punkin," he said. "How do you feel?"

"Okay. Tired. I hurt." She turned her face away from him, toward the window. He could see tears in her eyes, on her cheeks. "You hate me now," she said.

"No! No, I don't hate you. I could never hate you."

"I'm afraid Daddy," she said.

"You're all right now. The doctor—"

"I love him, Daddy. This wasn't his fault. He's . . . he's good. You don't know. Nobody here knows, but I do. I . . . I love him."

"All right," he said, patting her hand. She was okay. It was all right.

"You don't believe me," she said. "You think I'm just a child. But I'm not." She looked at him. "He didn't rape me. I don't care what Mama says. And he didn't do this. He had nothin to do with this." She started to cry then.

"Honey, honey," he said, patting her hand, not knowing where to touch her. He was flooded with relief; he felt connected to her again.

"Daddy, I'm scared. You've got to do somethin." Her voice was barely above a whisper. "She called that old man Rooster. Everybody says he's the head of the Klan. He's mean."

"Who? Your mother?" Anger again, bitterness.

"Yes. Yes, she called him on the phone. I heard her. She told him that Paul raped me. That he did this to me. I know . . . Daddy! Please. You've got to warn him. Tell him. Tell him to . . . go away. To go back up North. While he can!" She was crying now, sobbing.

"Honey, don't . . . calm down. You'll hurt yourself," he said.

"Please!" she said. "For me!"

"All right," he said. "For you. I'll go tell him." He was still gripping her hand. He suddenly saw her, in his mind's eye, not as his little girl but as a woman, her own woman, and the image pierced the fog of his despair like a shaft of light. He could not refuse her. He knew that he would have done anything she wanted him to right then.

"Hurry," she said. "I know those men will . . . please, Daddy."

"All right," he said. He stood up. He thought of Rooster, standing in his living room, the hateful, bitter look in his copper eyes. Ellen was right. The boy was in danger. He had to hurry.

"Please, Daddy," she said, "go now."

He squeezed her hand. He kissed her forehead. Something very profound touched him then: He heard something in her voice, something that he knew as love, but for the boy Paul. Love that he could not share with her. And yet the realization was not painful; it seemed to give him a surge of energy. He stood looking down at her for a moment, knowing her as he never had before.

"All right," he said.

＊＊＊

O.B. pulled his pickup to a stop in front of the Youngbloods' old house. It was quiet there, the huge magnolia tree in the front yard bathed in pale moonlight. Large, creamy white blossoms, like little ghosts, hung among the thick, waxy-green leaves. He could smell the tree, its sweet, pungent perfume in the damp night air. He sat there for a moment. The quiet in which the old house sat seemed ominous and foreboding.

O.B. opened the passenger door and stepped down. He got out, walking around behind the truck. He sensed danger in this whole thing, and he thought briefly of looking in the carrier, seeing if he could find something to use for a weapon. Something had already happened; everything was out of control, moving now with its own momentum.

He opened the carrier and got a flashlight, then he jumped the ditch and went through the sagging old iron gate and up the cracked sidewalk. He shone the flashlight on the heavy front door, the light reflecting off the fanlight above the door, a stained-glass peacock.

O.B. banged on the door with his fist. He tried the door, but it was locked.

"Shit," he said aloud. "What do I do now?"

He saw headlights in the street, then he watched as a police car rolled to a stop behind his truck. A tall figure got out; he could see his Smokey-the-Bear hat in the light from the streetlamp down on the corner. He could see his silhouette in the moonlight, the way his belly hung out over his belt like a watermelon.

"Hoyt Blessing!" O.B. called out.

"Whozzat up there?" the policeman said.

"O.B. Brewster," O.B. shouted. He watched Hoyt find the board laid over the ditch. He came slowly and carefully up the walk, stepping in the patches of pale light that filtered through the huge magnolia tree. O.B. could hear his leather belts squeaking, his handcuffs and equipment rattling and tinkling metallically.

"Lester said to meet him here," Hoyt said. "What you doin?"

"You seen Rooster?" O.B. said.

"Rooster Wembley?" Blessing said.

"You know any other Roosters?" O.B. said irritably. Something was terribly wrong; O.B. knew it now, could feel it in the damp night air.

"Naw," Blessing said, "I ain't seen him. Why?"

"Bang your nightstick on this door. See if you can roust anybody," O.B. said.

Blessing glanced at him out of the corner of his eye. He took out his billy club and banged it on the door. "Youngblood!" he yelled. "Open up! Police!" He looked at O.B. "These people is dope addicts," he said, "but even with their minds messed up, we'll play hell catchin em. Smart as whips."

A light came on in the stairway, glowing through the fanlight and through the side panels. The door opened, and Carl Youngblood stood there. His hair was mussed, his beard matted. He wore a pair of dirty blue jeans and no shirt. His broad, sloping chest was covered with thick black hair.

"What?" He looked at O.B., at the policeman, then back at O.B.

"Tell Siegel to git his ass down here," Hoyt Blessing said. "Now. We need to talk to him."

"He ain't here," Youngblood said; his voice was shaking as though his teeth were chattering.

"We can search this house. We got other men on the way. So tell him to come on down here," Blessing said.

"He's not here, I'm tellin you," Youngblood said. He looked at O.B. with panic-stricken eyes. The man was upset about something. He was hiding something, but not the boy. O.B. could feel it in bones.

"He's tellin the truth. The boy's not here," O.B. said.

"What? How the hell do you know?" Blessing said.

"He's not here. Get on the radio to Sparks. Tell him. Tell him to hurry," O.B. said.

"Hurry?"

"Tell him to come on," O.B. said, exasperation in his voice.

Blessing glanced at him again, suspiciously this time. He went back down the walk toward his police car.

"Where is he?" O.B. turned back to Youngblood. He was thinking

of Ellen, the sound of her voice, the pleading in her eyes. *The baby.*
Their child. He was the father of Ellen's child. O.B. tried to remember
what the boy looked like; he could not.

"You're Brewster, right? Ellen's dad?" Youngblood said. "Look,
I—"

"Where is he?"

"They got em. They got em both," Youngblood said, his voice
tense, tight.

"Who got em? Who?" O.B. felt the bottom dropping out; the old
boards of the porch seemed to sway beneath his feet. He knew who got
the boys, all right. . . . The pit of his stomach was cold and hollow.

"Some men. They were masked. Joe and Paul were packin the car.
They— God, it was awful. They were on us before we knew it. Didn't
want anybody but those two. They didn't lay a finger on anybody else.
They had . . . God. Shotguns, and chains." Youngblood ran his
tongue over his lips. "We just want to be left alone," he said. "Tell em.
Tell the police."

O.B. could see the man's terror in his eyes. "You need to tell em
what happened."

"I *told* em!" Youngblood said. "I already told em. I told Sparks. He
knows it!" His voice was a high whine.

"*Sparks!*" O.B. felt a hollow, startled sense of disbelief, but then he
knew the truth. "Lester Sparks?"

"The police chief. A little while ago."

"Jesus," O.B. said.

"Hey, y'all," Hoyt Blessing called from the street. He was standing
by the car. In the bright moonlight, O.B. could see the long, curled
cord of the radio mike snaking from his hand back inside the car.
"Sparks says for me to come on in. They searched the Siegel boy's car
and found a bag of marijuana, and Sparks has done issued an arrest
warrant for both of em on drug charges. Says them boys have left for
the North, hightailin it back to the Mason-Dixon Line!" They could
hear Blessing chuckling. "He says they've surely done crossed the state
line, and now they're the goddam FBI's problem!"

·~·~·~·

"**H**e's lyin," Sparks said, "Youngblood never told me nothing about
no masked men. He just don't want that house searched. It's prob'ly
fulla dope, too, and—"

"The car," O.B. demanded. "Why didn't they take the car?" He was
seething inside, his anger and frustration about to erupt any second.

He had driven downtown, parking at the corner, walking briskly around city hall to the police offices in the front of the little jail. Mac was there, in a short-sleeved shirt, sitting behind the desk, sweating, his pudgy hands flat on the top of the desk. Sparks stood against the wall, chewing on a matchstick. He looked relaxed, easy, but he was speaking rapidly.

"That heap of German junk?" Sparks said. "Shit. It probably wouldn't make it even to Atlanta. No, some of their organization, probably, came over from Mississippi, got em. They're long gone."

"How do you know that, Lester?" O.B. said, his voice thin, tight. He knew Sparks was lying, but what could he do about it?

"Look, O.B.," Mac said. "I know you're upset. Anybody would be. It was an awful thing. And they'll git em. Believe me, they'll git em. The dope-addict boy will pay for what he did to Ellen. You don't need to worry."

"I'm afraid he's already paid." O.B. felt deadened. His exasperation was like a cold lump in his belly.

"What the hell does *that* mean?" Mac said.

"I think you know what I mean."

There was a pause as Mac seemed to let O.B.'s threat hang in the air between them. His eyes shifted around nervously. "Now goddammit, O.B.," Mac said, "I don't know what all that son-of-a-bitch Youngblood told you, but I say he's makin it up. I don't know anything about the crazy story he claims he told Lester over there. But I can tell you this. We know the boys took off, ran away, because at last we was about to nail em for possession of drugs! I hate that it had to be somethin like this." He looked pained. "I wouldn't for all the world want nothin like this to happen to your daughter, but I warned you, O.B. Goddammit, I warned you. You ought to be glad they gone; now they can't do you any more harm!"

"Damn you, Mac," O.B. said abruptly, "cut the shit! You know it's true, don't you? You know it, and you're protectin Rooster and his boys. Both of you! Goddammit!"

"Now you wait just one goddam minute, boy!" Mac was sputtering, his rubbery lips trembling. He looked from Lester to O.B. "You better watch what you're sayin, boy," he warned. "You better be goddam sure you can prove that, because you're talkin some shit now."

"Somethin's happened to those boys, and you're coverin it up!" O.B. said, his voice rising.

"Easy, O.B.," Sparks said. "You're upset, man."

"Youngblood's not lyin. Why would he lie? What possible reason would he have for tellin that?" O.B. shouted, his face flushing with anger.

"Because he don't want to get arrested for dope hisself!" Mac shouted back, his own face red.

O.B. paused. "It doesn't make sense, Mac. That he would make up a story like that. But one way or the other, I'm gonna find out!"

"You just do that!" Mac said angrily. "Be my fuckin guest!"

"Fellows!" Sparks said. "Everybody's all upset. Let's all just calm down."

O.B. stood breathing shallowly. He glanced at Sparks. "Whatever you know or don't know, you need to find em, Lester," he said, evenly. "You need to get your men out there and find em. Before it's too late."

"I told you, O.B.," Sparks said, "they're gone."

"Shit," O.B. whispered, shaking his head. He knew they were lying, but he could not prove it. They had probably planted the drugs in the car, too. Could that be possible?

"You ought to go home now," Mac went on, after a minute. "Shit. We all need some rest." He looked down at the desktop, lost in thought for a moment, then he looked up, wearing a forced grin. "Tell you what, O.B. If them boys ain't caught up with, sooner or later—runnin like hell tryin to git back up North—I'll kiss your ass in Scales's window at high noon on Saturday!"

O.B. wanted to rest, but he wondered if any of them would rest now, until all this was over. He looked at Mac's sick grin. Then he turned and went out, down the sidewalk toward his truck.

When he got inside the cab, he sat there for a moment. He thought of Ellen, of the vanished child: a vague, abstract nothing that had ceased before it had begun to exist. And he thought of the boy, out there somewhere in the night, in the vast, silent dark, little more than a child himself, like Ellen, and he thought, All of us are so alone to face the world! And he knew that when he closed his own eyes to rest, he would see, in his mind, these eyes that would haunt his repose: Ellen's, in the hospital—hollow and feverish, aching with anguish and pain; Cora's, as her eyes had looked that afternoon while they'd been making love—dark and glinting with spring sunlight; and Eldon's as his eyes would look if he knew of his wife and his friend's renewed betrayal of him—red-rimmed, braced as though against an inward force that needed to absorb all the pain and agony in the world.

Chapter Twelve

AC PARKED HIS BUICK ON THE STREET IN FRONT OF ROOSTER'S house on North Walnut Street. He cut the engine, shut off the lights, and immediately he heard the chorus of crickets and tree frogs in the shrubbery and the trees lining the quiet street. Rooster's house was a white clapboard, one story, sitting back from the curb; a front sidewalk split the neatly trimmed yard, running up to a small front porch. A yellow bug light was burning next to the front door, and Mac could see dim lighting behind the curtained windows. He sat there a moment, listening to the night sounds. Despite what O.B. seemed to believe, Mac didn't know everything that was going on. He had heard only hints and vague innuendos that led him to believe that Youngblood might be telling the truth and that Lester Sparks knew more than he was telling about the situation. Sparks swore that he didn't, but lately Mac had been seeing, in his mind, the Jewish boy's blue eyes, the morning sunlight dancing in them that day—that seemed so long ago now—that he had met him on the street with Long. He got out and walked slowly up the walk; he rang the doorbell. He could hear it, a harsh, steady ring, way in the back of the house. He would just put it to Rooster simply and directly; they were so close with the paper mill, and yet so far at the same time.

After a minute, Rooster's wife, Mary Catherine, opened the door. She was a slight woman, thin and stooped; she wore her hair in a tight wave around her head, the kind of hairstyle that Mac associated with the 1930s. Her eyes were round and droopy, like two overripe plums, as she stood looking at him for a moment, holding a freshly lit cigarette between her fingers. Mac noticed that the mouth end was stained dark red.

"Evenin, Mary Catherine," Mac said. "Rooster home?"

"He's watchin the television," she said. Her voice was deep and throaty. She opened the door wider. "Come on in, Mac," she said. Mac recognized the music of *Peter Gunn* coming from the living room to his right. The sound on the television was turned up very loud. He moved to the doorway and looked in.

Rooster was sitting in a wooden rocker, staring at the screen; he didn't have his leg on. The right khaki pants leg was folded under him, so that there was just a stump, pointing directly at the television.

"Rooster, Mac McClellon's here," Mary Catherine said, raising her voice.

"What?" Rooster said, not taking his eyes from the screen.

"Mac's here!" she said, shouting. She looked at Mac. "Lordy, him and that Peter Gunn. You'd think they was cousins or somethin! Rooster! Mac McClellon's come to see you!"

"Set down, Mac!" Rooster said. Mary Catherine moved slowly out of the room, drawing on the cigarette as she went.

Mac sat on a narrow sofa. The music blared, but it sounded thin and tinny. Lacy and Dudley had that album, and when they played it on their hi-fi, it sounded rich and full. The gray screen flickered and flashed in the dimly lighted room. Peter Gunn was chasing a man down an alley; he stopped and fired his gun. There was a sudden picture of Peter Gunn's profile, filling up the whole screen. His eyes were angry. Then there was another picture of him running down the alley.

Mac's mind wandered. He didn't care for *Peter Gunn*. It was the kind of show that moved too fast for him, so that he was always missing some detail that rendered the rest of the show senseless to him. He was thinking instead of the phone call he'd gotten that afternoon from Montgomery, from a man in the Governor's Office. There were rumors that the two civil rights workers in Hammond had been abducted, kidnapped. Maybe murdered. The rumors wouldn't go away. The man in the Governor's Office had told him that one of the national networks was asking about doing a story on the boys' disappearance. Mac had told the man to tell them to look for them in Connecticut.

Mac wanted to believe what he'd told the governor's man. He realized that he wanted to believe it so badly that he had talked himself into thinking it was true. They were long gone and safe. Or . . . He had to know. *I have to know, and I have to show Rooster who's boss!*

◦•◦•◦•

The *Peter Gunn* show had gone off, and a commercial for Alka-Seltzer had come on. It featured the little man with an Alka-Seltzer tablet for a hat. He was dancing. Rooster watched him intently.

"Rooster, is the show over?" Mac said.

"What? Oh. Yeah."

"I need to talk to you."

"Mary Catherine!" he shouted. She had gone to the back of the house. "Come up here and shut off this damn television."

Mac stood up. "I can cut it off, Rooster—"

"Sit down! Let the woman do it." He rocked slightly in the chair as Mary Catherine came into the room, her shoulders stooped. She shut off the television set, and the screen went suddenly dark, the sound snatched away.

"What can I get y'all?" she asked.

"Coffee," Rooster said. "What you want, Mac? You want some whiskey? Mary Catherine, get him some whiskey. You want Seven-Up in it, or what?"

"Water," Mac said. "That'll be fine."

"You heard him," Rooster said.

Mary Catherine, her shoulders hunched, scurried out of the room.

"That Peter Gunn." Rooster shook his head.

"Yeah," Mac said. They sat there for a few moments, not saying anything. Mary Catherine came back in with a tray, a cup of coffee for Rooster and a drink, pale, in a tall glass with lots of ice for Mac. It looked as though she had put maybe a thimbleful of liquor in it.

The two men waited until Mary Catherine had left the room. Then Mac said, "Rooster, I got to know what happened to those boys." He took a deep breath.

"Yeah?" Rooster said, holding the cup before his face, blowing softly on the surface of the coffee.

"Yes, goddammit. Now listen. If you know anything—"

"Why? Why all of a sudden you comin in here—"

"It's not all of a sudden. Listen, I had a call today. From Mont-

gomery, member of the governor's staff. He . . . well, he offered to
send some state troopers in."

"Where?"

"Why, here. To Hammond."

"Why?" Rooster sipped the coffee.

"You know what I'm talkin about, Rooster! They been hearin stories. The talk goin around is that somebody took those boys. Abducted
em. Looks to me like that Youngblood fellow would keep his mouth
shut, but he told O. B. Brewster what he told Lester. And maybe he's
talkin it around. Anyhow, if you know anything about this, you better
just come clean with me right now." Mac paused. He looked around,
listening. He heard Mary Catherine puttering in the back of the house.

"About what?" Rooster said.

"Shit!" Mac felt himself getting angry. *Whoa. I can deal with this
bastard, but what about that secret, invisible gang of his?* "About what
happened to the goddammed boys," Mac snapped. He sipped the weak
drink. The man was infuriating, but Mac knew that if he didn't treat
him delicately, he could have a race war on his hands. It was all he
could do to keep his voice level and casual. "There was that story in
The Birmingham News, and some rumblin," he said. "Enough to
make folks get real curious. Now I got this election comin up soon. I
got to get out and talk it up some. I got a feelin the niggers are gonna
pull some more shit, just to disrupt things. And if you and your boys
are out havin you some fun, stringin up Yankee nigger-lovers or something, then I think I might call the troopers in."

"*What?*" Rooster said indignantly, as though he were being mistreated, and suddenly, Mac knew the truth as clearly as he had ever
known anything before in his life. What he had just said to Rooster was
exactly what had happened, and he had known it all along, and Lester
Sparks knew it, too. And O.B. knew it, and . . .

"Just to keep the peace," Mac said quickly, his voice trembling,
realizing that he was looking at a killer, a cold-blooded killer. It was
hot and stuffy in the house, and Mac was uncomfortable on the
straight-backed little sofa. "I'd rather not," he said, "but I'm between
a rock and a hard place, Rooster. I got to keep the niggers down." He
swallowed. He was talking rapidly, rambling, he realized. He took a
breath and went on, more calmly, "Gulf International—I know you
don't care about that, but a lot of other people do—they ain't announced yet. So I got to keep the niggers down. But I got to do it
peaceable like. I don't want to call anybody in. Period. Lester and his
boys might be able to take care of things, if we knew for sure that there

wasn't any other group involved." He paused again. "Goddammit, Rooster, what the fuck have you done?"

"Don't call anybody in," Rooster said. "We take care of our own."

Mac sat there stewing, his stomach burning and rumbling.

"What in the goddam hell do you mean by that? As if I didn't know!" Mac said.

Rooster's narrow eyes were like yellow slits. "Mac," he said thinly. "You've known all along. Don't say you ain't. So . . . call in the law. Put em on me," Rooster said.

"Huh?" Mac peered at him, squinting his eyes. He had a dull headache, hammering behind his forehead.

"Well, I just told you I know something about them boys' leave-takin, so I reckon you better arrest me. 'Course, now *you* know somethin about it, too, not that you ain't known it all along. So if you don't have me arrested and hauled in, then you become a accessory to the fact, as they say, not that you ain't already. It gets out what happened to them boys, the niggers gonna go on the attack, too. And, 'course, you let Lester Sparks lay one fat finger on me, you gonna see this whole goddam town go up in smoke. I got friends, you might say. You ain't seen a goddam thing yet, boy."

Mac realized, with crushing suddenness, that he had been ambushed. He sat there, unable to speak. *Why couldn't all this have waited until at least after the election? At least until after Gulf International had committed themselves? At least until I was safely a member of the Shady Grove Hunt Club?* The old man smiled at him, his yellow eyes twinkling in the dusky light of the room. *Goddammit! Why did I come out here in the first place?*

"You ask too many questions, you wind up knowin more than you wanted to know, ain't that right?" Rooster said. "So now, you can just live with it!"

Mac stood up. "You son of a bitch!" he said, gritting his teeth.

"Don't cuss at me!" Rooster said. "It's the pot callin the kettle black!"

Mac suddenly felt exhausted. He couldn't think of anything more to say to the old man. His mouth felt stale. The cheap bourbon had left a sour, bitter taste on his tongue. The bitterness was like the smoldering dread that he felt inside. "Tell me this," he finally whispered, "about them drugs? The marijuana?"

"What about it?"

"Was it planted?"

The old man smiled. "Now couldn't you just look at them boys and tell they's drug addicts? What more is there to know?" He nodded, his lips working slowly. Then, "Mary Catherine!" Rooster yelled. "Come show the mayor out!"

Outside, Mac breathed deeply in the damp, heavy air. The crickets and tree frogs roared in his ears. *Trapped.* I am trapped, he brooded, starting down the walk to his car.

~~~

O.B. found a metal tray in the bottom of the kitchen cabinet. He put a bowl of cornflakes and milk on it, together with a paper napkin and a spoon. He put ice in a large jelly glass, opened a Coke, and poured it over the ice. The foam erupted to the top of the glass. O.B. had to sip quickly at the edge to prevent it from overflowing. He waited, filled the glass to the top, and put the almost-empty Coke bottle on the tray next to it. He went down the hall with the tray, propping it against the wall as he knocked softly on Ellen's door. There was no response. He cracked the door and looked in. Ellen was sitting on the edge of the bed, looking moodily out the window. She wore wrinkled Bermuda shorts and a pink T-shirt. Her dark hair was pulled back loosely, pinned carelessly and haphazardly so that it formed a loose, unbalanced frame for her face, which was wan and drawn. It had been a week since the abortion, but she still had not gotten her color back.

"Ellen?" he called. She turned slowly around, looking at him with blue eyes that were lifeless and dull. "You hungry?"

"No," she said.

"You got to eat somethin," he insisted, pushing open the door and coming on into the room. He put the tray on her desk against the wall. "Cornflakes. You want me to cut up a banana for em? We got some."

"I'm not hungry, Daddy," she said.

"Punkin," he said, "you got to eat. You got to get your strength back."

He sat down in the little straight-backed wooden desk chair. On the desk were several loose-leaf notebooks stacked against the wall. There was also a framed picture of O.B. in his Yankee uniform, the pin-stripes, the NY logo, standing with his foot propped on the bumper of a 1936 Chevrolet. His grin was wide and forced. There was also a picture of Martha, one made shortly after her marriage. Her dark hair was short, and the picture was mostly profile, her face thin, her beauty girlish and delicate.

Ellen had refused to leave the house since she had come home from the hospital. She lay in her room, reading paperback books that O.B. knew she had already read.

"Come on," he said, "eat somethin."

"He's dead," she said. "I know he is."

"No. No reason to think that. They probably . . . roughed em up. Or somethin. He . . . he's probably at home." He paused. "Honey, did you know he was using drugs?"

"He quit when he came down here. I know he did. He promised me that, and he wouldn't lie to me."

"The police claim—"

"Oh, Daddy," she interrupted. "He's dead. Those men killed him, and because of me! They said he *raped* me! *Me!* And the drugs. They're tryin to frame him, Daddy." Her eyes were dry. It was as though she had cried herself dry, and now the words were a ritual, repeated as though the uttering of them would somehow make them untrue.

"You've got to quit torturing yourself like that. It wasn't your fault," he said.

"Nobody believes me," she said. "Not even you."

He could not get the drugs out of his mind. It all seemed too likely, too logical. She was not looking at him, and he knew she could tell what he was thinking. "I believe you, punkin," O.B. said.

"You do?" she asked. She fixed her pale eyes on him, then. They were sunken, with dark circles around them. Her cheekbones were high and prominent. He was concerned about how much weight she had lost.

"About the drugs, sure," he said. "But I know he'll turn up." She seemed to sense the lack of conviction in his voice. He was worried about the boys, but he tried not to think about what might have happened. He didn't know what he could do about it. He had tried. Maybe, if he were mayor . . .

He sometimes allowed himself now to flirt with the idea that maybe he'd win the mayor's job. Looking at his daughter, at how all this had wounded her, made him want desperately to do something about it. When he took over, he would fire Sparks. Sparks was covering up something. Mac was, too, probably. O.B. would call in someone who would find out what had happened. Conduct an investigation that would lead, he knew, directly to Rooster Wembley. He gripped his fists together, feeling frustration as he saw the pain in his daughter's eyes. It would do no good to accuse Rooster now, he knew. That would only lead to someone else's getting hurt. O.B. realized how much he hated that kind of intimidation, the kind that had always allowed men like Rooster to run things around here, ever since he could remember. Maybe if he were mayor, he could change that. . . . He had awkwardly tried to talk to several people about voting for him, but they had stared at him with curiosity, some with a kind of veiled amusement, and he was surprised at how angry their condescension made him. Several Negroes had come to him to tell him he had their support, that he would get lots of votes in the black community. And he had had a strange telephone call from Lyman Wells. Lyman had pledged support, had told O.B. that he would do anything he could as long as it was behind the scenes, but that he could not, right now, openly support him. "Maybe that'll change," Lyman had said. "Change?" O.B. had said, puzzled. "Yeah. I can't say any more right now. Okay?" The phone had clicked off.

O.B. knew that the odds were stacked against him. But the pain of Ellen's heartbreak—what he now realized was a lot more than puppy love for the boy—and his fear of what might have happened to Paul incensed O.B., made him long to act, to do something, anything. He wanted to find Rooster, or Red Kershaw or Bobby McElroy, and choke them, grind his knuckles into their eyes, and he feared that one of these days he would go out and do something foolish like that.

Ellen looked away, out the open window, as a slight, humid breeze came through the screen. It still had not rained, but in the afternoon it sometimes clouded up, and there was heat lightning and distant, rumbling thunder, as though the sky were teasing the earth. Watching her, O.B. could remember the years when, no matter how down she was about something, a word from him had made the sorrow disappear. She had been his child, but now she was no longer a little girl. It was frightening to him. It made him feel small and unworthy, uncertain about her expectations and incapable of meeting them, whatever they were. A sudden pang of guilt reminded him then of Cora: They had been together, just yesterday, at the old fishing shack in the woods. It was tumbled now, unkempt, some of its sideboards rotted, but they both still thought of it as theirs. And this had been a planned meeting, and they both had silently acknowledged that they were starting it all over again. And he had felt guilty and afraid.

He stood up. "At least drink your Coke," he said.

"Okay," she said, "I will. Just leave it there on the tray."

"I've got to go back out to the shop," he said. "Your mother's takin a nap."

"Okay." She looked at him, and he could see a spark of anger in her eyes. "Why did she tell Rooster that he raped me, Daddy? Why?"

"She . . . she thought she was doin the right thing."

"I'll never forgive her for that," Ellen said. "All this is her fault!"

"No," he said. But he knew that part of it was. He knew that in her twisted, sick mind, Martha had thought she should seek help from Rooster. And he hated her for it.

"You mustn't ever stop carin, Ellen," he said, but his words sounded hollow. Ellen's half-smile, the cynical, vacant look in her eyes, told him that they sounded that way to her, too, as he left her room.

❖❖❖

O.B. was lying in a kind of half-sleep, the night dark as pitch. Martha snored beside him. They were sleeping together now, but not making love. She had promised him that she would try to quit drinking, that she would taper off, and she seemed to be in a period when she was not drinking quite so much. He thought that she had been making the effort since Ellen had been in the hospital and then at home, and O.B. allowed himself to think that maybe she could pull herself out of it. Sometimes, in the past, she did that. She would just announce that she was quitting and go to bed for several days, finally getting up sober, vowing that she would never touch a drop again. O.B. always felt hope then, because he knew that she meant it, and they would get rid of all the liquor and beer in the house. Then it might be months, or even a year or two, before she became convinced that she could drink normally, control it as everyone else could, and it would start all over again, like a crazy, out-of-control carousel. Still, O.B. was grateful for the dry periods. They approached some kind of serenity then, almost a kind of happiness. He prayed that she might be entering a sober period. He could use her love now, what there was left of it. He just wanted her there while he made this race for mayor, he wanted her fully alive. He needed her support. He felt lonely and alone, and he needed someone, and she was not there for him. He thought of Cora, his eyes tightly shut in the darkness, his fingers gripping the sheet under him, trying to shut her from his mind, the picture of her lean, naked body the color of cane syrup, trying to concentrate instead on feeling the gentle night breeze across his naked legs. He did not want to think of Cora, although, now that they had resumed their secret love, his entire being ached for her, and he forced himself to will her away as he heard the soft, low whir of the fan. Gradually, as though out of a dark sleep, he began to hear another sound, a low, muted tapping. He listened, lying rigid in bed. Someone was knocking on the back door.

O.B. sat up. His first thought was of Rooster, the night he had pounded on the door, and he thought of getting one of his shotguns out of the front closet, but he wasn't sure he even had any shells. He had no pistol.

He swung his feet to the floor, listening, then got up and pulled on his green work pants that he had worn that day and thrown over a chair in the corner. He went out into the hallway, his bare feet padding softly on the cool wooden floor. At the kitchen door he paused. The kitchen was dark; light from a street lamp near the corner spilled in through the window, making leafy shadows on the ceiling. He heard the knocking, louder now, right on the other side of the back door. O.B. moved noiselessly across the linoleum, then turned the knob, checking. The door was locked.

"Who is it?" he hissed, trying not to wake Ellen and Martha. The knocking came again. Through the back window, O.B. could see the street lamp brushing pale yellow light on the leaves of the large old fig tree. O.B. crossed to the kitchen counter next to the sink, opened a drawer, and groped carefully inside until he found a butcher knife. He went back to the back door, where the knocking was weaker now, but still distinct. He turned the key in the lock. He opened the door a few inches.

He could see no one. He could barely make out the honeysuckle-covered fence of the old chicken yard, the old garage and the coal shed. "Who's out there?"

"Please," a voice said, and O.B. jumped back, startled, gripping the knife. There was a man slumped on the back stoop, his hand outstretched toward the door.

"Who is it?" O.B. held the knife in front of him, ready.

"Paul," the voice said, barely audibly. O.B. blinked trying to focus his eyes in the darkness. *Who? Some kind of trick?* "It's Paul. Please . . ." The voice trailed off.

O.B. switched on the porch light next to the door. The boy burst into full form then, and O.B. almost dropped the knife, his mouth dropping open, his face reflecting the horror that he felt. The boy wore only blue jeans, caked with mud. His face was thin and drawn, his cheeks hollow. His right arm hung limply, twisted grotesquely to the side beneath him. His eyes were feverish, his face contorted with fear and pain, and he was looking at O.B. like a wounded, trapped animal. "Please . . ." he said.

"Jesus Christ!" O.B. put the knife on the table, hearing it clack on the Formica. He squatted down next to the boy, peering at him. He had seen him before, but only at a distance. The boy seemed younger now, a beaten child. Disjointed thoughts rushed through O.B.'s brain:

This was the father of his daughter's child. A child that she was no longer carrying. This boy had brought his daughter pain, heartbreak, yet she loved him. He had taken O.B.'s daughter from him, and he had no right to even be here in O.B.'s home. He touched the boy on the shoulder. "My God," O.B. said. "What happened?"

"They . . . they broke my arm. Please . . ."

O.B. slid his own arm around Paul, holding him under the arms. Paul winced when O.B. got him half-standing, his arm swinging uselessly, and then eased him through the door, letting it close quietly behind him. He switched on the light in the kitchen, helping the boy across the floor, heading for the living room, someplace where he could lay him down. On second thought, he guided the boy through the hallway, into the front bedroom where he eased him onto the four-poster, letting him lie back on the plaid spread. He switched on a lamp on a dressing table in the corner. The boy was looking at him, his physical agony clear in his face.

"There was no . . . place else to go." The boy was breathing shallowly, his voice thick, as though his tongue were choking him. His eyes were burning. "The Negroes . . . they . . ." He licked his dry. "they were . . . frightened . . . took me in . . . but they were scared . . ."

"Okay, shhhhhh. Don't try to talk. I've got to get you to a doctor—"

"No! I can't . . . can't . . . they said I was charged with . . . dope. . . . They'll throw me under the jail!" He looked at O.B. "They planted it in my car. You gotta believe me. I wouldn't be that stupid."

"Who? Who did that?"

"The men. They . . . I can't . . . no doctor."

O.B. stared at him. "Water? You want some water?" he said.

"Yes. Please," the boy said. "They would kill me if they found me," he added, his voice trembling.

O.B. padded quickly back down the hallway toward the kitchen. He paused, listening. There was no sound, no movement, from the bedrooms. He found a glass and filled it with cold water from a pitcher in the refrigerator. The boy looked weak; he was probably hungry. O.B. picked up a plate with half a pone of corn bread that was sitting on the table, covered with a clean dish towel. He stood looking out the window, at the leaves of the fig tree. His heart went out to the boy, but really, he knew, to Ellen. The boy's arm had to be set. He knew, then, what he would do. Old Dr. Mason. He lived five houses down, on the corner. He would be there. He had retired, and his wife, who had been an invalid in a wheelchair, had died during the past year. For years, up until a few years before he retired, he had had an office in his home.

He had delivered Ellen, in the winter of that dark war year, in the very room where Paul now lay. O.B. shook his head. He carried the water and the plate of corn bread back up to the front bedroom to Paul.

·~·~·~·

The little white clapboard house was dark. O.B. pounded on the door until he saw a light come on toward the back, and he saw old Dr. Mason moving slowly toward the door. His wispy gray hair was mussed, and he walked stooped, wearing an old yellow robe with the waist cord trailing after him on the floor. He fumbled with the locked door, finally pulling it open as he put on the porch light. He stood staring at O.B., his eyes puffy and full of sleep.

"Brewster?" he said.

"I need you," O.B. said, "get your bag. An emergency."

"Call the hospital," Dr. Mason said.

"No," O.B. said. "I need you. There's . . . not time."

"I'm retired," the old man said, "I don't doctor anymore. Go on and let me sleep."

O.B. could see his wife's wheelchair sitting in the vestibule behind him. And she had been dead now almost a year.

"No," O.B. said. "Get your bag and come with me." The old man stood blinking in the dim porch light. "Now!" O.B.'s voice was harsh, and the old man flinched.

"What's happened?" the old doctor said.

"Someone is hurt, and you need to come. Just up the street. At my house. You can wear your robe. Put on some shoes and get your bag."

"All right," the old man stuttered.

"Hurry," O.B. said, coming inside, waiting in the crowded living room while the old man went back toward the back of the house. The house smelled dusty, musty, like a seldom-used closet; every flat surface was covered with papers and magazines and books, many of them open and facedown. "Listen," he yelled, toward where the man had disappeared, "you got any plaster, like for a cast, here?" The old man didn't answer. O.B. went down the narrow hallway, looking in the dark rooms. He passed the little converted side-porch area that had been the doctor's office for years; it still bore a faint clean, medicinal smell. Bright light spilled out of a bedroom, and O.B. looked in. The old man had put on his pants and was pulling on a shirt. His hair was still disheveled, tousled. "You got any plaster for a cast?"

"A cast?" Dr. Mason echoed. He still seemed only half-awake.

"Yeah. We got a broken bone."

"Arm?" the doctor said.

"Yeah."

"All right," Dr. Mason said. "We'll need several rolls of gauze. A couple of cans of powder. In my office—"

"Listen," O.B. said. "I'm sorry if I got rough with you."

The old man's eyes shifted back and forth. He kept looking at O.B. out of the corner of his eye.

O.B. touched his fragile shoulder. "I appreciate you comin out. I do. But nobody can know about this. You understand that? You can't tell a soul. I mean it," O.B. said. "We're gonna go over there and fix this boy up, and then you're gonna come on back here and go to bed and forget all about it. Unless I need you to see him again. If I do, I'll come get you. Otherwise, you don't know a goddam thing. Word gets out about this, and I'm comin after you. Now. You got that, or not?"

"I got it," the old man said. His eyes were full of suspicion, fear. O.B. could tell that he'd gotten through to him, that he was likely to keep it to himself, at least for now. "Where?" the old man said.

"This way," O.B. said, leading him, knowing that he had had no choice but to threaten the old doctor. He had cast his lot with the other side, with people that, eight or nine months ago, he would have described, if pressed, as the enemy. He hoped that there would be some solution, some fairly easy answer, but all his instincts told him that he had somehow made an irreversible, inevitable decision, taken on an immutable obligation from which there would be no turning away. He would never be able to explain why he'd opened his door to the boy to men like Rooster and Mac. To them, he would now have become, totally and completely, a traitor, subject to the quick, rough justice that underlay the very fabric of their way of life. He was, now, as marked a man as Paul, as Eldon.

He shivered in the night air, leading the old doctor back to the house.

⸱⤫⤫⤫⸱

The boy lay propped on pillows, his arm in a fresh white plaster cast lying on a towel. The boy had cried out in pain, sweat popping out all over his face, when Dr. Mason had set the arm. O.B. had been sure the noise would wake Ellen and Martha, but neither one of them stirred.

Standing at the door, O.B. had said to the old man, "Now listen, you don't say a word. Can I count on that?"

"Yes," he had said, "I promise." He had gone slowly down the sidewalk in the darkness, walking stiffly, carrying his worn old black leather bag.

O.B. was amazed that they had not awakened Ellen, but then, her bedroom was at the far, back end of the house. Martha slept soundly in her whiskey dreams. O.B. had poured some of her bourbon for Paul, and for himself, now they sat sipping it. O.B.'s limbs, especially his knee, ached with fatigue; soon, the first gray hint of dawn would appear in the western sky, and the day would begin, a new day with this boy in his house. Soon Ellen and Martha would be awake, and he would have to face them. He knew that Ellen would be greatly relieved, overjoyed that the boy was here. He did not know, and feared, how Martha might react.

Paul frowned as he sipped the whiskey. He seemed self-conscious and tentative as he lay back on the pillow. O.B. looked at him, pondering how this boy had been locked in adult love, in passion, or lust, with his daughter. Instead of anger, he felt a kind of peace that he was at least face-to-face with Paul, could see him as a person and not some faceless threat, a kind of relief that the boy and Ellen were battered and bruised but now safe, like boats finding refuge after having been tossed in a violent storm. O.B. even felt a kind of closeness with the boy.

"I can't tell you how bad it was," Paul said.

"The other one? What's his name?"

"Joe. Mancini." Paul closed his eyes, taking a sip of the whiskey. "Dead." His voice was a whisper.

"*Dead!*" O.B. said. "They killed him?"

"God, Mr. Brewster." The boy rolled his head on the pillow, tears glistening in his eyes. "They strung him up to a tree. Naked. They . . ." He turned away. "They burned him, all over. With a poker. And when he was still alive, they . . . They cut his balls off! His cock, and his balls, and he screamed, begging them to stop. He *knew* what they were doin, and he screamed. I never heard anything like that, I . . . it was so horrible. And he finally passed out, and he was bleeding, bleeding . . . and they left him hanging in the tree. I guess they were gonna hang me in the tree, too. They were saving me for dessert, I guess. They wanted to prolong it . . . calling me Jewboy, putting food in front of me and then taking it away, telling me I was next— Some of em sat around and watched when two of em broke my arm. Over a sawhorse, with their bare hands."

"Who? Who was it?"

"I don't know. They never said any names. They wore these masks made out of cotton cloth, like torn from sheets. I guess they were the

Ku Klux Klan. I didn't get a look at any of their faces, but they knew us, knew our names, knew what we were doing. They had seen us. They were men from here, this town, I know that. I still hear their voices when I close my eyes."

"How'd you get away?" O.B. gulped the whiskey.

"They kept me tied up; I never knew when they'd return to torture me some more. I woke up . . . it must have been around daylight one morning, and the guy that was guarding me was asleep. I don't know how many days I'd been out there by then. This was out near some cave somewhere, I don't have any idea where, but I'd know it if I ever saw it again. The ropes on my feet were loose enough that I was able to hobble off, get far enough away to shake the ropes loose more, and then I went through woods, like a swamp, with my hands tied behind me, the briars and bushes hitting me in the face, but I was running as best I could, because every time I closed my eyes I could see Joe, Joe's body with the blood running down his legs. And I finally got to these black people's house, and they took me in, they knew who I was. They doctored me as best they could, but they couldn't set my arm. They were terrified. They fed me, kept me hidden, but they finally told me I couldn't stay there anymore. See, they knew who had gotten me, and they were afraid. . . . After some days, they brought me to the outskirts of town. That was tonight." He turned away again, his face toward the black window. "I figured if I went back to the Youngbloods or to Eldon Long, I'd be walkin right back to the Klan. I knew once I'd gone they'd be looking for me, watching those places." He looked back at O.B. "I wouldn't blame you for throwin me to those people, but I didn't have any place else to turn. I know I'm . . ."—he shuddered as a sob racked his body—". . . puttin you, and Ellen, in danger, but I didn't have any other place to go," he said softly, between sobs, crying now, like a child.

"It's okay," O.B. said. "You did the right thing." The boy was really such a child. O.B. could not be angry at him.

"I'm sorry about . . . what happened. It was . . . well, I know you won't believe me, but I never used any dope, never once since I came down here."

"I believe my daughter," O.B. said. "She's told me about it. All of it. I don't like it, but . . . well, I don't like it a bit." It was something that he felt he should say.

"I'm sorry," the boy said.

"You ought to be sorry. But it seems like a long time ago. I don't know what's to be done, now."

"Yessir," he said.

O.B. took a sip of the liquor. The boy needed to be at home, with his own parents. Yet here he was, off down here, his very life in danger.

"Do you want to call your folks?" O.B. said.

"No," the boy said, quickly. "I can't. My . . . my mother's dead. And my father, well, he wouldn't understand. About the drugs. He'd never believe me. He didn't want me to come down here. I can't contact him about anything."

"What about the other one? Mancini?"

"He told me his parents were first-generation immigrants. They don't even speak English. He was in school on a scholarship. Besides, who's gonna believe me? They'll stick me with the dope charge! And the last thing the people in Washington said before we left was, 'Stay clean—get busted for dope, you're on your own!' " The boy wiped his eyes with his good hand.

O.B. sat very still. *Who can I contact, tell? Who can I trust?* He was too confused to think clearly; he kept running over in his mind: *I must do something! Something irrevocable has happened in this little town, the worst nightmare, and it could, it would, get worse.* His mind, his head, were pounding. He knew that he must not allow himself to relax, to think for even a moment that things were normal here. He trusted no one in authority. The federal government—someone beyond the state, the local, leaders—seemed a remote, indifferent entity. *Time.* He would play for time. He thought the boy was safe now, for the time being. He would keep him hidden. Then maybe he would try to spirit him away, in the middle of the night. That would make O.B. a criminal, too, but then he already was. He could take him to a bus over in Meridian. *What is wrong with me? What is happening to me?* O.B. sat looking at Paul's face turned softly to the pillow, the windows growing lighter now, growing gray in the first light of dawn. O.B. yawned, feeling the fatigue within his own body as he drank the last of the whiskey. He noticed that Paul had gone to sleep, his lightly whiskered face reposing on the fluffy pillow, his breathing long and regular, as though he were protected now, unthreatened and safe.

⋅⋅⋅

Ellen was up first, coming into the kitchen where O.B. sat at the Formica-topped table, drinking a cup of coffee. He watched her get a glass and pour some orange juice from an opened can in the refrigerator.

"You're not at work?" she asked. Nobody in their house made small talk in the morning.

"No," he said. "I didn't get a lot of sleep last night. They'll open up without me."

"Oh." She shrugged, sitting down at the table. She still wore the wrinkled Bermuda shorts, the pink T-shirt from the night before. It bothered him that she just slept in whatever she was wearing.

"Ellen . . ." he began, thinking he would make her feel better. "He's here," he said, watching her face.

She said nothing for a moment, looking at him with puffy, sleepy eyes. "Who?"

"Paul."

"What do you mean?" she said. "Here?"

"He's all right. He was in bad shape, had a broken arm, but he's seen a doctor, been fixed up. And he's here." He smiled, longing to see her face brighten, to see the slump of her shoulders lifted. "He . . . well, he'll tell you about it. He's in the front bedroom. He's alive." His smile felt stiff and frozen. "I guess we're hiding him."

"Daddy . . ." She looked around the room. "Ohh, Daddy. I don't believe it. I thought he was dead. I was sure he was dead." He could see tears standing in her eyes as she stood up, rubbing her palms on the sides of her shorts as though they were damp. She seemed confused for a moment, not knowing what to do, which way to move.

"You can see him," he said. "But let him sleep. He's worn out."

He followed her down the hall and watched her looking at the sleeping boy in the room that was bright now with morning sunlight. The heavy cast, completely dry now, curved across Paul's body. His hair was matted and dirty, his face reposed and calm in sleep. He slept with his mouth slightly open, his breathing slow and even. She stood there, looking down at him, and O.B. wondered about what horror, what pain, she must have felt all along, knowing that what Youngblood said was true. Then she sat in the chair next to the bed, leaning forward in what was almost a prayerful position.

"I'll let him sleep," she said, barely audibly. She looked up at him, her face soft, a gentle smile playing around her lips. O.B. breathed deeply, feeling sudden, unaccountable tears, as though he had found her and lost her at the same time, and he moved back, through the door, pulling it to softly behind him.

.~.~.~.

"I've decided," O.B. said to Martha, "I'm going to hide him. Until we can figure out what to do."

Martha sat there in the kitchen and looked at O.B. with disbelief. Then she got up and rummaged around in the cabinet, coming out with a bottle of Early Times. She grabbed a glass, splashed some whiskey into it, and took a long drink. She stared at him. He could see the fury building in her eyes. "Have you lost your mind?" Her voice was bitter and angry.

"What could we do, Martha?" he said.

"This is the man who raped your daughter. He's wanted for drugs. And you take him in like that? 'What could you do?' You could call the goddam police, that's what you could do!"

"They planted it on him. The Klan had him!"

"Says who? You believe what this boys says?"

"Yes! I don't know. Yes, for Ellen, I believe him," O.B. said, his voice rising.

"What's happened to you? Huh? You're not the man I married! I don't know what's happened to you!" She was screaming now.

"Just . . . just calm down, Martha," he said, suddenly aware that Ellen was up there in the front room, with Paul. They must be listening.

"No, I won't calm down!" She wore a white cotton dressing gown, and it swung out behind her as she turned back to the cabinet and got a glass, poured bourbon into it, and added water from the tap. "You want a drink?" she said.

"My God, Martha," he said, "it's eight o'clock in the morning!" *This is already out of control, as dangerous as a stampede.*

"So what? So fuckin what?"

"Jesus," he said. "Can't you . . ."

"Can't I what?" she spit at him. "No, I can't. This is the . . . the *goddamdest* thing I've ever seen in my life! He's a criminal! Well, I'm not gonna stand for it. I'm not." She drank deeply, the amber liquid running out of the corners of her mouth and dripping onto the white dressing gown. "I don't have to stand here and be insulted by you two. You with your goddam pathetic runnin for mayor! Against Mac McClellon, of all things! And your goddam slut of a daughter—"

"Shut up!" O.B. yelled, fury exploding inside his head. "Don't you say that!"

"Your goddam slut of a daughter!" she screamed.

He slapped her with his open palm, and she wheeled toward the sink, dropping the glass, which shattered on the linoleum floor. Her eyes were large, full of shock and anger, when she looked back at him. He saw her glance toward the hallway, and saw Ellen watching them, her face appalled. Martha's ragged breathing was the only sound in the room.

"You hit me," she said, softly, her hand slowly caressing her cheek. "You hit me." O.B. could not move. "That's it. Oh boy, that's it," she said. "You are somethin, O.B. You go along for years not even knowin I exist. Cold, like a lizard. And then you start to come out of it, and there's no place for me—"

"Martha," he said sharply, nodding toward Ellen.

"Let her hear. She knows anyway. I have my pride, O.B. How do you think it makes me feel? To know that you stopped lovin me a long time ago?"

"I . . . I'm changin. I . . ."

Her laugh was low and bitter. "It's too late, O.B. For me, you shoulda changed a long time ago." She stood looking from one to the other. O.B. could tell that she wanted to throw Cora at him, in front of Ellen, but she didn't. He was grateful for at least that.

Ellen just stood there in the doorway, her face open, agonized.

"How could we get all the way here after all those hopes and dreams?" Martha said. O.B. felt warm tears burning his eyes, and for a moment Martha was the girl he had loved all those many years ago. "We loved each other so much," she said. "We did."

O.B. could not speak. His tongue seemed swollen in his mouth.

"Well," Martha said, her face red and swollen. "I don't have to stay here. I won't be part of this. I can just leave you two here in your own hell! You *three*! God! I don't see how you stand each other!" She lurched toward the door, pushing Ellen out of the way. O.B. followed her, his heart pounding. The room seemed to spin around his head.

"Wait," he said, "you can't—"

She was gone down the hallway, and he ran after her, following her into their bedroom. She had ripped off the dressing gown, standing in a short peach-colored nightgown. "Martha," he said, "just calm—"

"Yes, I can!" she said. "I can leave this place! I've had enough."

"You can't go. Where the hell you think you're goin?"

"I don't know! Somewhere! I'll go to Meridian! What's it to you?"

He was afraid she would go straight to someone, to Mac or somebody, and tell him about the boy. He couldn't think straight.

"Martha—" He made a tentative gesture toward her, then just stood there helplessly. He watched her pull the gown over her head. She stood there naked, her round belly protruding, looking so much the way she had when she was pregnant with Ellen, her breasts so heavy and full, her nipples large and dark.

"I'll go home to my parents! Goddammit!" She had pulled clothes from the closet and the chest of drawers. He watched her struggle into a pair of panties and then yank a suitcase from the closet and throw it onto the bed. "You hit me, you bastard!" She glared at him. "Leave me alone!"

"You can't drive. You've already started drinkin—"

"I *can*, too! Don't tell me I can't drive. I can drive as good as anybody else! You're so 'perfect'! Mister Perfect! Hah! I just wish I was gonna be around to see you get humiliated in that mayor's race! God! That's gonna be somethin to see, the great O. B. Brewster crawlin home to lick his wounds after everybody shows him what they think of him!" She was throwing clothes into the suitcase. She grabbed up a double handful of cosmetics from the dressing table and threw them in.

"All right," he said, "go to Meridian, then." He heard his voice crack and thought for a moment that he would sink to the floor, his body lifeless and rubbery.

She stopped what she was doing and stared at him. She was still naked, except for the panties. "Hah! You don't think I mean it, do you? You think I'll come right back?!? Well, think again!" She had found a pair of Bermuda shorts and was pulling them on. Then she found a bra.

"Go to Meridian, but don't tell anyone about the boy," O.B. said. The strength seemed to flood back into his voice; it was firm and direct.

She was pulling on a blouse, buttoning it up, but she stopped, her hands frozen in front of her. Her smile was mirthless. She looked as though she were about to break down and cry.

"I'm serious, Martha," O.B. said, feeling a sick despair over what he was going to say next, but knowing that he had to do it for Paul's safety. "You tell anyone about the boy," he warned, so quietly and levelly that he could tell it got her full attention, "and I'll have you committed. So help me. I'll tell everyone what you are, and I'll have you put away in an institution. I mean it, Martha."

"Goddam you." She stood there, one hand on the suitcase, her eyes dull now, the flashing anger faded. "I know you would do that. You don't have to worry. I won't tell anybody. The criminal is yours and Ellen's." She paused a moment. "I don't want to go to jail with you! You're bound to get caught. You're a disgrace in this town, you bastard." She closed the suitcase with a slam. She turned away from him.

O.B.'s anger mixed with sadness was like hot liquid in his belly, but his head was strangely clear. He seemed to be seeing with a crystal clarity that surprised him. He looked at Martha in her wrinkled khaki shorts and light green shirt, her bare feet on the nappy orange rug. The green-and-white flowered wallpaper seemed sharply focused, its pattern acutely distinct in the brittle morning sunlight that poured through the window.

"All right then, go," he said. "Martha—"

"Fuck you." She yanked the suitcase off the bed and pushed past him, going down the hall to the kitchen, the suitcase bumping on the wall. Ellen was sitting at the table, and she looked up when her mother came in. O.B., following, could see streaks of tears on Ellen's cheeks. "I'll let *you* take care of him," Martha said, her voice now as quietly bitter as slow poison. "It's always been the two of you anyway." She took the bourbon bottle by the neck and went back up the hall, to the living room. They heard the front door open and then slam. O.B. got to the front windows in time to see her drive jerkily away from the curb, her old black Ford lurching as she let out the clutch, the engine resounding irately in the morning air.

O.B. felt relief tinged with regret. He did not move for a long time, looking out at the quiet morning street through his scratchy, itchy eyes, his body stiff and aching.

．～．～．

In the days that followed, O.B. tried to concentrate on his campaign for the mayor's office. He'd had some posters printed, with a picture of him in a coat and tie that Ellen and Martha had talked him into sitting for one Easter about five years ago. He had paid some teenage boys to put them up around town, but many of them had been ripped down within hours after they were put up. Some downtown merchants had point-blank refused to allow them on the outside brick walls of their buildings, where political posters had traditionally been hung.

"O.B., you just got to understand," old man Scales had said, peering at O.B. through his little rimless glasses. Scales's Dry Goods' two-story brick wall facing Washington Street was always plastered with advertisements for carnivals and auctions and high school football schedules.

"Understand what?" O.B. had said. "I'm runnin for mayor, goddammit, and everybody who runs puts up posters on the side of your building."

"Not this time," the old man said. "Listen, these are bad times, O.B., and you ought not to be gettin yourself all messed up in it. What you got against Mac's mayorin anyhow?"

"This is America, Mr. Scales," O.B. said, "and I can run if I want to."

"Sho now," the old man had said, "run if you're a mind to. Just don't put your goddam posters on my bricks. You understand?"

O.B. felt that he had wasted a considerable sum having the posters printed, but Eldon continued to be enthusiastic, as the election got closer, less than a week away now, telling him over the phone that he was going to win. O.B. knew better. They were not going to let him win. They were not even going to let him run a decent campaign, even if he had known how to go about it.

After a few days and some regular food, the boy was feeling much better. He stayed away from the windows, and during the rare times when someone might be likely to come by the house, he stayed in the front bedroom, the door closed and locked. Ellen had told O.B. that once Lacy McClellon had stopped by, and they had had an awkward, strained Coke in the kitchen. Lacy had wanted her to go riding, to go to the drugstore, but Ellen had told her she was not ready to go out yet. And the Avon lady had come by.

O.B. got home in the evenings, and they were there, sitting in the kitchen, talking quietly while drinking coffee or sodas, or else in the living room watching television, sitting on the sofa together, as though they were married. They treated the fact that they were alone there in the house together, day after day, casually and calmly, and O.B. tried to have that attitude, too, despite his paternal, emotional confusion over the situation. Ellen cooked for the three of them, with O.B. doing the shopping, stopping by the A & P on his way home.

Ellen seemed to enjoy preparing their meals. She did it with an ease that was foreign to O.B., and it seemed to be foreign, too, to the boy, who watched her with a rapt fascination. The simplest chores seemed to take on a kind of grace in Ellen's hands, and it achingly reminded O.B. of his early days with Martha.

He watched them at the table, with Ellen quietly aware that Paul was watching her every move, and O.B. felt the bittersweet knowledge that Ellen didn't belong just to him anymore, and that she needed him more than she ever had in her life.

Chapter Thirteen

❧

THE SATURDAY AFTERNOON HEAT IN THE SQUARE WAS STIFLING, but the people seemed to be enjoying themselves with their free hot dogs and soft drinks. Mac stood near the fountain and the goldfish pond, dabbing at the sweat on his face with a folded handkerchief as he shook hands, laughing and joking with the people who came by. He was enjoying himself, even though earlier he had felt resentful about having to fork over the money for the event. To hell with the money. He was glad now he had done it. He was going to be a rich man, anyway. Gulf International's announcement should come in a matter of days, and it looked as though it would coincide with his landslide election victory.

Mac had hired a couple of carpenters to build a little platform next to the goldfish pond, and Lacy and some of her friends had draped it with red, white, and blue crepe paper. Now he stepped up on it, looking out over the city square. He saw Belinda with her broad-brimmed white straw hat, over by the tables of food. She and the members of her two bridge clubs were serving. Everybody who was anybody was here. About twenty members of the high school band were over by the gazebo, tootling away, playing a ragged version of some Sousa march that Mac was familiar with but couldn't name.

He felt good. He had heard that O.B. had made an attempt at a speech in the square the other afternoon. Alston Scales had told Mac, laughing, that there was nobody there but "a few niggers and a coupla white folks looked like they was lookin for a handout!" He had heard that O.B. had spoken in several of the churches around town during the announcement period in the service. At the Presbyterian church, the morning he was there, Mac had been downright embarrassed for him.

"I just want you folks to know," O.B. had said, in a voice so soft it didn't even carry halfway to the back of the old stone church, "that I'm runnin for mayor of Hammond. I'd appreciate your vote. I know you got a member here runnin"—he had looked back at Mac, his eyes flat, with no energy in them, smiling slightly with just his lips—"but just give a new man some thought. Give him a chance." And he had sat down before he'd even begun. O.B. had looked thin, tired. He had taken all the business about his daughter and the abortion badly, and Mac didn't blame him. And then there was a rumor, later a confirmed fact, that Martha had left him. She'd been seen over in Meridian, where her parents lived.

Everybody was talking about the poor Brewsters as though they were white trash. Mac had to admit he felt sorry for his old friend O.B. All the anger that he'd felt at first over O.B.'s running against him was gone, dried up like yesterday's dew.

He stood looking out over people's heads. Every now and then, the unease that he had felt that night at Rooster's house would return, and he'd just turn his thoughts somewhere else. As far as he knew, Rooster had done nothing underhanded since he'd talked to him. And suppose the Klan *had* escorted the boys to the state line? Even roughed them up a bit? What was so bad about that? Mac realized that he could simply deny that he knew anything about whatever had happened.

Mac held up his hands to silence the crowd. "Y'all havin a good time?" he shouted, his voice booming out over the chatter and the laughter and the ragged playing of the band members. People turned to look at him, laughing, pointing.

"You ain't gonna make no speech, now, are you?" a stooped old man yelled, and people laughed. The old man's name was Winston Norris; he had been the vocational agriculture teacher at the high school until he retired over twenty years ago, and he was always present at events like this. He had been George Wallace's county campaign manager in the last election, when Wallace had lost to John Patterson.

"Naw," Mac said. "Just some words of greetin!"

"Thank the good Lord," the old man said. And there was more scattered laughter.

Mac squinted in the sunlight. He felt it beating on his head, sharp and oppressive, and he dabbed at his face with the handkerchief. "Friends!" he said. The faces tilted up to him, some of the jaws moving on the hot dogs. "I don't need to make any speech to y'all. Y'all know why I'm extendin my hospitality to y'all today. I can't make y'all any more aware than you already are of the times we're livin in. But I tell you, folks. Our side's winnin. At least here in Hammond! Our outside agitators are gone, and we ain't lookin for any more of em. And there's all this talk about so-called 'Freedom Riders,' comin in on buses and everything, but it sounds like just a lot of hot air to me. But if it's not, we're ready for em. If they want to come to Hammond, let em come on!" The crowd groaned and muttered. "We know what freedom is, here. We can show em a thing or two about freedom. We'll show em the World War Two memorial over there, with all the names of our native sons that died over there, defendin freedom!" There were several cheers. "We'll show em that Confederate statue over there, that commemorates the great wrongs done in the War of Northern Aggression!" Shouts of "You tell em, Mac!" and "All right!" Laughter at his calling it that.

Mac was aware of a stirring on the fringes of the crowd, some laughter, hooting. A disturbance at the corner. "I don't want to make a speech but there are some things you need to remember when you cast your vote for mayor in a few days," Mac continued as he peered in the direction of the disturbance. People were moving away from him, walking over in that direction, straining their necks to see what was going on. "What we got here?" Mac said, puzzled.

"Looks like a parade," someone said.

"Well . . ." Mac said. Everyone, it seemed, was moving away from his platform, leaving paper plates in their wake, the dull brownish-green grass of the park littered with paper napkins and wax-paper cups. Mac could see Belinda and her friends shading their eyes, looking in the direction of whatever was going on. The high school band members were all running over that way, laughing, holding their instruments. "Well, shit," Mac muttered under his breath. He stepped down and followed them.

He could hear jeering laughter as he pushed his way through the crowd, and then a sudden silence seemed to settle over the people as Mac got close to the street. He could see, above people's heads, even before he got to the sidewalk, a big dark green–striped watermelon, drifting along as though it were in midair. He swabbed his sweating face, breathing heavily, catching his breath, as the crowd parted so that he could get to the curb. It *was* some kind of parade, or march. *Niggers!* Leading the parade was a tall, fierce-looking old nigger man named Joe Bynymo, a hermit who lived back in the swamps across the river, who came to town occasionally to walk the streets wearing a long black overcoat in the summer and short shirtsleeves in the winter. He had on his overcoat now, despite the searing dry heat, not to mention a long black bullwhip slung over his shoulder, a wrinkled, smashed old felt hat on his head, and on top of that, the huge watermelon—it must have weighed at least fifty pounds—sitting steady, moving along with him. Mac had heard how old Joe could walk anywhere, even in the woods, with a watermelon on his head. People stood all along the curb, watching him, a hushed sense of awe hanging over the crowd, little children standing with their mouths hanging open. Following the old man were twenty or so niggers, carrying signs drawn with crayons on poster board. VOTE FOR O. B. BREWSTER the first sign said. BREWSTER FOR MAYOR, another said, and so on. Mac recognized Sally Long, Eldon's daughter, and the fellow Mark Price, who was going to find out just about the time school started that he didn't have a job for the year. There was an old woman, whose name was Hardenia something or other, and others, and they all carried signs. LET MY PEOPLE GO, one of them said. Mac shook his head. *Let you go? Where?*

The shock of seeing old Bynymo with the watermelon seemed to be wearing off the people. The crowd began now to jeer and laugh, pointing. "Git on outta here, jigaboos!" Mac heard someone—it sounded like a child—yell. The group in the street marched along, their eyes straight ahead, holding the signs so that everyone could read them. VOTE ON TUESDAY, one of them said, WE GOIN TO. *Like hell.* There were barely that many niggers registered in the whole county. Mac was grinning at the parade, but his face felt stiff. He was not amused. They had done nothing, of course, to take any votes away from him. They had probably *lost* any votes among the crowd that still might be considering O.B. But they had sure disrupted his carefully planned and expensive picnic. He had had more that he wanted to say, but now the people were drifting away, as though they had eaten and seen the entertainment and everything was over. He wondered if they even remembered who had invited them out here in the first place. "Shit," Mac muttered, watching the little parade move slowly on down the street, around the tall Confederate monument and away from the city square.

O.B. walked the four blocks down to the square. The sky was a cloudless white dome, and he noticed streaks of brown on the neat lawns and the dusty, wilted-looking shrubs. Folks watered their lawns after sunset every night, the thirsty ground greedily sucking up the water so that by midmorning of the next day everything was dry and parched again.

A small group of people had gathered in the shade, sitting on the grass and on a few iron-and-wood park benches. Eldon was there, sitting on the grass in his dark suit pants; he had taken off his tie and had the sleeves of his white shirt rolled up. O.B. was wearing a plaid shortsleeved shirt and khaki pants. He remembered, from this morning's image in the mirror, the dark, tired circles around his eyes, and he felt energyless, listless. His eyes wandered over the sparse crowd; there were twenty or so white people, old man Winston Norris, a lady who worked at Scales's Dry Goods, several more people who looked familiar to him but whose names he couldn't instantly remember, people he had seen around town for years but whose names he just didn't think about. There were probably thirty Negroes; he saw Sally Long and the old woman Hardenia. Of course, Cora was not there. *Cora!* He felt the muscles around his heart grip tightly. He had seen her on several occasions since Martha had left, and their lovemaking had settled into the same heated passion that he remembered, both of them plagued with guilt about what they were doing to Eldon all over again. He looked at Eldon as he walked by, and Eldon nodded to him and smiled. *He knows I don't stand a chance. He is doing this to get back at me, to wound and punish me, because he suspects.*

He remembered earlier that day, that morning, in the all-white First Methodist Church, the patronizing, almost laughing way the minister had introduced him, and how his tongue had seemed rooted to the roof of his mouth. The rows of people, dressed in their Sunday finest, their eyes church-serious, had stared at him as though he were a display in a carnival sideshow. *They knew he would not, could not, win.* He had stood there, seeing them as strangers, as people he had known all his life but had never known at all.

"Change," he had heard himself saying, his voice seeming to echo in his own ears from afar, the air in the church alien to him, its unfamiliar smells like something from another country. "Maybe it's healthy to change. For the future. I don't think any of us know what's gonna happen in the future. We've done things around here the same way for years and years, and maybe . . ." His voice had trailed off, and the silence in the church was stifling; a cough, a rustle of a cardboard fan or a bulletin, and the steady, politely expectant, yet closed and blocked eyes, like shields. He had swallowed, his mouth dry, feeling a sense of despondency but also of joy. He had blinked back tears. He knew now that he meant all this, understood it, and he knew that they could see it, too, if they would. "People were willin to starve," he had said, his voice trembling with emotion, "to not make their crops and starve, just to get the right to vote. I never saw anything like it. I went to see my old friend Buddy Ed Webb, and he opened my eyes to a thing or two. That old man . . . he . . . All us white people got a lot to learn, and we might as well get on with the business of learnin it. You all elect me mayor, I promise you I'll . . ." He paused. Some in the congregation were staring now with open hostility. "I'll . . . *we'll* all make those changes together. I can work with the Negro community. I can work with the white community. There won't be any need for these boycotts and such, which just hurt everybody. We can listen to each other, white and colored alike. You got to try to hear other people. You got to try to walk in their shoes."

O.B. stopped talking again, and the church was eerily silent, no traffic sounds outside on the Sunday-quiet streets, no birds in the humid outside air. *You are embarrassed for me*, he thought, but continued to stare at them, noticing old man Simmons White, sitting along the aisle. The old man, dressed in a dark blue suit and a crisp white shirt, seemed to squirm under O.B.'s level gaze. O.B. had the feeling that he was looking directly into the old man's heart and saw there disgust and hatred. The old man seemed to represent them all. *So this is what it is like! This is what Eldon wanted me to see, to feel. They look insolently at me, angrily at me, but they do not see me! They see only something to be feared, hated, as if I were colored. This is what Eldon wanted me to understand!* He knew that he was right, but that to be right would be lonely and frightening, and had sat down quickly, and after the service no one had spoken to him.

Now, in the park, he cleared his throat, feeling the sun on the top of his head as he prepared to speak. He hesitated as a pickup truck with a loud muffler went by on the street, halting him. O.B. could see a teenaged boy, leaning out of the passenger-side window, gaping curiously at the crowd, and O.B. tensed, thinking he was going to yell something, but the truck went noisily on by, the boy's pale, freckled country face hanging mute and empty, with only a look of mild astonishment and confusion and even anger that something was going on that he did not know about.

As the truck disappeared around the corner by the post office, O.B., following it with his eyes, saw three men standing. It was Rooster Wembley, flanked by two other men, and O.B. saw the flash of orange-red hair even as his eyes focused, and he recognized Red Kershaw, and the other one, Bobby Lee McElroy. They stood erect, stiff, in an almost-military posture, all three watching the group in the park, gazing intently and silently.

O.B., shuddering, looked at Eldon, and he could tell that Eldon had seen them, too, and Eldon just looked steadily at him, his red-rimmed eyes narrowed, his thin hands gripped across his knee. *Now I know what it is like. I am your brother. We have always known that, and even when Cain slew Abel, they didn't stop being brothers, did they?*

Eldon's eyes seemed to burn into O.B., and the tiny glints of his pupils as bright as the sun, making O.B. feel so full of hope and despair that his soul seemed about to burst within him. He thought of Martha and of Ellen, of Sally and of Cora. And he knew at last why he was doing this. It was because he could not do anything else. His whole life had been directing him to this very place and this very time, to be here and to stand up under the steady, intense gaze of Eldon and the watchful, threatening stare of Rooster Wembley.

O.B. pulled himself to his full height, feeling the hope, knowing at the same time the defeat that lay ahead of them. "A long time go," he began, his voice level, calm, "I was your brother. We were all brothers and sisters, but somethin happened. We let somethin so awful happen to us that we can't hardly bear even to think about it. I ain't an expert on sin, but ownin another man body and soul is a sin, and treatin a man or a woman like dirt just because the color of their skin is different from yours is a sin. It's just another form of slavery. And it enslaves the white people just as much as it does the colored, probably more. When I see how the hatred, the meanness, eats people up, I want to cry out, *Why? Why?*" He stopped. He felt inadequate, awkward, but they were looking at him, listening to him, so he pressed on. "Maybe we can't go back and change the wrongs, but we can try."

He could feel Eldon's eyes on him, and when he looked into them, he saw the pent-up range of centuries. *We will die. Some of us will die,* O.B. thought. *It won't matter. We can't let it matter. Yes. I am your keeper. And you are mine. And we may hate each other, we may kill each other. But we are brothers.*

∙~∙~∙~∙

A reporter from *The Birmingham News* called Mac early on a Monday morning, the Monday before the election on Tuesday, to ask him if he had any comment on Gulf International's plans to build a multimillion-dollar paper mill just outside Hammond. It had been announced that morning at a press conference in Mobile and was on the AP wire, and the *News* planned to "front-page it" that afternoon. Did Mac have a comment? the reporter wanted to know.

Mac had felt a mixture of exhilaration and anger that put him in a bad mood all the rest of the day. Gulf International could have let him make the announcement, or at least let him be in on it ahead of time, he thought.

The next day, election day, he and Belinda voted at Southside Elementary, and the *Hammond Times* was there to snap a picture of them coming away from the booth, grinning. The paper planned to run a special section on Gulf International, highlighting the economic impact it would have on the area, so there was no way the company could get spooked now, Mac figured.

That night, Mac was home, after supper, drinking bourbon and water, when he got a phone call about eight o'clock from Ashville, where the votes were being counted. It was Lester Sparks.

"Well, Mr. Mayor," he said, "you done it again."

Mac felt strangely emotionless; he had known, of course, that he was going to win, but now, instead of elation, he felt nothing but an inexplicable unease. "What's the count?" he asked, rattling the ice in his glass. Belinda, who'd come into the room, was watching him, a broad smile on her face.

"Lemme see, you got three thousand, one hundred and five, and Brewster got one thousand, one hundred and sixteen."

"That son of a bitch got eleven hundred votes?"

"Well," Lester said, "yeah, he did. But that ain't a third of what you got. Shit. You whupped him, boss! You kicked his ass!"

Belinda waited expectantly. "I won," he mouthed to her. She broke into a smile again, laughing happily. "Thanks, Lester," he said, hanging up the phone. He sat there in his uncomfortable brown corduroy chair, playing along with Belinda as she congratulated him, but his smile felt congealed. Instead of joy, there was dismay; instead of elation, dread. He did not understand it, as he sat there grinning like a moron, hating his wife, hating just about everyone he could think of.

·~·~·~·

Eldon didn't think he had ever felt as depressed as he did right now. He was sitting in the living room, the air close and sultry. A Bible lay open on the end table next to the chair, along with a yellow legal pad and a ballpoint pen. He had intended to work on his sermon, but he couldn't concentrate. The oscillating fans whined in the corners, and he fanned his face with a cardboard fan that he'd brought home from the church. He had talked himself into believing that O.B. would win the election, that there surely were enough white people to join in with the coloreds who were registered, but he must have known in his heart that it was a vain hope. ("You're dreamin, Eldon," Cora had said. "No way.") The boycott had all but petered out. From the very start, a few of the colored people had continued to trade at white-owned establishments, simply going about their business from force of habit. Some seemed not to understand at all what was going on, no matter how carefully he explained it to them in the citizenship classes. He understood now. So many of his people were resigned, burdened for so many generations with their hopelessness, that they accepted it as a part of their lives. He sighed, knowing in his bones how they felt. Some of them, he knew, would feel uncomfortable, frightened, *without* that feeling of despair. They were as addicted to it as people get addicted to reefer cigarettes and whiskey.

He was sitting with his shirt off, a tall, sweating glass of ice water next to the blank yellow pad. This heat. This drought. Every afternoon tall, bruised-looking thunderheads formed in the western sky, with distant rumbling and faraway flickers of lightning, but it did not rain, except for a few miserly, teasing drops. ("Like a little kitten done dribbled on your windshield," he had heard an old man describe it.) And the boys. Paul and Joe. They were both dead; he knew it in his bones. The police claimed not to believe Carl Youngblood's story, had refused even to investigate it, but Eldon knew it was true. Maybe it was true about the drugs, too. Young people these days . . . Of course, there was no proof that they had been kidnapped, only a powerful feeling. But who was interested in a black man's feelings? Or a man like Carl Youngblood's claims? From time to time, he found himself clinging to the hope they *had* left, gone back North, but then he knew in his heart that they had not.

·~·~·~·

He had called SNCC headquarters in Atlanta. Someone in the office there had sounded exasperated.

"Maybe we can send somebody down there," the man had said shortly. "But we've got more Freedom Riders comin in soon, all that."

"Won't do any good to send somebody else over. I want you to call the FBI. I want you people over there to—"

"Hah!" the man had said. "The FBI? Look, those boys were arrested for possession—"

"Not arrested," Eldon interrupted.

"All right, charged. Mr. Long, we're just gettin started in all this. We're reluctant to make waves where drug charges are concerned. We're takin the position that they're on the run."

"Well, they're not on the run! You don't know how things are over here! It's like . . . it's like Nazi Germany! There's nobody to turn to but you people!"

"I'm sorry," the man had said. "It's the drugs. It endangers everything we're doing."

"But—"

"I'm sorry."

·~·~·~·

Eldon had called the SNCC office in Washington. He had been shuffled around to several offices before he'd finally gotten a woman who listened to him. She had heard his story, listening patiently, the line silent.

"Of course we're worried about them," she had said when he had finished. "Did you read the statement his father gave out after that story about the boys fleeing the drug charges got broadcast? He's 'ashamed' of his son bein a 'pot-head' and an 'agitator.' Can you believe that?" Her accent was strange, Jamaican or something.

"Listen, they might be dead."

"That seems unlikely," she said. "The drug charges just sound too . . . authentic. Nobody blames them for getting out of there. It's just not big news up here, Mr. Long. It won't do anybody any good to overreact."

"You don't know. You don't know what it's like here. People take the law into their own hands. There are men here who think they're doin the world a favor if they *kill* somebody like those boys! You don't know!"

"I've heard," she said. There was a pause. He couldn't believe her calm. It seemed almost callous to him, a cold bureaucracy that he had not expected to encounter. Someday they would know. . . . But it made him doubt Youngblood's story himself. "Just hang in there," she continued. "For a little while. Something will turn up. I have a call on the other line."

Eldon listened to the dial tone with mounting fury, gritting his teeth.

Eldon had finally, with a sense of desperation, called the FBI office in Birmingham. He had explained the reason for his call.

"We are aware of the charges against the boys. I suggest you contact your local police department," the man had said.

"What good would that do? The local police are *in* on it!"

"Do you have proof of that? Because if you don't—"

"I am a man of God! A minister to my people! I can't sit by and do nothing! This is a deep moral and ethical issue!" He realized that he was rambling, trying in vain to be logical and practical in the face of what he was hearing. "I'm calling you to notify you that you need to look into the connection of the police with the Ku Klux Klan in Hammond!"

"They'll call us if they need us. Reverend Long, I'm sure you understand. It's a matter of jurisdiction. We're not in a position to respond to individuals, unless . . . well, I'm sure you understand."

He sat there, feeling the sweat in his armpits rolling down the insides of his arms, the sides of his chest. On top of everything, he had learned that the doctors had finally given up on Edna; she would never walk again, and although her sight had gradually returned in one of her eyes, she was blind in the other. She was still in the hospital, and God knew how long she would be in there. Thank God she was a teacher; teachers were among the few black people who had insurance.

He heard someone on the porch; the screen door opened, and Cora came in with a brown grocery sack. She wore a thin sundress, a green-and-white plaid that was soft and faded from many washings, and she had a cool look about her even though he could see a thin sheen of perspiration on her skin. She looked at him, her eyes dark, and passed through the room toward the back. He heard her in the kitchen, opening an ice tray. She came back in holding a tall glass of ice water and sat down across from him.

He looked at her eagerly, wanting to feel comforted. "At least she didn't die," Cora said. "She's gonna live. At least—"

"All right!" he said. He picked up his glass and sipped the cool water as he looked out the window at the harsh sunlight in their narrow front yard. Things seemed to have reached an impasse everywhere, and he felt a deep sense of helplessness. He had to narrow his focus, to think clearly.

She could read his mind. "God, Eldon, you knew he wasn't gonna win," she said. "Somewhere inside you, you must have known that he didn't stand a chance."

"Okay. Maybe so. But it was a hope."

Her eyes seemed softer as she sat looking steadily at him. "That's part of the trouble with hopin," she said. "The disappointment. Some things . . . well, sometimes it seems like things ain't gonna ever change."

"Maybe you're right," he said. "Maybe, now that Paul and Joe are gone, I ought to just throw in the towel. Just quit!" It had just popped out, and he was surprised and shocked that suddenly he was feeling better about quitting. The idea actually appealed to him.

Her eyes lingered on his face. "I don't think you *can* quit this, Eldon."

"Well . . ." he said, thinking of long, quiet days just writing sermons. Sermons that no one listened to. But he'd get away from this, this pressure. "I can, too. They . . . they don't care. None of em except the young ones care." He looked away. Quit? After all this? He felt the beginnings of tears in his eyes, and he didn't want her to see him cry, to see him be weak. "It's just that I feel all alone now. I can't get any help from anywhere I call."

"Call Reverend King," she said.

"I did. He's . . . he's got his own things goin. He . . . he can't do anything. There's nothin to rally around here. He said I need an event. Somethin big. He said he would be here if we—"

"Got somethin goin that would get in the papers. On the television," she said.

"Yeah." How sarcastic was she being? "What's wrong with that?"

"I didn't say anything was wrong with it," she said.

"He said he would come over and speak at the church in the fall. Said to remember that the autumn is the harvest! Said he'd do what he could to keep their spirits up. He said forget the boycott. Leave it officially in effect, but don't nag em none about it. He said it's natural they gonna be down about votin after the election. Even if we get the vote, that won't mean much for a long time, he said. So . . ." His voice trailed off. He was looking at the rag rug on the floor.

"You know, that boy," she said, softly, "Paul. I can't quit thinkin about it. He is the father of Ellen's baby. Little Ellen Brewster." She laughed wistfully, with an edge of bitterness. "There was a time when she was just like another daughter to me. Her and Sally, like sisters. Almost. I don't think they even knew back then that they *wasn't* sisters." She paused, thinking. "I asked Sally if she had seen her over there, at that house. She said yeah, some. She said they talked a little bit. They crossed paths." She looked at Eldon. He could not read the expression in her eyes, and he waited on her to continue. "Funny how folks always keep on crossin paths, ain't it? I mean . . ." She seemed to be groping for words, her forehead furrowed, "we were all born here. White, colored. Trash . . . everybody. We're all a part of this place, like it or not. Looks like *it's* us, and we're it. Like one of those mobiles, like that little wooden one with the carved birds on it that Sally had when she was a baby, remember? You touch one, and they all move. Nothin can happen to one of the birds without it happenin to all of em, in one form or the other."

"Yeah," he said..

"I . . . I've got somethin to tell you," she said softly.

"What?"

"Paul is alive and okay."

What was she saying? How did she know this?

"I . . . I just happened to see O.B.—he was comin out of the A & P—and he told me. He made me swear to keep it quiet, to just tell *you* and absolutely nobody else. Not even Sally. He thought maybe that family from out in Spocari had already told you—"

"Wait!" He felt a vast relief and excitement but also suspicion. "O.B. told you this?"

"Paul's at their house," she went on hurriedly, "and O.B.'s hidin him, because he figures if the police pick him up on that reefer charge, then he won't make it to the jailhouse before he'll be back in the Klan's hands. Because they killed that other boy—"

"Joe!"

"Yeah, they killed him, and then Paul got away, and those Rowsers out in Spocari helped him get into town. He had a broken arm. Anyhow, he's there, and he's gonna stay hidden till O.B. can figure out what to do. The boy's own father—"

"I know about his father." Eldon could feel the hoarseness and emotion in his voice. She was looking at him strangely, her head tilted to the side. "I called SNCC in Washington."

"He said I could tell you if you would swear you won't let it get out," she said. "O.B.'s scared. He said to tell you that they're playin hardball, and just to lay low about the boys for now. Paul's got nothin to back up his story, and . . ."

"Of course, praise God!" he said. Relief for Paul, grief for Joe, twisted together in his mind. And that old intense jealousy of O.B. The tears were rising behind his eyes; he could feel them, hot and stinging. Why did she have to even bring that man into it, bring him here? "Have you been over there to see him?" he asked, hearing the tremor in his voice.

"Who? O.B.?" She was staring at him. "No. No, Eldon. I haven't been over there." He looked away from her, covering his eyes with the flat of his hand. "I haven't," she said, softly and firmly.

"O.B. called me up, said he'd done what I asked him to," Eldon told her. "He said he did the best he could. He said Rooster had threatened *him*, and he was glad that it was all over." He looked back at Cora. He was aware that there was a thin film of tears in his eyes and that she could see them. She gave no sign if she did.

"Well," she said, "it may be over for him, but it ain't over for us."

He sat up straighter, peering at her. "All my good sense," he said, "tells me that there's only gonna be more killin and maimin. The federal government, they don't care. They 'can't do anything.' The police . . . shit! Nobody cares but us. And we ain't nobody. We just a rag-tail bunch of country niggers that don't nobody give a flyin hoot about! We already got Edna gonna be an invalid, half blind, all the rest of her life. We got one white boy killed, ain't no tellin what's gonna happen to the other one. And now we got to have an 'event.' We got to have some *reason*. Like years of bein treated like dirt ain't reason enough! Nobody cares about us but God, and sometimes I think He might of forgot about us, too."

"You're really down now, Eldon. Things'll get better. They—"

"If I thought we could just go back. To the way it used to be."

"How?" she said. "What you talkin about? And you can't go back anyhow."

"Cora?" He looked at her, weighing what she said. He felt his pulse quicken slightly. Had he heard right? "What you sayin, girl?"

"That's right. I'm ready now. I'm mad, Eldon. I'm ready to be with you, now. I'm mad about Edna. I'm mad about what happened to Joe Mancini." She was staring intently at him, her eyes sparkling.

He listened to the fans churning the hot air, a car going by on the street outside as her words sank in. He expected to feel a glow of happiness that she had come round at last. The irony that he didn't struck him as almost funny. "We don't have any help," he said.

"We don't need any help."

He wanted to go to her, to welcome her, but he seemed paralyzed. Just then the screen door opened, and Sally came into the living room. There were half-moons of sweat under her arms and beads of sweat on her face. She stood flat-footed, looking from one to the other.

"I was just tellin your daddy," Cora said, "that I'm ready to get with the movement. I'm ready to—"

"Well, congratulations," Sally said sarcastically.

Cora's smile faded then, her eyes growing hooded.

"Sally, don't—" Eldon said.

"What the hell you expect me to say?" Sally shrugged. "Now? Now she's ready?"

Cora sat stiffly in her chair, her hands folded in her lap. Eldon stared at his daughter, trying to deny to himself that she had expressed exactly what he was feeling.

"I want you to know, young lady," Eldon said, his tone sounding pompous and insincere to him, "that I was seriously considering callin the whole thing off. With Paul and Joe gone—"

"You can't call it off," Sally interrupted. "Ain't any way you can call it off. It's too big."

"The danger right now—"

"Fuck the danger," Sally said.

"Sally! Don't talk to your daddy like that," Cora said.

"All right, I'm sorry," Sally said. She fidgeted from one foot to another. Eldon felt a sudden sense of pride in his daughter; he admired her spirit. But he frowned. "Look, Daddy, nobody but you ever thought Mr. Brewster was gonna win that election. Folks laughed at you, you and him both, behind your back."

"I didn't think—" He paused. Sally was staring at him. "I just hoped, Sally. I had faith, like God tells us to. He's not just talkin about faith in Him, but faith in us, too, in good and justice! Folks have to have faith and hope."

"Yeah. Well. It doesn't make any difference to us. We're gonna step things up. We're gonna—"

"What are you talkin about?" Eldon said. He sat up straighter. He felt a sudden sense of alarm.

"Okay, just calm down," Sally said. "Look. I'm gonna keep on teachin the class, okay? I guess we owe that to Paul and Joe. My class with the kids. I don't know about the other ones. I'll keep on with that. But . . ."

"But what?" Eldon said.

"We're gonna do some more marches. We got the Greyhound bus station targeted now. That stupid segregated waitin room and the white-only lunch counter. We already got that down, gonna go for it right away. We've got to."

"Sally! Wait a minute. You can't—" he said.

"With you or without you, Daddy," she said. "We got to keep pushin, we got to force the crackers. We got to make somethin happen."

"They've taken Paul and Joe. They've probably killed em. You think they'd stop at that?" He had to make her listen.

"Cowards. Trash is all they are. They're tryin to scare us, Daddy. They can't scare us."

"They scare *me*," Cora said, raising her voice.

"Yeah. Well." Sally shrugged again. "All I'm sayin is, it's started. It's started, Daddy. *You* started it, remember that. And ain't no way it's gonna be stopped now." She looked from one to the other. She hesitated for a moment then went out the door, toward her room.

Eldon realized that he was clasping his hands tightly together. He felt light-headed. He released his hands, grasping the cold, sweating glass. He took a gulp of the soothing water.

"You need to talk to your daddy," Cora said, her voice barely above a whisper.

"What? Who?" he said, irritated. They heard Sally's radio come on, too loud, in her room.

"Your daddy," Cora said, more emphatically. "Go out and see him. Talk to him. This is too much for you, Eldon. You take all this on your own shoulders! You always have. It's gonna kill you—"

"All right," he said to make her stop. Her words hurt his ears.

"You stay so wrapped up in all this that you won't let *me* be close to you. I've tried, Eldon. I want to try now." She was almost yelling over the sound of the radio.

"I said all right," he said. Her face looked frightened and tense. Only seconds ago it had looked relaxed, smooth. "Call em and tell em to come to church Sunday. Come to Sunday dinner. I ain't goin out there."

"Okay," she said.

"I don't want to go out there," he repeated, more to himself than to her. "I don't think I could stand to go back out there, Cora." Surprised, he felt the tears rekindling in the edges of his eye. *I left a part of my very soul out there!* He sometimes felt guilty that he had risen above his parents' level of poverty, and he knew how irrational that was, how silly it was. But he still felt it, an intense, aching guilt. All he had to do was think of his father and his mother, and it was like the years were pushing down on the top of his head like a huge fist.

⋅~⋅~⋅~⋅

He sat at the table in the kitchen, looking across at his parents. His father sat leaning back, patting his ample belly, grinning. His mother sat delicately in her chair, her blue bandanna on her head, her light, feathery body poised. He had watched her mash corn bread and black-eyed peas and fried chicken torn from the bone into a mush with the back of her fork and then spoon it into her almost-toothless mouth. The four of them had just finished an entire lemon icebox pie that Cora had made that morning. Eldon felt stuffed and slow and uncomfortable.

"Where Sally?" his mother said.

"She . . . hangs around with some other young folks," Cora said.

"She got her a boyfriend?" Blount asked, smiling, tiny crumbs of corn bread clinging to his chin.

"Yeah, she does," Eldon said. He did not want to talk about that.

"Who?" his mother said.

"You probably don't know him. A town boy."

"What his name?" His mother was peering at him like a fragile bird.

"Nathaniel Pierson," Eldon said. "Works out at the veneer mill."

"Bet he Ray Pierson's boy," his father said.

"She sho look pretty at the churchhouse," Punchy said.

"Hah," Cora said. "That's the only time she'll wear a dress. I guess she does it for us. you ought to see her the rest of the time. She dresses like a field hand."

"Like me, then," his father said.

"I didn't mean . . ." Cora's black eyes flickered to Eldon, then away. "I didn't know you were a field hand," she said quietly, standing up to clear the table. Eldon watched keenly what was passing between them.

"I been a field hand all my life," the old man said. "Chopped more cotton than the law allows. Proud of it, too."

"Uh-huh, sho is," the old woman said.

"You been a dairy man for years now, Daddy Long," Cora said. She was putting dishes in the sink. She seemed irritated all of a sudden. She was not looking at any one of the three of them. "That's all I meant," she said.

"Ain't nothin wrong with bein a field hand," the old man said.

"I didn't say there was," Cora said. "I only said that Sally . . . you said she looked pretty. Okay? That's all I was talkin about." She started running water in the sink.

"Can't that wait?" Eldon said. She shut the water off and stood looking into the sink, acting extremely tense.

They had talked, over dinner, about the boys' disappearance. They had talked about Edna Blanks, the two old people murmuring an occasional "uh-huh." They had talked about the election. ("Mister Billie one crazy white man," Blount had said, laughing. "What he know bout bein a mayor?")

Eldon had almost despaired of communicating with them. He knew that Cora was feeling some of the same frustration, but she seemed to be annoyed, even angry, with *him*. His father sat working on his teeth with a wooden toothpick.

"I sees on the television where the peoples sendin in the Freedom Riders," the old man said suddenly. "What the Freedom Riders, Eldon?"

"They . . . they're comin in on buses. Integrated groups. They may . . . come down Highway Eighty. I don't know."

"Peoples just ridin on the buses?"

"Yeah," he said. "What do you think of that?"

The room was still and quiet. Cora, still standing at the sink, turned and looked at them at the table.

"Think of it?" The old man seemed puzzled. Eldon's mother was looking sharply at him, her face tilted to the side like a sparrow; the look in her eyes, her very bearing, reminded him of Sally. His mother's body was bent, her spine curved, like an ancient tree worn down by years of harsh elements. As he looked at her, he could see the sunken mouth, the liquid eyes, so weak and feeble, and he had the dizzying, frightening sensation that she was aging before him, and he looked away.

"Eldon's thinkin of givin up," Cora said suddenly. "Callin it all off."

Eldon shot her a hot, quick stare. The two old people sat motionless, staring at him. "It's . . ." he faltered. "Sometimes I don't see how we can win," he said, his voice constricted and thin. "It'll just get worse." All three of them were looking steadily at him. "I don't . . . don't want to be responsible for killin. People gettin hurt. You, maybe."

"We old. Ain't nobody gonna bother us," his mother said.

"I don't know," Eldon said. "I worry about you. You're out there, alone. People who hate me could . . . to get back . . ." He trailed off.

"I worry about everybody I know. I even worry about O.B." Eldon tried to smile, but he knew it was a sickly half-grin.

"Mister Billie? Whut you worry bout him for? He a white man. Ain't no sense worryin bout no white man." His father shook his head. His chair was tilted back, touching the wall. The room was getting warm, the midday sun beating on the roof, the air still and unmoving. "I done tole that man," his father went on, "I tole him when he come to see us—"

"He came to see you?" Eldon said, surprised.

"Uh-huh, sho did," his mother said, "weeks ago now."

"—I done tole him, say, when the time comes, us gone go right on up there and put our marks down and vote! He say he glad. He say he right proud of us."

"He did?" Eldon looked over at Cora. She turned slightly, her eyes focused out the window over the sink. She seemed distant, lost in thought. At that moment, he knew that she somehow had known that O.B. had been to see his parents.

"Sho did," his father went on. "Us proud. Tole Mr. Hubbard, too. He say don't make no difference, ain't nothin but crooks over there in Montgomery noway, just a buncha hogs rootin at the trough. And up dere in Washington, too. He say a politician ain't got his hand nowhere but in your pocket, white and nigger alike!" The old man chuckled.

Eldon was watching Cora, the way the afternoon light came through the window, burnishing the clean line of her neck and her bare arm like polished mahogany in the sleeveless gray dress. Her expression was moody, her thoughts on something far away in space and time.

"I tole ol Mr. Hubbard," the old man went on, "I say it ain't gone happen in our time, huh-huh, say he gone go right on to the white heaven, all right, and us gone go on to the nigger one. He laugh like a hyena. I tole him our grandchillen's chillen, though, ain't gone be nigger and white. He say that's right. Say it called the mongrel, or somethin like that, and he laugh like a hyena again and throwed his arm around my neck, then he give me a drink of whiskey out'n that bottle he carry round in the dash pocket of his pickup. He say, 'I tell you what, Blount. I hope they's a heaven for just old broke-down farts like us'n, cause I sho would miss not havin you around with me for the eternity.' " The old man laughed. "Sho did. That's what he say. He a mess!"

"What did O.B. want?" Eldon said.

"Huh?" his mother said. "He just come to see us. Just come to say hello."

"He didn't want nothin," his father said.

Cora turned from the window, as if she'd sensed his probing eyes. She turned on the water. "I need to wash these," she said, "fore it gets so hot back here. Y'all go on up where the fans are."

He watched his parents make their way slowly up the narrow hallway. His mother situated herself on the couch, spreading her skirt around her. She picked up a cardboard fan and fanned her face. His father sat in a chair, his legs spread, his hands on his knees. He and his father watched his mother get her snuff can out and put a few pinches inside her lower lip. She leaned to the side and spit into a wrinkled, brown paper sack sitting on the floor. Eldon knew that there was an empty coffee can inside the sack; one of his earliest memories was of sprawling in the bony, yet somehow soft, lap of his mother, rocking before the fire, his mother spitting from time to time into a coffee can in a sack on the floor beside her, the chair creaking, the fire popping and crackling as his eyelids grew heavy, so weighted down that he could not even force them open, feeling himself desperately, finally—tired and worn out from the day—surrendering, dragged against his will down deep into restful, sweep sleep.

"You can't quit now, boy," his father said, startling Eldon, forcing him harshly out of the brief reverie. He looked at the old man, at his tired eyes, his placid, loose face. He could hear Cora in the kitchen, the dishes clinking, the sound of swirling, splashing water. "You ain't got no business startin somethin you ain't gone finish," the old man said.

"Why do you say *I* started it?" Eldon said. "It's bigger than me. Rosa Parks started it."

"She started that over there. You started this over here. Both of you are instruments of the Lord. That's all."

"Uh-huh," his mother murmured. "Amen."

"The Lord started it. He gone finish it. All you got to do is finish yore part," the old man said.

"Uh-huh," his mother said.

"How will I know when I'm finished?" Eldon said. For a moment, he felt like a child again, a boy, looking up, asking. It was almost as though he were not just remembering but actually *was* the child again, his father towering over him, flat-bellied and broad-chested, powerful and dark. The feeling was so vivid, so intense, that for a moment he smelled the sweat of bodies, the scent of new-mown hay, the rich odor of manure baking in the sun. It made Eldon shudder, the way years could telescope, evaporate like light from a suddenly darkened room.

"When the Lord calls you home," his father said, his voice like gravel, "then you'll know."

Yes. When He calls me home.

.~.~.~.

When *the Lord calls you home.* Eldon sat in his office, staring out the window at the dusty, dry privet. The afternoon had darkened, and he had been hearing the thunder, an almost steady rumbling that he had thought at first was a jet plane. He had put the yellow pad aside, locking his fingers behind his head, leaning back in the swivel chair, watching the heavy air grow darker and darker. He felt a sudden breeze burst through the open window. It felt damp, almost cold, smelling of loam and reeking faintly of ozone.

Large, syrupy drops, seemingly heavier than normal rain, began to pelt the stiff privet leaves, turning them immediately from a light, pale green to a deep, rich color, like that of a tropical forest. The shrubs began shaking and swaying as the wind came up abruptly. Lightning crackled across the sky, followed by sudden, heavy cracks of thunder, and Eldon stood and looked out, seeing the dark fury of the storm, the trees down the street bending in the wind, the rain heavy and thick now, driven almost horizontally in sheets across the yard of the church and the limerock-strewn street.

The drought was breaking with a furor, a tumult. The sky was as dark as midnight; everything on the ground that Eldon could see was outlined in a pale silver light that seemed to come from within, from inside the very walls of the houses and beneath the bark of the swaying trees. He could see no break in the clouds. He though of the parched, dry cotton, the rows of corn that had baked day after day in the fierce, unrelenting sun. The farm ponds, their surfaces still and unmoving as glass, their edges wide bands of caked and cracked dry mud, and the grass in town, withering and dying, twisting up tightly like a starving baby's tiny fist. He thought of the rain out in the thirsty country around Hammond, lashing over the fields, shaking the heavy and dusty trees. The thunder rumbled. Remember: *Autumn is the harvest.* Have faith, and the rains will come. *The desert will bloom again.* He had once heard Martin King preach that no matter how hot the summer got, autumn would always come, and he felt it in the damp breeze, saw it in the thick, swirling muddy water now filling the ditches beside the street. The heat had broken like fragile glass; the air through the window was suddenly chilling as winter. He stood watching the rain, smelling the freshness, remembering that one of the last times he had seen rain on these leaves had been the time O.B. had come here to tell him he would run for mayor; it was the first time a white man, other than Paul and Joe, had ever set foot in the office, or any other part of the church . . .

The storm had reached the height of its fury. Water stood in broad puddles in the churchyard, the puddles' surfaces peppered with the persistent downpour. *And the Lord shall show forth his handiwork.* Eldon could feel the power of the storm beneath his feet, through the floor, and into the very center of the earth. *Autumn is the harvest.*

Eldon sat back down. He prayed. He had had faith, had known that the earth would renew itself. The rain had settled into a steady pounding now, the thunder distant, the lightning only flickers against the roiling sky. He sat observing the rain for a long time. He had his sermon now. *The desert will bloom again.*

Later, as he walked home, the mud squishy beneath his feet, the earth silvery and shiny in the late sun that peeped intermittently through the clouds, he sensed someone watching him. He turned around, his eyes darting up and down the deserted street. Slowly, a red pickup with three men in it moved out of a side street and stopped next to him. He did not recognize the white man who was grinning at him from the passenger side. The truck sat there, its motor idling, and then the door opened, and the man who was grinning at him stepped down. He was big, with muscular arms bulging his T-shirt. He wore tight, greasy denims and heavy boots.

"Evenin," he said, nodding to Eldon.

"Evenin," Eldon said, feeling his heartbeat increase. Why now? he thought. *They are feeling victorious, cocky. They think they have us down, think they are about to beat us.* The driver's door had opened, and a man had stepped down, coming around the front of the truck. Eldon recognized him. He was Rusty Jackson, a wiry man who used to work for O.B. Brewster. He stood there, looking at Eldon, his eyes naked with hate. The other man continued to grin. The man who had been sitting in the middle slid over, and Eldon saw a splash of red hair and knew him to be Red Kershaw. Red stepped out onto the running board, standing in the open door, holding a can of Sterling beer.

"What you doin, Reverend?" Kershaw said. He sneered on the title.

"On my way home," Eldon said.

"You goin home to fuck that good-lookin nigger gal you married to?" Jackson said.

Eldon said nothing. He felt strangely calm, except for his pulse;

there was an inevitability about this, something that he had run through in his mind many times before.

"I hear she likes to suck a white man's dick," Jackson said. "Hell, I *know* she does, cause I was out fishin the other day and seen her going down on old O.B. Brewster!"

Eldon, stunned, tried to look them in the eyes. *He is just saying that. How would he know to say O.B.?*

"What do you want?" he said. He wanted to show calm, not fear.

"We want to fuck your wife," Jackson said, "like O.B."

Eldon did not look at him. He felt his knees growing weaker. He focused on Kershaw and the other man, who continued to grin at him. Kershaw's pale green eyes seemed flat, uninterested; his skin was pasty white, freckled, with a reddish tint, as though the color of his hair bled down his face and down his neck. His hand, gripping the beer can, was rough and heavily freckled.

"Listen, nigger," Kershaw said. "I got a message for you."

He leaned over and spit into the road, a long globule of spit that dangled for a moment and then dropped into the muddy ruts. He wiped his mouth with the back of his hand.

"What?" Eldon said, almost with relief. *Yes, give me your insulting message!* Because he suddenly knew it was the truth about Cora and O.B. that they were together again, making love again; he had been knowing it in his heart for some time, and the obviousness of it now hit him like a blow between the eyes. *White skin, brown skin.* Of course he had been talking to her. Of course he had told her about Paul, and they had talked about Ellen, too. He saw it with a clarity that blinded him.

"You gittin smart with us, nigger?" Jackson said.

"No," Eldon said.

"No, what?" Jackson stepped forward, blurred in the edge of Eldon's vision.

"No, *sir*," Eldon said, without looking at him.

"You look at me when you talk to me, nigger," Jackson said. Eldon looked at him then; he and Jackson were about the same height, both small and wiry; the other man towered over them. Jackson's eyes were like pools of dirty motor oil. His face was narrow, like a weasel's. "That's better," he said.

"What's the message?" Eldon said. The image of O.B. and Cora together crowded his mind, and he wanted to get on with it, force their hand.

"Just this," Kershaw said. "You and that nigger-fuckin friend of yours, Brewster, been fuckin things up around here long enough. Now his mayor shit is over, right? He can't do nobody no harm but you. If he wants to fuck your wife, then I reckon that's his business. But we want *you* to stop all this shit you doin. That clear?"

"I cannot stop destiny, Mr. Kershaw. God's will be done." Eldon's voice trembled. *Beat me! Kill me!*

"Don't hand me that shit, nigger," Kershaw said. "All this integration shit. We're sick of it, tired of it. And we want you to know what's gonna happen to you if you don't stop."

Eldon stood there. His lips were dry and chapped. He swallowed.

"You can kill me, but you cannot kill God," he said. "Was there anything else you wanted?"

"This," the big man in front of him said, and he drove his fist into Eldon's stomach. Eldon felt the breath go out of him, felt the sudden, shocking pain of the blow. His knees buckled under him, and he went down onto them in the mud of the road, reaching out instinctively for support, and he felt the man knock his arms away. Eldon gasped, gulping for air, and the man slapped him across the face, the blow stinging, bringing tears to his eyes.

"Listen, you black piece a' shit," Kershaw said, "you better put a stop to all this crap goin on. We know it's that goddam church of yours. And if it don't stop, all of it, that goddam church ain't gonna be there. That's the message. You got it?"

Eldon gasped. Kershaw's voice seemed to come from far away, through the fog of pain and anguish that Eldon was feeling, through the bitter taste of his jealousy and fury at O.B. and Cora. *Again! I forgave, and you have betrayed me again!* He could not speak, could breathe only shallowly, and he could not focus his eyes.

"You got it?" Kershaw said. Eldon tried to nod.

The man slapped him again, with the back of his hand this time, and Eldon's head snapped the other way. He felt the salty, warm taste of blood in his mouth, almost a respite from the other, deeper pain, and he tried to nod his head, tried to respond. They could kill him, right here in the street. At that moment, death seemed a reprieve.

Eldon knew that everyone along the street was huddling behind closed doors and windows, and he prayed that they would stay there. That no one would be foolish. That no one would—

The man slapped him again.

"Goddam niggers," he heard Kershaw say, his voice echoing, muffled and distant. "You better hear this, and hear it good, Long," the voice said, "any niggers git outta line around here gonna wind up dead. You got that?" Eldon felt his head move, nod. He was still on his knees, his ears pounding, his body tense and shaking. "All right," he heard the voice say.

The man hit him again, with his fist this time, and sparklers exploded inside Eldon's head. He felt his body swaying, his balance gone, and he put his hands flat in the mud, trying to hold himself up. He heard their laughter, heard the truck doors slam. He heard the idling motor suddenly rev, and the horn blasted near his head, a raw, shattering metallic sound that rocked him almost as badly as one of the physical blows. The truck's tires spun in the mud, the back end swaying, and he heard it roaring down the street, turning the corner, the horn blasting again as the sound of it died away. He whimpered involuntarily, still gasping for breath, feeling himself sink slowly toward the muddy surface of the street.

How many times must I forgive? Seventy times seven? I cannot. I am only a man.

The only sensation in his arms and legs were weariness, a fatigue so powerful that it seemed to come from the very marrow of his bones, and he was dimly aware of footsteps running toward him. He felt himself drifting, then sinking, the side of his face nestling itself against the cool, mushy softness of the black mud. And then he slept.

PART 4

AUTUMN

Chapter Fourteen

MAC PUT THE PAPER DOWN, SO SICK OF READING STORIES ABOUT the so-called "rights movement" that he thought he would vomit. At least none of those "Freedom Riders" had come to Hammond. He remembered seeing pictures last spring of the riots in Anniston and Birmingham, had seen the footage on the television news. *What in the hell is going on in this country? What are they doing to the South?* In the fifties, the federal government had sent National Guard Troops into Little Rock to get one or two little nigger children into a white school, and now they were standing by watching these rabble-rousers from up North ride around the country on Greyhound buses and set up housekeeping in nigger-towns everywhere, causing riots and trouble wherever they went.

Mac shook his head as he struggled to get out of his uncomfortable chair, then stood, stretching. The drapes were open, the windows up; outside, he could see the barest, faintest change of color in the leaves. He knew that almost overnight they would become a blazing fire of oranges and yellows and reds, and the air would turn as cool as spring water. The air was already pleasant, smelling hazily of woodsmoke, the nut-warm, fruity smell of autumn.

That smell always made Mac think of football, giving him a tingly sense of anticipation in his belly. His season tickets for the Crimson Tide's games had come just the other day, the same day, as a matter of fact, that those young people had tried to integrate the waiting room at the bus station. Lester had joked that they were probably just trying to copy the Freedom Riders in other parts of the state. The whole thing had been puzzling to Mac, who had thought that things were pretty much settled down, but all of a sudden, there they were: Mark Price, who had accepted his firing without saying a word, and Sally Long, Eldon's daughter, and that boy Nathaniel Pierson and one or two others, sitting at tables in the lunchroom and on the white side of the waiting room. But no Eldon. No grown people. They had arrested the kids without much trouble, and Lyman Wells had showed up to pay their fines.

Even though the Gulf International announcement had been made, Mac was still worried that the company might change its mind. Carleton Byrd hinted as much over the phone; Mac could tell that Byrd enjoyed keeping him on a string. And every now and then Mac would find himself wondering about those two white boys. They sure got away clean. A month now, and nobody's seen hide nor hair of them. It seemed they had just vanished.

"Don't worry about it," Lester Sparks had said to him. "If we find out somethin, we'll take care of it."

"Take care of it?" Mac had said. They were sitting in Sparks's little office at the jail. Sparks had shifted around in his chair, holding his pulpy matchstick in front of his face.

"If we find out somebody bothered em, we'll arrest em, is what I'm sayin," Sparks had said.

"I *know* somebody bothered em, Lester," Mac said. "Just how much, is what I worry about."

"Well . . ." Sparks said. "All I'm sayin is that it ain't surprisin that two dope addicts like that would just up and run. They probably headed for California or somethin." He put the matchstick back between his lips and looked away, not meeting Mac's eyes.

"Goddammit, what have you heard?" Mac said. "You've heard somethin. You know somethin you ain't tellin me. I can tell."

Sparks looked back at him then, his flinty eyes narrowed. "The scuttlebutt's around that the Klan is plannin somethin. It might be just talk. You know them people. But the talk is they plannin somethin."

"Somethin? What?"

"I don't know. Somethin big, though. They gonna show the niggers once and for all."

"Shit," Mac had said. His stomach had been sour and acidy again lately, and he pulled out a package of Tums and popped one into his mouth. It was dry and chalky on his tongue. "Shit," he had said again.

Now he stood looking out the window of his house across the neat lawn, hearing his wife and son and daughter chattering in the next room, sitting down for the evening meal. He was not hungry. He knew that if something *was* afoot, Rooster would know about it. *Hell, he would be at the very center of it.*

⋅⋗⋗⋗⋅

Later in the week, Mac saw Rooster Wembley sitting alone at a table in Maud's, and he sat down next to him. Rooster was finishing a piece of pecan pie, his dinner plate with its neat pile of chicken bones pushed to the side. It was late in the lunch hour, and not many people were in the restaurant. Rooster looked up at Mac as he sat down.

Alda Mae hovered at Mac's elbow. "Bring me a grilled-cheese sandwich and a glass of sweet milk," Mac said, without looking at her. She moved away, her rubber-soled shoes noiseless on the tile floor.

"You ought to try the squash casserole," Rooster said.

"How you been?" Mac said.

"Tolerable," Rooster said. He chewed the last bite of his pie, a look of ecstasy in his copper eyes. "Ummmmm-ummmph," he said. "Is there anything better than pecan pie on the face of God's green earth?"

"I don't know," Mac said distractedly.

Rooster arched his eyebrows; Mac could see his tongue playing about on his teeth in his closed mouth.

"What's on *your* mind, Mac?"

Mac looked around the room. Maud stood behind the cash register, her deep crimson hair glowing in the overhead lights. Several men sat at the counter, their backs to them. There were people at a couple of tables up near the front. He looked back at Rooster, who was inspecting him curiously, a twinkle of amusement in his eyes. Sparse gray whiskers dotted his chin. His jaws still worked slowly, as though savoring the last tastes of the pecan pie.

"I don't like what I been hearin," Mac said.

Rooster frowned slightly. "What's that?" he said.

Mac leaned closer to him. "There's talk," he said. "Scuttlebutt that the Ku Klux Klan is about to do somethin big," he whispered and saw Rooster's eyes waver slightly.

"I wouldn't know anything about that," Rooster said. There was a flat, rising anger : : his eyes now. "Why you tell me that?"

"Come on, Rooster," Mac said.

"I don't know anything about any Ku Klux—"

"I been out there to that huntin lodge, Rooster. You talkin to *me*, remember?" Mac sighed deeply. A slow, burning ire ate away at the linings of his stomach. "Look," he said, keeping his voice calm, "things are better. For some reason, Long's holdin off. We ain't had any of them goddam Freedom Riders in here. There ain't any need for whatever the Klan is gearin up to do. You want to git the goddam FBI in here? Start em pokin around, askin questions?"

"They can't come in here unless you call em in, and you know it. They don't have no jurisdiction in nothin like that. Besides, I don't know anything about this. You talkin to the wrong person. You don't know me. I ain't ever seen you at any huntin lodge, cept to shoot deer at Thanksgivin, and you ain't seen me, either." Rooster blinked his eyes, staring calmly at Mac.

"What is it, Rooster?" Mac said. "Goddammit!"

Just then Alda Mae came up with his sandwich and his glass of milk. She sat the heavy white plate on the table with a thump. The bread was toasted brownish yellow, and a slice of pickle lay in the center of the sandwich, where it was sliced from corner to corner. Both men stayed quiet until she was back behind the counter.

"What are they plannin to do?" Mac said under his breath. He picked up half the sandwich. He had no appetite, even smelling the tart smell of the melted cheese, the faint hint of mustard.

"I told you," Rooster said, "I don't know nothin about it."

Mac bit into the sandwich and chewed. It tasted like dry cardboard, but then most of his food tasted that way lately. He swallowed and took a drink of milk. It was cool and sweet. At least he could taste that.

"I tell you what," Mac said, looking at the wall, his jaw working slowly, "anything happens to fuck up this Gulf International business, there's gonna be hell to pay."

"Come on, Mac," Rooster said. "That dago is where nobody will ever find him."

"Shut up. Goddammit," Mac said, looking around.

"Oh!" Rooster said dryly. "I forget, you don't really know nothin, do you?" His eyes narrowed. "But goddammit, you do!"

Mac detested the man. How could he have ever gone along with anything with him, even looked up to him in some kind of peculiar, odd way? Rooster was evil.

"You need a haircut," Rooster said. He winked at Mac.

"I'm tryin to be serious, goddammit," Mac hissed. "I'm tryin to appeal to somethin decent in you, if there is such a thing!" He had raised his voice, and he saw Rooster's eyes go flat again, saw them quickly scan the room.

"Ain't no reason to yell at me," Rooster said. Mac could see anger tinged with contempt in Rooster's yellow eyes. "You come to my house that night. I told you what I knew, what I had heard. Now you come in here while I'm eatin my dinner, carryin on like a crazy man." Mac started to speak, but Rooster held up his hand. "Shhhhhush! Just listen, cause you asked me a question, and now you're gonna get your answer. I'll tell you somethin." He paused. "Somethin I only *heard*, now. You gonna cross your heart and hope to die if you tell anybody? Cause this is a secret." Rooster's voice was low and menacing, angry and controlled. "Listen close now. One of them boys, the wop one, has done met with a untimely passin. He has done gone to the great spaghetti factory in the sky. His greasy body is under about two hundred feet of good black Alabama dirt, over where they're buildin the new innerstate bridge, up near Eutaw. I got this on good authority."

Mac knew his mouth was hanging open. He was as shocked that Rooster was telling him this as he was at what he was hearing. "*Dead?*"

"Yeah. But the other one? The Jew? Well, he got away. Ran like hell. He probably ran all the way back to Israel." Rooster leaned back, his expression caustically amused now. "So, you ask questions, you git answers, cept they might not be the ones you want to hear, right? Now you know even more about it, don't you Mister Mayor? 'Course, you've *really* known about it since the night you come to my house and watched *Peter Gunn* with me. I don't know how you would explain that."

"Wait! Wait a minute," Mac cut him off. "You mean one of those boys is dead, and the other's out there somewhere?"

"Somewhere, yeah."

"Good God, Rooster." Mac felt his face flushing, the blood rushing to his head. It seemed hot in the restaurant all of a sudden. "He escaped, and he knows . . ."

There was silence. After a minute, Rooster said, "Well, I don't know what he knows. You'd have to ask him that. I'm just tellin you what I heard. Overheard. At the barbershop. I heard they whupped up on both of em pretty bad, then the Jew, the rapist, got away, ran off durin the night or somethin. I'm just tellin you what I heard. I don't like knowin it no more'n you do." Rooster's eyes seemed to twinkle with a kind of venom. "I tell you," he said to Mac, "whatever those old boys do is bound to be one hell of a somethin, don't you think?"

"What? Huh?" Mac said.

"These Ku Klux Klan you talkin about," Rooster said. "You said they gonna strike soon. Gonna do somethin sho-nuff big. Make even a thick-headed nigger sit up and take notice. Huh? I wonder what it's gonna be? Reckon what they gonna do?" He stood up, adjusting his leg awkwardly under the table, dragging it behind him as he moved slowly away. "Oh," he said. He rummaged around in the pocket of his baggy pants and came up with some change. He counted out thirty cents and, leaning back clumsily toward the table, grunting with the effort, put the coins next to his plate. "I like to forgot to tip Alda Mae," he said. "I'll see you around, hear?"

Mac, watching him cross the tile floor, saw some of the men at the counter turn and speak to him. He pushed his uneaten sandwich away and fished in his pocket for his package of Tums. Everything had now gotten irretrievably and completely out of hand. How in hell had he gotten into all this? Images of the Shady Grove Dear Drive, vivid and colorful, leaped into his consciousness and then started to fade, and Mac felt as though his insides were being painfully twisted and pulled in ten thousand different directions at once.

Eldon stood on his little screened front porch, trying to enjoy the tranquil cool of the Sunday morning; he had been trying to concentrate on his notes for his sermon. For over a week now, he had lived with a simmering rage, a consuming anger that was confused with the fear he felt when he considered confronting Cora with the evidence of what she was doing. *What evidence?* He wanted desperately to believe that the men had been lying, making it up just to get at him. He dreaded accusing her of such a thing, partly because tensions had been running so high in their household lately that, if he should be wrong, she might never forgive him. And partly because he was afraid that it was the truth. He had thought of going directly to O.B., but something was holding him back on that. *Please Lord, let it be a lie. But I know in my bones that it is the truth.* He could tell by looking at her; he knew her that well. But he knew he had to be careful, with both O.B. and Cora, because it might just be an ugly lie. But it was not. It was—

Then the bomb exploded. He was suddenly confused, his mind a blank. He would remember that he seemed to feel the vibration first, a slight sense of vertigo, as though the earth were unsteady, about to move, and then came the hot blast—a sudden perception of a vacuum, filled immediately by a violent noise so deafeningly intense that he felt

it piercing his eardrums. The house shook and then become abruptly
still as the penetrating loudness died away, leaving an oddly clamorous
quiet.

"Eldon!" he heard Cora call out. He stood numb, paralyzed with a
quick terror. Then he was looking around frantically. Trying desperately to get a bearing. *The church!* He could see a thin wisp of dark
smoke rising into the clear air, rising over where he knew the church
to be, and he felt a sinking inside his chest. *Sally!* She was there,
getting ready for the citizenship class. But it was early. Maybe she was
not there yet. Maybe—Cora pulled open the door; she had her dark
blue church dress half on, her hair still matted from sleep, her face a
mask of terror and shocked disbelief. "Eldon?" she said. "*Eldon!*"

"It's the church!" He opened the screen door and stepped out into
the yard. He saw someone, a man, running down the street toward the
church. *Let it not be, Lord! Let it not be!* He took a couple of steps,
moving jerkily. His legs did not want to work. He stood still a moment,
taking a deep breath. *She's all right! Everything's all right!* He ran
through the yard, jumping the ditch into the street.

"Eldon!" he heard Cora calling.

He was running now, his feet pounding the soft dirt and gravel. The
leather soles of his shoes slipped and slid, but he ran with a smooth,
steady gait, rounding the corner, seeing people gathering, seeing at the
same time the gaping hole in the corner of the church where the
educational building had been added, flames and smoke boiling out of
two upstairs windows. All the windows in the church and the building
were cracked and shattered, the innocent morning sunlight sparkling
on the shreds of remaining glass, and the churchyard and the street in
front of it were littered with debris: bricks and paper and pieces of
wallboard, chunks of cement, glittering shards of glass. His breath
came in gasps now, and he was sweating under his long-sleeved shirt.
The crowd that was gathering seemed to part for him, divide automatically as he ran up, hearing their voices, their weeping and moaning
and hysterical chatter.

"It's all right!" he shouted. "Everything's gonna be okay!"

"My baby, Lord, my baby," he heard a woman's voice sing a mournful cry above the others' voices, and he shut it away, denying immediately that he had heard it.

"No," he said. "Nobody's hurt." He ran toward the crater in the side
of the building, stumbling on bricks, pieces of wood.

"Reverend Long!" someone was shouting. "Don't—"

He was pushing his way through the opening, hearing his breath rasping in his throat against the acrid, smothering smoke hanging in the air. He could not see for a moment and had to grope his way, then the smoke cleared and he saw electrical wires dangling and the hallway next to the Sunday school classrooms choked with caved-in debris. He heard flames overhead, could see them eating at the ceiling, but he pushed on through, shoving aside a piece of wallboard.

He was dimly aware that someone was with him, then two other people, all of them whimpering and panting, shoving aside shattered furniture, random piles of little preschool desks that had been stacked against the wall, working frantically and deliberately to clear a way into the room. Eldon could hear the crying now, a child's crying, and then he could see her, a little girl, her hair done in tiny red ribbons, her face soot-streaked and her white dress torn and stained. She was standing, looking at him, holding out her arms—Paula! Paula Whitfield—her name popped into his head, and he cried aloud. She was all right! He saw one of the men with him grab her, wrap her in his arms.

Coughing, his eyes burning, he pushed on into the smoke- and dust-filled room. Then he saw her; his stomach seemed to turn over. He thought he felt someone's hand on his arm, but his body was deadened from the shock, his mind sedated even as his vision became clear in the chaotic, hellish room. Sally was on the floor, sitting, her back against the wall, her arms splayed out as though she had been flung there like a discarded rag doll. Her eyes were open, dulled already from the bits of dust and smoke that had begun to settle in them. The lower half of her face was gone, and in the dimness he could see the bright red blood, wet and slick, shining with a light of its own making, as it covered the front of her white-and-pink flowered dress, the blood already beginning to coagulate and turn darker in the folds and crevices of the fabric. He could not move, and he felt a vast emptiness inside himself, and then that hollow void slowly, agonizingly, began to fill with a throbbing ache, a pain so intense and deep that he knew that he would never be able to stand it, and he dropped to his knees, and his ruined daughter, his Sally, looked back at him with sightless eyes.

⋅∾⋅∾⋅∾⋅

Maybe, he thought, the human soul can bear anything. The house was quiet. Cora was lying on their bed, a wet washrag folded across her closed eyes. His parents were at the funeral home. He envied them for their stoicism, their calm, their ability to cry and then move on dry-eyed. His own sharp anger burned, and he wanted to lash out, to hurt, to kill back. He wanted revenge.

He was standing in the living room, still in the sweat- and dust-stained shirt, his pants torn and smudged; he could smell the acrid smoke, the harsh, sulfurous reek of the dynamite in his clothes and on his body, but he did not want to change clothes, did not want to rid himself of the odors. There would be something final about that. He was clinging to the stink of death in a kind of perverse hope that for as long as what had happened remained in the present it could somehow be changed. He stood looking at a row of pictures on the little false mantel, all of Sally, mostly snapshots, with a couple of portraits made at the little studio on Strawberry Street. Sally—staring out at him, smiling, innocent, and alive. The portraits had been made to give to his parents. His parents. Thinking of them, he thought of Cora's parents long dead and now all but forgotten. It was funny that he would remember them now, at this moment, how her mother had been so fat that she was unable to get out of her rocking chair during the last years of her life, and the little cabin reeking of urine, and Cora's father, angry and mean, with a long razor scar down the side of his face, killed in a fall at a planing mill and everybody saying good riddance. Especially Cora and her sisters. Her sisters were all dark, squatty, and passive like her mother, and Cora had been tall and beautiful. It had been her own will, something strong and powerful in her that even her father, that angry and mood-stricken man, had respected. Or feared. *Cora's will . . . Cora and O.B. So many miseries to contend with . . .*

Eldon tried to blank his mind by staring at the pictures, at Sally's delicate features so like her grandmother's, but then he had to turn away. Or soon he would be breaking down.

◦~◦~◦~◦

The house was so quiet, he thought as he sat down on the sofa. He picked up one of the cardboard fans, looking at the picture on the back. He had seen it many times, reproduced on Sunday School cards, done in stained glass in church windows. It showed Jesus, dressed in a long, softly flowing blue robe, holding a lamb, while sheep curled around his feet, rubbing against his legs like cats. A golden halo surrounded his head, his soft-looking clean hair, his delicately featured white face. Eldon felt no emotion, nothing, looking at the picture. He felt drained and dry, devoid of all feeling. He narrowed his eyes, staring at the picture, the bright colors forming cloudy blobs, and when he opened his eyes fully again, he was startled to see that the face on the picture, the face of Jesus, was now the face of Cora's father, hot-faced and resentful, the smooth, raw scar raked angrily down his cheek. Eldon blinked his tired eyes, and the face was once again the unwrinkled, unblemished face of the white Jesus.

He dropped the fan to the floor, rested his head on the back of the sofa, and let the tears come, his eyes clamped shut, his hands gripping the edge of the sofa. He could cry now. There was no one here to see him.

.~.~.~.

The phone rang, startling him. It was Hardenia Moon. She told him that a television station out of Birmingham was in town, along with the one out of Meridian. They were taking films of the church, and talking with people. Eldon thanked her for the call. There seemed to be a quietly understood conspiracy, stretching from Sparks to his neighbors, to shield him and Cora from the reporters. And yet he wanted to talk with them. He *would* talk with them, when he could, when he had the strength. But first he had had to be with Cora. She had been frighteningly silent at first, and then a kind of terrifying, subdued hysteria had taken over, so that she shook all over, restrained tears oozing slowly from her tightly closed eyes. His father had had the good sense to bring a jar of corn whiskey into town with him, and they had practically poured the crude, sharp-smelling clear liquid down her throat. It had acted like a strong sedative, so that now she slept, with a cool rag across her face.

.~.~.~.

It was Gus Levy, at the funeral home, who told him about the newscasts on television. The story had even made the national network news. Eldon listened intently, thinking that he ought to be focusing on all Gus was saying, but he couldn't. He peered at Gus. He was light-skinned, with a salt-and-pepper mustache, probably the wealthiest black man in Hammond.

"The coffin can't be open," he said to Eldon in a low voice. "You got to talk to Cora."

"I can't do nothin with her," Eldon said. His eyes felt scratchy; he had not slept; Sally's ravaged face loomed before him every time he closed his eyes.

Gus put his hand lightly on Eldon's shoulder, guiding him down the hallway. There were mirrors on the walls and dimly lighted sconces as they passed a little mourning room, where he saw his parents quietly sitting, his mother with the familiar brown paper sack at her feet. Cora was in the "chapel," a large room with folding chairs. The heavy-looking gray coffin sat at one end, the soft light in the room glinting dully on its surface. Cora sat in a chair in the front row. She stared at the wall, lost in her own grief; she wore a dark blue dress, and Eldon could see that the buttons up the back were fastened crookedly.

"Cora?" he said softly, and she did not answer, did not turn, gave no indication at all that she had heard him. "Cora?"

Then she turned slowly. Her eyes were wide, a surprised, inquisitive look, as though she had stumbled by accident onto some scene that mystified her, that she did not understand at all. "What?" she said, "what?"

He sat down next to her. Flowers were already arriving, and the room smelled sticky-sweet; the air was close and still, like a tomb. The faint scent of her jasmine perfume, which he loved, mingled and blended with the heavier smells of the funereal flowers. She smelled cool, like the outdoors, like trees. "Honey." He put his arm around her shoulders. The room, the entire place, was quiet, as still as midnight. "We need to talk," he said. He swallowed. Everything he said seemed hopelessly out of place, totally inadequate. She stared at him, a trusting, childlike expression in her dark eyes. "We don't need to worry bout the coffin." She seemed confused, not comprehending what he was saying. He looked at Gus, who was standing just inside the door, his face a familiar mask of compassion and condolence that Eldon had seen a thousand times at the funerals where he had preached and Gus had managed. "We can't open the coffin, now or at the funeral."

"I want to see her again," she said.

"See her, then," Eldon said, nodding his head toward the coffin. He meant the portrait, a framed eight-by-ten that his mother had brought in, a picture of Sally in her white cap and gown, the last picture that had been made of her. Her high school graduation. Her commencement. The picture sat on top of the coffin. Sally was looking out, beneath the white mortarboard, the tassel hanging at her ear, a half-smile, a kind of cocky half-smirk, on her lips. The expression was so like her. The photographer had somehow captured Sally's very essence in the portrait.

⋅∿⋅∿⋅

Cora stared at the photograph. "I'll never see her again," she whispered.

"She's with the Lord," Eldon said, his voice trembling. The idea was of no comfort to her now, but she knew he knew that.

"Why did it have to be her?" Cora said. Her words sounded dull and faint in her own ears. *Why couldn't it have been me? I am the sinner, and You have brought the retribution for my sins down upon my daughter's head!* She felt weighed down by an abiding anger at God and a sense of helplessness like none she had ever known before.

Then she became aware of a soft, throaty moaning coming spontaneously from deep within her, and she felt Eldon looking closely at her. She knew that her eyes were wide, fixed on the photograph. She could not help herself as her moaning increased, becoming more like elongated groans, a rhythmic, almost primitive singing, without words, without notes, a singing that seemed to come from so far deep inside her, so far in her past, that it was as natural and as involuntary as breathing.

Eldon held her. She moaned, rocking back and forth. Slowly, the song seemed to end of its own accord. She felt his strong arms around her, and she knew sadness so deep that she did not think she could endure it. Eldon loved her, and she had betrayed him again, and now God was punishing her, punishing them both, for *her* sin! She felt the warm tears on her cheeks. *I must confess. And I must ask him to forgive me. Again. One more time.*

"Eldon," she began her voice so hoarse that it was only a faint breath. "Eldon . . ." His arms tightened around her. "I have . . . I've betrayed you, again."

The room was silent. She felt his arm grow more rigid, then relax. It was a moment before he spoke.

"I know." His voice was soft but full of agony. She could not look at him. She realized that she had known that he knew.

She went on quickly. "I know I can't ask you to forgive me again. But I have to. I love you, Eldon, and God is punishing me, and I must ask Him to forgive me. And I have to ask you. I wouldn't blame you if you—"

"Shhhhhh," he said.

"If you love me, you'll give me another chance. I don't deserve it, Eldon, I—"

"I've known it for a while," he interrupted. "The night they beat me up. Kershaw and them, they told me. They had seen you and him, they said."

They had seen us! Her heart sank, making her dizzy.

He went on. "But I knew it before then. I think I must have known it the first time it started again. It's like I just . . . knew. The night you and O.B. came to get me out of jail, and I saw you there together, I knew—"

"But that was—"

"Shhhhhh," he stopped her. He spoke slowly, his voice full of pain. "I have known for thirty years, Cora. Maybe I have known for a hundred years, for centuries. And I have forgiven you. Both of you. Over and over in my mind, and I knew God was testing me. He was sending me the fire and telling me to survive it if I could—"

"Eldon." She could hear the anger in his voice. It sounded like a sermon, and she knew what he was covering up. He meant every word of it, but it was his way of dealing with his remorse and his hurt. "Eldon, you must promise me . . ."

"What?"

"If you love me, Eldon, you won't try to get revenge on O.B." He did not respond. "It was my fault, Eldon, my doin. I tempted him, it was me—"

"Don't be a fool, Cora," he said.

"Promise me!" She stood up then, looking down at him. "It would just make it worse. Don't you see?" His eyes seemed sunken. He looked as tired as she'd ever seen him. "If you love me, Eldon. Forgive me and let's try to pick up the pieces and go on from here. For Sally." Their eyes locked. "I'm sorry, Eldon. How can I ever tell you how sorry I am?"

Love for him, for Sally, flooded her. She felt a strength, then, looking down at him. He stood up. He opened his arms, and she moved close to him, and they stood there, both crying quietly in the room with Sally.

⋅∿∿∿⋅

It was important to them all to have the meeting in the bombed-out church, and they came from all over, almost every colored person in town; there were pickups and beat-up cars parked up and down the narrow streets, and there were even some wagons, with their ambling, slow mules, tethered in nearby yards. Eldon had watched them picking up what was left of the debris, covering the gaping hole with black tar paper, even cleaning and sweeping what was left of the education building. It was in ruins, naked, scorched rafters outlined in the dim lights from the church itself and the street lamps. The windows at the side of the church were covered in thick, translucent plastic. There was no way everyone could get into the church, so they stood around outside, in groups.

It was Nathaniel Pierson who had first mentioned the meeting to Eldon, earlier, outside the funeral home. Inside, the boy had sat for a while with Cora and had been surprisingly gentle and calm, but outside he had approached Eldon roughly, jerking his arm, hurting him so that Eldon winced.

"We're havin a meetin to decide what we gonna do," the boy had said, staring down at him, his eyes glinting.

"We will have no violence, no bloodshed," Eldon had responded.

The boy's pain and anger had flashed in his eyes. "Tonight. At the church. You be there."

It had sounded like an order, and Eldon had to struggle to control his own anger. Then he saw the boy's despair, his suffering, in his eyes. He realized with a start that he had not thought Nathaniel capable of such grief, had not really tried to know him at all.

At the church, Eldon had not known what to expect. He was shocked and dismayed as he crossed the yard toward the front door to see several men holding shotguns and rifles, their women standing quietly and passively beside them. They broke off their talking as he passed, watching him in silence, gaping at him, as though Sally's death had somehow formed an aura around him. He stood for a moment, looking at the church; a seared, singed smell hung in the air. Then he went up the front steps and through the front doors. The inside of the church was crowded, the air close and heavy, the smell of the fire thick and hanging here, too. People talked excitedly, a steady, buzzing murmur, and Eldon made his way down the aisle, accepting condolences from some, some simply touching him, shaking his hand. Hardenia Moon stood and hugged him. He felt lightheaded, nervous, full of a kind of vague anxiety; he sensed that the situation was now beyond his control. He did not know if he had the strength or the will to wrest the control back, but he knew he was determined that there would be no more bloodshed, no more killing. Conflicting emotions warred within him. He was exhausted by his anger at O.B. And he was angry at Cora as well. His rage seemed like a permanent part of his heart now, and yet he forgave them, he knew he did. *I know what I am made out of! And like the Lord, I forgive them, because He does. He made them weak, he made us all weak! Yet he challenges us to be strong. That is what it is all about.* He saw some of the people looking at him. *I love her. I must be strong.*

The pulpit was empty. They were waiting on him to preside, even if he had not called the meeting. He mounted the podium, looking out across the crowd, which began to fall silent. He could see Nathaniel, over by the window, where he had been sitting that winter night when he had introduced Paul and Joe to them. That had been the last time the church had been this packed, the last time he had felt this sense of anticipation, of nervous excitement, on their part. And on that night Nathaniel had sat there with Sally . . .

Eldon's despondence and his misery were overpowering. He shut his eyes, trying to clear his head.

"—git em and string em up! The only thing we got to decide is how and when!"

"Yeah!"

Eldon opened his eyes. Nathaniel was on his feet, waving a pistol over his head. Eldon could see Mark Price standing next to him. *Sally? Where was Sally?* It was hot and stuffy. Eldon's suit coat felt scratchy on his shoulders and arms.

"We got guns just like they got," Nathaniel said. "For every one of us that dies, a cracker dies. They owe us one goddam cracker!"

"Uh-huh! Amen!" Mumblings and shouts across the crowd.

"Please." Eldon's voice was little more than a whisper, but some of the people down front looked up at him, and a hush fell over the crowd.

"Please," Eldon said again, his voice louder now. "You are talkin about war!"

"You goddam right!" Nathaniel yelled. There were other shouts in support of him, but still other shouts: "Listen! Listen to the preacher!"

Eldon felt as though all his strength had gone out of him. He struggled to find some power somewhere, something to propel him. Suddenly, it was there, like a burning coal, his rage and his jealousy driving him. The young men moved and spoke with a driven energy, an energy that Eldon now began to feel. His grief and his fatigue seemed to lift. *I hate O.B. I must confess that, know that in my heart. I hate him and yet I love him, too, because he is my brother. He is a part of me, like one of my hands that I cannot chop off, even if it is diseased and pains me.* He pulled himself erect, blinking his eyes to chase the dizziness away. *Look into my heart, Lord. Angels and devils are battling for my soul. Lord, give me strength!*

"Wait," he said, raising his hand.

"We been waitin too long," Mark Price said. "We been waitin for generations. We ain't gonna wait no more!"

"I'm not . . . I'm not tellin you to wait for justice. Justice will come."

"Shit!" Nathaniel growled. There were loud mumblings of support for him around the church.

"It will! It will!" Eldon said. "You can't win this way. They'll crush you! And even if you did win, you'd be worse than them if you won that way! Don't y'all see that? Don't y'all understand? Godamighty!"

There were more rumblings and grumblings. Then an expectant hush gradually settled over the crowd. He saw rows of faces, eyes turned to him. He called on whatever was left inside. *Lord, be with me.* "It ain't gonna never change if you hate," he said. *Make your face to shine upon me!* "Hate eats you up. It gets in your heart like a boil, it tears at your insides. It—"

"Your daughter is dead!" somebody yelled. "Your own daughter is dead! And you stand up there—"

"I stand up here tellin you I know my Sally is gone from us! You don't think I know that? You don't think I cry it in my bitterest heart? I hate, too! Lord knows, I want to take whoever put that bomb there, take his redneck throat in my hands and choke the evil life out of him! Lord, I hate! But I can't win by hate. It was hate that killed her! The white man hates! That's what they know. They got to hate us so they won't hate themselves!"

"Amen! Uh-huh!"

"You got to love! You got to—"

"Love is for Jesus and sissies!" Mark Price yelled. "I'm a man. I can't be no—"

"Jesus was a *man!*" Eldon shouted. His voice echoed to the far reaches of the church, strong now, full-bodied. "He was a man, boy, and don't you never forget it! You think it didn't take a man to go through what he went through, and then still love us, love *you?* How many times you think he wanted to give up, huh? How many times you think he wanted to just lash out at the unbelievers? How many times you think it went through his mind to just whup up on somebody, maybe to kill em, maybe to just say to *hell* with em? How many times, boy?"

Shouts of "Uh-huh!"

"Yeah, I hate. I hate the evil people who did this to my Sally. I hate the country that allows that evil to happen! I even hated God! Yeah! I got mad at him! I'm mad now! But you know what? God can handle that! He's bigger than that. He don't mind. Cause he loves me. Cause I'm gonna come outta this . . . we all gonna come outta this . . . on the other side, and that love is still gonna be there, like sunlight on a flower, like a rose openin up! God understands my hate. And He tellin me, He sayin, 'Be like me!' " His voice fell into a rhythm, a pattern; he was suddenly aware that it was like the song that Cora had sung at the funeral home, and, thinking of her, his eyes misted over, his voice choked. " 'Be like Me!' We got to hang on even in the face of death! We got to go on lovin them that hate you, that persecute you and revile you, because we gonna come out the other side."

He paused. The church was deathly still. They were all watching him, the air expectant, hushed.

"For the Lord's sake, put down your weapons. For Sally's sake. For the sake of us all. He who lives by the sword *dies* by the sword. Those men who did that to my baby are dead, dead to eternity, their souls withered like dry seeds on concrete. The Lord has already punished em! Their hearts are blackened like ashes; they are sufferin in their own misery. Have pity on em! Give em your compassion. Feel *sorry* for em, because they know hell, they are in hell! Hell is hate! Hell on earth. Don't match their senseless violence with your own. They ain't worth killin. They ain't worth any more dyin. Any more sufferin. But *we* are! *You* are! Nonviolence! Remember what Paul and Joe taught us. Think about Reverend King, over there in Montgomery. If we all keep on, things are gonna change. I know it don't seem like it. And when we git spit on, kicked and maimed and even *killed*, it seems like we fools not to git up and kick back, but the way to beat the kick is not to return it. Turn the other cheek. Forgive seventy times seven! It ain't easy. It's the hardest thing on earth! It take a *man!*"

The church was hushed. Eldon swallowed. Every eye was on him; no one moved.

"Brothers and sisters," he said, "give it a chance. The road is long and hard, but ain't none of us ever had it easy. We the most equipped people on the face of this earth to suffer for what we know is right. We sho have had the practice. And we gonna win. In the long run, we gonna win. I talked to Dr. King on the phone. They gonna start marchin in Montgomery. In Selma. Real soon, we gonna march on the city hall, we gonna block the streets, and when they try to move us, we gonna forgive em and tell em we love em! But the white trash want us to fight em their way. They know they can beat us their way, with the hate and violence and the meanness! Don't give in to em. Dr. King said, Think about Sally! Think about her life! She with Jesus now, she restin in love. They can't change that. Let em know that, finally, this is one place where *they* ain't callin the shots." He paused and took a breath. He felt exhausted. They all stared at him. He smiled, then, in relief, in a sense of hope that surged within him. "They already so confused they don't know whether to shit or go blind," he said, and he saw them smiling in return. "Return their white hate with black love. Forgive em their meanness. And we gonna win. I promise you. With everything in me, I promise you."

His words hung in the hushed air. "Amen," he said. He stood there for a moment, his throat scorched and dry, tasting the acrid air on his tongue. Then he walked down from the podium, his legs weak and shaky, trembling with each step, going up the aisle. The people crowding the aisle moved aside, giving him room, all eyes watching him as he tried to keep his shoulders back, to keep the weary stoop out of his walk. He pushed open the door, feeling the cool night air hit his face, feeling the tiredness in his bones. The door rattled to behind him. There was still no sound from the church. The groups of people who had spilled over stood here and there, looking at him. He nodded to them. He crossed the churchyard, walking slowly, turning down the street toward home.

·~·~·~·

In his exhaustion, Eldon was sitting on the lawn chair in the darkness, before going into the house, breathing deeply in the night air, when he was suddenly aware of the steady, insistent ringing of the phone inside.

He dragged himself out of the chair, his bones stiff, his muscles tired. He slowly crossed the yard in the shadows, stepping carefully, guiding himself by memory.

The phone sounded louder when he pushed open the door. He snatched it up, barking into the phone.

"Hello!" he said, too loud, angry.

"Eldon? This is Martin King again."

"Huh? Oh. Yes."

"I wanted to call you again to see how you're doing, Eldon. It's terrible. Please tell Cora. Tell her be strong. Tell her Martin said be strong."

"I will," Eldon said. King had called immediately, when he'd heard about Sally, and Eldon had been too numb to talk to him, hardly knowing the source of the voice on the other end of the line. He sat down, holding the phone to his ear.

"You sound hoarse. Take care of yourself. I know it's hard gettin through a time like this. The Lord is with you. You're in all our prayers." King's voice was smooth, mellow, like warm syrup.

"All right. Yeah. Thanks," Eldon said.

"Are you all right, Eldon?" King said.

"What? Yeah. Well as could be expected."

The line was silent. Eldon could hear the long-distance lines humming. He had nothing to say and waited for King to speak.

"Eldon? Tell me, when's the funeral?"

"I don't know. End of the week. Sometime. We got some people comin . . . our people. . . ."

"Yeah," King said.

Silence. Then Eldon suddenly remembered whom he was talking to. "You comin over? It would mean a lot to us, to Cora and me, if you—"

"Yeah, Eldon. I'll be there. So will a lot of other folks."

"Who? Who you mean?"

"Haven't you seen the newscasts? This thing is all over everywhere. I think you ought to do it up big. Plan somethin big."

Eldon was distracted, half listening. "Plan somethin?"

"Yes. Her funeral. A procession or somethin."

Eldon didn't answer. The line hummed. Then King spoke, gently. "This is your *event*, Eldon," he said.

"My what?"

"When we talked? Don't you remember what I said? You've got to have an event, a cause for folks to rally around. Like the buses over here. Those lunch counters up in Greensboro. You've got it now, Eldon."

My event. Eldon's pulse quickened. Then, "I don't know, Martin," Eldon said, his voice shaking. "Sally . . . it's just . . ."

"I know how you feel," King said. "It doesn't seem right. But let me ask you. Where's the good going to come from in this thing if it doesn't come out of that evil? How're you going to make that awful thing right? Pray about it, Eldon. Get with God about it. Turn it back on those people who did it. Make it work against them."

Eldon sat holding the phone, his entire body aching and stiff, weak with fatigue. He realized, suddenly and frighteningly, what King was saying. He said nothing.

"This is it, Eldon," King said. "This is your event."

The words seemed to reverberate in Eldon's ear, and he licked his dry lips and blinked his scratchy eyes. The image of Sally was there, hanging in the air before him.

"All right," he said, almost a whisper. He felt a twinge of excitement, of revived energy, somewhere inside. "Lord give me strength."

"Lord give you strength," King said.

.~.~.~.

Ellen parked her father's pickup in the small parking lot of Levy's Funeral Home, in Shortleaf. She cut the engine and sat there for a moment, thinking of the other colored funeral home, Stoner's, in Frogbottom, where she'd had her abortion. For a moment, she could again smell the pungent, sweet alcohol, feel again the sultry, stuffy heat. She shook her head to clear it, breathing deeply the crisp, early autumn air, so clean with its hint of coolness.

Levy's was a new concrete-block building, with a gravel parking lot. Several cars were parked in front. She recognized the Longs' black Chevrolet and shivered, looking away from the gold-and-black hearse parked nearby. She opened the door of the pickup and stepped down, gripping her purse, her shoes crunching on the gravel as she crossed to the front door.

Inside, on a table near the door, was a small, hand-lettered sign, LONG, with an arrow pointing down the hall. She followed the softly lighted hallway to a large room filled with rows of folding chairs. The entire front wall of the room was a bank of flowers. Sally's coffin looked dull as unpolished silver against the bursts of colors. Ellen looked around in the dimness, her eyes becoming accustomed to the muted light, and saw Cora sitting motionless and still in the back row, her eyes seemingly fixed on the closed casket.

Cora wore a light yellow dress, almost off-white. Her hair was cut short, shorter than Ellen had ever seen it. Ellen could not remember when she had last seen Cora to talk to her. She remembered the night earlier in the year, back in the winter, when Cora had come to the back door to ask her father to go get Eldon and Sally out of jail. Ellen had sat there at the table, watching her mother's fury, confused and perplexed by it all, and especially puzzled by her father's reaction to Cora's presence. That night Ellen had sensed that there was so much hanging in the air that was not expressed or even acknowledged in her family, had felt it as palpably as a change in temperature against her skin.

She stood looking at her dead friend's mother. Cora seemed ageless; she looked exactly as she had back when she'd been working at her parents' house, taking the two of them, Ellen and Sally, to the park or playing three-handed Hearts in the backyard under the shade of the huge old fig tree. What had happened to stop all that? Ellen vaguely remembered, like a scene from some old picture show, or some re-called dream that could be remembered only in fragments, an argument about how Cora should have known better, that somebody had complained; Ellen's mother had been embarrassed and angry. It seemed somehow to have been her father's fault, though she couldn't remember anything being said directly to that effect. Ellen remembered that it was common for Negro housekeepers to take white children to the park, and that it had never seemed to occur to any of the three of them that there would be anything wrong with Sally going along. *Or had it?*

Now Ellen squinted her eyes in the dim light, focusing on Cora, whose unwavering gaze was fixed on the coffin and the bank of flowers. It dawned on Ellen that Cora must surely have known the rules, that there was no way Cora could not have been aware of what she was doing.

That's what had so angered her mother; Ellen could understand that now. But why was it her father's fault? Surely he didn't encourage Cora to do it. Did he defend Cora? *Why?*

The questions hammered at her brain. She thought of her father. She had heard just yesterday, from Mr. Leach, that she had gotten a full scholarship to Middlebury, one of those last-minute ones that often go unused, Mr. Leach had said, because people are already enrolled somewhere else. The teacher had urged her to take it. School was starting, but he had talked with them about letting her enroll late, and they had agreed to a few days. The thought of leaving her father, and Paul, right now, was intolerable to her. She ached with the pain she had seen in her father's eyes when she had told him about the scholarship.

"You can leave all this. You'll have a chance," he had said. "Sometimes, when I think . . . when I look back . . ." His voice had dwindled, his eyes drifting off out the window. She'd known what he meant and sensed that his regret was so private that he could never share it with her.

Cora seemed to sense her presence in the room. She turned slowly to look at Ellen. Cora's dark eyes were wide and dry, her face vacant and impassive like polished leather.

"Cora?" Ellen's voice seemed overloud to her in the silence. Cora did not react for a moment. Then her face seemed to relax, her eyes softening.

"Ellen," she said softly.

Ellen moved toward her, reaching out. Cora's hand felt cool and smooth. Ellen slid into the chair beside her. The older woman gripped her hand tightly. "I'm glad to see you, Ellen."

"I'm so sorry, Cora," Ellen said. Cora's large, intensely black eyes were steady on her. She felt the tears filling her eyes; then as the immensity of the moment struck her, she began to sob.

Cora put her arms around her and pulled her close. Ellen felt Cora's body begin to shudder. They held each other, their crying quiet and steady.

"It's all right, it's all right," Cora murmured. Ellen let herself go, thinking *And I've lost a child as well;* feeling the tears like a purging surrender to her grief over everything that had happened the past year. She could remember Cora comforting her years ago—a skinned knee, a yellow-jacket bite—and even though she was now a woman, she was still the child, too, and she let herself be that child, feeling Cora rock her in her arms, whispering calmly and serenely, the older woman humming a wordless tune whose melody seemed to come from their very breathing, their collective mourning for all the losses that they'd endured.

⌒⌒⌒

They sat for a long time in the chapel, in silence. Finally, Cora watched Ellen as she got up and walked down front and stood looking at the coffin, staring at the framed portrait sitting on top, of Sally in the white graduation costume she had worn the night before Ellen had donned one of some other color to graduate across town from the other—the white—high school.

After a while, Cora followed her down and stood next to her. "Eldon says she's with God now," she said quietly. Her throat ached from the crying.

"Yes."

"I suppose she is. Sometimes, though . . ." Cora paused. "Sometimes God seems like just another word. Just a hollow word. Like all the others. Sometimes He's not somethin you feel. You know?"

"Yes," Ellen whispered.

"Love," Cora said. "You feel love. It's not concrete. It's just somethin you feel." She sighed. "If you show it, people will destroy it. Hold it in your heart, nobody can get at it." She looked at Ellen then. *You are the daughter of one of the men I have loved for over twenty-five years. Do you know? Is there something passing between us that has no words?* "We women keep on doin it, though, don't we?" Cora said. "We keep on showin it, and people keep on destroyin it. It's the oldest story in the book. Older than Eve. She knew the truth of it. Both Marys knew it. I think all women do. We can't hide our love, even if we have to watch it get destroyed."

Ellen looked at Cora then. The girl's eyes were wide; they seemed to glow with a dawning of new knowledge. Cora felt a sudden jolt in her heart. *Lord, I can see him in your eyes!* "Sometimes you have to just keep it in your heart, though," Cora went on. "Because you hurt people. You hurt the people you love. I don't know why God made it that way, but he did. Maybe because he's a man, you reckon?" *I am free now,* she was thinking. *Your father will always be a part of me, but I love Eldon; we will find peace. I know we will. When I lie down at the end of my life, I will not lie down a sinner.*

Ellen was smiling. Cora felt the tears stinging her eyes again. Ellen put her hand on her shoulder and squeezed gently. The room was quiet, the smell of the flowers overpowering, like splashes of cheap perfume. Cora watched Ellen looking at the coffin. The girl's eyes were dry now. Her lips were trembling, her hands gripping her purse so tightly that her knuckles were white. Cora guessed that she was thinking of her own vulnerable future, so frightening in its uncertainty, its promises and its pain. *Poor Ellen . . .*

Cora tried to pray, but her mind seemed like an arid desert. She recited, by rote, under her breath, "Our Father, Who art in heaven, hallowed be Thy name . . ."

Chapter Fifteen

~⚭~

ELDON STOPPED HIS CAR IN FRONT OF O.B.'S SHOP. BEFORE HE could get on with the rest of this week, he had to do this. O.B.'s pickup was parked at the side, the only car in the lot. Most of the building was dark, but he could see a light back in O.B.'s office, and he got out, slamming the door. *Am I giving him a warning? Is that why I slammed it?* Eldon took a deep breath. The sky was pale blue, the air gray with evening twilight. Eldon pushed through the front door, crossed through the parts department, and stopped in the office doorway. O.B. was sitting behind his desk, scribbling on a pad.

He looked up, and for a moment neither man spoke. "Workin late on inventory," O.B. said. "Going over some figures."

Eldon came into the cramped office and sat in the same chair he'd sat in that winter afternoon that seemed a century ago. He unbuttoned his coat and crossed his legs. O.B. peered at him, his blue eyes steady on Eldon.

"We've got some unfinished business, O.B." Eldon's voice was firm, the words hovering in the air between them.

"All right." O.B. tossed the pen down, crossing his arms over his chest. His chair squeaked as he leaned back.

Eldon stared at him. "You know why I'm here."

Their eyes locked for a long moment. "Yes," O.B. answered.

"I want to tell you a story," Eldon began.

"Look—" O.B. interrupted, and Eldon held up his hand, stopping him.

"No, wait. You're gonna hear this, O.B." Eldon knew that his voice was tight; he felt the heat of his rage, boiling just under the surface, and he fought to control it. "You're gonna listen to this story." O.B. said nothing, just looked at Eldon expectantly. "When I was a boy, I came home one day and found my daddy cryin. Now you know my daddy, and he wasn't a man to cry. That was the only time I ever saw him cry. He wanted me to know what was goin on, because he wanted me to know how things worked in this world.

"You remember my mama was old Mrs. Hubbard's cook, and round the house she'd been noticin Mr. Hubbard lookin at her in this peculiar and familiar way for some time. What was she gonna do? Huh? Daddy had a good situation share-croppin with Mr. Hubbard; the man was good to his tenants, you know that, and there wasn't anyplace else for my folks to go, anyway. Mama and Daddy were both scared, knowin he could just up and run em off the place if he took the notion. They didn't have nothin to really call their own then. And Mama wasn't gonna accuse Mr. Hubbard of nothin, since you know what would happen to a nigger that accused a white man!"

The little office was silent. Eldon went on, "Daddy said it like to drove Mama crazy, waitin, expectin him to make a grab at her, and when he finally did, it was almost a relief." Eldon paused again. The office was quiet. Then he continued, "Anyhow, the day I found Daddy cryin was the day that white devil Hubbard forced my mama into his bed. And Daddy told me wasn't a thing we could do about it, none of us, because if we even told anybody, the evil men in the white sheets would come and get us, and they *would* have, too. That wasn't any fairy tale. And if they didn't, wasn't any way the police would arrest a white man on the word of a nigger. Nothin we could do. Cause even if she didn't let him have his way with her, he could sic the Klan on us anyway.

"Well, I knew what *I* could do about it: I wanted to kill the bastard. But I knew I couldn't. God had already spoken to me, you see, and He had told me, 'Thou shalt not kill!' He had told me to go out amongst my people and set em free. Free from this kind of hate I felt in my heart. To spread His Gospel and His love amongst the world." O.B. was staring at him, and he went on in a low, tense voice. "But I made a private vow. A vow that I broke. I swore that my wife would never work in the kitchen of a white man, to be demeaned like that. But one time, when I was too young or too stupid to know any better, I let my wife work for a white man, because he was my brother. When we were boys, we had slept in the same bed and drunk out of the same cup. So I trusted him, even though I knew what had happened in the past. I trusted him, because he was my brother, and he betrayed me. He betrayed me then, and he betrayed me again. Just like what happened to my mama."

"Eldon—" O.B. started.

"Let me finish. My daddy was powerless, O.B., but I'm not. I'm snatchin my power. I'm takin it. Maybe my people here in town ain't come all that far in a year, but *I've* come miles and years! And so will they, eventually, they'll be where I am. You betrayed me, O.B., but God was testin me, and I passed the test. You couldn't really hurt me. It ain't in your power to hurt me, unless *I* let you."

"Goddammit, Eldon," O.B. growled. He stood up, towering over Eldon. His eyes were now full of fury. He seemed about to burst, and the words came slowly at first, then seemed to erupt from deep down inside him. "Eldon, I . . . I love her, goddammit, I love her!" His hands were flat on the desk, his arms tense and trembling.

The words seemed to hang in the air between them. The only sound was O.B.'s labored breathing. "You finally admit it," Eldon said thinly. "But it's too late. Surely you know it's too late."

The silence was long and tense. Eldon watched O.B. breathing deeply, his eyes full of pain.

"I'm sorry," O.B. whispered. "Maybe . . . I'm sorry." He looked as though there was so much more that he wanted to say. Finally, he pleaded, "You have to believe I'm sorry, Eldon. You have to understand that I love her." He faltered. "I know now that I have always loved her. That ought to make a difference." He paused again. He seemed to call on all the strength he had. "I want you to forgive me." O.B.'s face was a mask of anguish.

"I will," Eldon said. He felt a surge of power. He stood up, still looking up at O.B. "Someday."

O.B. flinched as though Eldon had hit him.

"You can't have her, O.B. You never did really have her, and you never will. You white cracker son of a bitch."

O.B.'s eyes flashed with anger. "You nigger bastard!"

They stared at each other, their eyes riveted. Eldon's rage was like a thin, smoky heat at the front of his brain. "All right," Eldon said softly, little more than a whisper. "All right." He nodded toward the door. "Let's go outside," he hissed.

He turned his back on O.B. He went out the front door, hearing O.B. following him, taking off his coat as he went. Outside in the twilight, he yanked the tie from around his neck, and in his fury blindly flung both the coat and tie to the ground. He turned around, facing O.B. He held his arms up, feeling the satisfying tenseness of his fists, the airy lightness in his arms.

O.B. stood gingerly before him, on his toes, moving smoothly; he still had an athlete's body, and he circled Eldon. Eldon blinked, his vision distorted by the rage filling him like a flood. Suddenly, as though out of nowhere, O.B. jabbed, and the punch caught Eldon on the nose. Sharp pain tingled, and tears shot immediately into his eyes. Eldon swung wildly. The blow caught O.B. on the side of the head, and he grunted, stepping away, his foot slipping on the gravel of the parking lot. He regained his balance quickly, circling, panting.

"Goddammit," O.B. said, "goddammit!" He swung, missing, Eldon hearing the whistling fist go by his face.

Eldon jabbed, hitting O.B. in the chest, and Eldon heard the breath go out of him for a moment. Eldon blinked back the tears, tasting the warm, salty blood seeping into his mouth. He was quicker than O.B., and he punched again, catching O.B. in the eye, and O.B. staggered back, his eyes wide and rolling like a panicked wild horse's. O.B. swung with abandon then, his fist crashing into the side of Eldon's head, a blow that Eldon felt only as a crushing force as his head snapped to the side and his eyes went out of focus and then back in. He saw O.B. moving in. He stumbled forward, weakly throwing his fist, and his arm went around O.B.'s neck, and both men went down together.

O.B. rolled, Eldon holding him in a headlock. O.B. kicked, whimpering, getting a grip on the back of Eldon's collar, pulling him backward, and Eldon heard the cloth of his shirt ripping and tearing away. They bucked against each other; Eldon felt O.B.'s fists hit his back a couple of times, and then both men were still.

They lay that way for a long time, their bodies pressed closely together, their breath coming in labored gasps, and then slowly becoming more regular. Eldon heard a car go by on the highway. O.B. finally stirred, and Eldon moved, allowing him to sit up. O.B.'s eye was beginning to swell, and his shirt was covered with Eldon's blood. He sat flexing his fist. Eldon's nose throbbed regularly. He wiped his mouth with the back of his hand.

"I swear, O.B.," he said, after a minute, "one of these days, I guess I'm just gonna have to kill you. Or you me." The passion of his fury was gone. O.B. breathed easily now, looking into Eldon's eyes. It was as though they were bound together as surely as from birth, as though the same womb had nurtured them both. Eldon could read clearly in O.B.'s eyes that he felt it, too, knew it as deeply as Eldon did.

O.B. lay back, his eyes focused at the gray sky, at the few faint stars now visible in the dusk. "Naw," he said softly. "We could never kill each other. We both know that." Then he closed his eyes.

Eldon's rage had left him exhausted and washed out. He felt weak, unsteady, lying in the dusty gravel. *There. I feel cleansed.* He thought of Cora. There was no white skin in his vision now. *The line of her neck. Her eyes. Her smell.*

I have forgiven.

***

Eldon looked at Mac McClellon across the desk. The white man seemed agitated; his eyes were narrow slits, his color a dull glowing red. *You do not frighten me anymore,* Eldon was thinking.

"No," McClellon said, "I will not give you any such permit." He sat stiff in his chair, his fingers rigid on the edge of the desk in front of him. "I understand your grief, Long. I have children, too. I think I know how you feel. But by damn, man. This is your daughter you're talkin about. This is makin a mockery of her . . . her funeral. You're not thinkin straight."

"It's an old tradition," Long said. "The funeral procession. We just want to do this one on foot." He wanted to do this right, to go completely by the book. He was determined to get the parade permit.

"No," McClellon said. "I know what you want. You want a demonstration, a march. I've seen all those people camped in front of your church. I've heard the rumors about King and E. D. Nixon and that Parks woman and the others comin in here. I've been warned, don't think—"

"Yes," Eldon said, "the March for Dignity." He felt proud, knowing that it had gone too far now, and there was nothing McClellon could do about it.

"Say what?" Mac said.

"The March for Dignity. Sally would have wanted it. It's not making a mockery of her memory. It's dignifyin her senseless death, her murder."

"All right," McClellon said, holding up his hands. He seemed pained, nervous, and Eldon fixed him with a steady gaze.

"All right you'll give us the permit?" Eldon said.

"All right I hear you," Mac said. "No. No permit."

Eldon shrugged. "Then we'll go anyway," he said.

"No. You'll be arrested. There are two hundred state troopers on their way in here right now. And I have access to other deputies. No way. These are . . . public streets. People use em. You can't—"

"That's my point," Eldon cut him off.

"What?"

"We are people, too, Mr. McClellon," Eldon said firmly. He detested this white man, hated his stubbornness, but he would try to lead him to righteousness.

McClellon drummed his fingers on the desk. The large knot of his red tie stuck out in front, and his collar seemed too tight for his neck. Eldon had seen him on the network news last evening, being interviewed by a correspondent from up north. "We *have* no racial problems here," McClellon had drawled, with a benign smile, "this is all the doins of so-called outside agitators. The whites and the coloreds in Hammond have gotten along nicely for many years, thank you; we appreciate the help, but y'all can just all go on back up there and see if you can't solve all the problems in Harlem." He had looked self-satisfied, as though he knew he had the final word.

Now Mac looked away, far less confident, Eldon thought. "Why are you threatened by all this Mr. McClellon?" Eldon said.

"Because this is . . . this is *anarchy*, Long! You people have gotten it into your heads that you want to go around breaking laws all the time. What about the good, decent, law-abidin citizens? Don't they have rights, too?"

"You mean white people?"

"Well, yeah, and good colored people, too. I don't notice *all* your folks fallin in line behind you like little tin soldiers!"

"Watch the procession on Friday and see," Long said. In spite of his frustration about the permit, he was enjoying McClellon's unease, his distress. Anyway, Eldon had discovered that if he focused his attention on something else, like the March, he did not have to think about Sally. "People, white and colored, from all over, will be here by Friday. It's a simple funeral procession, to pay homage to the life of one little colored girl who lived and died in this backwater town. But it'll be on the television. Everything you do, everything those troopers do, will be on the television, for everybody to see."

"The troopers ain't gonna do nothin, because there won't be any reason for em to do anything. They'll be here to protect you! From whoever blew up that church, and burned those crosses. Can't you see I'm doin this for your own good?"

"You doin it cause you don't want Gulf International pullin out," Eldon said, staring at the man.

"That's right! What about it? I'm responsible for the economic welfare of all the citizens—"

"Bullshit!"

"—of Hammond! What did you just say to me?"

"I said, 'Bullshit,' " Eldon said.

"Well, that's a fine way for a preacher to talk," McClellon said, and Eldon laughed.

"You mean a fine way for a nigger to talk to a white man, don't you?"

McClellon's eyes narrowed until they were little more than glinting slits in his face. "Tell me," he demanded after a minute. "What makes you so goddam cocky all of a sudden?"

"I don't mean to be cocky." Eldon leaned back in the chair and looked around the spacious office. "I'm just confident," he said.

"Listen." McClellon leaned forward, his voice low. "You pushin this thing too far, you hear me? You had that goddam boycott that didn't work. You brought those civil wrongs workers in here, and they turned out to be drug addicts who up and ran off and left you high and dry. What makes—"

"The boycott *did* work," Eldon said, quickly. "Some of the white community suffered badly—"

"All right! I'll grant you that. But the damn thing petered out. You can't sustain somethin like that. I'd think you'd learn from your mistakes." McClellon leaned back in his swivel chair then, his hands locked behind his head, gazing steadily at Eldon. "What makes you think this thing is gonna work any better?" McClellon continued. "If I *gave* you the permit, which I *won't*, what makes you think you'd accomplish somethin? I'll tell you what you'd accomplish: nothin! But maybe, somebody *else* killed. Maybe more bloodshed. You want that? Good God, man. Your own daughter dead, and you want to push on some more! Nossir! No way. You already got blood on your hands! I don't want any on mine! No way. No march, no nothin. You got that?" McClellon's expression, craggy and fixed, seemed carved in stone.

Eldon's smile felt stiff on his face now. He thought, This man is not going to budge. *Well, you don't know what you're up against this time, white man!*

"We are going to march, Mr. McClellon," Eldon said.

"No, you are not, Mr. Long," McClellon said.

.~.~.~.

Well, at least he called me "Mr.," Eldon wryly thought, as he drove home. He turned down Ashe Street, slowing as he approached the church, on account of the people spilling over into the street. The front lawn of the church had become a campground, with small pup tents, sprouted like mushrooms, and tarpaulins attached to the several small trees. Eldon had no idea where all the people had come from: There were several nuns, dressed in their habits, and a couple of priests who had told Eldon that they were Episcopal from Nashville. And there were groups of young white college students. They tended to have shaggy, unkempt hair, and some had beards. No wonder McClellon was nervous. People, some of them colored people from surrounding towns, were staying in homes all over Frogbottom and Shortleaf. People just seemed to appear out of nowhere. From the start, everything had felt beyond his command, ever since King had first put the idea of the procession into his head.

As he drove slowly past the church, he could see several cook fires, the smoke rising straight up into the clear air; he could smell the food, roasting hamburgers and wieners, and he could hear laughter and guitar music. He could feel the sense of anticipation, and he felt restless, tense, thinking of McClellon's threat. But excitement tingled in his body, too; there was something reckless about all this that stimulated him. Everything was so new and frightening. He guided the car on past.

Cora was standing in the living room when he came through the front door.

"What'd he say?" she said.

"No way," Eldon said. "But we go anyway."

"Eldon . . ."

"We walk behind the hearse. Up Ashe Street, across Washington through downtown, then up Jackson to Shortleaf Cemetery. It's all set." He made his voice firm, steady.

"Without a permit?" she said after a minute.

"Yeah," he said.

She sat down. "I don't know, Eldon," she said. "I'm so tired. Everybody's so tired. How long can a body go on?"

He took off his coat. He sat down next to her on the sofa. "We have to do this, for Sally," he said.

She looked at him then. Her eyes seemed drawn, weary. "Who are all these people, Eldon?" she said.

"People who care about Sally. Who care about us."

"You sure?" she said. "Why do they care about us? Why?"

"Because they believe in what we're doin," he said, "They're willin to get their heads bashed in. I guess we oughtta be, too."

"Again?" she said, her voice soft. "Again? When will it end, Eldon?"

"I don't know that either." He studied the way the lamplight played over the soft skin of her arms. "Maybe this is just what life is for us."

"It's not fair." She said it as though it were merely a statement of fact. She seemed without emotion as she said it, without surprise. She hurts so, he was thinking. But I must not let her bring me down.

"No, it's not fair," he said. The love he felt for her, for the memory of Sally, was so intense that it blinded him, shut out everything else for a brief moment of peace. For a moment, he wanted just to protect her. To make her life—all their lives—better. But all the time he was feeling that, he knew. In order to do that, he had to risk those very lives. *Lord, will it ever end?* He put his arm around her shoulders, and they sat there together, content for the moment just to have one another in the still room.

⋘⋙

For years, O.B. had kept a bolt-action .22 rifle in his office. Tonight he had it with him when he drove home in his truck. He was uneasy about what was happening in the town, the people coming in, the sense of impending danger in the air. He kept two shotguns at home, a sixteen-gauge for shooting birds, which he rarely did anymore, and a twelve-gauge that he had used for deerhunting when he had the time. He knew they were there, in the front closet, if he needed them.

Just that morning, his secretary Paulette had asked him if he had heard the rumor about the boys.

"Everybody's talkin about it," she had said. "They say one of em got killed by the police in a shoot-out, and the other one escaped. They say it was . . ." Her voice faded.

"Yeah?" he had said, "what?"

"That it was Paul Siegel who got away. My husband said somebody said he was still around here. Hidin out. That's what he said."

"Is that right?" O.B. had hoped his expression masked his nervousness. "How could the police keep a shoot-out a secret? *Why* would they?"

"It's probably just a lot of talk," Paulette had said, looking away. "Folks say they went back up to the North."

He had waited until everyone was gone and then had gotten the rifle and put it in the pickup. Now he stopped in front of his house, looking up the walkway; it was first dark, but no lights were visible from the house. Nervousness, fear, ate away at him. He thought about Ellen and Paul, in the house together. Her life was hers now, separate from his. He knew he had to let her go, let her get away. What was there for her here? It was time to act, to clear the way for her.

He looked up and down the deserted street, then he got out and went up the walk. A rifle was a common sight in Hammond, especially in the fall. Nobody would have questioned him about it, yet the fact that he needed it bothered him deeply. He twisted the doorknob; the door was locked. He fumbled in his pocket for the keys, then unlocked the door, noticing the glow of light spilling down the hallway from the kitchen. He locked the door behind him.

Ellen and Paul were sitting at the Formica-topped table, the kitchen curtains closed, one of the back windows covered with a towel. They both looked at the rifle when he walked into the kitchen.

"Take that down," he said abruptly, more harshly than he had intended, pointing to the towel. "It's a dead giveaway. Why would somebody hang a towel in the window?" He regretted his tone immediately. It had been almost a month, and *he* hadn't thought of that before.

"Okay," Ellen said sheepishly. She stood up and took the towel down, closing the curtains as much as they would go. She stood holding the towel.

"Just stay away from the windows," he said to Paul.

"What's the matter, Daddy?" Ellen said.

"Nothin," he said, "nothin's the matter."

They were all jumpy, nervous with each other. This was no way to live.

He smelled food and walked over to the stove; there was a boiler, with wieners and kraut, heating on top, a loaf of white bread open on the table. Paul was spreading margarine on a piece of bread, and O.B. watched him cram half of it into his mouth, using the arm in the cast with dexterity. He was still thin, but his eyes were alert, bright. Both of them were staring at him, Paul's jaw working rhythmically. O.B. put the rifle down across the end of the table.

"Is that loaded?" Ellen said.

"No," O.B. said. "Not at the moment, anyway."

"What's goin on?" Paul said, chewing.

O.B. sat down. "I hear they're goin ahead with the march. The city wouldn't give em permission, but they're goin ahead anyway." He was looking levelly at the boy. "They're still comin in. People from all over. They say Martin Luther King's gonna preach at Sally's funeral. Then everybody's gonna walk, behind the hearse, all the way through town to the colored cemetery out in Shortleaf for the burial."

"What'll happen?" Ellen said.

"I don't know," O.B. said. "I hear the Klan's gonna be out in full force." Ellen sat stiffly in the chair. Her face was scrubbed and without makeup. Her hair, tousled and loose, was not quite dry from a washing. She looked so young to O.B. So fresh. He still could not bear to think about all she had been through. Looking at her, he was suddenly reminded of Martha, but he forced back the sudden, surprising feeling of loneliness. He would have to get used to that. He had not heard from her, and he would not allow himself to call her. He had made up his mind that there was no hope for them anyway.

"There's a rumor goin around," he said. There was no response in the eyes of the young people. "There's talk that you're still around here, Paul, maybe even in Hammond. I think we need to get you out of here."

"What?" Ellen and Paul said at the same time.

"I have an old pickup out at the shop that the mechanics use to go out into the country in. It's not much, but it runs good; it'll get you to Birmingham. You can catch a bus—"

"Daddy—"

O.B. looked away. He could not bear the ache in Ellen's eyes.

"But maybe," Ellen said, "With . . . with the television and everything. Maybe we'll get help."

"I don't know. Who knows what's gonna happen? All this is too dangerous."

Ellen was staring at him, her eyes wide.

"Eat your supper, Paul. And get whatever you need to take. We need to get goin."

There was a silence as the two young people stared at him.

"Are you sure, Daddy?" Ellen said. He could read her face. Suspicion that he was doing this to get rid of Paul. She still doubted him. She looked at him peculiarly all the time now, and more than once he had wondered what Martha might have told her about him and Cora. *That is just my own guilt I'm feeling. She knows nothing. She is a child.*

"Yeah, I'm sure," he said. He *was* sure. He wanted only happiness for her now. A life. He had no idea what was going to happen in the coming days, and he had already decided he would head Paul north on Highway 43, through Tuscaloosa, to Birmingham. He had a hundred dollars in cash from the shop to give him. The boy would be safer where nobody knew him. And Ellen would be safer if Paul was not with her. That was a certainty. There was always the future. For *them.* He stood up. "I'll eat later," he said. "I'll leave you two alone for a little while." He paused, looking down at them. "This is for the best, believe me."

Paul looked frightened, and there were tears in Ellen's eyes. O.B. turned and went up the hall, through the living room and out onto the screen porch. The night was pleasant, the air a hint of autumn. He stood looking through the rusty screen at the starry night, feeling hollow, empty, thinking of Cora, and he bit his lip. *I must do something. Eldon is leading them—and Cora—into a trap.* O.B. knew that Mac held all the cards, and getting Paul out of town was just a beginning, because there were the drug charges against the boy. He knew now that they were bogus, but they were there. And if Eldon tried to go without the parade permit, there would be a riot, he was sure of that. There would be bloodshed. He knew now that there was no way that Eldon could not march. The only real answer was to get help, to call in outside law, to get federal marshals in to stop the violence and to investigate poor little Sally Long's death. *If I were mayor . . . If I were in charge . . .*

O.B. felt an overwhelming sense of sadness and helplessness, alone on the porch in the cool night air.

〜〜〜・

Paul rode with Mr. Brewster out to his shop on the highway. Neither spoke as they moved slowly down the deserted streets, and Mr. Brewster pulled his truck around back, next to an old blue Chevrolet pickup, and parked and shut the lights. Mr. Brewster told him to wait while he went inside to get the keys.

Paul's dreams, asleep and awake, were haunted all the time now by the image of his father's face, stern and unmoving, slowly dissolving and reforming as the face in the dingy white sheet with the hacked eyeholes. He had slept fitfully since his abduction, lying awake much of the night thinking of the presence of the men behind the masks in the town, waiting patiently to move in and pounce when he closed his eyes or turned his back. The image of Joe Mancini's naked body, strung up in the tree with the blood running down his legs, his eyes wide in astonished and unbelieving anguish, was so indelibly stamped in his vision that it was there constantly: when he watched television with Ellen, when he tried to read the newspaper, when he closed his eyes for a moment to rest them.

The entire experience was like a prolonged nightmare, beginning when he had first come to this place. He had clung to Ellen as the only bright spot in the darkness, the only speck of real decency he could find. He did not understand these southern Negroes. Even after all these months, their world still seemed remote and closed to him. They were suspicious of him, even Long, and many of them remained hostile. He still believed in what he had come to do, but now it seemed even more confusing to him, more complex than he had ever imagined. Now he was both relieved and frightened to be leaving, saddened as well. He was relieved at the prospect of being out from under the brooding threats that seemed to hover in the air around him, and yet the highway, stretching out in its dark loneliness, terrified him. He imagined it lined with men like the ones who had kidnapped and almost killed him. And where did it lead? He had no place, really, to go. *But if I ever get away, I will never return to this place!* And then he thought of Ellen, and a sudden dim, confusing weightlessness, like grief, washed over him.

She had stayed at the house. They had clung to each other in the kitchen, both mumbling promises, promises that he did not know if he would ever have the strength to keep. *I love her.* But what did that mean? He knew that he did, but he needed, most of all, to be away, from this town, these people, even from her. Because she was a part of it. *No. She is not. She is like an angel in the midst of hell.*

Mr. Brewster came back out with the keys. He had not turned on any lights, and Paul could see his face only in shadow.

"This is dangerous, but you know that," Brewster said. "You understand . . ." He paused. Paul said nothing. He did not know what the man was trying to say. "I mean . . . well, this town is no place for you now." He paused again. "It wasn't way back last winter, either, if you want to know the truth."

"Look, I know what you must think of me, but—" Paul began.

"No, now. It's okay." Brewster was leaning against the truck, his eyes in darkness.

"I do love her," Paul said. "I wish I could change what happened."

"I know you do, Paul," Brewster said. "I don't blame you. Quit worryin about it."

"I mean, I plan to see her. When she comes north to school. I hope you—"

"All right," the older man said. He paused, and Paul waited. "Just park the truck in the bus station parkin lot, the Greyhound, there on Eighth Avenue downtown." His voice was thick with emotion, as though the details of his directions gave him an outlet from what he was feeling. Paul wished that he could see his face. He was a tall man, impressive, and Paul knew that by declaring himself, by making that run for mayor against bitter odds, he had alienated himself forever in Hammond. What he had done took courage, and he might pay for it for the rest of his life.

But Mr. Brewster would never leave this place. He would stay always. Paul watched him toss the small bag of his few clothes into the back of the pickup and put a loaded shotgun in the cab. "Just in case," he heard him mumble. *Just in case.*

"Listen, I don't know how to thank you for everything," Paul said. He held out his hand in the darkness, but the older man did not take it. Paul could not tell if he saw it or not. He dropped it back to his side.

"Okay," Brewster said. Then, after a minute, he said, suddenly, "I'm gonna get those charges dropped."

"Huh?"

"The drug charges. I've figured out a way. It's been comin clear to me the last few days. A plan. It'll be risky, but it might work. It might just solve a lot of problems at one whack."

"How?" Paul said.

"Never mind. Don't worry about it. You got enough on your mind. You know how to get on Forty-three, toward the river bridge?"

"Yeah," Paul said.

"Just go on through Tuscaloosa on Highway Eleven, it'll take you right to Birmingham. You'll be okay there."

"Well," Paul said, "thanks." He sensed then, more than saw, that Brewster was holding out his hand, and he grasped it, and the two men shook. When Paul pulled his hand back, it contained folded, crisp bills.

"Let us hear from you when you get to safety," Brewster said.

Paul had a sudden urge to embrace him, to cling to him. He turned away quickly and climbed into the truck, jamming the keys in and turning the starter. The truck roared.

"Don't stop for anything, till you get to Birmingham," Brewster said, and Paul nodded. He backed the truck. He could dimly see Brewster, standing beside his truck, and he waved. The truck smelled heavily of motor oil and grease, and the seat was hard and uncomfortable, but the engine purred like a sewing machine. He pulled into the highway, following the signs, driving back through town on the quiet, deserted streets, careful to observe the speed limit. His hands trembled on the wheel, the cast awkward and heavy, and he swallowed several times, trying to ease the sudden dryness in his throat. Soon he was through the edge of town and on the highway going north, and as he climbed the high river bridge, the old truck body rattling around him, he looked into the rearview mirror, seeing the few clusters of sparkling lights receding into the distance—the town, everything, fading farther and farther away behind him.

·~·~·~·

Back at the house, Ellen had been waiting for him in the kitchen. O.B. now sat at the table, waiting for the food to warm back up for him. He could tell Ellen had been crying, but she sat straight now, calm, her eyes dry. They sat in silence for a long time, neither needing to say anything. Finally, Ellen said, "You can come up and visit me in Vermont."

"Sure. I will," he said. He stood up and moved toward the stove, sniffing the sharp vinegar smell of the kraut. He looked at the curtains over the sink, his eyes misting as he thought about Eldon and Sally—Cora, Martha—the sorrow swelling in his chest like a hot balloon. "It was an awful thing, about Sally Long," he said, after a moment. "How can human beins do such a thing?" O.B.'s voice was low and pensive. "It's almost beyond belief."

"Yessir," Ellen said.

"I don't think I can feel the way I used to about this town, these people, ever again," O.B. said. "It's like findin out you've gone through your life with blinders on. You think, Was that me? It's too much."

"Sally used to say it was ignorance. A way of life that was based on ignorance," she said.

"I'm so sick of all that. I don't belong with that," he said. "I belong way out yonder with old Buddy Ed Webb, walkin along behind a mule and a plow, smellin the earth turnin over under my boots." He looked away from her. She was so young. She did not know what he was talking about, had no way of following what he was saying. "I belong out in a little tumbledown fishin shack alongside Chickasaw Bogue. I shoulda never left it, shoulda never given up what I had there." He thought again of the recent times he'd spent in that shack with Cora. "But I guess I had to. I had to just be a human man like everybody else. A human *white* man." He turned back around. Ellen was looking at him strangely, her face cocked to the side, her eyes questioning and curious.

"You mean," she said, after a minute, "when you were a boy?"

"Yeah," he said. "When I was a boy." He stood very still, looking at her, at the deep blue of her eyes, like blueberries in the summer, her dark hair framing her thin face. There was something piercing in Ellen's eyes now, an acute understanding. Then it suddenly hit him, with a certainty that startled him. *She knows! And she has probably known for a long time, maybe even from the beginning!* "It seems a long way away now," he said, as casually as he could, turning away.

"Daddy . . ." she said.

"I don't think I can talk about it anymore, Ellen," he said.

"All right," she said.

．～．～～．

Mac was tense and anxious all day, trying to do business as usual at the bank, trying to pretend around the lobby that things were normal. But all the customers wanted to talk about was what was going to happen tomorrow. *The niggers!* His stomach bothered him, and his phone rang all morning long, Lester calling several times to report on what was happening around the church and on what he was hearing from the other camp.

"Everybody says them ain't real nuns," Lester had said. "I tell you. This is some kinda rag-tagged bunch a 'folks. Juvenile delinquents and beatniks.

"And it *is* official. That nigger King—Martin Luther Coon—he's gonna preach at the funeral. Probably whup em up into no tellin what kinda frenzy. We got to decide what we gonna do, Mac. We got to have plans."

"Tonight," Mac had said.

"The Grand Exalted Dragon is here, too. He's stayin in a motel over in Meridian; thank God he ain't stayin out here. Ain't no tellin how many of them bastards will be showin up. They're havin a rally tonight. I ain't found out where yet, but I will."

"You doin a good job, Lester," Mac said.

"Well," Lester said, "I just want to stay on top of it, git ever'thing straight with the fellows from Montgomery, the troopers and all. I want this thing to go smooth, whatever happens. I think every goddam television camera and newspaper reporter in America is showin up on the streets of Hammond!"

.~.~.~.

By early afternoon, Mac knew that he couldn't concentrate on anything in his office, so he told his secretary he was going home. As he walked out to his car, he looked at the high, pure blue sky, inhaled the freshness of the September air. The first football game was coming up Saturday, and he was looking forward to going over to Tuscaloosa to see the Tide play Mississippi Southern. The Bear was loaded this year, and they were talking a national championship. *Jesus! Why did all this have to interfere with that? Was it asking too much to just let a man enjoy his football?* Lacy was getting ready to go over there tomorrow, to start her freshman year. She was excited about it. She and Belinda had been up to Birmingham shopping several times, and Lacy had so many trunks and things she couldn't get everything into her car. He and Belinda were going to carry some with them on Saturday—

Suddenly, like a quick blow to the gut, he though of Long's daughter. He shook his head, forcing away the sharp feelings of guilt that edged about in his mind. It was not his fault. *I had nothing to do with it.* Why, just a year ago at this time everything was normal, everybody was content and happy, and now things were so chaotic and tense. People just couldn't let well enough alone, he brooded. It was that crazy Long and his pushing, pushing!

He decided to drive by the church again, just to see the zoo. He was trying his best to see the humor in it, making wisecracks and joking with people in the bank all morning, but a cold, hard knot of tension lay like bitter bile in the pit of his stomach. Mac turned his Buick down Ashe Street, forcing a smile, trying to remember the jokes that he'd heard all his life about how long colored people waited to bury their dead, sometimes over a week, in order to allow all the family to gather from as far away as "Dee-troit." He remembered that old local radio program, *The Sick and Shut-in Show,* that he and his family had listened to on the car radio on the way to church on Sunday mornings. He remembered Dudley's mocking the announcer, mimicking the way he pronounced certain words. *"Internament* will be in Mount Hebron Cemetery, Levy Funeral Home in charge."

Mac could sense the carnival atmosphere around the church from a block away. It made him uneasy. Something bad was going to happen. He knew it. His ass was in a crack. Even his worry about Gulf

International and his investments seemed secondary now. He had begun to worry in earnest that he and Lester might really be just as guilty as Rooster Wembley and those boys who had murdered the Mancini boy, that if this thing blew up, got out of hand, then people would say they had known and covered it up. But they *hadn't* known. *He* hadn't really known anything. He didn't really know what Lester had been privy to; he hadn't asked, and he didn't plan to. But who would believe him? He had trucked with Rooster Wembley, and when you lie down with dogs, you get up with fleas! If he got tied in with all that, he would be ruined in Hammond; his reputation would be shot. He would be denied that feeling of contentment and well-being that he knew would come when he propped his boots on that stone fireplace out at Shady Grove Plantation, a glass of bourbon in his hand, surrounded by the smells of tobacco and barbecue, the sounds of the calm and stately dialogue of powerful men like himself. Never to know that! He shuddered.

He slowed, guiding the car carefully along the narrow street by the church. He couldn't believe the dregs of humanity that seemed to have gathered here. It was like insects flocking around an opened jar of jam. He could have understood the niggers coming in, but who were these white people, and where did they come from? He felt a sense of righteous anger at them: The very idea of their thinking they had a right to come in here and tell *his people* how to run their business galled him, made him so furious he was speechless. Especially *these* people. He could hear music and singing coming from a group gathered on the front steps of the church. *Shit*, he thought. What were they so goddam happy about? This was supposed to be a funeral, after all. Mac shook his head, gritting his teeth, his fingers squeezing the steering wheel. He had stopped the car, and now several white young folks were gazing at him with smart-aleck looks on their faces. One of them, grinning broadly, gave Mac the finger. *Damn!*

He gunned the motor and felt the big car drift easily on down the street, turning the corner, passing Eldon Long's little house, seeing him standing in his front yard. Long had exchanged his severe black suit for a pair of khaki pants and a blue shirt—it looked like a denim work shirt. he watched Mac go by with no reaction showing on his face, and Mac thought *Lord, now's the time he ought to have on the suit, getting ready for a funeral, instead of finally starting to dress like a nigger!*

He drove home faster than he normally did, down his street, and into his driveway. The configuration of cars was there; Dudley had just gotten in from school, was just now going in the front door. Mac watched it slam behind him. They would have more parking space starting tomorrow when Lacy left for the university. He went inside, draping his coat over a chair, expecting to smell dinner cooking, and then realized that he was much earlier than he usually was. Dudley was slouched on a sofa.

"I'm not gonna make it this year, Dad," he said. "I've got Miss Minnie for English. I'm a dead man."

"Who? What?" Mac said.

Dudley looked at him, his eyes narrowed. "What planet you on?" he said.

"Listen, I've got my mind on a thousand things," Mac said. He went over and looked out on the sunporch. It was empty. "Where's your mother?"

"How would I know?" Dudley said irritably. "I just got home."

"I'm right here," Belinda said, coming into the living room. "What are you doin home at this hour, Mac?"

She had on a black dress with large white polka dots and round white earrings like small saucers. She was holding a big black straw purse.

"Nothin's goin right today," he said.

There was a long silence. His wife and his son looked at him questioningly.

"Well, I have a study club meeting." Belinda shrugged. "Why don't you go up and take a nap?"

"I don't want a nap," Mac said.

"I'm late," she said. "I'm sure there's nothin to all this, Mac—just ignore it and it'll go away." She was moving toward the door, the purse under her arm, pulling on long black gloves. "You didn't block me in, did you?"

"No," Mac said. "Shit."

Belinda stopped, giving him a dirty look. "By the way Lynn called from the bank. O.B. Brewster was trying to get in touch with you. She said she told him that you had gone home."

"Did he call here?" Mac said.

"No. Did he, Dudley?"

"Don't ask me. I just got home. Shit," Dudley said.

"See?" Belinda said to Mac, her eyes flashing. She went out, slamming the door behind her.

"If the goddam World War Three was startin, she would go to a study club meetin," Mac said, and Dudley laughed, throwing his leg over the arm of the sofa, his dingy blank canvas shoe dangling in the air.

Mac went to the kitchen, thinking he would have a drink. Melvinie was sitting at the kitchen table, peeling potatoes. She looked up.

"Lawsy," she said, "what you doin home, you sick?"

"Naw," he said, "I ain't sick. I'm tired." He looked at her soft gray dress, her blue bandanna tied around her head. She was peeling new potatoes, putting them into a red bowl. He sat down at the table. "Listen," he said, and she looked up at him, her eyes spent, red-veined, her heavy, broad face a mask of indifference. "Listen," he said, "you plannin on marchin in that parade tomorrow?"

"Uh-huh," she said. "I sho is." Her hands continued to work with the short knife. She could peel the potatoes without looking at them, her eyes fastened on Mac's face. "I don't go to Rev'ren Long's church. But I know him. I know his peoples. Yassuh. I be there."

He sat there for a moment, watching her hands on the potatoes. He was irritated with her, but he didn't know how to respond. The thought of threatening her with firing flickered through his head. He looked back at her broad face, and she was staring at him, her watery, aged eyes boring into him. He had a sudden, fleeting sense that she could see into his soul, see his guilt there. *Guilt? What guilt? I had nothing to do with anything!* He almost blurted that out before he caught himself. *I'm just tired.*

Then he heard the front doorbell ring, *bong-bong. Bong-bong.* He thought he heard voices, then he heard Dudley's shoes shuffling down the hallway. "Dad," he heard him say. "Dad?" He stuck his head in the door. "A man to see you."

"Who?"

"Mr. Brewster." Dudley came on into the kitchen. He opened the cookie tin and rummaged around.

"Git yo nasty hand outta there!" Melvinie said. "Ain't nothin in there for you!" He opened the cabinet next to the refrigerator. "Git outta there, boy, fore I snatch a bald spot in yo head!" Melvinie said. She waved the little paring knife at him.

Mac stood up. *O.B.? Maybe he'd come to his senses. Maybe I can talk him into calming his buddy Long down, talking some sense into his nappy head!*

.~.~.~.

O.B. stood on the sunporch. He seemed nervous and uncomfortable. The door to the living room was closed.

"What can I do for you, O.B.?" Mac said.

O.B. looked steadily back at Mac, staring at him with his pale eyes. His blond hair was shaggy, needed cutting. He looked tired. Maybe he was beginning to show his age, at last. O.B. took a deep breath. He seemed to have rehearsed this, thought it out carefully.

"Well," O.B. said, "I came over to see if you might want to call in some help."

"Help?" Mac said. *What the hell is he talking about?* O.B. just stood there. "It ain't me that needs help. That crazy fucker Long is goin right on with that big march tomorrow. Ain't any way I can let that happen. I made the decision: no permit. We got troopers comin in, if we need any 'help.' I been on the phone to Montgomery. I talked to John Patterson hisself! He says if they break the law, stop em! That's what the troopers are for. Help?"

"Okay." O.B. held up his hands.

"Listen, now," Mac said, leaning forward. "I *know* for a fact that the Klan is plannin on stoppin em, too! I hear they've brought in the Great Grand Holiness Bullshitter or whatever the fuck they call him, from Louisiana, and *they* want to make a big fuckin deal out of this, too! People have lost their fuckin minds, O.B. The only help I need right now is somebody to help me make Long see the light and cancel this shit. Otherwise, I'm caught right in the middle."

"Why?" O.B. said.

"Huh?" Mac was perplexed at the way O.B. was acting. *What the hell is he talkin about?*

"Why are *you* in the middle, Mac? All you got to do is call in the federal marshals. Turn it over to em—"

"Shit!" Mac felt his fury mounting. "Don't talk to me about the federal government! Look at that asshole Kennedy. I feel like I'm sittin on a goddam keg of dynamite, O.B., and it's about to go off!"

"Calm down, Mac," O.B. said.

"That's easy for you to say. You ain't the goddam mayor, in case you forgot."

"Just turn it over to somebody else. That's all—"

"I can't *do* that, O.B.! I would be goin against what the people in this town want, and you know it."

"The white people."

"The *majority* of the people! The folks who own the property and vote and run the schools and everygoddamthing else!" Mac felt his breath getting short, felt his temples pounding, and he took a deep breath. He sat down in one of the low-slung chairs, breathing evenly, and O.B. stood there a moment, then followed suit and sat. Mac realized he'd been rattling on like a maniac. He felt that same distant and confusing and nagging sense of guilt, which he willed away. "O.B.," Mac said, after a minute, "I guess I just thought it would all just . . . go away. Take care of itself, you know? I mean, I figured these niggers stirrin up would git tired of it, lose interest. They probably will. It's just takin em longer than I thought it would. I mean, all this marchin to the cemetery and stuff. It's like it's . . . catchin on. They all got to git in on it, like it's some kinda fad or somethin! Jesus."

"No, Mac," O.B. said, "it ain't a fad. It ain't gonna go away."

What did he know? Mack cocked his head to the side, peering at O.B. "You been talkin to Long?"

"I don't have to talk to Eldon to know it. What you don't realize, Mac, is that this ain't anything new. I bet the first black slave that was ever brought to this country was thinkin about this, had it in his mind even way back then—"

"Shit, don't tell me—"

"—because that's what it means to be a man, Mac. Eldon's not a nigger. He's a man. Just like you and me."

Mac shook his head and sighed, feeling weary. "I've heard all about these goddam theories! But a nigger is a nigger, and a white man is a white man, and that's the way it's always been and the way it always will be. You can't change it by pretendin otherwise. I got nothin against em. But they got their place just like I got mine. And society won't work unless you learn your place and stay in it. Try to change nature, and bad things happen. That's how people like Long's daughter get killed. I would expect you to know that, O.B. I would expect you to tell your buddy Long that."

"No," O.B. said, "I won't tell him anything."

"Oh, now, O.B.," Mac said quickly, "there's some things you're forgettin here—"

"Matter of fact, I'm thinkin of marchin in that funeral procession tomorrow myself."

Jesus H. Christ! "Are you a white man, O.B.? Or what? Go to him and—"

"No, I said. We been through that."

"Wait a minute," Mac said, "wait a goddam minute." *I'll bring this goddam nigger-lover to his knees.* "You still got that note comin due, don't forget that. I'm willin to—"

"Fuck the note!"

Mac was stunned, dumbfounded. "Huh?"he blurted.

"I don't care about that, Mac." Mac sat there, uneasy now. He knew there was some big reason O.B. had come to the house this way—it was unlike him. Something just told him that he didn't really want to know what the reason was. O.B. looked self-satisfied, smug. He was a fool. Wasn't he?

Mac spoke tentatively, hesitantly. "We talkin about your business, O.B. We talkin about your livelihood."

O.B. smiled at him. "I'm free of that, Mac," he said.

"Free? What you talkin about?"

"I'm talking about . . . bein free." He seemed to be picking his words carefully. "Bein able to do whatever the hell I wanna do. If you wanna take this business from me, fuck it. This business ain't me. You want it, you can have it. Welcome to the headache!"

"Wait a minute now," Mac said, quickly, sudden fear gripping him. "I don't *want* your business. I never said that." He sat looking at O.B. with alarm, beads of sweat on the skin of his face. His arms were flat on the arms of the chair, and his body seemed to be tense and straining.

O.B. couldn't tell if he was trying to pull himself out of the chair or push himself back deeper into it.

"Just sit there a minute, Mac," O.B. said with outward calm, and Mac peered questioningly up at him. O.B. could see bewilderment mixed with fear in his eyes. "Just hear me out. Listen to what I got to say before you say anything."

Mac slowly nodded, his eyes full of suspicion.

O.B. had agonized over this plan, all the risks involved, the rightness or wrongness of it. Suppose Mac wouldn't buy it? Then what? It was a calculated risk. And O.B. was going to have to lie, to tell a blatant lie, to make it work. It could easily be disproved later, but it was the immediate moment he was counting on. He stared at Mac, watching his eyes dart nervously about. Mac was frightened of all this, terrified. He was being destroyed by it; O.B. could see it happening. And now he would apply what could be the final blow, and it was a lie. A *lie!* Where, he had finally asked himself, lying awake in the dark night, where does good come from if not from evil? Maybe two wrongs *can* make a right. He had to do it. There was no choice. He had to take the chance.

"I want you to do four things," O.B. said tightly. "First, I want you to call in the FBI, to look into that church bombing and the kidnappin of those boys—"

Mac was shaking his head, muttering under his breath.

"Wait now, goddammit," O.B. said. "Second, give Eldon that parade permit. Three"—O.B. held up three fingers before Mac's face—"call in federal marshals to oversee the march and see that nobody gets hurt."

Mac laughed harshly, almost a snort. There was a moment of tense silence. "Jesus Christ," Mac said, "what the hell is the fourth?"

"Have those phony drug charges against Paul Siegel dropped."

"I can't—"

"You can, too. All you got to do is make a call to the D.A. down at Ashville."

"Wait! Jesus! You crazy, O.B.? What the hell is this?"

"Because you want to stay out of jail," O.B. said.

Mac stared at him for a moment. He seemed to squirm in the chair, his eyes darting about. Then he chuckled uneasily. "You've lost your goddam mind, O.B.," he said, his voice choked and raspy.

"I have a signed, sworn statement," O.B. said, "from Paul Siegel that says you were one of the men who kidnapped him and Mancini and murdered Mancini—"

"No—!"

"He recognized you. And it goes on to say that you also bragged openly to him about plantin that dope in his car, along with Rooster Wembley and some others who're named in this statement!"

"But . . . it's not true." Mac's voice was shaking. "I . . . I wasn't there. You can ask anybody. I . . ."

"I don't know about that," O.B. said, "all I know is what he said. He's alive to testify to it, too, and the signed statement, one copy of it anyway, is in my safety deposit box, right in your own bank." O.B. could see Mac's eyes turn inward. "And if you try to go in there and get it and destroy it, then there won't be any doubt—"

"He's lyin! The son of a bitch is lyin!"

"He overheard y'all talkin about bombin the church, too, makin plans for all that—"

"Goddammit, O.B., you got to believe me. I wasn't . . . I wasn't . . ."

"But if you do what I ask, those four things, then I'll tear the statement up. Paul will go back North, and you won't have to worry about it anymore." O.B. stood looking down at Mac. He didn't know how deeply Mac was involved in everything, but he remembered the look on his face that night at Lester's office, after the boys had disappeared. He was gambling that Mac was in deep enough that he couldn't take a chance, but not so deep that he wouldn't call in the FBI and the marshals. "They'll find that boy's body eventually, Mac, and all this'll be pretty hot for you. You know too much. The other boy is safe. There's no way you and your buddies can get him—"

"Stop this 'my buddies' shit, O.B.," Mac said, trying to be tough, his voice shaking.

"Wake up, Mac," O.B. said. "This is your chance to get out from under this, turn it over to somebody else." Mac just sat there, his eyes focused on the black-and-white tile of the floor. "We both know that it doesn't matter whether you were *really* there or not. You might as well have been. You've known all along what was goin on, and you didn't do a goddam thing about it. How you think that's gonna look if you keep on coverin it up? It's gonna come out, Mac, sooner or later. The truth. And how's it gonna look?"

"Hold it, goddammit," Mac said. His lips were trembling, and he wiped the perspiration from his face.

"Sally Long's blood is on your hands, Mac, as surely as if you'd lit the fuse!"

"I said leave me alone," Mac blurted, his voice shrill now, childish and churlish, and he looked around the sunporch as though he was confused, disoriented, desperate. O.B. waited. Then Mac spoke. "All right. All right," he said softly, almost a whisper, "who you want me to call?"

O.B. was aware that he had been holding his breath only when he let it out in a long sigh. Relief flowed through him. "Start with the FBI office in Birmingham. They'll know who to call next," O.B. said.

•~·~·~·

Ellen caught glimpses of the hearse from time to time, but she mostly saw only the backs of those marching ahead of her and the placid, smug, and sometimes startled looks on the faces of the people lining the streets. When they recognized her, they would punch the person next to them, then laugh, point, call out: "Hey, Ellen, what you doin with the jigaboos?" or "Hup, hup, hup, hup!" She was thinking of Paul, wondering where he was, if he was safe. She wondered where her father was.

Her father had seemed so tired this morning when he'd told her simply that Mac McClellon had "seen the light." He had sat at the table, his shoulders slightly hunched, his large hands curled around a cup of coffee. She had noticed the puffiness in his face, the lines around his eyes. His blond hair was tinged with more gray now than she had ever before noticed; it was almost as though he had aged overnight. His eyes seemed tormented but resigned. And when he looked at her, they were full of pain. She knew how much he still suffered over the abortion, but they didn't talk about it. They did not have to. She would see him stealing glances, quick, agonized stares at her as though he were trying to fix her image in his mind. Her heart went out to him. She knew what a lonely man he was. How hard it was for him to see her go.

She thought she must have known the truth about him and Cora for a long time, since she was a little girl, but it had been buried somewhere, lost. She did not know how long it would take her to deal with all of that. She could clearly see that they must have loved each other deeply, and she knew without asking that the rumors she heard were true, that it was still going on, and it was all tied up in her mind with her and Paul. It explained a lot about her mother to her, and she felt a pang of sadness, of missing her, and she vowed to try to see her again, to see her now as another woman. But it made her, even more, want to get away. She understood completely her father's locking in on his youth, his not being able to turn loose his youth with Cora; and she must have known what was not being said, what could not be put into words, spoken aloud. She knew the pains of that kind of separation, the helplessness and insecurity of that kind of uncertainty. She knew it now. As her steps fell steadily beneath her, on the hot pavement, she felt as though she were walking through time, as though she were somehow present and witnessing her own birth, entering an irresolute existence full of incertitude and danger. She knew she could not know what lay before her. She was certain that Paul would call, would be there, and yet she knew that, somehow, even now, she did not completely know him, was not sure of him, and she wondered if she would ever be. She wondered if a person could ever be sure of another human being, could ever really know another person. She did not think she would ever know the answer.

They turned the corner onto Jackson. The sun was higher now; she could feel its warmth on the top of her head. Up ahead, beyond the hearse and the police car, she saw a line of men clad in white sheets and cone-shaped headdresses. They carried the U.S. and the Confederate battle flags, and they waved them back and forth, back and forth. They seemed to be blocking the street.

Then she caught sight of her father, at the edge of the street, just ahead of the police car and the hearse.

O.B. watched the police car turn the corner, and then came the hearse, glinting low and sleek in the morning sunlight. He looked back up Jackson Street where the men in the white sheets were. Their costumes looked almost comical in the sunlit morning. There were about thirty of them, carrying brightly colored flags, their faces peeping through round holes in the headdresses. He would bet money that Rooster was there. And Rusty Jackson.

Two rows of state troopers in their riot gear, their Smokey-the-Bear hats perched on their heads and gas masks hanging from their shoulders, lined the street on both sides of the group of Klansmen. There were also men in business suits whom O.B. knew to be federal marshals watching things. The air was tense, a hushed expectancy settling over the Klan, the federals, and the sparse crowd of spectators as the procession rolled closer. Then the robed Klansmen began talking loudly among themselves, laughing and pointing down the street toward the procession.

O.B. had moved all day in a kind of haze, a dreamlike state in which he seemed to be outside his own body. He knew that his fatigue came from the weeks of tension, his long, futile attempt to run for office, something that was so outside his nature that just thinking about it had worn him out. He was tired from last night, the phone calls to Ashville and then to Washington, his taking over as Mac grew more and more despondent, sinking ever deeper into a paralyzing depression, finally into a state of immobility in which he stared silently at the floor.

And now that was over and done with. He was already deeply missing Ellen in anticipation of her leaving. He strained to see Cora in the crowd as the marchers began to go by, feeling his breath quicken even as he thought of her. Through it all, he had had Cora constantly on his mind. His feelings for her seemed to settle in an aching desire to return to the past, to go back and know that everything that had happened, over the years, had never happened at all. Maybe it was his wish that he could somehow go back to that innocent, glowing time that propelled him off the curb to fall in with the marchers, near the front. Those close to him looked at him curiously, questioningly. The Klansmen had begun to move forward now, toward the police car. O.B. saw the blue light on top of the patrol car come on, beginning to spin around. The cruiser picked up speed, scratching to a stop a half-block in front of the Klansmen. The procession moved on slowly behind it, the hearse's taillights blinking red in the sunlight, O.B. hearing the shuffle of footsteps on the pavement, the breathing, the

muffled comments. A policeman got out of the car; O.B. saw it was
Hoyt Blessing, hitching up his pants, looking self-consciously around
at the spectators and at the sheet-clad men in the street. Three other
men, dressed in dark suits, got out of the car. O.B. knew they were
federal marshals. They stood in the street as the funeral procession
came on slowly up the street and the group of Klansmen moved toward
it. One of the marshals held up his hands toward the group.

"Halt right there!" he said loudly, his voice barely audible back
where O.B. was. He had on a brown suit, buttoned tightly across his
belly, and a flat salt-and-pepper crew cut. The group of robed men
came on, straggling, several of them holding Confederate flags and
stepping boldly out, some holding back. "Halt, in the name of the
United States government!" he said again. They came to a ragged halt.
The funeral procession moved slowly up the street; O.B. felt its power
behind him, like a deliberate flood. They were close now, only the
police car and the hearse separating them. "You are to disperse immediately," the man said, standing flat-footed, his hands on his hips.

"We got just as much right—" a voice said, and O.B. recognized it
as Rooster's. He made Rooster out now. The man was standing at the
front, the clumsy costume not hiding the leaning, tilted way he stood
now that O.B. knew which one he was.

"These people have a parade permit; you don't," the marshal said.
"I am an agent of the United States government, and I am ordering
you to disperse, peacefully and quickly. Do you understand?"

"Shit. . . ." Rooster drawled, and there was some laughter and snorting from his men.

"Sergeant Weathers?" the marshal called, and one of the troopers
answered.

"Yes sir?"

"Disperse them," the man said.

"Wait a minute—" Rooster said. The troopers were moving into the
street. O.B. could see Eldon and Cora in the front row, straining their
necks to see what was going on.

He didn't know who moved first. He heard shouting and then heard
crashing glass as the windshield of the hearse was shattered by a rock,
splintering into millions of sparkling shreds of glass still locked in the
frame. Women began to scream. There was scuffling in the middle of
the street as several of the Klansmen and troopers grappled hand-to-
hand, the Klan's oddly feminine-looking white gowns flopping around
their pants legs and muddy boots. Some of the troopers flailed away
with the sticks at several Klansmen who were throwing chunks of bricks

toward the marchers. The procession had broken ranks, and O.B. saw several young black men, led by a muscular young man in a dingy, stained T-shirt, surge forward.

At the same time, several of the Klansmen waded into the crowd of mourners, some swinging sticks that they must have had hidden under their robes. O.B. was rooted to the spot, hearing the screams and cries of pain. He was shocked as he saw several elderly black men fighting back feebly, saw a gray-haired old woman go down to the pavement, her arms over her head. He could see the young black men fighting with the Klansmen, pulling their headdresses off, pounding their startled faces with their fists.

The chaos swirled around him, and now the sounds of gunfire. *Firing into the air! Surely, they are firing into the air!* The two groups were merged, now, and the air was filled with the acrid scent of gunpowder. The siren on the police car went off, an abrupt *whoop, whoop, whoop.* O.B. felt a sudden, frenzied passion to be with the angry black boys, and without thinking, he impulsively ran forward, grabbing the first whirling mass of white he saw and pulling the headdress away. He held tight as he looked into the flinty eyes of Rusty Jackson, and O.B. swung his fist, all the pent-up rage and frustration within him behind the blow, and as if in slow motion, he saw his fist crash into Jackson's face and saw the bright red blood spurt from the man's nose as Jackson sank to the pavement. O.B. backed away, flexing his throbbing fist as he searched the crowd, looking for Ellen. He saw her, back in the rows of marchers, watching the fighting with round, frightened eyes.

Somebody swung at O.B. from behind, but he sensed it and ducked in time, staggering away. He heard a low popping noise, like a firecracker, then another. The troopers were firing tear gas. Grayish-green clouds were already billowing. He ran for the lawn at the edge of the street and saw people stumbling, covering their faces; he saw Rusty Jackson, bleeding, crawl into the gutter. The breeze picked up the clouds of gas, swirling them toward the blue, cloudless sky. The frenzy seemed to subside immediately with the spitting gas.

O.B. saw several Klansmen, their gowns now ragged, retching, vomiting onto the pavement. The troopers, wearing gas masks, waded through the crowd, pulling men to their feet, handcuffing them, leading them away.

O.B.'s eyes burned, and he could see others rubbing their eyes; he could see Eldon and Cora now, safe behind the hearse, watching as the Klansmen were being subdued and the troopers were regrouping.

The gas shells were sputtering out and the tear gas drifting off into the air. O.B. saw Rooster, his hands handcuffed behind him, and several of the other Klansmen, their robes torn and muddy and bloodstained, being led away by the troopers. Among them was Jackson, his head down, his wiry body as tense as a bow as blood dripped from his face. O.B. saw the young black man, also handcuffed; his black face was contorted, smears of blood staining the front of his shirt. O.B. remembered him then as being Sally's boyfriend. He had seen him in the parade from Maud's, at the theater. He remembered the fierce anger in his eyes. The street was littered with dirty clumps of white cloth, pieces of rocks, troopers' hats. Nobody had bothered with O.B. They were arresting only those who were still fighting. He melted into the crowd.

All the spectators and the marchers were hushed now, an eerie quiet settling over everything. The police car was parked at an angle across the street; the hearse with its crushed windshield glinted in the high sunlight. There was only the sound of the moans, with some sniffling and gasping from the gas. O.B. looked up and down the street. It had become quiet Jackson Street once again, with tiny St. Thomas Roman Catholic Church sitting back from the sidewalk and old Mrs. Virginia Stabler's huge three-story house on the corner. The police car moved out slowly, its left headlight shattered, its driver's side door dented. The hearse was moving again, too. O.B. saw Gus Levy driving it, his face out the opened side window so that he could see around the ruined windshield. The marchers began to move then in the eerie quiet, the only sounds their uneven breathing and the shuffling of their feet on the pavement.

Then, almost in time with the sounds of their feet, someone began to sing, a lone voice at first, quickly picked up and softly echoed. O.B. stood still on the sidewalk, his arms hanging limply at his sides, listening to the ancient chant: "*I looked over Jordan and what did I see . . . comin for to carry me home . . . a band of angels, comin after me . . . comin for to carry me home! Swing Low . . . sweet chari-oh, comin for to carry me home . . . swing low, sweet chari-oh . . . comin for to carry me home . . .*"

O.B. was one with the rhythm, as though it were coming from inside his head, as though he felt it in the pulse of his own blood. Numb, moving as though he were under water, he eased back into the street and fell into step with the marching mourners. He was aware of the sun on his head, and then suddenly, he felt *the nearly physical sensation of the smooth hoe handle in his hand, with the promise of cool water at the end of the row.* He could see Eldon and Cora ahead of him, and his eyes misted over in that moment—for both of them, he realized. The sound of the singing echoed and reechoed in his brain and in his soul as he marched: A *band of angels . . . comin after me . . . comin for to carry me home. . . .*

•~•~•~•

From where Eldon stood, his arm around Cora, he could see down a hill covered with rows of gray-white tombstones and, beyond that, across a railroad track to an open field where the rest of the Klansmen had gathered, standing with their flags, the sunlight reflecting off their white robes. The smell of violence, of the tear gas—the belly-tightening fear that he had felt—lingered with him, but now he focused on Martin King's words, so melodious in the early afternoon air.

"He that raised up Jesus from the dead will also give life to our mortal bodies, by His Spirit that dwelleth in us. Wherefore my heart is glad, and my spirit rejoiceth, my flesh also shall rest in hope." There was silence. A lone cough nearby, subdued crying. Across the way, in the field, he could hear the harsh voices, the rough laughter, distant and small and irrelevant. "In sure and certain hope of the resurrection to eternal life through our Lord Jesus Christ, we commend to Almighty God our sister Sally, and we commit her body to the ground." He felt Cora tense. His own heart was swollen in his chest. Eldon looked around the crowd gathered at the raw grave, the mound of moist black earth poised and ready to cover her forever. He saw his father, his paunch sagging, his eyes liquid, his arm around his mother, who was bent over, her body like dry, fragile sticks; she had walked the entire way, bless her. He had worried that she would be hurt, but she had seemed impervious, the hatred swirling around her like a breeze, ruffling her but not touching her. ". . . earth to earth, ashes to ashes, dust to dust," the voice went on, "The Lord bless her and keep her . . ." Eldon felt the sun on him, like a warm hand; he heard crying, a low, steady weeping around him. Thankfully, the rude noises from across the railroad tracks were faraway and removed. "Rest eternal grant to her, Lord, and let light perpetual shine upon her."

Eldon's eyes moved slowly over the crowd, and he saw Ellen, dabbing her eyes with a wadded Kleenex. Hardenia Moon's face was a mask of grief, two shiny tracks of tears down her cheeks. He remembered the grimace of hate on Nate's face as they had led him roughly away. And closed his eyes. He could smell the moist pungency of the turned earth, the cloying sweetness of the flowers; he could smell

Cora's salty body, her faint scent of jasmine, and he felt the searing tears welling up inside him, but he choked them back, listening to King's voice like velvet, as tender and soft as the old shuck bed that he had slept in as a child.

"May her soul, and the souls of all the departed, through the mercy of God, rest in peace. Amen."

When Eldon opened his eyes, he saw O.B. The mourners had begun to sing now. They were holding hands, the rows of people around the grave, crossing their arms across their chests and grasping the hands of the two people on either side, as they sang louder still, some of them humming, drowning out the Klan's protests. They swayed back and forth, a slow, almost tantalizing rhythm, growing louder and louder. "My Lord He calls me . . . He calls me by the thunder . . . The trumpet sounds within my soul . . . I ain't got long to stay here!"

Eldon sang along. He had learned the song years ago, in his boyhood, at the country frame church, and at the dingy little wood-frame training school in the Flatwoods. It now had a new meaning to him. He felt Cora's hand grasping his tightly, heard her voice in his ear, and when he looked at O.B., their eyes locked. O.B. stood apart, by himself. He was not singing. Eldon thought for a moment that O.B. was standing barefoot in loose, faded overalls, his hair shaggy across his forehead, but when he blinked his eyes, he saw that O.B. had on a tie, knotted loosely and crookedly under the collar of his wrinkled white shirt, and that his eyes were not the eyes of a youth. *He is my brother. He is my mortal enemy.*

Eldon could tell, could almost clearly see, that O.B.'s eyes moved back and forth, back and forth, from Cora to him, and back to Cora.

Always, back to her.

⌁⌁⌁

The house seemed so empty with Ellen gone. O.B. sat at the table in the kitchen, looking at the few dirty dishes sitting on the drainboard, trying to summon the energy to wash them. The Sunday paper was scattered on the table, the funnies on top; O.B. had finished reading it, and now the day stretched before him, as barren and unfilled as the house. He thought of maybe driving out into the country to see his folks. He had not seen them for a while, but the idea depressed him even more than he already was. They would be full of platitudes, superficial things to say about all that had happened. He would be reminded of how little they understood him.

Bright morning sunlight slanted through the windows. The weather had turned cold all of a sudden, the leaves everywhere blazing, brilliant and intense. O.B. had taken to driving aimlessly for hours at a time, listening to his thoughts and the pickup's motor purring gently.

He had to sort it all out in his mind, try to think it through, all that had happened to him and would happen to him now. Where would he go from here? Mac had resigned the mayor's office. O.B. had heard that he was in some kind of hospital down on the Mississippi Gulf Coast. Everybody around town whispered that he had had a nervous breakdown, that he had been driven to it by all "the nigger business" and the fact that Gulf International Paper Company had announced that it was changing its plans, pulling out, not building the plant in Hammond after all. Lyman Wells had called O.B. and asked him if he might consider being appointed interim mayor, and then later he could run for the office when a special election was set up.

"Some of us have been anticipating all this for a long time, O.B.," Wells had said to him. "I was delighted that you were willing to run for the office when you did, and I hope you'll consider it now. Whattayasay?"

"I don't know," O.B. had said. He was flattered, but the idea still frightened him.

"Well, you can count on me," Wells had said. "Listen, why don't you come round some time, and let's talk? Okay?"

"All right," O.B. had said. Then, suddenly, "Listen, I will be the interim. I want to."

"You do? Great!"

"And then . . . who knows?" O.B. had sat there thinking of his future. *Yes. I will keep on doing what I can.*

"I hear your daughter's off at school, right?" Wells continued. "It's not good for you to be there all alone like that. Huntin season's comin up—I'll be callin you. You still like to hunt deer?"

"No, not really," O.B. said.

"Well, the Shady Grove Deer Drive is in a couple of months; you'll get an invitation, anyway. We sometimes manage to . . . well, do a lot of business out there. And drink a lot of bourbon, too." Wells laughed. "You play poker?"

"Sometimes," O.B. said. "I don't know about the hunt though. Let me get back to you?"

"Sure thing, Mr. Mayor," Wells had said. "Listen, you sound down. Anything I can help you with?"

"Well, to tell you the truth, yeah," O.B. had said. "I've got this note that's overdue at Planters and Merchants. And Mac . . . well, before he left, he was gonna foreclose and all, and I—"

"Hey, O.B.," Wells said. "There are other banks, all over this part of the state. Don't worry about it. I'll make some calls, okay?"

"Okay," O.B. said.

As the phone had clicked off, O.B. had been once again surrounded by the quiet and the loneliness of the empty house. The driving around helped. He knew that Martha was never coming back; he had not heard from her since he had had Lyman send her the divorce papers. He knew that she was as relieved as he was that it was finally over. She knew how he felt about Cora, and she could not live with that. That was all. He thought of the town; it would never be the same again, after all that had happened. Rooster and Rusty Jackson and Kershaw and several others had been arrested and charged with the murder of Joe Mancini and the kidnapping and attempted murder of Paul Siegel. Mancini's body had been found under tons of dirt at an overpass on a new Birmingham-to-New-Orleans superhighway that was being built across Greene County up north of town. One of the men had confessed and led authorities to the body. It had been Red Kershaw who had broken down and told all, even confessing to planting the drugs in Siegel's car and having a hand in the bombing of the church. He gave a list of names to the FBI.

O.B. heard a knocking at the back door. He eagerly moved to answer it. Nobody had visited the house since Ellen had left for Vermont, almost three weeks ago. He pulled open the door, and then he just stood there unable to move or speak.

Cora stood on the back steps. She wore a dark gray wool dress and a white sweater. The sunlight glinted on the grayish highlights in her short-cropped hair as she looked at him, her eyes dark, almond-shaped. *The back door,* O.B. thought. *She had come to the back door.* The blood quickened within him.

"I wanted to talk to you," she finally said.

He didn't answer her, his tongue feeling large and dry in his mouth. He stepped back from the door then and nodded to her.

"Come on in," he said. She followed him into the kitchen, and he gestured toward the chairs around the table. "Sit down." He found he could barely look at her.

"That's okay," she said.

She stood very straight with her hands clasped in front of her. He had thought of her constantly since the funeral. Her dark eyes, the line of her neck. The way she had looked, standing there next to Eldon, her back straight, gazing off into the distance as though she were untouched by anything earthly, untouched by any of the pain and years.

"I needed . . . I wanted, to tell you," she said, "how grateful we were that you were there. It took courage."

"No," he said, "not much."

"Yes, it did. Don't think I don't know. I have to live in this town, too. And Eldon told me about you goin to see Mac McClellon. He said someday y'all'll be able to get together and laugh about it—"

"Why do you and Eldon stay here?" he said then, almost blurting it. "You don't have to, you don't—"

"Because!" she said. "Because it's our home." She looked away from him, resting her hand on the vinyl-covered back of one of the kitchen chairs, her fingers tracing circles across the top.

There was a long, tense silence. Suddenly, she broke it. "I don't know," she said, her dark eyes flickering over him. "I don't know what I want to say." She hesitated. "You remember that time, when we were kids, in the fishin shack," she asked softly, "that last time when we talked, all those years ago?"

"Yeah," he said, his entire body aching with the memory.

"You ever think about that? All we talked about and everything?"

"Yeah, I have," he said. He could feel his own pulse, and he sat down at the table, inspecting her face, so conscious of her nearness that he felt almost faint. "Of course I have," he said, looking up at her, his voice a whisper.

"Things might of been different, if . . ." she said. "I mean, I think you might have really loved me, back then, even though . . ."

"Yes," he said.

"But we never could have changed who we were, could we? Even if we'd run off up North somewhere, like I wanted to, like I dreamed about, we'd've still been us. Carryin who we were with us."

The room was silent.

"I might not have known it," O.B. said, "but I loved you then. And I still do." He reached out toward her, but she took a step back.

"I don't see how that coulda been love," she said, a curious, pleading look in her eyes. There was a tentative, youthful air about her now, a kind of innocence. "I just don't question it, O.B. All I can do is face up to what it was. What it is. We'd of always been us. We were who we were even before we were born. Like you said back then." She crossed her arms across her breasts, hugging herself, moving away into the middle of the room, her shoes creaking on the linoleum. "Well, there ain't any use worryin about what might have been, is there?

Besides . . ." She stood very still, her eyes focused out the window to where the sunlight played on the brownish-red and dying leaves of the fig tree. "There's all this other stuff," she said absently, after a minute. Then she chuckled. "That's funny. That view out that window. It ain't changed in over fifteen years. I saw the seasons change out that window. Washin white folks' dishes." She chuckled again, a low, throaty laugh that rumbled up from deep in her chest.

"We could . . . we could maybe still go," he said, his voice barely above a whisper. "Up North." He knew how hopeless it was as he said it.

She turned and looked at him then, fixed him with a steady, black-eyed gaze.

"No." She shook her head. "It's much too late for that. There's all this other stuff. There's Eldon." She paused. She seemed to take a deep breath. "No, that's not why I came over here. I just wanted to tell you that I appreciated you bein there. Eldon did, too. He knows I'm here. He told me about the fight. Everything." She paused again. "I wanted to thank you. That was important to me—"

"You coulda told me that anytime. You came over here—"

"To tell you that, that's all. I needed to do that. To . . . round it off. End it."

His heart was pounding. He could barely breathe. "It's not too late," he said, his voice rising, "we *could* go. I'm free to do it, now, I'm—"

"But *I'm* not!" she said. "Goddammit, O.B., think about me! For a change, think about *me!*"

He nodded, seeing her as the young girl she'd been, her printed, flour-sack calico dress clinging to her breasts, her hips, the hair around her face damp from creek water as she bit into a plum, the sticky juice running from the corners of her mouth. Her eyes had once sparkled in summer sunlight. . . .

"Sally's dead. I'm all Eldon's got now," she said, her voice startling him out of his vision, "and he's a good man. He's been good to me. We can have peace. He loves me." She paused. "About love . . . Well, I don't worry about what love is anymore. I just know now that I want to be with Eldon for the rest of my life. I reckon that's enough."

He heard her sigh and knew she was looking at him. He sensed that she longed to hold him and comfort him, but maybe he was just confusing his own longings for hers. He saw her moving toward the door, and he began to cry. If she heard him, she did not let on as she went out the back door, letting it close gently behind her.

He rose quickly, moving to the window to watch her cross the sparse grass of the yard, her stride determined, steadfast. She moved with a grace like that of a doe gliding quickly and silently through the woods without the ripple of a single leaf. He stood at the window, watching her cut through the narrow gap in the back fence, through the privet and the honeysuckle vines still dark green and thick. For an instant, he could see the white sweater, glimmering and spectral, and then it, too, disappeared down the alley and she was gone, vanished like a haunting, faded dream that is forever lost before it can even be remembered.